# AS WORLDS BURN

## A Tawdry Tale of Inspired Healing

### James Dwight

Bob

From one writter to
Another! Enjoy the
ride!

Jim

This is a book of fiction. All characters and events portrayed in this
novel are either fictitious or are used fictitiously.

As Worlds Burn
A Tawdry Tale of Inspired Healing

Edited by Beverly McGuire, Jeannine Mallory and Tyler R. Tichelaar

Published by Aviva Publishing

Aviva Publishing
2301 Saranac Avenue, Ste. 100
Lake Placid, NY 12946
518-523-1320
www.avivapubs.com

Library of Congress # 2008938736
ISBN 978-1-890427-50-4
Printed in the United States of America

www.asworldsburn.com

# **Preface**

by

Tyler R. Tichelaar

author of *The Marquette Trilogy*

I am not a fan of introductions because I think readers are better served first by reading the novel and coming to their own conclusions about the work. In general, most introductions would better serve as afterwords. However, I was pleased to be asked to write a preface for *As Worlds Burn* by James Dwight because I fear readers who are not fans of science-fiction will dismiss the book because of it being designated as part of that genre. While the book does take place on alien planets and there is some initial need for the reader to adjust and learn about the alien worlds, once readers move past the first few chapters, I believe they will find themselves engrossed not only in the storyline and the characters, but also in the philosophical questions the novel asks, questions all people ask themselves about the true nature of humanity, its place in the universe, and the meaning of its existence. It is this questioning in the novel, beyond the intergalactic battles and adventure-filled pages of most Science Fiction, that makes *As Worlds Burn* literature as well as enjoyable reading.

The title of *As Worlds Burn* by James Dwight suggests an apocalyptic tale, but such a designation is far too simplistic. While it is a science fiction novel of war on another planet that takes place after what appears to have been a great catastrophe, the reader will discover the focus is upon a very philosophical and even spiritual story about what it means to be human and the role God plays in our lives. Never falling into simple allegory or a veiled commentary of the twenty-first century, *As Worlds Burn* presents

iii

situations that resonate with our culture today while reflecting a fictional world needing redemption from its own social conditioning where no easy solutions are provided.

The novel begins when Verbolana, a member of The Chosen people, dies in the war against The Wretched. At the moment of her death, she experiences what her religion has taught her to expect—a sled coming to take her to Heaven. However, what she expected ends there. Heaven is not what she was taught it would be, and she soon learns her planet and the culture she was raised in are also far from what they had seemed during her lifetime.

Verbolana's story becomes one of a journey through Heaven, trying to find meaning, happiness, and an understanding of God. While at first she hopes for the Blessed Amnesia that will make her forget her earthly life, instead she comes to understand her previous existence in new ways while meeting numerous people in Heaven who help her try to find answers to her questions about the meaning of it all.

Dwight alternates the novel's scenes between Verbolana and Trake, the man Verbolana loves. Trake survives the battle in which Verbolana dies, but only to end up stranded among the Wretched, ultimately learning their ways, and discovering that what The Chosen taught him about the Wretched and the history of the conflict between the two peoples has been a series of lies.

Dwight's fictional world at first appears to be a commentary on what could happen to our own planet if we do not take better care of the earth. The Chosen live in open skyscrapers they call towers, never venturing down to touch the earth, or Father, as they call it. Father has been wounded and must not even be stepped upon so he has time to heal. Generations earlier, the people had been warned they must leave Father's surface. The Chosen went into the towers, but the Wretched remained on the earth; for disobeying this dictate to let Father heal, the Wretched have ever since been despised by the Chosen. Yet what appears to be an environmental disaster may only be a distorted message—one that makes the reader wonder how much of what our own media tells us is also manipulated for political ends.

More interesting than the environmental concerns to me was how *As Worlds Burn* reads like a science-fiction version of *What Dreams May Come,* providing a spiritual exploration of what life after death might be, and what life on earth actually means in relation to it.

At the novel's center are questions about God and Truth. In Heaven, Verbolana meets Paul, a man who lived in California on the earth familiar to readers, which he calls Terra in the novel. Just as the Chosen's religion has been full of lies, Paul points out the problems with religion on earth:

They were all anti-logical as far as I can tell. And I don't mean illogical, but anti-logical. Because most of them follow logical paths of thinking in order to make sense of non-logical issues. That to me is anti-logical. Now that I think about it, it's amazing how so many Terran religions got so much of it right but ended up being so incredibly wrong.

Paul even discusses Jesus directly, rejecting the idea of a Virgin Birth and explaining that Jesus's message was too broad for people so they had to make it definitive and turn Jesus into a God. God himself tells Paul he has sent 852 messengers to earth to help humanity, but since humanity never understands or accepts what the messengers have to say, it is unlikely God will bother to send any more.

The voice of God throughout the book is especially compelling. He talks to Verbolana and Paul and anyone else in Heaven. Whenever they want something, God makes it happen for them—such as changing their hairstyles or letting them view scenes from history—but what God does not do is tell them all the answers.

He admits he doesn't know all the answers himself. Instead, Paul and Verbolana are left to figure things out on their own. Dwight's fictionalized God is the God of modern science, the idea of an expanding and evolving God who changes and grows as people change and create him—he fits our twenty-first century notion of quantum physics and an expanding and vibrating universe, with a God who matures and expands in correlation with humanity and all the universe.

Readers who are strict Christians may be offended, and a few graphic sexual scenes may turn off some readers. *As Worlds Burn* is for the open-minded, for the reader who enjoys thinking—the reader who wants more than just an action-packed adventure novel—although there are several episodes to fulfill the desire to be entertained. Readers who like to question the meaning of existence will find kindred spirits in Verbolana, Paul and Trake. Readers may even question and reevaluate their own lives and the beliefs their culture gave them. Whether you enjoy reading science-fiction, fantasy, philosophy, or self-help and spirituality books, *As Worlds Burn* is not one easily forgotten, but a book to be savored and to be given a second or even third reading.

# CHAPTER 1

Verbolana struggled to her feet, disoriented and frightened. For a moment before, she had dropped behind the fallen log in blazing pain, three arrows protruding from her chest. Yet now she stood, her pain gone, her eyes clear. With a quick glance, she spotted her attackers slinking through the deep forest, arrows notched in their bows, eyes intent on their quarry. But they didn't shoot; didn't even seem to see her. She looked at the ground around her with growing detachment. Trake, her Honored master, lay face down in the weeds, the back of his shaved skull a ghostly white against the trampled grass. Verbolana wanted to shake him, for he seemed oblivious to the approaching danger. Then she understood. There, staring up at her, eyes grayed, body crumpled and bloodied, was her own dead face.

Relief washed through her; body-rich, cleansing relief. Her Gods had not abandoned her. All the sins she had committed in the last few hours had not turned Them against her. She would see her Encore, her sweet afterlife.

The Trials! Her momentary relief vanished into the stinking air that clung to her withering planet. Eternity hinged on her performance in the coming hours. If The Humble Magician, her most feared God, was not pleased with her performance she may well spend enernity picking up after those with leading roles.

Frantically she scanned the forest around her. There, a few feet through the thick undergrowth, off to her right, her glorious sled

1

waited, just as the Holy Drama promised it would. Floating just above the brambles and vines that clogged Father's skin, the gaily-decorated divine transport bobbed on the slight breeze, waiting to whisk her up to the Second World. Stamping in midair beyond the ornate sled stood the fabled Beasts of Ansett, straining at their harnesses, ready to fly her away from this miserable world. Her life here was done. The Blessed Amnesia would soon wash her soul of all but the memories of her Gods.

Verbolana looked back down at Trake. He was moving now; the huge winged Vipeon tattooed across his shirtless back seemed to take flight as his lean muscles reacted to his commands. She watched, filled with a new private dread, as he crawled to the side of her earthbound corpse and brushed the tuft of long blonde hair back from her dead eyes. Panic piled on panic. *The Gods are watching*, her mind screamed. Then, with sudden resentment at the man she had secretly loved all her life, *haven't you done enough? You lead me out here with your stories of divine guidance, jeopardizing my Encore with your selfish desires, and now ... Shut up! Don't say a word!*

"I am nothing now," Verbolana heard Trake whisper. "You were my only reason for life, and I have killed you. I care nothing that you are a Blessed servant and I am an Honored warrior, my dear Verbolana. I will never know you and yet I have known you all my life. I know from your eyes, from the way I saw you walk, and sit and laugh. I know from the way you cared for your girls. I saw you sparkle behind that curtain we all must draw around ourselves. I have loved you for as long as I can remember. You stole into my dreams before I even knew to dream. You have lived beside me all these years and I have wanted no other. And now I have killed you with my wanton, covetous desire. As an Honored warrior, I will receive no Encore. Now is my only chance for happiness, and yet the Gods conspire to make me miserable." Trake dropped his head to her bloody chest, mixing his tears with the spreading stains. "And I have lied to you in our last moments together, our only real moments together. I was not ashamed of what I did. I was not sorry. My only sorrow comes from not having told you how I felt—what you have meant to me all these years."

The Trials! Flooding panic dumped through Verbolana's body, wobbling her knees and making her fingers quiver. She could not listen to his words, his blasphemous words. The Gods would punish her for even hearing such treachery. She could not stay another moment. She must run! Run from the selfish, treasonous plan he revealed to her only hours before. Yet even through the panic, she felt his love. She stuffed her bubbling compassion down with anger and fear. The Gods would see whether she faltered, see whether she were not worthy. Eternity was at stake. Her Encore of bliss and contentment waited.

And the Blessed Amnesia. In a matter of minutes, none of this would matter. She would be free. Free from the pain, free from the cloistered, ragged, self-deprecating life that the Chosen, both Honored and Blessed alike, were required to live. Free from their crippled Father, her planet so abused and worn. And away from their battle with the Wretched, those sinners who still scurried across Father's skin, not letting him rest, not listening to the Gods who know the sacrifices all must make.

This was no longer Verbolana's world, no longer her battle, thank the Gods. She reached down and touched Trake's head as if to signal her departure. Deep in her core, below the anger and fear, an ember flared with the warmth of his skin. Buffered and coddled by the ashes of her cruel life, she had kept this glowing coal hidden from the prying eyes all around her. But now, in these last few moments, on a world she would soon forget, a subversive fire threatened to ignite. With all her strength, Verbolana stuffed

3

this elegant burning back into its place. Trake did not react as her fingers ran through his hair. He was of a different world now and she needed to concentrate.

With shaking limbs, Verbolana stepped around Trake and over her own lifeless shell, and then took the few steps to her waiting sled. Groping for the reins, she focused her concentration on the unfamiliar task of balancing on the rocking platform. She dared not look back. She whipped the beasts to speed with a force of will that started at her anchored feet and shot like steel through her determined body.

To her astonishment, the thick forest opened before the straining animals. Trees parted to either side or merely vanished before her magical path. Then, as she topped the forest and sprang into the gray sky, the full force of the noonday sun warmed her frigid limbs and dazzled spots before her eyes. The sudden glare activated a haunting memory: her first sunrise, the pain of unfiltered sunlight, the glory of the open sky and an endless green horizon. She had been seven, she remembered, with Wexi and Treena, her two best friends even to this day, by her side. She frowned at the vision, for this was like no memory she had ever experienced. Every detail stood in her mind as if she were living it anew. She tried to reject the visions, dismiss them from her mind and concentrate on the evolving vistas all around her. The lake was just coming into view as the sled gained altitude. Then, on the horizon, her home, her tower, appeared, as if emerging from the depths of the lake it was built over. She fought for control of her mind. She had never before seen her home from the outside.

Wexi's pain-contorted face loomed before her eyes, blocking her view of the advancing tower.

"It wasn't your fault," Wexi's voice rang in Verbolana's ears as if Wexi was right next to her. "We wanted to come. We wanted to

4

see the sunrise as much as you did." They hung, strung up by their wrists, their toes barely scraping the deck. With the buffer of time removed from the memory by the hand of one of her Gods, Verbolana clearly saw Wexi's tiny back bared; blood and pus oozed from the linear welts left by the public whipping the girls received from the Director.

With a scream of horror, Verbolana shook the image from her eyes. She concentrated all her will on the developing sights. As her sled drew closer to her home, she marveled at the size of the tower; the clouds marching across the sky seemed of equal proportion. And the blimps! Three giant battle blimps floated, moored to the top deck, straining mightily against taut cables.

Then Treena's frightened eyes unexpectedly superimposed across the sky. Evidently, the Gods had something urgent to say. With unwanted clarity, Verbolana saw it had all been her fault, coaxing her two friends into the dangerous adventure.

The sled was much closer to her tower by the time she was able to refocus. Apparently she had traveled at great speed even though the sled had settled into a gentle rhythm. Verbolana now saw the rusted girders that held floor after floor of her exiled cousins. Not all cousins of course, but that was how they thought of themselves. And the gardens, this time of year a patchwork of matte grays and yellow-greens against the deep browns of wet soil, each floor assigned a different set of crops. Verbolana had no idea which floor was hers, the floor where she had spent her entire nineteen years until a few short hours ago. She pictured Treena on a deck three-quarters up the tower, waving from the railing after breaking every rule by sneaking through the filters and across the gardens just to say goodbye.

Not Wexi, though. Wexi would have passed this way hours ago. Poor Wexi, the pleading in her eyes; the forbidden speaking of love. Verbolana sent a silent prayer, for she knew Wexi's time had either come or gone. She would be done with her Trials by now and she would have either passed or failed. And after this life of torturous sacrifice, failure was unthinkable.

Deep in the shadows of each deck, like dirty sponges left to dry, Verbolana now discerned the Za filters. It was hard to believe she had never seen a Za spider until the night of misadventure that was trying to steal her concentration. The Za spiders were saviors of her people and were therefore sacred. But that night, as they tiptoed through their filtering webs, intent on seeing the sun rise from the outside of her deck, they had run across many of the night-loving Za, gorging on the human filth their webs had gleaned from the air more than a century after the Great Cleansing.

Verbolana winced at her juvenile stupidity. In her haste to savor the forbidden, she had not thought her plan through. After sunrise, the three had realized their predicament. They could not crawl home under the cover of darkness. They were literally trapped in a web of Za filters without an excuse. Verbolana relived the horror, not only for herself, but for her two draftees as well. She relived their decision to walk brazenly from the filters, hoping no one would notice.

People noticed. With perfect vision, as if she had actually regressed those fifteen years, Verbolana waited with her two best friends for the Director to arrive, corralled as they were by aghast adults. After the Director discovered the truth, Verbolana felt herself manhandled to center stage. Again, she felt her smock unlaced down her back as she locked eyes with her horrified friends. Guilt, then anger, washed through her resurrected heart. *We were just children,* Verbolana screamed into the dirty sky. But the whip was not forestalled. Different screams rang in her ears. Pleading, indignant screams that she had caused. Guilty, humiliating screams that she tried desperately to break away from.

Screams that, to her now-mind, burrowed deeper than the Za whip that had slashed across her back.

The tower was gone. She wrenched her concentration back to the sled. What was happening? The Blessed Amnesia, where was it? Was this the beginning of her Trials? Was she to show repentance? Was that the purpose of these memories? Was she expected to remember all before she could forget? No one had prepared her for this.

Trake's face entered through the hole in her heart and her stomach tumbled. She shied. Do the Gods really know my most private thoughts? Of course they know, silly girl, and they will soon confront you. Repent! Now! You must! She hadn't the courage. Repentance would imply some sort of control where she had none.

She pushed the sinful visions away, but they reemerged. Verbolana could not keep from remembering. She saw Trake's eyes, so different from the others, steeled for sure, yet somehow soft and fragile. There was something in his movements: a reluctance or hesitation that screamed his desire to question. She knew he was different, more like her.

But that could not be true, she realized now. He was a man, crude and base. "Gods, you are right!" she screamed to the sky. "Men are for men, women for women."

Verbolana concentrated her now-mind on the powerful, straining winged beasts ahead as they pulled her sled to new heights. She ventured a glance back at the tall speck sticking out of a perfectly round smudge of blue. Her brutal home lay quiet and benign, its illusion of tranquility shocking to her eyes. She could hardly imagine that a world of such suffering seemed so beautiful from afar. The smoky haze could not hide the deep greens of the continent below. The scars her people had rent upon the land seemed mostly healed. Even the emptied cities were only speckled patches of graying concrete from here. The colors of nature had reclaimed so much.

And the ocean! She marveled as it came into view on the horizon. She had heard stories of how vast it was, though they were wrong about its coloring! Sun-swept blues and tumultuous greens melded and mixed with the billowing whites and dark grays of marching clouds. From here everything looked robustly healthy, not the sickly gray-green of the Director's stories.

Then nightfall rushed toward her. Verbolana watched the shadow line as it marched across the curved horizon and she knew she needed to concentrate. She had failed miserably in her life and now in her death, she had this one chance at redemption. The Humble Magician hated incompetence and defiance, and Verbolana had displayed both in her final days. The Magician would forgive all if she could muster enough strength for the next few hours.

Now over the rippling ocean, she watched the Magician's Mists forming just ahead of her speeding sled and she knew from all the stories what waited ahead.

*Am I ready? I have been preparing all my life and still I am afraid.* In panic, she pulled on the reins, ordering the great beasts to veer from their course. But they plunged ahead, into the Mists that hid the Second World from the eyes of all but the knowing.

The concealing fog cleared almost as soon as it had closed and the Great Hall stood tall before her, its doors open for her arrival. She could never have imagined such a sight had she not been schooled from her earliest memories to recognize the splendor her Gods had laid out for her.

The Orchard of Falmar appeared as well, framing this most holy of meeting places with the colors of harvest. As she descended now into this new land, she distinguished the Fruits of Bliss and Contentment hanging heavy from the straining branches of the magical Orchard. Verbolana longed to sample her way through the trees, tasting all she had been denied. Yet the animals pulling her would not be distracted. They passed the enchanted trees and then over the Ponds of Abundance, teeming with still more sensations for her to wallow in, when, or *if*, it became her time. She recognized many of her uncles and aunts, lounging in the dappled sunlight, draped in colored gowns of the finest Za cloth. She longed to join them. She waved but they did not see.

And there he stood, draped in a shimmering robe, waiting with arms outstretched, as her sled entered the enormous hall. Before the wild beasts skidded to a stop, Verbolana leaped from the sled, rolled twice across the unforgiving stone floor and came up in an aggressive battle stance. She took a moment to assess her situation. Attacks could come from any corner. Her head swiveled as her feet slid noiselessly, always grounded, always centered. Daring a glance back at the Magician, Verbolana breathed smoothly through her surprise. The Magician approached with arms still outstretched, a cautious smile on his face. And something else, something so alien Verbolana could not immediately identify the incongruity. Then she instinctively leapt and rolled again to gain distance. The Magician's skin was brown, his features heavy and thick. Only through abject fear and relentless training could Verbolana manage her deep bow of respect and reverence. Something was wrong.

Her most fearsome God approached quickly and helped her rise, his actions chilling her more than the nine remembered lashes that still hung to her back. This was not his way.

He stood her close to him, his face inches from her own. "You have been brought to your Second World in the way you expected, but now it is time to end the illusion. God, the creator of all humankind, has chosen you to enter this afterlife He calls

Heaven. However, it is not the Paradise you were taught to expect. The Humble Magician does not live here. No Gods of man's creation live here."

The imposter waited until Verbolana's eyes came back to his before he continued. "All of humanity craves to understand the ways of the universe, so they invent Gods to fill the void of what they cannot understand. As it turns out, however, people cannot create Gods; we cannot see them, hear them, or know their intentions. We cannot write their words or interpret their signs. We cannot build monuments to please or displease them. Those things are not within our power as humans." The man spoke softly now, like the breathed words of her people in the quiet hours.

Verbolana looked up at what had to be her God, too stunned to speak.

He continued. "I am here to ease your transition. There are very few who do not have a difficult time with this news. You will need time to adjust, to learn your way, and time to accept that what you were taught about divine life was only the one you call The Author telling his people what they needed to hear and believe."

The man paused. Heavy silence added pounds to Verbolana's shoulders and bowed her head. The entire hall seemed to fall into sudden twilight.

"If this is just an illusion, then where are we, really?" The words emerged flat and halting. Confusion fought with suspicion and fear for her attention.

"If this place gives you comfort, then you can stay here. You can walk through the doors and live out your years languishing in the Orchards and Ponds of your expectations. However, you must know that this is only one of your choices. Your choices are only limited by your imagination and the imaginations of those around you."

"Where are we—*really*?" Verbolana's mind had latched onto the only safe concept she could conceive. Fighting would have been so much easier than this.

"We are in your own personal universe, your realm, as we like to call it. God gives one to everyone upon arrival. Without your input, it is smaller than a deck on one of your towers, much smaller. If you ask God in the way that he accepts, it can become anything you desire: A home, a world, a universe. There are almost no limitations."

"I did not tell him what I wanted," came her suspicious response.

"He took this experience from the teachings of your people. He decided this was the most comforting way to bring you here, to give you what you expected during your transition. It will not happen again. From here on out, you must ask for what you want. For now, you must ask aloud. You must say, 'God, I wish,' followed by whatever you wish for."

"God, I wish you would leave me alone and let me get on with my Trials. What have you done with the Magician? You will not trick me with your games." Verbolana pushed away from this usurper, convinced now that this was the first test.

The man stood with a bland expression, his arms frozen in place where he had held her. "My name is Alcot. I am your Weaver. If you truly wish that I leave, then I must do so. This is your universe and you have absolute control of everything and everyone inside it."

"Be gone!" She had come back to her defensive posture and scanned the room for new threats.

"If you ever need me, just ask God. Either I or one of my profession will come to help you." He turned to walk away.

Panicked, Verbolana blurted, "Wait, this is all so confusing. What if I forget your name?"

"You will not." He smiled back at her. "That is one of God's ultimate blessings here. He blesses us all with perfect health and perfect memory." Without looking back, the false Magician strode across the smooth stone floor toward the dais. In mid-air, about halfway to the altar, a door appeared. With a flourish of fluttering robes, the man disappeared behind the door as it closed.

# Chapter 2

Verbolana sat alone on the cool stone floor, mentally exhausted from her fruitless ranting at her echoing new home. She heard, outside, the giggles and squeals of her cousins from just over a tantalizing grass-covered hill where she had spied the Ponds of Contentment during her arrival. These furtive, vague chatterings, caught on the occasional breeze, were the only handholds that helped her distinguish one moment from the next, one hour as it passed or one day that was no longer a unit of time, for the sun had not moved since she arrived. Her new prison was neither hot nor cold, she had determined, and she did not feel tired or hungry even though she had not eaten or slept in a very long time. She didn't even feel the need to relieve herself. Nothing. She felt nothing but alone and afraid—and very confused. She was afraid even to feel afraid. How dare she feel anything but the rapture of being in the presence of her Gods?

She refocused for the millionth time; sat in perfect comfort, not a stiff muscle or errant pain to complain about. The walls of the Great Hall exemplified the solidity she must show now, with their solid cut-stone patterns of sun and moons, crouching or leaping animals for which she had no name. The Vipeon she knew, its scales glimmering with gold-leaf splendor, its eyes alive with ruby colored stones the size of her fist. The air was clean and fresh, with just a hint of tempting perfume from the ever-blossoming Orchard just outside the open doors.

"My faith is strong," she declared aloud. "I will await my Trials, or live through these, if these are my Trials. Humble Magician, I am your warrior, ready to follow you to the Cleansing of the Universe. I obey your every command. I am not here to question or challenge the wisdom of my Gods."

A perfect, full-color image of Trake's roguish face blossomed behind her open eyes like a flower unfolding inside her skull. One slow deep breath and a muttered mantra dissolved the illusion. She waited. Another vision popped behind her eyes. Another breath and another prayer. "I am your warrior," she proclaimed, her youthful voice bouncing off the distant walls. "I will await your orders." Giggles and splashing from outside intruded into her beautiful prison. "You want the Strength! I will give you the Strength!" she finally yelled in defiance. "After only two years of training for the Home Guard, I passed the Ruthon on my first try. I say again, I will fight for you. The Strength flows strong in me. But I am not perfect." She stood suddenly, her limbs immediately limber and quick. "Is that what you need to hear? I am not perfect. You know that! I know that! This man—this man I have no business with—have never had business with, invades my thoughts. Graceful Dancer, God of Passion, tell me what this means!"

Silence. Heart-shrinking, terrifying silence. Infuriating silence. *Hold on*, she coached herself. *This will pass. Eternity awaits. Your Trials are almost over. You were always told that the Gods abhor weakness, that they honor discipline and fortitude. Now is your time to show them your spirit.*

Behind the dais, the multi-colored floor to ceiling banners fluttered with a puff of wind, their bottoms snapping against the stonewalls. Verbolana held her breath. Had they arrived? Stone-still silence was all that greeted her for another hour or two. Or maybe it was three minutes; she could no longer distinguish.

Fruit-blossomed fragrances reached into her blackened reverie. Whirling toward the door, Verbolana settled into a perfect defensive posture, expecting battle finally to commence. The unfiltered sunlight beyond the aching doorway flashed brilliant white across her eyes. Then Wexi's animated smile blossomed across the void. Unlike any dream, Verbolana reviewed another spontaneous memory, every detail exactly as it had been only a few days ago, every nuance available to her scrutiny. Wexi stood in front of her, giggling with excitement.

"Vee," Wexi bounced beside her. "You passed. You must be thrilled. Congratulations!"

Like Verbolana, Wexi was as trim and quick as a sea serpent coiled to strike. In perfect remembrance, Verbolana felt herself wondering whether her own military haircut looked as silly as Wexi's. Though she had never seen her own face, except for a few fleeting glimpses in the shiny, rusted metal of one of their ancient stoves, she certainly knew all that was left of her long straw-colored hair was a perfectly round foot-long tuft at the front of her scalp. The rest had been shaved away by the Militia recruiter. And just as Wexi's haircut destroyed a piece of her innate femininity, Verbolana was sure this military tradition, originally reserved only for men, did nothing to help her appearance either.

"Thanks." Vee felt herself smile with a flat affectation, just as it had been on that day only a short time ago.

"What's wrong?" Wexi exclaimed. "If I had passed the Ruthon at twenty-two, I would have swung the ropes. You have one more color on your tattoo and you will graduate."

Verbolana's hand went instinctively to the back of her shaved skull, to the scabs of the new full-color tattoo perched on her left shoulder, ready to strike. The Director had chosen a Night Hawk, much to Verbolana's unspoken protest, for its grace and dexterity as it swoops down to pick off its prey.

From somewhere outside the memory she felt her thoughts form as if she were thinking them anew. *To what?* she had thought to herself, *to what will I graduate? I can now kill without effort, slice the Wretched while hanging upside down from a battle blimp. How is this something to celebrate? I am a teacher! How can the Humble Magician ask this of me?*

"Alcot!" she screamed in desperation, for with that memory, Verbolana had no doubt why the Gods had abandoned her here. She deserved every stretched moment of her incarceration. She had not pleased her Gods and they had left her with even their punishment ripped away. Maybe they would come back once she contemplated and repented her every sin. She longed for the focus brought by the lash at her back, for the harsh reprimands of her teachers. Anything, anything to remove this hollow death. There was nothing to lose now. This was her eternal punishment. Why not call for the silly salvation the strangely colored man had promised?

More time passed as she swung frantically from hope to despair and back again. An hour, a day, a week? She could not tell.

From a crumpled heap on the floor, she heard the hollow footsteps of someone approaching through the empty hall. With her eyes hidden behind her arm, and her stomach dumping new acidic fear, she pulled herself from yet another waking full-color dream to peek through the gloomy hall.

Anger was her first response. Through clenched teeth she blurted, "You came?" It was more of a question. "I don't understand. Would you have come earlier?"

"Yes," Alcot, her Weaver, answered with casual ease. He walked to her and stood beside the heap she had become. "You needed time, though. Everyone has demons to exorcise. Folks from your planet need more time than most. Do not be ashamed. Everyone has anger. It is one of God's gifts." Alcot knelt beside her and stroked the short blonde hairs that now covered her aft scalp, his brown hand a stark contrast to her alabaster skin. She flinched at his touch. "What you have told me is true?" Verbolana ventured, still dreading whatever answer he might give.

"Yes, but I have more to tell you when you are ready to listen." His expression was softer than a newly spun Za filter.

"Can we leave this place?" She croaked. The question dumped more acid into her empty stomach.

"I think that is an excellent idea," Alcot answered. "Do you know where you would like to go?"

"I only know this place and one deck of one tower. Will you take me somewhere?"

"Of course." Alcot paused. "Do I have your permission to change the setting?"

Not fully understanding, Verbolana nodded.

"God, please recreate my home here and set us in the great room." Instantly Verbolana found herself curled in a deeply cushioned armchair, her feet tucked under her legs, her head pillowed into the softness of the arm of the chair. She had never felt such comfort. Across from her sat her new friend, similarly pampered, eyeing her expectantly.

Verbolana ventured a little look around. Nothing in her imagination could have prepared her for what she saw. She froze in renewed fear as her first thought emerged through the haze of her dazzled mind. "You are Wretched?"

Alcot smiled in what appeared to be genuine amusement. "I didn't think of that when I brought you here. I know your people well and your reaction should have occurred to me." He paused to appreciate his cavernous living room. "To put you at ease, no, I am not one you call Wretched. I come from another world. God has created life on 143 different worlds. My home world, like yours, has suffered many disasters. My people have lived underground since a meteor struck our planet eight hundred or so years ago. The surface is still uninhabitable."

Verbolana perched on her elbow to give the room her full attention. There was nothing even a bit familiar in anything she saw. Dark, wet earth and snaking wood seemed to make up most of the domed ceiling. The deck seemed to be of polished flat stone, wet in spots from where the roof leaked down rivulets of water. Thick rugs led down domed earthen passageways at every angle, lit by contained flames that popped and sizzled in their housings. Furniture littered the enormous room, low tables and cushioned seating scattered about as if thrown by a giant hand, to rest where their slidings ended. Bottles lined one wall, lit from below so their contents glowed in a thousand shades of a hundred colors. What looked like freestanding, painted Za filters stood haphazardly around the edges of the room; some had splashes of bright colors, whereas others depicted dark, gloomy subjects in gloomy rooms of their own. But of all the alien sights, the one that struck her hardest was that they were alone. Such space, empty of teeming cousins. She did not know whether to scream with delight or despair, but scream she wanted to.

And Verbolana was desperate for answers, so she did not scream. If her Gods did not exist, if this man were telling the truth, then she must learn. "Can you tell me what I see?" She would try to be the best student, hopefully this time without the lash.

"Our homes, when possible, are excavated from under the great Balsat Trees. Their enormous root systems hold the roofs firm, so there are fewer cave-ins. My people believe our Gods speak to us through these magnificent displays of roots and minerals," Alcot explained, pointing to the ceiling. "When I built this grotto, I asked God for a ceiling that would foretell of great successes and even greater deeds for me in this new world;

18

accomplishments that would silence the critics who haunted me in my previous life. I asked the Falstafs, the conduits to our Gods, to read my ceiling. The tangling of the roots, the precious stones trapped here and there, the rivulets of rainwater, how they flow and drip—all told of an enchanted future. But to be honest," Alcot bowed his head in humility, "the fabrication did not help. All that I was not in my previous life had followed me here. There were no shortcuts to my work." He paused and sighed. "Wonderful fairy tales for the ignorant, a silly little reminder for me." His eyes dropped to his interlaced fingers lying placid in his lap.

"So you are human? You said you are a Weaver. I thought ..."

His eyes bounced up with obvious amusement, saved from his past. "Ah, Weaver, baker, sculptor. We are all human here, except God, of course. We just choose different roles. The human condition does not allow many of us to exist without purpose. I enjoy meeting those new to this world. And I enjoy helping them create a place of comfort for themselves, if that is ever possible."

"Why do you call what you do a 'Weaver?' Weavers have no particular distinction where I come from." Verbolana's audacity amazed her. She spoke as if she actually believed his wild stories.

"You can ask God for anything you want. Anything—barring nothing. Anything, anything." He paused.

She tried to absorb this, but the words meant nothing. *Anything, barring nothing?* What could that possibly mean?

"Many people are overwhelmed by the possibilities and an equal number are hardly impressed at all, thinking this is the way it should always have been. But it turns out that everyone, and I mean everyone, ends up confused and frightened by the prospect. Some do not even have the imagination necessary to figure out what they want, while some can imagine more than they dare. A Weaver, like interlacing the threads of a blanket, helps people

19

through the maze of their desires to, hopefully, a place of peace. From there, many blossom."

Verbolana looked at the ceiling. The view did not help her sudden sensation of vertigo. All too well, she saw the tangle of her own mind; the stilted desires, the chopped dreams, the diverted emotions. A wild thought popped into her head. Tentatively she probed, "Could I go back?"

Alcot smiled again as he met her eyes. "Many do. Reliving parts of your life can be very healing. Continuing where you left off can also be useful, but it is more difficult than you might think. Knowing the truth about God will change how you react to those around you. Also, with just a wish, you can manipulate anything. Few can resist the temptation to change events more to their liking."

Verbolana fought through the dangling ropes that cluttered her mind. She saw Trake, the injured embarrassment in his eyes from their last encounter. Her heart fell and she almost retched. "But I don't know how," came her anxious whimper.

"To go back?" Alcot asked.

"That too, but more." She struggled with a dozen thoughts colliding, until they coalesced into a single desire. She could not believe what she was going to say. It was like she was standing at the center ring and jumping for a rope, for if she were wrong, she would have eternity to lament. "I don't know how to love the man I love." She squeezed her eyes and awaited the lash. Her heart and stomach rose to her throat, threatening to choke back the words. *Courage, you stupid girl, courage! Just say what you have to say.* Finally, "Will you teach me?"

Alcot smiled. "I would be happy to teach you. It is one of my favorite things."

# Chapter 3

Verbolana laid snuggled into Alcot's thick shoulder, a full inch of blonde hair now covering her head where for the past two years, ever since being called to the Home Guard, her lieutenant had shaved her scalp weekly.

"I have done bad things, Alcot," Verbolana admitted from inside a comfort she hardly believed was now a small part of her. "Things I didn't like doing. Things that hurt other people ... children especially," she finally eked out.

"I know your world," Alcot responded to the curved ceiling of his bed-grotto. "As I have said a hundred times already, you had no choice."

"I could have stood up to them," she whined. "I could have told them I just wouldn't do it."

"From what you tell me, you tried that and have the scars to prove it." Alcot shifted his head around to lock eyes with her yet one more time. "It is not your fault. Even your Director could not have changed what he did." Verbolana felt Alcot's eyes sink deep into hers. She felt him searching her eyes, needing to know his words had meaning for her. But she also felt her cloying resistance, as if his advice lay captive on the skin of a sticky Ka melon, never sinking into the flesh of the damage she held so dear.

"I keep waiting for the curtain to fall on this little charade. My Gods are jealous Gods. They do not like to share the limelight."

"Your Gods never existed," Alcot pressed, this time with less compassion, more insistence. Verbolana felt his intensity, his passion for her understanding.

"But, Alcot, if what you say is true, the things I have done are a hundred times worse. You leave me with nothing to hold onto."

The comfort of their snuggled moment vanished. Images flashed and settled behind her eyes as an old memory appeared yet again, this time a petite back lay before her, red welts already rising in rows that criss-crossed scars from previous indiscretions. She studied the memory. She felt her then-mind, necessarily detached from her actions, as it compared, with dispassionate interest, the differences between the Za whip, with its fine braided strands, and the springy switch from the Warset vine. The Za whip cut deep and ragged, tearing flesh not only when applied, but also when pulled back. The switch, whether lashed at the back or the legs or the arms, was more of a bruising, concussive blow that left large swollen welts, though smaller, finer scars. Her now-mind willed her arm to stop, willed her ears to plug from the muffled whimpers that came with each stroke.

"Where are you?" Alcot's voice interrupted the remembered scene.

"You can always tell, can't you?"

"Your body gives you away," he responded. "You flinch when it's the whip."

"I want to stop. I was promised the Blessed Amnesia."

"You were promised many things," Alcot smoothed her furry scalp with a gentle hand. "But you can stop. You know how."

"It doesn't seem to help," Verbolana complained, realizing they were still face to face, eye to eye. Unwilling, or unable, to withstand his scrutiny, she sat up and instinctively pulled on the sheet to hide her naked form. Failure was all she heard from his simple statement. "I can't change what I have done. I understand that much from your endless meddling."

"But you can change how you feel about it. Accept. Separate. Forgive. You know how."

With annoyance and resentment clear in her voice, Verbolana complied. "God, I want to go back to the scene I just witnessed; to the beginning of that day's trouble."

The gloomy bed-grotto vanished. Verbolana sat in the half-light of her home deck, claustrophobia gripping her now-mind as it did every time she went back. Taking a moment to adjust, she brazenly surveyed her surroundings, immediately altering the remembered scene to this new fictional version of what could never be. With force of will, she settled into the scene, intent on letting the events run as they had on that day.

Verbolana, the teacher, sat cross-legged on the cold deck across from her young charges, her focused green eyes picking up every detail. They had chosen a spot close to the maze of floor to ceiling Za web filters. Verbolana made sure their spot was also close to the training circles. Her girls sat in two small groups, two Honored in one and six Blessed in the other. Their postures were correct, with legs crossed, backs straight and heads bowed, reading from the two Holy Dramas borrowed from the Deck Director.

All was as it should be. Verbolana took a moment to steal a peek around the deck. She bowed her head to let the only hair she had left fall into her face to hide her eyes from prying neighbors. She roved each training circle. Her stomach slowly soured as her search continued. Trake, the graceful instructor she could learn so much from, was not there and he should have been at this hour. If he was not in training, then he was out on patrol. She wanted to pray for his safe return, but she dared not. If the Gods dug deeply, they might discover blasphemy and her Encore could be lost.

Verbolana refocused on her little circle of girls. It was her job to instill in these girls what her teachers had failed to instill in her. They needed discipline of mind and body. They needed clear, unwavering focus on the performances before them. All her people did, or they would all die.

"Stasha!" Verbolana barked, as she smacked her green, springy switch down hard on the cold deck. The sharp noise startled no one. There had been too many switches over too many years. Verbolana bore the scars of her own instruction on her back and arms. "Tell me what you have just read."

Stasha, a Blessed child of eight, straightened from her reading and locked her eyes on Verbolana's. "The Humble Magician, God of Battle, commands the Chosen to fight and we are honored in his asking. He provided us with our towers to separate the Chosen, both Honored and Blessed, from Father's skin during his time of healing. All those who remain on the surface are Wretched and we must cleanse them from our Father's body. From his words, 'All that dwell or so much as trod upon Father must be severed.' Our duty is clear." She spat her words with the proper venom and Verbolana smiled.

"And what else have you read this morning?"

Stasha's snarling face softened. "The Blessed serve the Honored in this lifetime. They postpone pleasure for their Encore in the afterlife." Verbolana watched as Stasha bowed to the two Honored girls in the circle.

Verbolana's switch slashed hard on Stasha's back, slicing through the thin material of her uniform, raising a wicked, long welt.

"And?" Verbolana was horrified. Stasha, her star pupil, had left out the scripture that defined the lesson. Such an omission was unthinkable at her age.

Stasha did not flinch at the unexpected blow, did not suck in her breath from the pain, and certainly did not cry out. "And, from the lyrics of the Harmonious Minstrel, God of Nature," she continued, "'all will be rewarded in their time, as the natural order is restored.'"

"Ventra," Verbolana continued, as if her heart were not weeping. Stasha was such a crystal-eyed child with so few marks; Verbolana had to assume she herself was somehow to blame for the girl's lapse. Regardless, she continued without pause. She could give no quarter, no matter what the girl's history or status. "What else can we learn from the verses of our Gracious Songster?"

Ventra was not such a sparkling child and Verbolana knew her back and arms told that tale. In the two seasons since Verbolana had inherited this group, she herself had marked Ventra half a dozen times. Ventra's manner was slow and deliberate, bordering on insolent. At least, that was how it seemed to Verbolana, so the girl paid the price.

"The machines of our past tricked us into thinking they could give us everything, that even with our endless appetites we could live without want or need. The machines and those who built them lied. Our forefathers sucked our Father until he could give no more. Now he lies deflated and crippled, so we must let him rest."

Verbolana interrupted here. She had no desire to whip anyone else, and she was not sure Ventra could quote the proper scripture.

"Allura, what else does this tell us?"

Allura, an Honored Breeder, raised her eyes to the sky she had never seen. She did not meet Verbolana's eyes; it was not appropriate. "We, every one of us, are born to covet not only the possessions of comfort, but also the respect and admiration of our fellows. We must train ourselves to quiet the voices in our heads that attempt to steal our resolve. The scripture says, 'You need no audience beyond our ears. We, your Gods, command you to recite, line for line, your parts, without invention or explanation.'"

"Very good, Allura. Please, all return to your reading." Verbolana accented her request with another swipe of her switch to the deck.

The training circle drew her eye again. *Trake,* his name surfaced without her consent. Panic gripped her. *Your skill is great,* she continued as if it were her original thought. *And the Strength runs swift with you, more than any on the deck. It is why my eye roves to you. My training has given me new insight, new appreciation, and I see that, even though we are Honored and Blessed, man and woman, we are equally blessed. Humble Magician, make true this man's hand and focus his eye. Graceful Dancer, God of Passion, help him to focus on the needs of the many and not the comforts of a few.*

Deeper, closer to her heart, she shrunk from her other more deviant thoughts. It would not do for the Gods to see these, for every deviant reflection the Gods unearthed added another challenge to the Trials and Verbolana feared her list was already long enough.

Verbolana shifted her position on the hard deck, hoping the discomfort would bring new focus. With disciplined eyes, she surveyed the closest living circles. Her eyes skipped over two, for they were male, and settled on the next, a scene familiar though not necessarily safe. Even in day use, pillows lay strewn across the deck. A few Blessed servants scurried about, tending to this and that, while two other Blessed sat curled over close work. It took Verbolana only a moment to recognize what they were doing. Her sister's latest child needed two servants, it appeared. As Verbolana had observed a hundred times already, her twin sister, an

Honored Breeder named Zaluma, was supervising everything to do with her children with an active switch in her hand.

Verbolana looked away before anyone caught her gaping. Zaluma had no patience for her Blessed sister and often reacted violently if they happened upon each other. Verbolana stifled her ageless question and converted it to prayer. *Clever Choreographer, God of Creation, thank you for choosing Zaluma for the lead role. Without your constant vigilance, I might have been born first, a dancer with not nearly her skill. Though no one desires the climactic drama of cross-pollination, Zaluma has been a wonderful choice.* Then added as camouflage and proof of her piety, *And Graceful Dancer, God of Passion, thank you for my cousins and the dances you have taught us. They are pleasing to the eye and heart and bring great comfort.*

Two of her young girls squealed and a few hundred eyes turned to the commotion. *Swack!* Verbolana lashed out with her switch. The offending girls pulled their damaged hands to their laps as a small beetle scurried to safety.

Verbolana's switch was not finished, however. She slashed out again and again and again, delivering six wicked blows to Ventra and two to Daira. They both required punishment. Their lack of focus was appalling. Ventra, however, had added immeasurably to her own sins. She had attempted to deny something to an Honored.

Daira sat stone-faced as Ventra struggled to resume a proper sitting position. Verbolana heard the commotion build around her as Daira's birth supervisor approached, summoned by the crowd. The horror of the situation was lost on no one.

Verbolana leaned forward, her chest to her knees, and opened the back of her loose smock to bare her own back. The teacher was responsible for her Honored charges.

"How many swipes did my charge receive?" The supervisor was furious.

"Two."

"And the other girl?"

"Six."

The woman slashed Verbolana eight times, dropped the switch and walked away without another word.

The hundreds within eyesight strained for a view. Verbolana's now-mind remembered her only relief had been that Trake had not been witness!

# Chapter 4

Trussed shirtless in his woven battle harness, Trake hung suspended by a single rope, watching his breath cloud in the predawn chill. Verbolana's now-mind sat just behind his eyes, as she had always envisioned her Gods creeping into her own thoughts. With morbid fascination she had decided on a new course of therapy. As if Trake's eyes were her own she saw, a few feet below him, Erox, working the ropes and supervising the training exercises.

With his free hand, Trake gained Erox's attention through the nearly complete darkness. "Hand me a Talsartt," Trake signed to his best friend, using the language of stealth still reserved for Honored warriors.

"Sure," the burly Sailing Master mouthed and signed his silent response. "Then I'll hand you a one-way ticket to join the Blessed grunts in the filthy air of the gardens."

"I'm not going to kill them," Trake complained, looking around at the eight men who hung around him flailing with their long staffs that simulated the very same weapon Trake requested. "Just motivate them a bit. You know, the way Mortoff used to shake us up fifteen years ago. What would the Deck Director do, anyway? If they're making us train these Blessed servants for battle, it is proof they need every Honored warrior still alive."

"If not the gardens, which will eat at your lungs, then certainly the whip." Erox continued his line of thought as if he were actually going to hand Trake a weapon. "I think the Deck Director would love to make an example of you."

"Me?" Trake mocked, then resumed his complaining. "But it is useless. These Blessed draftees will never learn to do battle while swinging from the ropes. Swinging from a sacred battle blimp is for Honored warriors, not these hapless servants."

"These 'hapless servants' have their afterlife to look forward to. Since the Gods deny us an Encore, let these Blessed idiots face the blades head on," Erox returned. "The Wretched have swollen their numbers with forbidden procreation. Their terrorist ways must be expunged. We must use our every asset to do the will of the Gods."

Trake felt a familiar stab of resentment freeze his heart. Erox spoke words he hardly needed to hear, or hardly should have, anyway. As if to swing away from his dangerous feelings, Trake released his hold on the rope that held him suspended from the rusting girders supporting yet another floor of Chosen refugees and pivoted downward in his harness until he grabbed the thick rope with his bare feet. His braided foretuft of thick, black hair now dangled below him as he hung head down.

As he refocused on the job at hand, Trake ordered aloud so all his trainees could hear, "Erox, give us a jolt to simulate a cannon blast." Then, to the men hanging around him, Trake intoned, "Use the recoil of the blast to get you swinging again. You're a gnat in a Za web if you're not moving. Time your body shift. You have to imagine the battle blimp floating above you. In combat, the blimp will be moving, always. Use that movement, anticipate it, and you will never be left hanging. You are a 'swing crew.' If you're not swinging, you are dead."

As the jolt came, Trake shifted, flipped and swung in a precise example of what he expected. He looked away. He could not bear to watch his charges flounder. He would scream if he did. It was not their fault, he knew. Like all Honored warriors, his instructors had dangled him by one foot over his mother's tit as his first lesson. He was not sure why, but no one had anticipated that the Cleansing of the Wretched could go so wrong. No one had imagined the Honored would need their Blessed servants to join in the fight. The Directors had always told the Honored that the job was almost finished, that they had all but purged the Wretched from Father's skin. Now, Trake feared, it was they, the Chosen, both Honored and Blessed alike, who would be purged.

Instead of watching his men, Trake allowed his gaze to wander across the crowded metal deck, still littered with the sleeping masses of the Chosen, almost all of whom were cousins to one degree or another. With the Strength flowing through him, each slumbering form appeared to him as a glittering bundle of energy. Without looking, he felt the men around him struggling to perform their prescribed movements. Ignoring his duties of instruction, Trake let the Strength gather with increased intensity in his eyes and ears. Movement and the creaking of ropes drew his attention through the still, stale air to the central ring of this deck that had been his home for all of his twenty-three years. Eight or ten men were already at their hauling stations, pulling at the ropes that would soon deliver buckets of water from the lake far below. In a few minutes, as the sun rose, Trake would be able to see all the way to the far-side Za filters, their dense webs shimmering white and gray between the red-rusted steel of the deck above them and the cluttered tans and browns of the sleeping Chosen, littered across the deck before him. He thought for a moment about the outside world, Father, his skin alive this time of year with the brilliant greens of new winter grasses, his skies as scrubbed as possible by the rains that would one day scour the last remnants of the filthy legacy left by their ancestors. It was almost worth it, Trake thought, to face the bows and blades of the

Wretched to escape this gloomy, shadowless tower his people called home.

As most of Trake's cousins slept, sharing warmth under age-thinned blankets, Trake spied a few Blessed servants rummaging in their living circles, preparing for another day. A few other Blessed picked their way through the masses, maybe heading for the commissary to start on the morning meal. Soon, the all too familiar aroma of roasted Milnox porridge would wash across the deck, helping Trake put a name to his dangerous longings — remembering the days not so long ago when the great blimps left them by their ancestors were used for trade with distant towers instead of constant sorties against the Wretched terrorists.

With subtle movements, Trake rotated in his perch. Two living circles within easy sight held his unhealthy fascination. First he spotted his own circle. He was pleased to see Gratton, his wrinkled lead Blessed, already at work. Hard-muscled Erox had spent the night, bringing his servants with him to join into one large circle. Trake watched Gratton and one of Erox's Blessed servants folding and stowing their bedding, preparing their expanded camp for day use. Fronton and Erox's strongest Blessed, Arment, were missing. No doubt they were already lending their backs at the hauling stations with the intent of commandeering the first load of water for their masters. Trake and Erox had learned long ago that if they pooled their resources and used their whips liberally, they could bully or cajole almost anyone on the deck, except the Deck Director or his cronies. Trake noted his and Erox's little bevy of Blessed companions were still lumps of bedding. Trake shied from his immediate wanton desire. Coveting Erox's possessions was a sin that could well keep him from his next promotion and that would not do. Trake could earn a prettier, more pleasing boy on his own.

As if in boredom, Trake's eyes wandered casually to the left, sighting the other circle that held his smothered fascination. It was a female circle, four circles down from his, and it would not do for the Gods, the Deck Director or even Erox to catch Trake showing interest there. All Chosen were very clear on this, their most sacred sacrament. Men and women lived separate lives. The Gods had spoken. Beyond directed procreation between Honored Breeders, the sexes did not mix, did not speak, did not even acknowledge one another.

Trake shrunk his thoughts from this blasphemous perversion. He tried not to look, reminding himself the Gods saw all. Though even as he looked, he wondered what drove him. Did he have a secret desire for the whip? Was he angry with the Gods for not inviting the Honored to the Encore? Was he perverted from birth, damaged beyond repair? Whatever the answer, his compulsion consumed him, controlling his gaze.

There she was, crouched, rolling her bedding. Trake watched as she stood, fascinated that her military haircut and nearly completed tattoo did not help him ignore her. Who would have ever dreamed of Blessed women training for the Home Guard? Especially this slight beauty with piercing green eyes, a mischievous smile and an apparent penchant for the whip. Her performance must have been exceptional, Trake conceded as he watched her move, for her tattoo to be so far along after only two years of training. The thought evoked a mixture of emotions he tried to bury immediately: he was thrilled and revolted, hungry and afraid, angry and forgiving. What was it about the swell of her hips that made him forget all the pleasures hard muscles brought? And what of her mounded breasts, which served no function since she was not born to breed? Were her lips so much more luxurious than those of his Blessed companions? Were they, even in the remotest way, knowing of a man's needs? He thought not.

The fascination must lie in her eyes and smile, Trake concluded. There was no other explanation. Those instances, over the last twenty years, when their eyes met across the crowded deck, had cauterized their own space in his heart. Isolated, protected, cherished. Moments when, before she dropped the protective Za web across her face, he saw her buried spirit. Dangerous defiance is what he saw at times, loving compassion at others. He even thought he might have seen appreciation or attraction. That would have been too much to ask. Those memories he must have built from his own desires.

"Trake, what's next?" Erox demanded, annoyance clear in his muffled voice.

Warmed and somehow revolted at the same time, Verbolana switched her now-mind to the slight figure rolling her bedding.

Shivering, Verbolana finished rolling her bedding and stood, her ancient, earth-toned smock falling to the tops of her bare feet. She combed her fingers through her tuft of stringy yellow hair, then let them wander back over her freshly shaven aft skull and the scabs of the tattoo that was still in progress. Her explorations confirmed what her mind still had trouble believing, that the Deck Director had chosen her for the Blessed Home Guard. Ten years ago, even a Blessed male in the military would have been unheard of. The massive Wretched insurgency had changed all that. So many were called now, even obstinate young teachers with the whip marks to prove it.

"Vee, where are you going?" The almost silent words floated through the frigid air.

"Where do you think?" came Verbolana's snarled response, loud enough to wake a hundred Chosen. "Do you think I would abandon your warmth for fun?" She quieted. "Training calls and if I'm late I'll get the whip again."

"You love the training and you know it," sweet-faced Treena shot back, resentment obvious in her voice.

"I love the training, the physical challenge, but I don't love leaving you. And I don't like to think about what I am training for. Can you imagine the Wretched here, overrunning our tower?"

Treena stuck her tangled mop from under the covers. "No! And how could they ever get this far up, anyway? The Gods built these towers to keep the Chosen safe while Father healed. Those Wretched might be able to climb up to the first deck or two, but we would just pull the ropes up. How could they climb and conquer us way up here? It's absurd."

"They wouldn't need to," Verbolana hissed in defense. "All those terrible sinners would need to do is keep us from dipping our buckets in the lake. The Gods built our towers over lakes so that we would have enough water to survive while Father healed, but apparently the Gods did not anticipate that there would be so many survivors from the Great Cleansing. These Wretched are truly diabolical. Without water, surrender would be within a matter of weeks." Verbolana allowed herself to calm before she continued. "Sometimes I think the Directors should call everyone to the Militia. Then you'd understand how vulnerable we are."

Treena's sparkling face fell in defeat. "All I wanted to say was that I miss our mornings. It was the only time they gave us and now that is gone, too."

"I know." But something distracted Verbolana. She felt eyes on the back of her head. Her newly acquired Strength prickled the back of her neck. She looked off across the crowded deck to the raised dais of the Deck Director, sure that he had his ugly stare on her, but his attention was elsewhere. Movement to the right caught her eye. A swing crew was training. The man in the center was looking at her. From across the short distance they locked eyes. A warmth of excitement flushed through Verbolana's body before she could control herself. Trake was staring at her again.

Verbolana's now-mind yearned to take control, to rush across the three or four living circles that separated them and leap into his arms. There was no confusion now, no lingering doubts, but she had made that mistake a few times already and the outcome was never satisfactory. Anytime she tried to apply her new understanding to an old situation, the results had been catastrophic. Someone always ended up getting whipped or beaten. Once even worse. Verbolana remembered taking a short sword to the Deck Director and then having to fight off half the deck, including Trake, before she could ask God to get her out. No, it was best just to watch and learn.

She remembered her reaction to Trake's interest. Could it be coincidence, or was his interest something deeper, something more sinister? She looked away, and wondered. She had spent her entire life on this deck. For twenty-two years, she had lived within a rope's length of this man and still had no idea what he thought or how he felt. She had never spoken to him and yet his voice filled her dreams.

"Vee, you'd better go." Treena's voice broke through her thoughts.

"Of course. See you tonight?" It was the appropriate question. The Gods did not allow settled Blessed couples. Their assigned Honored took priority. Verbolana felt lucky that her Honored master preferred older, less exuberant companions.

"That's the plan. I'll have to wait to see. Harta has been a little unpredictable," Treena responded, referring to her own master.

Verbolana bent and gave her friend a kiss on the forehead. "I'll miss you if you can't make it. I'll probably invite Wexi just in case."

As Verbolana walked off, she thought of Treena and Wexi, but Trake also snuck into her thoughts. Rumor said his battle blimp was going on patrol tonight. Her eyes strayed again to his training circle. His back was to her now, which made it so much easier to walk away.

# Chapter 5

Verbolana awoke alone in the large bed of Alcot's bed-grotto, her sheet and blankets crumpled and piled around her, a buffer to the world outside. She didn't need the sleep, at least her body didn't. With a little prayer to her new God, any weariness could be removed in a flash. It was her mind that needed the sleep, needed the escape from her constant searching.

Confident that Verbolana had the skills she needed for now, Alcot had excused himself, content to let her explore on her own for a while. And Verbolana was grateful for his departure. Her self-absorbed indulgences came close to sinful coveting in her mind. She was spending hours upon hours lost inside someone else's head, literally. She had gotten very good at this quiet observation, so good she was now concerned these constant forays had become an obsession. But the knowledge she had gained was helping her heal, helping her accept that her dreams and desires had been more the reality than her waking thoughts had ever been. And she was determined to dig deeper, to learn more about what she had forever left behind. If she were never to be granted the Blessed Amnesia, then she would need something. With a simple prayer, she was off again.

For more than three hours, Trake and his assault force had floated silently through the starless sky toward the crumpled city where they hoped to cleanse another large number of Wretched from the skin of Father.

Now that dawn finally approached, Trake crouched at the foremost porthole of what used to be the giant blimp's cargo bay. Four long lines of groggy, nervous warriors sat on the cold floor of the coach behind him, all intent on their meditations. The jagged-toothed serpent heads tattooed to each side of Trake's shaved aft skull seemed to peer around his ears, as focused as Trake on the scene before them. The two-headed, winged Vipeon was the most feared warrior in all of his world's mythology, and for some reason the Gods had chosen Trake's back and head for this fierce symbol to ride on. Trake had never been sure why. The acidic fear that crept up from his belly in moments like this seemed strong enough to devour the creature from the inside of his skin. Yet Trake knew the importance of this talisman for his men, so even in the frigid predawn air, he led every battle bare-chested. His squared shoulders held both his and the animal's graceful necks tall and proud; his broad, long-muscled back gave the creature's body a life of its own, moving as he moved, adding strength and vitality to his own body already hardened by the life of a born soldier.

Trake swallowed hard and took a slow calming breath, reluctantly pulling the filthy air deep into his lungs. The mask that covered his nose and mouth did little to filter the stench of his burned-out world.

As he heard Erox descend the metal ladder from the wheelhouse above, Trake pulled his attention away from the broken jumbled landscape ahead and turned to await Erox's arrival.

"We passed the old dome foundation thirty-two minutes ago, sir," Erox breathed. "We will be over the city center at sunrise, just as planned."

Trake's thoughts momentarily flitted to the enormity of what had been one of many great cities that had once dotted Father like so many insidious cancers. It was said that the dome that had covered this city was more than fifty-four miles across and fifteen-hundred feet high at its center. "What of the winds?" Trake asked his old friend. Like Erox's, his words carried silently on his breath.

"Standard for predawn, sir. Southwest at thirty knots. We are cruising at a thousand feet, heading due south at fifty. Below five hundred feet the air is bone still."

Trake leaned his head out the porthole and let a large dollop of spit drop from his mouth. He traced its course through the different wind currents until it disappeared under the bow of the giant blimp. "Is there shear?" Trake asked.

"Sharp, right above five hundred. We will need a quick descent to keep running silent. We have frost. No clouds from horizon to horizon."

*Good news about the frost,* Trake thought. The cold air would improve their maneuverability and lift. In the summer, or even on a warmish winter day, this beast could wallow like a heavy load dangling from the ropes with not enough backs to lift it.

"Very good, Sailing Master," Trake commanded, using his friend's formal title. "Pass the word, missiles launch in three minutes."

"Perfect." Erox smiled his excitement before picking his way back down the ranks toward the wheelhouse, spreading the order as he went.

Trake surveyed his troops as his eyes followed Erox's departure. Blessed draftees were almost all he had left. They were well trained, but nothing like his Honored warriors. Trake prayed, *Humble Magician, God of War, please, set the stage for a rousing performance; give us good wind, steady hands and keen eyes to do your will.*

The flattened, broken city stretched to the horizon before him; this place of evil, this site of so much corruption, both of mind and of body. He shuddered to think what his ancestors had done behind these walls — collected, coveted, consumed and bred themselves into oblivion. Just like the Wretched who would soon die. The thought that the Chosen and the Wretched had come from the same stock was almost too much for Trake to comprehend.

He felt the deck of the great blimp drop as they began their descent. Groggy-eyed soldiers, now tense with fear, turned to him. He flicked them a signal with his fingers. As one, the long lines of men rose to squatting position. Another flick and the men in the outside rows pulled and affixed the ropes that raised the well-oiled porthole hatches. Frozen air dumped through the open holes as the men in the center rows pulled open and laid flat the hatches their great-great-grandfathers had cut into the floor. They traveled on the wind. There was no sound of their passage.

As they descended, the blimp buffeted through the shear. Two men toppled; the clatter against the metal floor froze hearts, pumped adrenaline. All knew the racket would scream their arrival through the frozen air. *Oh well, if they have not seen us coming, they have heard us now,* Trake acknowledged. With haste, he raised his right arm and pumped it down twice. Smoke off a full minute before he had planned.

*Thuwuph, thuwuph, thuwuph!* The compressed air cannons commenced the battle. The massive coach lurched back with the recoil of the great guns. Frantic clanking filled the air as the gun crews ratcheted their compressors for another salvo. Behind him, Trake's men drew arrows and fitted them to the slots of their crossbows.

Trake watched the smoke missiles streak through the dark gray sky. Two disappeared into the hollow of their target; one wandered wide to port and ignited against a crumpled pillar that had once been a major support for the sports arena they now attacked.

"Damn, one wide to port! Check masks; prepare to take on smoke." They dropped fast now, closing to fighting distance. "Guns one and two, load smoke. Gun three, load shrapnel. Fire smoke when ready. Hold shrapnel!"

One gun blasted, the second only moments behind. Both missiles disappeared into the mouth of the makeshift cave. Trake threw his hand high, fingers spread wide, the signal for "all stop." Erox, in the bridge two hundred feet behind, flared the air brakes, and the ship wobbled to a halt, directly above the entrance to the old loading dock.

"Dip arrows." Trake always waited until the coach settled to give this order. He had seen firsthand the death that came from one scratch of this stuff.

*Thwack!* A short-lived scream gurgled through the coach. Trake glanced over his shoulder. An arrow protruded from the neck of one of his men. Trake recognized him as a cousin; second or third, he wasn't sure, but he was Blessed.

"Careful," Trake ordered. "Strip, dump, replace. Observation, report!"

"Starboard thirty by fifteen forward," came a clipped voice from the deck above. Trake followed thirty degrees down from the horizon and fifteen degrees forward from the center point of the coach. Rubble and a lone tree were all he saw.

*Twang, twang, thwack!* Two arrows bounced off the metal shell of the coach. The third hit its mark. Another down. "Strip, dump, replace!" Trake needed to remind these Blessed troops every time. Their comrade might appear merely injured, but there were no nonlethal wounds in this business. "Report!" he screamed.

"Port forty-five by thirty aft."

"Helm, pivot hard left rudder!" Jets of flame from the no-longer-understood engines pushed the nose and tail of the mammoth balloon in a static spin. The coach lurched, throwing three to the deck. In the middle of the maneuver, a stripped corpse dropped from the coach's belly. Another followed shortly.

From the loading dock below, a great roar erupted. The Wretched were pleased with their kills.

Driven by the smoke and crouched low, the Wretched swarmed from their cover. They scattered in every direction like skitterbugs at first light, heading for whatever cover the gray cement rubble all around them afforded.

"Scramble ... fire at will!" Trake shouted. "Target the breeders and the children." He watched the Wretched drop as his men fired ... ten... seventeen ... thirty down in the first minute. He heard the return fire bounce off the coach shell and the enormous balloon that kept them aloft. He silently thanked his ancestors for the strength of their vehicle. Though no Chosen living understood what the blimps were made of or what powered them, so far, 130 years after their construction by the machines, they still performed flawlessly.

Trake counted forty-six dead before the swarm had dispersed, with only those first two causalities on his side. Still, an entirely unacceptable ratio. *These heathens will breed that many tonight,* he reminded himself. *We probably won't breed any. I've got to bring my numbers up before I head home. I'll never get the final color in my tattoo this way.*

"Bring us up to two-hundred. Ahead quarter speed. Remember to lead your targets. Cannons fore and aft, load shrapnel. Fire at will!" he commanded.

Assuming every hit as a kill, Trake continued counting ... *fifty-eight ... sixty-five ...*

*Pwamm!* Trake's head smashed into the bulkhead. He hit the floor, a thousand suns dancing before his eyes. Screams of pain and panic filled the coach. "Report!" Trake screamed as he lay on his back, gaining his senses. No one heard him over the turmoil.

He pulled himself to a squat on the heaving floor and took stock. Almost every one of his men was sprawled across the deck. One kneeled over a hatch screaming, "He fell! He fell!"

Trake looked down from his porthole. Two more of his men lay broken in the rubble below. "Anyone see anything?" He would mourn the dead later.

"Port side, forty-five by zero. Something big."

*No shit,* Trake thought. He looked back through the coach. There was a man-sized dent in the side of his ship. *What?* "Helm, left hard rudder. Full ahead!" Whatever the cost, he needed to find what had done this. "Rig the slings. Swing crews prepare. Observation, talk to me!"

"It's the size of a large tree, sir. Looks like they're ratcheting it back."

"Observation, direct the helm. Put our nose straight into it. Distance?" He was already running for the rear exit door.

"Three-hundred fifty yards."

"Fore cannons, rapid fire! Target the gun crew!" Trake screamed.

The Wretched had never developed any weapons on their own. This new advance could change everything. What if they brought this new weapon against a tower? It was unthinkable. Trake thought fast. "Drop grappling hooks fore and aft, starboard and port, with fifty feet of rope. Helm, bring us to sixty feet. Rig slings for a running landing." Trake waited for five beats of his racing heart. "Lads, listen! We're going down to grab this thing, whatever it is. We need cover fire. Shoot anything that moves."

"Sir, they're preparing to fire," announced Observation.

"Fore cannons, I need three minutes! Blast those Wretched animals."

By the time Trake stumbled through his warriors to his aft position, one of his crew was holding his harness ready for him to slip into and cinch. His dual swords protruded from the back, crossed for quick draw. "Sailing Master Erox, you're in charge. Bring me back."

"Aye, sir!" Erox yelled from the bridge. "Approaching sixty feet."

*Thawoom!* Something huge streaked by the port side, the displaced air enough to buffet the coach violently.

"It's a long arm with some sort of trailing basket!" shouted the lookout. "I don't know if we'll be able to lift it."

Trake ignored the man, motioned to the five others now ready in their harnesses and swung from the door.

Verbolana pulled herself from the remembrance. She knew what was coming and for at least a moment she wanted to wallow in Trake's Strength and courage. With visceral intensity she fell into Trake's mind again, his Strength her Strength, his determination her determination. What had she been doing at that moment? On a whim, she switched scenes, now as natural as focusing on a new object in the room.

Her bare feet slapped against the metal grate of the bustling deck as she cut through one living circle after another and made her way back to the commissary. Sweat from her training session still dripped from her aft scalp, leaving dark smudges on her threadbare gray smock.

Sunrise and the hour or so after was Verbolana's favorite time of day, the only time she felt even the slightest influence of her home's languid sun. Not that the sun was at fault, she reminded herself. The poor thing labored tenaciously to reach her here in the middle of this large deck, hidden behind layer after layer of the floor to ceiling Za spider webs her people used as filters for the putrid air. The smoky air still clung to her sorry world, eight generations after the Cleansing had begun. Nevertheless, Verbolana appreciated the moment, for soon the sun would rise further in the sky to leave everyone in the gloomed shadow of the deck above.

As she skipped along, Verbolana could not let the still-sleeping forms of the Honored she stepped over and around foul her mood. She prayed, *Oh Righteous Narrator, God of Virtue, give me patience. The Honored have their roles to perform in this play, and I, as a Blessed servant, have mine. I do not deserve to know the climax of our performance. Give me the strength to ignore the critics that dwell in my soul and listen only to the direction you give me.*

Buried in her heart, deeper than the Gods could read, Verbolana acknowledged, as usual, that the prayer did not help. The laziness of the Honored still irritated her and as she stepped across another sleeping form. To get even, just a little, she accidentally brushed her bare toenails over the figure's exposed leg. She moved on quickly. Getting even was a dangerous game.

As Verbolana approached the central ring of the tower, she slowed. Some Blessed were busy at the ropes, hauling dried grain to the stone mill a few levels down or fresh vegetables to the decks above. At the railing, Verbolana stopped to watch. The view from here was still inspiring, even though she had seen it nearly every day for the past twenty-two years. When she looked down, she still had to hold onto the railing to forestall the awesomely magnetic feeling of vertigo that always overcame her. The diminishing rings of deck after deck, falling almost endlessly to the lake below, dangling ropes and ever-smaller cargo nets made her head feel like the solid metal she stood on was dancing in the winds. Sometimes she wondered how far it was to the lake below and though every school child knew they were forty-six floors up, she still had no idea how far that might be.

Mathematics had no place in the lives of the Chosen. Mathematics led to discovery, discovery led to advancement and advancement led to doom. And if the Chosen fell into that trap, they would be as guilty as the Wretched. Father needed to rest; his seemingly endless vigor had been sucked dry and all needed to honor his time.

Pohta, a third or fourth cousin, stood by the rails, also watching.

"Waiting for something?" Verbolana asked casually.

Pohta bolted to attention before she turned to the voice. "Oh, it's just you." She let out a long breath.

"Glad to see you too," Verbolana snickered, her innocent face crinkling with mischief.

"No, no, it's just that … Well, you know. I don't need the whip today. My Honored Breeder is anxious for her bath. I have been sent to commandeer the first load of water."

"Do you think she has any notion how many backs it takes to bring her precious water up this many levels?"

Pohta flinched and stepped away from her cousin. "Who's looking for the whip now?" She didn't wait for an answer. She slid over toward the loading dock to wait in peace.

Verbolana couldn't blame her. *Why do I have to be such a troublemaker? The Righteous Narrator will have his way – eventually.* She knew the answer and she knew the consequences. She also knew she could no more hide from her impertinent nature than ascend to the top deck and bask in the light of the sun. No matter how many lashes she took, she could not help but question and wonder – and yearn. She looked over at the straining backs of her cousins in their pulling stations and her heart went out to them. The pain of a lifetime at the ropes was unimaginable. Two years ago, she had spent four grueling days pulling, as punishment for her stubborn ways, and that was more than she could take.

# Chapter 6

Trake swung from the protection of his craft into a shower of arrows. It took every ounce of Verbolana's will to stay focused and not deflect the onslaught of flying barbs. She felt his prayer as it bubbled through the welling panic. *Harmonious Minstrel, Lord of Nature, forgive me for trespassing here. I touch the skin of our Father only to protect him, like sterile gauze cleansing a wound. Know that my visit will be short and my footprint light. Help me protect our Father from those who refuse to see. Help me restore the balance and bring our Father those who will live with him in harmony.*

Ever since the Chosen had abandoned the evil machines of their ancestors, they had learned about using ropes. It was simple for Trake's blimp crew to swing all six warriors smoothly to the ground on a dead run to their target. Each man unhooked his harness and drew his swords before he had taken five steps. Trake dove behind a chunk of broken cement to take stock. His Honored squad fanned out behind similar cover.

*Thuwuph, thuwuph, thuwuph!* Cannons blasted above him. Screams of pain and confusion erupted somewhere in front.

Trake took a moment to gather the Strength. Here, touching Father's skin, the power he felt welling from the core of Father still shocked him. Springed steel now replaced wobbling legs, while whipping speed invaded his arms. The Strength was so much stronger here, actually touching Father. This was only his eighth time to his skin, and he took nothing for granted, not like the Wretched.

All panic dissolved as the Strength overtook him. Trake gave a knowing smile to his men and signaled for a straight-on assault. By his calculations, they had almost no time before the crude machine would strike again.

Trake advanced at a dead run, his swords crossed ahead of him, his shaved aft skull glistening, making the tattooed heads of the ferocious Vipeon come to life. If he could capture this new weapon, his superiors would surely award him with his final tattoo color. Maybe even move him a deck closer to the sun.

Together, the Honored squad rushed through the broken landscape. The Strength changed everything. Arrows now flew in slow motion. Trake sliced them in mid-flight with his flashing blades. He wondered for a moment why the Wretched did not feel the Strength. The Author said it was because they were nonbelievers, but Trake was not sure. The Strength was so powerful; how could they not feel it?

A Wretched battle cry startled him as he rounded a column of jagged cement and twisted metal. Trake raised one blade to block the attack as his other blade arced low at an unprotected belly. The man screamed no more. Back to Trake's right, another Wretched advanced and another died. Trake was almost jealous. Their Encore would be so sweet, even if they did not believe. Trake had only this life, he knew. No matter how sweet his Blessed servants made his life, how could anything compare with the promised afterlife? He ran on.

Jab, swing, twirl! The wicked machine was now in view. The thing was huge, made of rusted steel and frayed cables, ratcheting cranks and a swinging basket. It looked ready to fire. Trake glanced to his left and right; four Honored still advanced. Enough to handle the hooks.

Trake signaled overhead to his blimp and heard the jets' throaty response. Erox would fly down the mouth of a volcano if asked. Slash, duck, pivot! *Encore! Encore! Send the Wretched to their Encore,* his mind sang. He saw another of his brethren fall, cleaved nearly in half by a crazed, axe-wielding heathen. Three remained. He would have to handle two of the hooks himself.

*Thawuuunk!* The great machine loosed another huge chunk of cement. Trake followed its arc. Wrong trajectory. The missile sailed under his ship and off to raise destruction on the already decimated landscape. With the arrival of the blimp and all its firepower, Trake watched the cowardly Wretched abandon their machine, scurrying through the rubble like Blessed children under the eye of the Deck Director. But now, with the Wretched's field of fire cleared of comrades, enemy arrows flew unabated from the cover all around them. Trake dove low and rolled, turning his face to the sky. His ship floated directly above, grappling hooks dangling. He signaled "All fire." Glorious barbed rain showered the ground ahead of him. Trake hoped someone was keeping count.

Ten beats he waited, then peeked out. He was no longer a target. The Wretched were in full retreat. Trake scurried around and through the rubble to within thirty feet of the contraption. Neither of his troopers was apparent. Sheathing his swords, Trake bolted for one of the dangling hooks. Grabbing it at full speed, he swung the rest of the way to his goal, found a solid perch for the hook and attached it to the Wretched machine. A satisfying clink confirmed its purchase as Trake heard one of his men bring another hook home on the other side. Running for the next hook, Trake willed his winged totem to give him speed.

Arrows thunked all around, but Trake's eyes were on the next hook and the next perch. He leaped and grabbed the hook, his momentum swinging him high onto the back of the machine.

Frantic glances told him he stood on what looked like the loading deck, with nowhere to attach the hook. He yanked hard on the rope, but it gave nothing. An arrow ricocheted off the deck at his feet. He would not survive long up here. All signals forgotten, he waved desperately to his ship. He heard the jets flare and the rope gave slack. He snaked his hand under the deck to find what he hoped was a solid beam. He hooked the rope in place and looked to his right. Recker, an Honored ensign, gave him the thumbs up, indicating that the last hook was set. Trake signaled the ship, hoping Alken, his third remaining squad member, had made it to the machine.

The jets above flared and Trake appreciated their heat as Erox pointed them downward for maximum lift. Trake felt the thing jolt and groan and fidget. Could the jets lift this monster? Would the ropes hold? Finally, the load broke free from Father and swung forward. Trake grabbed for leverage as the deck pitched with the uneven load, his hands slick – with blood.

* * *

Trake flew through the freezing morning sky clinging to the heaving platform, transfixed by the jagged gash in his arm. Life was so unfair. His moment of glory, the heroic capture and the celebration that would follow, ruined by the simple scratch of an arrow he thought he had blocked. This was not the way to die. A thrown battle-axe to the chest, his mates above groaning at the sight – that's how it should end. But, no, he would not even let it end there. No axe could stop him. Trake fantasized himself staggering, an axe-throwing Wretched approaching to finish him off. Standing tall, the axe still embedded in his chest, they would battle. Amidst flashing blades, Trake would realize that his armor had taken the brunt of the blow. Dramatically, he would rip the axe from his chest to astonished cheers from above. With a mighty backhanded swipe of the man's own axe, Trake would relieve his Wretched foe of his head. Another roar would explode from the blimp above and as Trake grabbed for the dangling hook, he would stagger back from another fatal blow, this time from a cowardly arrow loosed by a hidden Wretched.

Barely able to push forward, Trake would signal the ship. Give me more slack. If I can't set this hook, all will be lost.

*Thawack!* Another arrow, this one through his leg. *Thwack! Thwack!* Two more sunk into the chest. He would give a mighty tug, falling forward finally to set the hook. With the last of his Strength, he would then roll, ignoring the pain as the arrows pushed deeper by his movements. With his last breath, he would signal his ship. Mission accomplished.

That was his death, not this paltry scratch that would bring him no honor, just a delirious fever, a rasping liquid cough and a shameful looseness of his bowels.

Let go! Let this heaving deck throw you to your death, he said to himself. Some will see – and all will mourn.

Suddenly Trake envisioned a new death. He realized his mission was not over. He could still die with honor. The blimp crew needed his direction. What were they to do with this Wretched machine? They couldn't take it to their tower. Surface dwellers had been crawling all over it and it was contaminated. However, this new weapon needed to be studied, its threat analyzed. The Generals would want to know its range, its payload and its accuracy. If any more of these abominations existed, his people needed every scrap of information they could glean.

The answer to both of his problems was horrible yet glorious. Trake would have to land the machine somewhere on the surface, close to his tower, then defend it until all the proper analyses had been completed. His only hope was that the poison in his system would allow him this final honor. Moreover, he hoped Father would understand. For setting foot on his skin for more than a few moments was, in itself, a death sentence. To place a blasphemous machine on him was unthinkable. Unthinkable, yet necessary.

So Trake held on, his new course set in his mind. The frigid air blued his fingers and his face, but he failed to notice. Once set, his mind traveled deep into his body, to a place the Humble Magician had shown them: One finger below the bellybutton and halfway to the back. They called it Dahr, the center, the point that vanished. It was the same place he had gone to find the Strength, but with his feet not on Father's skin, this meditation now had only a fraction of the power.

"Commander," a voice filtered through his meditations sometime later. "We're approaching our tower."

"Thank you, Ensign." Trake pulled himself immediately alert. He took stock. Good. Alken, the third member of the squad, had made it aboard and sat wrapped around a pole close by. Recker had crawled through the machine to come to Trake's side. He stared at Trake's open wound.

"We're going to have to put this thing down. We can't take it home!" Trake yelled through the wind, watching the impact of his words. He saw his team hadn't made the same logical connections he had. "I'll need help guarding it." Their confusion melded into horror. Both men thought they had survived another day.

"I figured we'd drop it in the lake," ventured Recker. It was an equally horrific suggestion for Father, but one that they would survive. At least for those who were unmarked by battle. "The Honored are so few. We are needed." Ensign Recker presented another logic. Alken nodded in agreement.

Trake sized his men up by locking eyes with each as he considered their proposal. How many Honored would die in the face

54

of such a machine? Not for the first time, he wondered how the Gods had chosen the Honored for such duty. In the old days, before the Wretched posed any real threat, the life of an Honored male was sweet. Blessed servants hauled their water, braided their ropes, forged their weapons, grew and cooked their food, even scrubbed the sweat from their backs. All that was required of the Honored men was to train for battle and fly out for a little target practice now and again. No life was easy since the destruction of the machines, but the Honored had the best of what there was, in exchange for receiving no Encore. Now, with death so close, the trade-off seemed unfair and impractical. The first to die were the ones with the most to lose. Even the Blessed at the hauling ropes outlived the Honored these days.

So be it. Their questions changed nothing. Necessity had set Trake's date of death as well as that of the two who rode beside him.

Trake looked away from his men, unable to voice his decision. He focused on his now lost home, as their tower came into view through the tangled structure of the weapon. Perched above a perfectly round lake of shimmering blue, Trake realized they must be struggling through a strong headwind, for only a westerly gale could have scrubbed the skies so clear.

A glorious day to die? Trake's heart sank as he watched his sacrificed life loom larger in his vision and his heart. His suddenly beautiful tower appeared, shimmering with iridescent glory. Protective Za spider webs cocooned almost the entire structure, breaking the midday light into its component pieces, blasting rainbows of color to eyes accustomed to the drab realities that otherwise filled Trake's life. This was not the day to die. The normally brown skies sparkled blue. Even the spiky trees that rushed below him showed deep shadowed greens, contrasting with the brightness of new growth.

Trake's world never looked like this. He scrambled to his knees, still clutching the Wretched machine, his resentment growing. As the tower loomed larger, details he had long taken for granted assaulted his new sensibilities. The gardens, with their deep greens and rusty browns, popped in contrast against the stark white of the Za filters. Every deck had something growing, even at this time of year. Trake realized he didn't have the slightest idea what those crops might be. All he knew was he always had enough to eat and every scrap of waste, including his own excrement, went back to the gardens. He also realized he didn't care. The gardens were Blessed work and he was Honored. They would ascend to the Ponds of Bliss and Contentment and he would be decomposed to be added to the gardens. He was supposed to get his bliss and contentment here! To die here, now, was wrong.

Trake took note of another great blimp floating above his tower, moored with straining cables to the top floor landing field. Marveling maybe for the first time, he noted the size of the once luxurious vehicle. He looked above to confirm that his own command was of equal size. Why, his thoughts suddenly spat, were they only allowed to occupy the lowest decks of the cargo bay of these great ships, when above them lay deck after deck of who knew what?

He had heard the stories, just like he had heard the stories of the upper floors of the towers. The Gods could not stop rumors of the empty wasted rooms that spread out above him, especially when the stories were so tantalizing. Walled rooms with carpeted floors large enough for an entire living circle to spread out in secluded comfort. Other smaller rooms specifically designed for evacuating and cleansing one's self or one's lover. Trake was not sure he believed such stories, but why else, why else would the Directors bar so much of their battle blimps from exploration?

Sure, there were probably sinful machines and corrupting niceties, but were not the Honored evolved enough to see past such traps? Could they not, as a special treat or performance enticement, wallow for a day, or just an hour, in what the Chosen had given up for the sake of Father many generations ago?

With death waiting for him before this day was through, Trake fearlessly examined what he had never let his mind explore. *Gods be damned, I have been cheated!* His mind screamed. *You have withheld luxurious comfort from those who deserve it.* Then aloud, "Look, look at that blimp. It is huge and we are crammed on its lowest decks. What are we missing?" He released his white-knuckled grip to point at the distant moored blimp, almost losing his balance in the process. Staggering with sudden grief and anger, Trake continued his tirade to his astonished charges. "Look at that magnificent vehicle. Rows upon rows of windows, luxury beyond belief, serving no purpose, all abandoned. Imagine the cloistered spaces, insulated from the cold and the heat. Room, gentlemen, room to live in comfort and ease! Room for each of us to have our private pleasures. All wasted. Did the Gods not teach us that waste is sinful?"

Recker shot his face skyward. "Gods, the fever has come. Our commander knows not what he says." Then, backing as far as he dared from Trake, he screamed through the wind, "Commander, you must jump! Soon you will disgrace yourself further. Save yourself. Save Father with your sacrifice!"

"Ah ha!" Trake screamed back. "If this is the fever, I want more. I see so clearly, feel so strongly, yearn with such passion. If this is to be the day of my death, then I will grab and suck and flail to the end. I will vent my frustrations and contemplate whatever I wish. I will spit at the Gods if I must, to expel what needs expelling." Trake's focus suddenly turned. "The Wretched," he screamed with diverted passion. "Someone must pay for my squandered life. If it weren't for the Wretched, who knows? Father might have healed before my lifetime. It is the Wretched, not the Gods, who have stolen my life."

Frantically, Trake waved his arms as the deck of the machine pitched wildly beneath his feet. "Erox! Erox! Turn around! Turn around!" He grabbed for a handhold. He started signing his orders with the assumption someone was keeping a lookout. The blimp started its turn almost immediately as Trake tried to orient himself with the landmarks available.

"Commander," Alken came to life. "You are fevered. You do not make sense. We cannot drop this contraption on Father. There will be retribution, such retribution. We must unload, climb to the blimp and drop this thing in the lake. It is the least offensive course."

"What if the Wretched retake it?" Recker tried another tactic. "If we put it down on dry land, all our efforts, our very lives, could be wasted. I agree with Alken. The lake is the least offensive, and the safest for all the Chosen."

Trake ignored his men's arguments while he surveyed the forest for the best spot to put down, somewhere defendable. From this altitude, though, all he saw was a perfectly flat blanket of dense green foliage. Trake remembered Mortoff spouting on their training sorties. The machines had done this. Everything from horizon to horizon, and beyond, had been diabolically engineered by the machines to optimize crop production. What had once been rolling hills had been flattened and sloped, to the perfect pitch, so irrigation water could roll with the ultimate efficiency from its sources above into the holding lake he had lived above all his life.

Trake searched his memory. The old maintenance yards would work. The machines had poisoned that land so efficiently that the black oily ground was still mostly dead. Trake knew the rusted sheet metal of the dilapidated sheds harbored the Wretched, and though other gunships were assigned to keep them empty, he was still nervous. The great roads were another possibility — the long ribbon-like scars that criss-crossed Father seemed never to heal. However, they were too thin for good defense, with sickly forests close on either side.

Trake could think of nowhere else. Long ago, the machines had flattened and fenced, de-rocked and cultivated, drained or irrigated, mined or amended every square inch of this land. The landscape now resembled a prized garden gone awry, clogged with unruly growth, the ground too perfect for growing a healthy forest, Mortoff had said.

A maintenance yard seemed his only option. Trake signaled to the blimp, then explained to his men what he was looking for and sent them off to the far sides of the machine to look. Within a few minutes, the blimp's observation crew had spotted a site. It was on the shore of Lake Oswigg, their home lake. They saw, in the distance, the top floors of their own tower on the horizon, seeming to rise from the shimmering surface of the lake like a glowing island. A forlorn, forgotten island as far as Trake was concerned.

Trake signaled his ship and they made a long slow circle around the compound. Nothing moved.

Trake thought it unlikely the Wretched would choose to hide within eyesight of a tower, but one never knew. The Gods had decreed long-range eyepieces as machines when the Chosen had first taken the towers as homes, so there was no immediate disadvantage, even though they were within sight of the tower. The Wretched had learned generations ago to hide their tracks and their cooking fires.

Trake signaled his ship again and the quiet, midday air exploded with cannon fire. Steel-piercing shrapnel clattered and thudded into the dilapidated compound. Trake watched a long-eared, unnamed creature scamper into the open, bewildered with panic. The next cannon blast pulverized the poor thing. Damn the Wretched. At least his people felt the price and mourned the innocent. He shuddered with the next thought. If there were any Wretched within ten miles, they would probably find the corpse of the dead creature and eat it. Impossible! How could the Gods grant such wickedness an Encore? Trake would never fathom such injustice.

The ship signaled Trake after two strafing rotations. Observation had seen no movement. They also indicated that they were running low on ammunition. Trake reluctantly gave the order to put down. Even in the midst of his seething frustrations, he hoped landing on this black scab would minimize his insult to Father. However, Trake knew this was unlike setting foot in the city. The Gods had deemed that necessary. And though Trake saw this, also, as necessary, he felt certain his Gods would not. There was no middle ground with them. The nature of man, they said, would not allow it. Too many times humans had proven the contrary. Avarice, gluttony, hoarding: These are what man is made of. Only discipline to the Performance could save them, and Father.

Trake's perch bounced to the ground. He did not bother with prayer. The finality of his death was all his mind chewed on. He stared at his chosen mausoleum: greasy black gravel; an occasional stunted tree, bare and forlorn; twisted sheet metal and the rusted disembodied guts of machines.

His resentments continued to surface. The Gods had chosen poorly. *I am of much greater value than any death I might encounter here. Gods, give me a sign! Tell me what I should do!* The gash in his arm throbbed. Remembering the poison in his system and its slow, unstoppable progression, he realized negotiation was useless.

Trake had longed for much more for his life. He had imagined himself ascending the decks with honor and glory, into the outstretched arms of a life softened by favor; sun-kissed fruit from the northern towers, peeled and sliced by soft-clothed smile boys; tubs of warmed water large enough to accommodate three or four slippery bodies; and so much more. He had even heard they used Za webs as screens for privacy much like the blimps used metal and wood. What he could do behind such screens. In his mind, he had spent days arranging and rearranging the pillows of his hidden nest, selecting his harem, sampling virgin flesh, suckling and being suckled. Trake had even dared to imagine his most secret desire coming to him in the quiet hours, stealing silently to his side, somehow knowing his desire and feeding him with her soft wet folds. Yet it wasn't just the folds he ached for. Smooth hot skin, deep curves and jutting red-tipped mounds fascinated him. He longed, even now, especially now, to bring this unspoken need into the light of day, to gaze into the liquid searching eyes of a woman. It was the eyes, he knew, that held the true temptation. Not like the eyes of his male lovers. Those male eyes could hold desire or lust, they could show satisfaction or approval, but they couldn't give Trake what he longed for, that softly yielding, vulnerable anticipation that he had seen once, just once, in the eyes of one of his cousins. He knew it wasn't any woman he wanted, but just one woman, Verbolana.

"Commander, we have company," Alken breathed in his ear.

Trake immediately signaled the blimp. He wanted forty Blessed Militia landed and the swing crews to stay as long as possible. A glorious death was all he had left.

Verbolana opened her eyes to the tangled roots of Alcot's ceiling, tears spilling from her lost eyes. He *had* loved her, once she dug through all of that male garbage. She closed her eyes again and imagined Trake's hands gliding over her bare hips, lounging gently at the junction where her chest began swelling to breast. She felt her nipples respond in anticipation, felt her heart warm under his hands. Anger exploded unexpectedly. Bolting upright, she screamed at the ceiling, "You stole my life, you idiot God! He *did* love me and you kept him from me with your perverted fairy tales. Trake, oh Trake. I rejected you in our last moments together and you were right all along. And now you are lost to me forever. Can you ever forgive me?"

Verbolana found herself in a room with gleaming metal boxes, stone floor and a close flat ceiling. It was a part of Alcot's home she had never been in before. Apparently she had flung herself from bed and ran as she raged. Her red and swollen image stared back at her from one of the metal surfaces, the details lost, but the meaning clear. Without thought, she knew she must escape or fall helplessly into self-pity. She crumpled to the floor where she stood. "God, show me what I was doing while Trake was about to enter battle."

"Vee, if you have any more trouble, you could be sent to the gardens or even the ropes." Treena, Verbolana's very favorite lover, breathed the words into her ear as they lay in total darkness. Wexi lay snuggled at her backside, caressing Verbolana's scalp and neck while avoiding her damaged back. The quiet hours required absolute silence, but that did not mean human activity stopped. Total darkness could hide so much.

"You could be sent outside the filters. The sun and wind would eat you up and spit you to your Encore before your time." Both knew the gardens would shorten Verbolana's life. The smoke of eighteen billion lives and their possessions still clogged the skies these many years later. "If you fail as a teacher, anything is possible. 'A Blessed who fails *must* be punished.' Those are the words of the Magician."

Verbolana put a finger to Treena's lips. She knew her predicament and she appreciated Treena's concern. She also wanted to forget, to feel the comfort of her cousins without the reminders.

She reached out and stroked Treena's shoulder before reaching back to pull Wexi closer. Distraction was impossible. As their lips met, she imagined Trake's bristled chin. As her hands caressed, she longed for hardened muscles instead of the soft curves she encountered.

What do I expect? Men have no use for women. Trake would never come to me. Why would he? His lovers know his needs as they know their own. It is the same with me. Can a man know me as well as my female cousins do? I don't think so. All is as it should be. The Graceful Dancer is right; the flowers of passion grow in clumps with each variety finding protection among its own kind. Only an Honored Vessel and her surrogates need feel the loneliness of cross-pollination.

All three girls lurched as urgent voices erupted in the dark. Off toward the central ring, a torch burst to light and soon after, the ropes set their pulleys to creaking. The girls looked at each other in amazement as other torches came to life, illuminating the central ring and spilling light across the deck. No one interrupted the quiet hours, not in this way.

Verbolana's excitement soured when an impossible thought crossed her mind. She hadn't seen Trake's blimp crew return. They were always back by sunset. She sat up with feigned curiosity. It would not do to reveal the depth of her panic.

The call went out for more Blessed haulers. Verbolana watched through the flickering torchlight as young men struggled beneath their blankets to don pants and scamper to their stations. Soon Erox and a handful of Militia unloaded from a lift.

"Where are the rest?" Verbolana couldn't keep the alarm from her voice. "What has happened?"

"Looks like we'll know soon enough," Wexi commented sleepily over her shoulder. They watched as Erox conferred with the Deck Director at center stage. The Director climbed the steps while still in conference with the Sailing Master. He straightened to address the alarmed deck.

"Our blimp crew has had incredible fortune. They have managed to capture a new machine that the Wretched planned to use against one of our towers." He paused for a moment to let the erupting rumble die down. "Commander Trake and the rest of the blimp crew are camped a short distance from here. We need all Honored warriors and Blessed Militia to report to the training circles immediately."

"That's all?" Verbolana screeched when the Director stepped from the stage. Her discipline would not allow her to scream. *Camped! What does that mean? There are no towers close by. Are they on the surface? They can't be!* At least Trake was still alive. She had gained that much from the announcement. But on the surface? They would all be sacrificed. He was lost to her forever.

"What is this machine?" Wexi's thoughts went to the practical. "The Wretched have built a machine? How can *that* be?" Then, "Come on, Vee, let's get over there. Treena, come with us. You can stand outside the circle."

The crowds were already thick around the circles. They let Verbolana and Wexi through because of their shaved aft skulls, but Treena could not squeeze through. She had no way of knowing this was the last time she would see either of her two closest friends.

Vee and Wexi edged into one of the circles, hand in hand.

The Director was already speaking. "Our ship, as well as two others, is being re-armed as we speak. We are stripping another for a speed run to Drandmont for reinforcements. The threat is as of yet undetermined. We have placed this machine and a small contingent of men on the surface. All archers, ordnance and swing crews are to report to the landing deck immediately."

Verbolana and Wexi turned wide-eyed to each other. Neither had ever left their deck and neither ever guessed they would be.

As female Militia, their training was for home defense. Now they were to fly *off the tower*. An hour ago, they would have said it was impossible. Both eagerly grabbed long-handled Talsartts from the weapons rack and headed to the central ring and the ride of their lives.

As she stood in line to board the lift, Verbolana's thoughts again turned to Trake. He was still alive *and* lost to her forever. She couldn't quite fathom what that meant. Never to see him again was more than her heart could grasp, so instead she thought the opposite. She *would* see him again, soon, as she swung from the blimp, her razored Talsartt trailing her coiled form. She saw him battling, outnumbered, three to one, his Strength failing under the onslaught. Out of nowhere, a slashing Talsartt sliced one, then two of his foes. Rejuvenated by the timely assistance, he finished the third.

Trake would then look up. Verbolana would see the surprise in his eyes turn to appreciation: Appreciation for her skill, for saving his life, for her masked beauty. As she swung closer, he would grab the shaft of her weapon and pull her in to him. At the moment their lips met, arrows would fly again, piercing him and her in the perfect moment for lovers that was never meant to be, that never could be.

# Chapter 7

Verbolana jumped ahead to another moment that stuck out. "Vee, I am too scared. I can't get to the Strength," Wexi breathed. The wind buffeted the coach again, forcing Wexi to reach for balance even though she already sat on the cold steel.

Verbolana opened her eyes, also frightened by the unfamiliar sensations. She had never had anything but solid steel beneath her and the constant movement of the blimp disoriented her. The Za mask Verbolana wore hid the grimace Wexi's words provoked. She eased her mouth to Wexi's ear, knowing the whip would follow if she broke anyone else's concentration.

"If you keep interrupting me, I'll never get there either." Then, with a softer tone, "It's the floor, the constant movement. It's stealing your energy." Though Verbolana knew that wasn't her only problem. Instead of seeing the swirling vortex, all she saw was Trake's face—sometimes panicked and sweat-streaked, in the throes of battle; sometimes with sparkling eyes and an impish grin, in the throes of passion.

"You think that's it? This mask is tickling me, too. I've never worn one before," Wexi rattled.

"If you want to swing first, keep talking." All Verbolana wanted to do was get back to her vision of Trake.

"I'll try," Wexi agreed.

When Verbolana closed her eyes again, she realized how foolish she was. If she wanted to help Trake, she needed to concentrate. She needed every advantage she could get. With reluctance, she pushed his face aside and took her mind to that magical spot behind and below her bellybutton. Tonight she saw it glow scarlet with silver flecks. Letting her mind fall into the vortex created by Father's swirling energy, she chased the ever-falling vanishing point. Her mind dropped through the metal deck she sat on and out into the cold night air. Her imagination twisted and pulled, giving her a familiar moment of overwhelming vertigo. She had never been unrooted from Father. The moving blimp, the freefall down to Father's connecting love—Verbolana focused harder, collected and reformed the vortex, and as soon as it coalesced in her mind, shot it to Father's skin. There she burrowed deeply into the comfort of stone and soil. She saw and felt Father accept her offering, pull it fully into his core and connect the power of the individual to the power of the whole. Then Father gave the offering back, ten—even twenty fold.

Rooted now to Father, Verbolana pulled her mind back into her body, with the fire hose of the Strength blasting through her. She watched, almost as an observer, as the energy filled and spilled from her body, first through her arms and out her relaxed fingers, then her legs and out the arches of her feet and lastly out through the crown of her shaved skull.

"Swing crews to your stations." The man to her right breathed the silent order.

Verbolana turned to Wexi and repeated the order before the Strength nearly exploded her to her feet. She peered forward through the dark. A large Honored warrior stood with a harness ready and nodded in her direction. Was he telling her she was to swing first? How could that be? They would want their strongest fighters in the first wave. She took Wexi's hand and they picked their way forward.

As they approached, the Honored soldier grabbed her shoulders and pulled her close—the first time she had ever been touched by a man. Verbolana felt their energies melding. "Father loves you, young one. You will swing first." It was all he said before he set to work strapping her into the woven harness.

Verbolana switched her vantage point again, the transitions becoming almost second nature. Or did God anticipate her requests, sense the patterns? She could not tell.

* * *

"Thank the Gods they do not have the Strength." Alken shivered at his side. The night had brought a damp, clinging fog. "I would not be able to see them if it weren't for the Strength. Their energy signals give them away."

"And the noise they put off. Who would have thought we would use the training our quiet hours have brought us," Trake returned. "These creatures would wake a tower with their fumblings." He paused for a moment to switch subjects. "How many do we have left?"

For Blessed Militia, Trake knew his men had fought well; he could find no fault there. But they had been outnumbered. Who would have guessed so many Wretched lived outside the cities? He doubted they could last until the blimps returned.

"We're down to five," Alken reported. "Two are badly wounded. They will feel the fever soon."

Trake flexed his own arm in response to the report. Apart from the pain of the wound, he felt no ill effects. "We must hold out as long as possible. If the blimps return into the teeth of this monster, we will lose more tonight."

69

"Aye," Alken agreed. "What do you think they're waiting for? They have us backed to the ring."

"Who knows what those animals are thinking? They scurry around like rodents to grain, without thought or plan. It's the only reason we have survived as long as we have."

"Looks like they're scurrying again, Commander." Alken nodded in the direction of the tree line.

Sure enough, Trake detected shapes moving among the darker tree trunks. "Bring the other boys around. See if they found any salvageable arrows. If they didn't, we'll have to wait for blade distance." Alken disappeared as Trake waited and watched. And wondered. Would his decision to stay and protect the machine have been different if he had known his wound had come from a jagged edge of the machine itself? He was not infected, at least not with the quick death of an arrow or blade. He might well survive his wound, only to be slaughtered by the Wretched. He liked to think he would have stayed no matter what, but he was not sure. He had not yet tasted one morsel of sweet life, and now it was over. How could the Gods give him such a small, worthless part? Trake heard Alken slither forward with the rest in tow. They fanned out across the jumbled machine, each finding cover where he could.

"We have twelve arrows among us," Alken reported.

"Twelve?" Trake tried to keep the discouragement from his voice. "We'll hold fire until sixty feet. I'm thinking they may not fire at us if they think we're out. They won't want to give us anything to salvage."

"You may give them too much credit. I have seen no subtlety from them yet."

"Do you have a better idea?"

"No," Alken admitted. "I guess we'll see soon."

Clanking metal interrupted them. Trake flinched and whirled. Someone was behind them, climbing onto the machine. Trake motioned his men to hold their positions and bolted back through the supports and trusses. With the Strength guiding him, Trake picked his way back. He saw shadowed shapes—three, now four. He hoped the gloom of tower life would continue to play to his advantage. He found a spot halfway through the machine and crouched behind a beam. Somehow he would take them one at a time.

The silence of the night evaporated. Trake heard the roaring onslaught of the Wretched charge and the whooshing of an arriving blimp at the same time. His prey looked up at the sound, and Trake rushed. Three bounding steps and a thrust. One down, he counted. Three more steps, and he swung on a second. The man blocked, and out of the corner of his eye, Trake saw another man circling. The trusses clanged with his every move, his sword hitting metal, not flesh. He dropped the blade and pulled his long dagger from the sheath on his leg. He lunged, stepped, feinted, and lunged again. Two down. The third close at his back.

Verbolana switched her now-mind, desperate to learn where she had gone wrong in the next few minutes.

Verbolana took a huge gulping breath and jumped from the coach into the smoke the cannons had just blasted to hide their arrival. Blind terror stole into her Strength and wobbled her arms so much she was amazed she still held her Talsartt. As the ground approached, she sensed panicked movement. From her years of practice, she twisted, pivoting in her harness. Now, upside down, with Talsartt cocked, she swung at the first shadow she saw. Surprisingly, she felt her weapon connect and sink into yielding flesh. She drove the blade deep and felt herself career off course.

Suddenly the rope wrenched her back. Her feet lost their grip on the rope, and she twisted into a crazy spin. She pulled her Talsartt in and hugged its shaft to her, hoping the razored blades would not slice her rope. *Wham!* Her body smashed into something hard and she lost what breath she had. In panic, she fought for air, but her lungs felt useless. She sucked, but no air reached her lungs. She sucked again in panic, to no avail.

Through the concealing smoke, she glimpsed a large man hanging beside her. She noticed his Talsartt flashing at vague figures below her. As her lungs finally accepted her frantic attempts, she saw the man looking up, studying the ropes above them. "You tangled us, you idiot! Cut yourself free, or we're both dead."

When Verbolana hesitated he commanded again, "Cut your rope, damn you! We are bugs in a web dangling here."

Verbolana gave his command no more thought. He was an Honored warrior. His words, his experience, must be right. She dropped her Talsartt, pulled her dagger, and hacked at her rope. Arrows pierced the air around her, and she gave what Strength she had to the blade in her hand.

The rope finally cut through with a jerk, and she fell hard to the ground, driving her right shoulder into the ground. She looked from her back as the ropes untangled from their own weight. The Honored warrior swung free, his lifeless body a dead weight. An arrow pierced through the seam of his harness.

Verbolana lay for a moment, more aware of her surroundings than she had ever been. How could things have changed so completely in a matter of a few hours? A life, so relentlessly predictable, had veered irretrievably off course without a single thought to her wishes.

Her Encore was close. Her Trials and Rewards would come to her today, she was sure of that. And the next moments would speak so clearly to her eternal life. Those thoughts galvanized her, there on her back, in the concealing smoke. A wave of pure energy coursed through her body. The Strength filled her, stronger than it had ever been. The pain in her shoulder vanished. The wobbling fear that gripped her a moment earlier was gone.

Verbolana rolled to her belly and surveyed the scene. Maybe she would not die immediately. Maybe she would prove herself as no other Blessed woman ever had. She still clutched her dagger, and her Talsartt was only feet away. However, there were many moving shapes around her. Wretched! Ragged-haired Wretched everywhere. Verbolana rolled to her stomach and inched her way through the smoke to her Talsartt. The Strength grew within her. Every movement around her seemed amplified. Without thought she could tell the Wretched from the Chosen.

Crawling, she grabbed her Talsartt and slashed out low and hard, feeling the free, pulling contact as her blade sunk deep again and again. Hidden by the smoke, she revealed herself only by her attack. With one leg cleaved, one of her victims fell to meet eyes with Verbolana. She flopped away, horrified by the indignity of such an intrusion. She stabbed at the man's belly relentlessly with the dagger end of the Talsartt, ending the encounter. Clean death was the Honored way, not the pleading weakness that confronted her.

Time passed in a haze: swinging blades, pounding feet, whizzing arrows swatted from the air, the mingled auras of Wretched and Chosen. Dizzied movements blended, becoming one confused flow.

Somewhere in time, the Wretched numbers thinned. She had to find Trake.

Completely engrossed, Verbolana shifted on the cool stone floor, but when she realized she was completely without pain from her awkward position, she continued.

Trake spun and caught the dull eyes of his enemy. His training told him not to look into the eyes, *watch the shoulders and the hips* was his constant tirade to his recruits. The body could not lie as the eyes could. Now he was stuck, drawn in by what he saw. Anger, a deep seething rage. He jabbed his knife forward. The man flinched. Yes, there was fear there, too—and determination. What had he expected?

The two combatants moved, eyes locked.

"Why do you kill us?"

Trake jolted back, but the man made no movement forward.

"I would like to know before I die. I do not understand why we fight. I only know that you come from the sky, slaughter without thought and then flee to the safety of your lavish homes."

"You have heard the words of the Gods." Trake spat his response. "You do not listen."

"Many of my people think you come for sport," the man continued as if not hearing Trake's response. Then, "What is this of Gods and their words? You speak with the Gods?"

Trake glanced quickly over both shoulders. This must be a trick. The man spoke such nonsense. There was no one sneaking behind him, so he looked back at the man. "The Declaration was made generations ago. All heard the words. 'Father is sick, and all must vacate.' The machines carried the Declaration across the world, to every home, to every ear."

"The machines came to kill us," the man stated flatly. "And many died those days. Cities crumbled; domes fell; mothers and children were slaughtered. That cannot be what this is about. It was more than a hundred years ago. What threat can we pose to you now? There are so few of us left; there is plenty for all."

Trake could not believe his ears. How could this man be so stupid? He was Wretched, of course, but he *had* heard the words. Everyone knew that! It *was* a trick. No more talk. The battle raged and this idiot was keeping him from it. Trake smiled and lunged. The man jumped to the side, so Trake moved again, slashing wide and true. He felt the man's blood, warm on his fingers. Twisting the blade, he pulled up, stopping only when bone blocked his way.

Trake looked back into the man's eyes.

"Spare my children," he managed.

Trake pushed the man off his knife and watched his knees buckle, watched his pleading eyes gloss.

"Foolish men deserve no Encore. I would take your place in a heartbeat, you imbecile."

Verbolana opened her eyes. She was seated on the cold stone floor of Alcot's living room, her face buried in her hands, her mind reeling with new insults. The Wretched. She hadn't even given thought to them! How many had we killed? Billions, she had been told. Every city on the planet, every single soul who was not Chosen. And those who escaped the slaughter. They were hunted down, the breeders targeted, the mothers. In the name of what? Lies, all lies. But she could not stop now.

She picked herself up off Alcot's floor and wandered the halls of his cavernous home. For a moment it occurred to her that she was taking up Alcot's space; his home. She wondered where he had gone. Vaguely, through volume upon volume of new information, she picked a perfectly clear memory from the stacks. This was her realm, just made up to look like Alcot's. She could have anything she wanted, but what did she want? A Za-shielded suite on an upper deck? A Wretched hut on Father's skin?

She harrumphed at the distraction as she plopped down on Alcot's couch. She knew what was to come. Was she stalling? Was her mind telling her that enough was enough? With a fluttering heart, Verbolana asked God for the next scene.

# Chapter 8

Verbolana could have lived a hundred lifetimes and not needed to see what she now saw. It was her most spectacular sunrise: bright streaking pinks fading to deep maroons of smoke and haze, framed by the shrouded greens of arrow-tipped trees that marched to the horizon. If she only could keep her mind on the view above, with its vast liberating openness, life was glorious. But her eyes felt sucked down to that oily field, littered with the kills of the night. She knew which were hers, still pictured the pleading eyes as they faded to black. Why had they not closed their eyes, she asked herself again? Why did they have to explode with so much blood? She let her anger bubble to the surface, felt its power again, saw herself swinging her Talsartt again and again in the rage of the unexpected.

"Have you ever seen a sunrise?"

The voice startled her, and she sat up straight, dried her eyes and nose with her sleeve before she realized she had merely smudged the speckled blood into rosy swirls. What should she do? Men and women did not speak. But he was Honored. If she ignored him, would he whip her? It was *his* voice. Her anger doubled. Had she not given enough? Lost enough? How could this longed for moment come on the heels of such ugliness? She swallowed her anger, as they had taught her to do all her life.

"No, sir, not like this. From the tower, things are very different." Verbolana tried desperately to sound light, not to drive him away with her rage. What else could she say? She needed to stay connected. His voice felt like a lifeline. "Everything is so open, it is a bit frightening. The wind blows free; the sky is large. I never thought you could actually smell the trees." She could not look back, ashamed of the blood that covered her.

"I have seen you before." Trake stammered, now standing directly behind her. She longed for his hands to rest on her shoulders. She willed herself to slump back against his legs, gaze up at his face, reveal her shame, but she could not. She sat frozen, staring ahead, hearing the hovering blimp for the first time.

"My name is Verbolana, my Honored sir," she recited.

"And I am Trake," came his stilted response. Then his voice softened. "Please excuse my impudence, but extreme times call for extreme measures. We don't have much time. The Generals have arrived. They want to see the machine in action. My men are all busy and the Directors choose to send women into battle. So, I'll need your help."

Verbolana refocused on the sunrise. Its first rays peeked through the branches. What did it matter, time, if she could not ask for what she needed? What did it matter if the platter, laden with delight, perched within her reach, could not be grasped? Of all the moments of misery she could remember, this was the worst. The joy that should have filled her with his very words was hollow as she realized what would never be. The fantasy that made it worthwhile to rise in the morning evaporated as if the sun burned through her eyes and into her brain.

Movement on the battlefield caught her eye. An Honored soldier walked from body to body, checking for life. Something nagged at the edges of Verbolana's mind, something she needed to remember. Her muddled brain attempted to sort the images, the collage of movement and terror that assaulted her. There — freeze that image — above her — dangling. It was Wexi, swinging,

78

jerking, pleading with her eyes. The snaking rope followed her lumped fall. Wexi was hurt, lying somewhere close by.

Verbolana looked up with new focus.

"Wait," her voice croaked. The man's blade hovered above a crumpled form, petite next to the others. "Wait!" she shouted with more force this time. The man looked at her, his eyes hollowed. "Is that a woman?" She willed him not to say yes. He nodded.

Verbolana stood on snaking legs. "I'd like to see her before …"

"It's not a good idea." Trake's voice slowed her momentarily.

Ignoring his advice, Verbolana picked her way across the body-jumbled landscape, still pooled with blood, to her friend. She felt Trake close behind. The other man looked down, shrugged and moved on to the next.

Unexpected rage swept through Verbolana as she knelt next to her friend. The glories of death, just another lie. Her friend's waxy, sallow skin told a different story, one of pain and depletion, the draining of glory from a glorious creature. Verbolana dropped to her knees next to the crumpled form, placed her hand on a bloodied arm. She was cold, not Wexi anymore.

"Wexi," she pleaded. "This isn't fair. Just last night …" Verbolana's soft, eyes filled with the beautiful remembrance of their quiet night together with Treena. Their lazy satiated moments after another hard day. Wexi's languid body snuggled close, naked and warm.

Verbolana shook her gently, and when she gained no response, rolled her to her side. The softest of moans gave Verbolana hope.

"Wexi—girl—come back to me." Verbolana's voice was soft, yet urgent. "It is not your time. The Humble Magician has enough recruits for today." Wexi's eyes fluttered at the words. Verbolana saw the struggle behind them.

"She's been marked. The fever will come," Trake intoned over her shoulder.

Verbolana's anger erupted. "Go away! I don't need your help."

"If you wait too long, she will become contagious. You will have to go too, then."

"Go away!" Verbolana screamed. At that, Wexi stirred, and Verbolana forgot all else. "Wexi, come back to me. There has been a mistake. It is not your time. Do not get on the sled."

Wexi's eyes fluttered open, their deep blue curtained behind web. "Vee, you're alright. They said you went down. I was frantic. I pushed — I had to — it was harder — are you all right?"

"Wex, you shouldn't have." Verbolana realized her friend lay in blood because of her. "Why?" she asked, knowing she would have done the same.

Wexi gave her a weak, sad smile. "You know, I've always loved you, Vee."

Her declaration jolted Verbolana. One foot on the sled, and yet she spoke of love! It could not be. She put a finger to Wexi's lips. "The fever has begun," she said over her shoulder to the Gods and in case Trake still listened. Then back to Wexi, "Best not to talk; save your strength." Especially talk of love. Love begat possession, and possession begat coveting. And coveting begat eternal death. Death without Encore.

"All are gone." It was a man's voice above her, talking over her head. Trake *was* still there. Had he heard?

She looked back. He nodded at the Honored executioner. She screamed, "Nooo!" As she turned back, the pike already buried deep in her friend's chest.

"You bas ...!" but her words cut short with horror upon horror as Trake buried his sword into the gut of his compatriot.

"We all must go. We have trespassed on Father for too long."

It was a simple statement, spoken with finality and compassion, and so appropriate for Verbolana's new reality. Trake shook his blade free of the crumpled man and helped Verbolana to her feet. Suddenly she felt free, just knowing it would soon be over. Soon she would step on her own sled and, shortly after, stand among the Trees of Plenty, with the Blessed Amnesia that came with Encore. So she would no longer look upon this world; she would focus her sights on an eternity of Bliss and Contentment. "But we have a few more chores before our time comes," Trake continued.

They walked back to the machine, his touch constant at her elbow. A touch that an hour ago would have filled her world. A touch that now she hardly acknowledged. His calm brutality had turned him alien. Verbolana wanted to hate him, but she was numb. She wanted to reach out and shake him, bring him back to match her fantasy, but that would have taken too much energy. So she followed by his side, removed, floating, hollow.

"Everyone has left. They have finished their inspections. The Generals have asked us to fire the thing one more time so they can observe it from above. Then they will haul it off somewhere."

There seemed no response necessary, so Verbolana stood mute and waited.

"I need you to help me crank the bucket back."

They climbed onto the machine and worked the levers to-gether, their silence broken only by the occasional instruction. When told, she climbed from the machine and stood with the corpses. She watched, detached, as Trake signaled the blimps to fall back, and sometime later the machine gave one final throw of its great arm.

It all seemed so futile. Life was just not precious enough to get so worked up about. Leave Father to himself. We can all abandon him; what does it matter? The languid thoughts mired in the sludge of her brain. She noticed a blimp's return, Trake's hurried movements, attaching hooks at the corners, the lift-off and Trake's final signals, but they all seemed so silly. What was the point?

Then Trake stood before her, with the sound of a blimp still somewhere overhead. The sun had just crested over the spiked greenery that lined the clearing and its warmth coated her back like a blanket. They locked eyes, and a smile played across Trake's lips before it hardened into resolve.

"Lie down and be still."

She followed his instruction, never breaking contact with his eyes. If the Gods truly read her every thought, she was doomed anyway. So, bouncing between emotions deeper than unformed words, she drank from his well, quenched a thirst that tickled her very core. She sucked from his eyes the milk that all said was poison, milk that she knew was nourishment she could not live another moment without.

He bent to her, adjusting her arms, his fingers brushing more than seemed necessary.

"I always hoped we would meet some day, but not like this. You seem different from the rest. I adored watching your eyes when you teach." The words thundered through her and she fought for control. Her sled waited; she could not respond. She sucked the words and the feelings they evoked away from her mind into her gut, where she hoped they would be safe.

"Please close your eyes."

She felt nothing as his sword plunged deep.

# Chapter 9

Verbolana squinted her eyes open. She expected to see the Magician's Sled, with its lathered beasts ready to pull her skyward. What she saw instead was Trake still standing above her, pulling his long dagger from the sheath attached to his calf. Without hesitation, he plunged it to himself and crumpled on top of her.

"Do not move; do not make a sound," he breathed. "The blimp will probably make one more pass to make sure we are dead."

It was only then that Verbolana realized that Trake's sword stuck in the ground between her arm and her side. She lay with his full weight crushing into her, his foretuft of hair tickled her arm, the smell of dried sweat and blood filled her nostrils. She listened to the drone of the engines and the pounding of her own heart. Through it all, she felt distinctly cheated. An unimaginable dream had somehow come to pass. The man she had loved since she knew how to love was on top of her. He had just confessed feelings for her and all she could think of was the oblivion of death, the sweet amnesia of her Encore.

Verbolana, however, was accustomed to the cheats of life. So she lay until she was told to rise. She ran when he grabbed her hand and pulled her to the forest. She hid when he told her the Wretched were following them. There was nothing else to do. She was not called until she was called. She knew that much.

Slowly, ever so slowly, Verbolana's anger asserted through the black tar that had become her brain. *Trake has cheated me. I should be riding the sled, journeying to my Encore, preparing to meet the Humble Magician in the Halls of Valdor.* Then the confusion that so often came with the ways of the Gods: *But I was not called. Surely the Gods stayed Trake's hand. There must be a purpose beyond my understanding.*

Verbolana had to unbury the truth. Her eternal life depended on it. She looked up at Trake. They were huddled in a thicket, Trake intent on the sounds of the forest around them.

"What are we doing?" Her voice croaked, afraid of the answer.

"Shhh!" He breathed before looking down at her. His face spoke of fear and caution.

She ignored him. "What have you done? The Gods will curse us. I will see no Encore." She hoped she was wrong, but she had nothing on which to base her judgment. Her training had never envisioned anything like this.

"*I* will see no Encore," he hissed back. "Never. I am Honored! I am offered nothing but this life, and I am not ready to give it up."

"So you have kidnapped me to keep you company? Tell me the Gods have spoken to you."

"The Gods have spoken. Now quiet before they hear you." Trake's attention returned to the bushes around them. Then Verbolana heard what he heard. She struggled with her new situation. If she called out, she would surely cause a battle. She would not defend herself and one of the Wretched would send her to her Encore. However, the Magician would not be pleased at that. There were prices for incompetence, even in the Encore. Moreover, who was she to say Trake was not reading from the Script? She remained quiet and listened as the rustling diminished into silence.

"I am thirsty," Trake stated flatly after the danger had moved on. "I need water."

Verbolana stood. "And I am a teacher," she stammered, her anger rising again. "I do not know where to find water any more than you do."

"This will be hard." He sounded almost apologetic. "Father hides his gifts, especially from the undeserving."

"You think we are undeserving? You are following the Script. Everything happens for a reason." It was time to take charge. She had decided to follow his lead, she had not called out, so now it was time to believe. Believe what she had never been able to believe before. "Let us explore her skin and find her treasures." She took his hand, as a teacher leading a pupil, and left the thicket.

They did not get far.

"Simply move your mind away from the pain, like when you're getting the whip." He was seated on a fallen log. Verbolana sat on the ground, tending to his feet.

"I've never gotten the whip. I never did anything to deserve it."

"Deserve it," Verbolana mocked. "I never did anything to *deserve* what I got, either. The whip just came." She watched Trake wince as she pulled another thorn from his foot. "We're not going to get very far if we can't find protection for our feet. Father's skin is not like the metal deck of home. This is very unforgiving."

"I noticed the Wretched wore coverings. The few times I have been on her skin, I wished for something for my feet. You're right; it's not like the deck." He stifled a cry as she probed for another thorn.

"Do you think we can find our way back to the battlefield?"

"What would we do there?" he asked.

"The fallen Wretched must have coverings."

"Augh, the Wretched wear dead animals. How can you even suggest it? It's unthinkable. No wonder you got the whip."

Verbolana bristled. "We are here now, trespassers. We cannot take a step without sinning. How many Za webs have we broken just walking through this forest? How many tiny lives have our feet ended by stepping on her skin? The Gods spared our lives for a reason. They directed your hand. We must do the best we can."

"I will not wear dead animals. I am not Wretched."

Verbolana had said all she dared. Giving an Honored options was one thing. Giving Trake a direct order could only end in punishment. She pulled another thorn from his foot and waited, head bowed in a show of respect.

It was then she heard the leaves rattle and sensed impending doom. She felt Trake stiffen and reach for his sword. She looked up and caught his signal. As instructed, she silently brought her feet up underneath her and came to a crouch. With the Strength, she sent the pain from her damaged feet away and started a low run through the brush. She was not skilled at forest stealth, and the racket she made brought two arrows almost immediately. They missed by inches as she brought herself up behind a tree. Information flooded her brain. The arrows' trajectories registered in her mind like frozen lightning. She felt the crouched men, ready for another shot. She looked back at Trake for instructions. She was to continue her dash while Trake lay in wait.

Verbolana gathered the Strength and the courage that came with it and bolted again. She ran fast and low, dodging behind whatever cover she could find. The forest was thick and she heard arrows thunking into trees all around her. Searing pain sliced into her side and then her arm, but she kept running. Finally, she heard Trake's battle cry. She was dead anyway; the poison would take effect soon. She might as well go back and help him. She looked down at her punctured body. Both arrowheads had gone completely through her and protruded out the other side. Her first instinct was to break the shafts and see whether she could pull them out. She pushed hard against her side and used her other hand to grasp the shaft and wrench it for a quick snap.

Unfathomable pain erupted from the wound and Verbolana dropped to her knees with a primitive groan. Her head spun; her last thought was to stay upright. She crumpled and vomited.

Verbolana awoke warm and cocooned, the pain in her arm and side secondary to a new sensation. She felt a body nestled tight to every curve, strong arms holding her still, hot breath on her neck. She lay perfectly still, opening her eyes to slits. Trake's arms held her. Trake's hands cupped her—her breasts. She pictured the Gods, seated across the front row, scowling as the scene unfolded. Her mind shifted back to matters more urgent. As her body awareness grew, she felt what must be his manhood, hard and long against her backside. She arched her back, trying to relieve the pressure of his thing tight to her. Stabbing, blinding pain halted her struggle. She was trapped in treasonous repose with this man.

"Trake, please!"

He shifted behind her and groaned himself awake. By the time his eyes opened, she had struggled to her back, nauseous from the pain. She leveled an accusing stare, burrowing into his eyes.

"You were cold," he whispered. "I was cold. I was afraid for you. You did not wake, even when I removed the arrows. The fever will come."

Verbolana wanted to grab his extended monster and scream, *What is this? What are you trying to do, leave me with eternity in the wings with no Encore?* She couldn't bring herself to touch it. She waited, seething, not satisfied with his explanation of an act that could exile her from Paradise forever. She watched his eyes as sleep evaporated and reality filled in. She could not decipher everything, but she saw his eyes flicker down and his face redden before he jerked away, and turned his back on her.

He lay for many moments before speaking. "I—I was—sleeping. I dreamed," he stammered. That seemed to be all he was going to say for a long while. "I have no excuse. My dreams should not have taken me there. I do not know what is wrong with me. It will not happen again."

Verbolana, too, fought for control. Errant thoughts, blasphemous thoughts surfaced from deep within her heart; thoughts of compassion and maybe even understanding where only horror and revulsion should reside. She pushed and pulled at her brain, knowing the Gods watched and waited. She feared again they would see her as lacking. Or worse. Was she damaged beyond redemption?

With blinding pain, she rolled away from him. *I must collect myself. The Gods are testing me. They see my weakness and they probe.* She gingered up to all fours and with her good arm, pushed herself to her knees. *I must compose myself.* She stood, and new pain exploded. She looked down, expecting to see blood pouring from the wound in her side. She saw something else instead. Protruding from her chest were the shaft and feathers of a brand new insult. As she watched, another joined it. She dropped to a strangled cry behind her.

"Veerrrbbbolllaaannnaaa!"

Afraid her emotions would overtake her, Verbolana slipped into Trake's mind and continued to watch.

# Chapter 10

**M**y last words were lies," Trake repeated. "I will love you always." He kissed her cooling forehead, then reluctantly came to a crouch. "But I was wrong about one thing. I did not kill you; these Wretched did. And they will now follow you to their Encore."

Through angered grief, Trake searched for Father's Strength. The pain in his heart seemed to block his mind. Sudden panic dumped acid into his stomach and watered his bowels. *Father has abandoned me. She does not approve.* Cold determination pushed at the fear and heartache. With quaking limbs and his heart threatening to strangle him, he managed a deep calming breath that filled every crevasse of his lungs with calming pressure. Then a long and slow exhale. Again, a deep breath. His mind reached down through his mired confusion tentatively to touch his center. Panic resurfaced. He pushed it down again with his breath and his mind. *Stay with me, Father. I will serve you here. I will take many Wretched from your skin. That, I promise.* He felt a break, a crack, in his molten fear and dove past his belly to find his center. Immediately he started the spin of energy and imagined the whirlpool of his vigor form. Before questions could pop, he dropped his mind down and connected with Father. Digging deep, he burrowed to his core, amplified his gifts and hijacked his might for his own.

*You are still with me.* He smiled with relief. As he pulled back more Strength than he had ever felt, Trake envisioned his feet healed and nothing but smooth deck on which to run. Awareness rushed back to his head, and he visualized his attackers. From his place behind the fallen tree, he easily sensed each man's energy, even felt each man's rapt focus.

They knew where he hid, Trake realized, and they were closing. He had to move. He bolted like an accelerated swing from the fastest battle blimp, and picked a retreat line dense with trees. He saw loosed arrows as streaks of his attackers' extended energy. Some flew close; most embedded into shielding trunks or tangled in thickets. Finally out of sight, he slowed and circled.

*Father, you answer my prayers. You want me to kill these foul creatures. Why did I not ask for your help before? I could have evaded and conquered without endangering Verbolana.* Verbolana's lithe running form flashed before his eyes. He bucked his mind from the sight. *She is safe now and she is free. The fruits of Bliss and Contentment juice her mouth, and the Ponds of Abundance soothe and tantalize her. Thank the Gods this evil world is lost to her. But what of me now? I have no Encore. I sin beyond sin, yet Father still loves me. Maybe if I ask, he will show me his secrets. I will keep to the Cleansing, and he will honor my sacrifice, show me water and berries to eat. The skin I tread on will bring him closer to the healing he needs.*

Trake refocused, revenge and righteous rage coalesced in his calming mind. He picked out each attacker's signal with ease. Three Wretched were close. Trake watched as one took point. Another, keeping his distance, fanned out to the right. The third took the left flank, with the final two providing cover from the rear. Trake knew little of surface warfare, but he was impressed. He was certain they would soon attack from three angles.

Now was not the time for revenge, Trake reasoned. He would have to run so he could attack on his own terms. Night would come, and no doubt they would cluster. With the urgency of battle fading, the pain in his feet returned. *If I am to live, I must follow*

*Verbolana's sage advice and find coverings. I must become Wretched, if only to kill the Wretched.*

Trake stood still, taking stock. Where is the battlefield? Which way did we run? I have no idea. Where was the sun when we fled? I didn't pay attention. Can Father help? He again slowed his breathing and stilled his mind. In spite of his predicament, he smiled with new revelations. With each breath and each release, he felt the Strength returning. His pursuers had picked up his trail; he felt their confidence grow as they discovered each broken twig. Trake searched further into the empty forest, breathing and releasing. On the breeze, faint but distinct, came the answer. Maybe not from Father and maybe not from the Strength, but the answer came nonetheless. A sweet, tangy stench carried on a whisping breeze. Excrement, mixed with the heavy metal scent of blood. *Follow the breeze.*

Picking his way through the thick undergrowth, Trake followed the pungent trail. Progress was slow and frustrating, for every step threw roaring crackles and snaps through the echoing forest and sent slivers of pain up his legs. With part of his mind constantly on his pursuers, he stood for long stretches allowing the pain to subside in order to gather Father's Strength. *Are you leaving me to these savages, Father? I am your protector. Now, if ever, I need your Strength.* He stepped, and the pain started the sapping of his Strength again. His betrayal infuriated him, and his next kiss from Father would be that much shorter. He had no time to wonder further. He must survive, with or without him.

Trake's pursuers were gaining, and he was at a loss for what to do. Hide and ambush, run and possibly head straight into their army, somehow hide his trail? None of the options appealed to him. His tactical training had not prepared him to fight like this.

Then it occurred to him, the simple solution hiding behind ignorance. *All I have to do is fight one of them, if I can strike quickly*

91

*and silently. Once I have his bow, I can defeat the rest.* Time was the problem—time, and his trail. They were following his trail. If it ended suddenly, they would stop and search. Any surprise would be lost. *Think Trake, think. Could I backtrack and split off? They are close. I must sprint forward, ignore the danger in front and then backtrack.*

He took off without further thought. The racket was horrifying; twigs snapped like cannon blasts under his feet; even his own heart seemed to pound out an echoing crescendo to his flight. Also, the stench was getting stronger. Any moment he expected to crash into the clearing and face hundreds of his foes.

*That's far enough. Stop, backtrack. Careful, you fool! Forget the pain, tread lightly, don't break a twig, dislodge a leaf. Where are you going to hide, you idiot? You didn't think of that. Could be your death. Over there, the thicket at the bottom of that tree. You need to go for the last attacker so others will not see. How far apart are they? It's not far enough, find another spot, fool.*

Trake crouched into the best cover he could find. Totally inadequate, he knew. Prayer simmered inside him with every step. *Father, you are still with me. I feel your love. But Magician? Dancer? Narrator? Would it be too much to ask? Can you see the benefits? I am your man on the ground. It is what we need,* he stated with sudden insight. *Wretched roam free among the trees where we cannot swing at them. Their numbers seem so strong, even when we fight them every day.* He held back the truth, as if that were possible. He stuffed the words that entered. *I have saved myself because I am afraid to die* did not enter his brain; however, the words felt wedged in his heart. *I will not die before I have lived* seemed lodged in his soured gut.

Checking on the men's progress, Trake realized his position would not do. The men hunting him had fanned out further than before. Good for his plan, but he would need to reposition. He surveyed the thick forest and bolted twenty feet, then halfway up the trunk of a tree, where he reached out to pull himself into the lower branches. The canopy was thick, hiding him well. He sensed each man's concentration and almost saw their heads swivel as their focus shifted. With poised sword, he waited. A swing with perfect precision and timing was his only chance. Tracking all, the moment came. From his perch, his blade whispered the applause of Encore to the back of a pursuer's head. Following the strike, Trake swung from the limb and landed on his victim. Now open to reprisal, he lunged for the quiver of arrows and the dropped bow. Before his assailants could get off a single shot, Trake stood behind the trunk of his tree, fully armed while the Strength told him each man dodged for cover. One still scrambled in the open. Trake leaned, aimed and loosed the arrow. Two down.

Movement ceased in the forest. Trake waited and listened to a gust of wind in the top branches, the crashing of a large animal in the distance, his pounding heart. Nothing else. He felt one of his adversaries, the furthest, drop to the ground. Trake ventured a peek, too much underbrush for a shot. Maybe he could do the same. He crouched low as a voice in his head screamed *No, where would you go? Think, Trake, think like a Wretched. If you stay here, you'll be picked off. Move, you have to move!*

Keeping the tree between himself and the closest two, Trake ran straight and fast. He felt and heard them react, felt the circling foe stand and aim. He dove and rolled through the brush, twigs snagging and scratching, his new bow almost ripped from his hand. One arrow flew over his head by inches as another was being notched. Trake crawled frantically for the next tree. Two arrows embedded in the dirt close by; another grazed his arm, tearing flesh and muscle as it passed. He had gained nothing with his maneuver. Each pursuer had merely repositioned. Trake tested his arm; fine, the pain would come later. But what of the poison? Was this his death sentence? If so, he would take these Wretched with him.

Trake bolted for a nearby tree. They were ready this time. Three arrows flew close. *This will not do. Think!* He felt them gesturing to each other, making a plan. If they were to keep up with him, they would have to advance. Trake stopped and settled. This was his chance. Two would cover one's advance. He felt the two stand clear of their cover and take aim on him, felt the third running low. Trake exposed himself and both loosed simultaneously. A mistake. Trake ducked for cover and, before they could notch another arrow, he came around with a perfect chest shot for his running foe. Three down.

His last kill was not dead and not quiet. The coward bleated his pain to the others. Trake sensed their attention shift to their fallen comrade. Trake took advantage and snuck to the next tree. No response. He took the next tree. One covered him while the other advanced to his friend. A gift. With the tree as a shield, Trake bolted at full speed, claiming outrageous victory. He had a new weapon and three fewer adversaries.

Once well out of range, Trake halted his retreat. Through the dense foliage, he observed the discipline of his foe evaporate. With grateful astonishment, he felt the remaining two assailants crouch to tend to their fallen. *What is the point? The poison will soon kill them. Or will it? I feel no ill effects beyond the pain. Should I finish these fools?* He watched as the two idiots gathered a fallen, each over their shoulders, and stumbled off in the opposite direction.

Baffled, Trake established a safe cushion and followed with bleeding feet and a dozen hastily harvested leaves pressed hard against his wounded arm. He had realized in those moments of quiet that he would not survive long without food and water, and since he had no forest skills, following these men was the obvious choice.

For the first time since stepping on Father, Trake had a chance to reflect and plan. If he lived through the poison, his options were mostly unknown. The only scenario he saw was not a pleasant one: hiding close to a Wretched camp and stealing what he could. That was all his limited imagination presented. *Maybe if I could sleep, I could think more clearly. I have never been so long without sleep. Or food! I should be home now, lounging in glory. My greatest battle, and I will never hear the applause. I am stuck here hobbling behind men I should kill, men who killed my only hope for happiness here.*

*Verbolana, I am sorry I have been too busy to mourn you.* Her twisted death mask jumped before his eyes. *I am sorry I was so stupid. We could have defeated them with the Strength. I acted in haste and now you are gone. I will stay alive, if only to feel the shame of failing you.*

Through his fresh grief, Trake noticed the stench of death growing thick in his nose. He thought he had traveled away from the battlefield, but perhaps not. The realization buoyed him just a little. If he were careful, he could find bindings for his feet. For if he intended to steal Wretched food and water, he may as well get used to the idea of wearing Wretched clothing.

Commotion—shouts of distress and concern—diverted his thoughts. Trake crept closer. He had found the battlefield. Hundreds of Wretched milled about the tarred earth of the clearing, collecting clothing from the dead, nursing wounds, tending children. Children? These heathens brought children to battle? What kind of dim lanterns were these people?

A crowd surrounded the two surviving assailants. One hugged a wailing woman to his chest; the other held a grubby long-haired child on his hip. Shouted questions interrupted their reunion and they responded simultaneously, recanting in voices for all to hear the chase and various battles. Trake listened with no small amusement to the tale as it grew. He watched others gather to listen as the various battles escalated in scope and complexity. His and Verbolana's bumblings evolved into a flawlessly executed ambush with at least fifteen marksmen cleverly concealed throughout the forest. Shouts of triumph erupted at every incredible shot or slice and all seemed to visualize each death with vivid detail. The men were true heroes, having vanquished one of the most cunningly planned attacks in months.

What fascinated Trake more than the exaggerated tales was the interplay between the men and women. These Wretched acted as if everything was normal: speaking, laughing and even touching each other. He twisted and squirmed, as if a thousand Za spiders crawled beneath his britches. He pushed his own desires deep with the expectation of the Gods' retributions. There was no way these hedonists could find their way to the Encore. None of them. It had been a lie to make the killing easier, or maybe the Directors didn't know. Maybe these abominations were more than the Directors could envision. Children running wild, screaming as they saw fit. Women, some swollen with the evidence of random procreation, tending fires built directly on Father's skin. Trake even witnessed two men bring a lanced animal into camp. They dropped the poor creature on the black ground, then dug into it with their knives. Surely with the blood of Father's creation on their hands, they would not be allowed into Paradise. He witnessed a man and woman actually mashing lips, their hands roaming freely across each other's body, yet the Gods did not strike them where they stood. Wretched indeed.

Hidden, hungry and stiff with pain, Trake watched as the hours dragged. The Wretched made camp, brought water and cooking pots from stashes in the forest. They piled the stripped corpses of the fallen and called all together to hold hands and wail in a synchronized lament. It was almost as though they were praying, Trake realized, but that could not be. What God would listen to such heathens?

Darkness finally approached and as the tedium wore on, Trake had nothing left to divert his mind from the stiffening pain of his wounds except the growing hunger pains and the chill that had overtaken his muscles, sending him into fits of chattering shakes. The lightheadedness from fatigue and hunger was almost a relief, though he feared he would soon be too weak to call on Father for help. He knew he needed to stay alert to stay alive, yet he had no training for such a battle. Honored, he now realized, were much too pampered for a fight such as this. The realization came with shame, and the shame buoyed him with anger. He was stronger than these Wretched. He had the power of his Gods, and his Gods would not abandon him.

Knowing the Chosen would not attack at night, the woods seemed to empty as streams of Wretched arrived. The younger men brought tents and bedding along with yet another surprise. Through the gloom of twilight and against the fires that now blazed, Trake glimpsed what had to be animals with large packs attached. *Would the blasphemies never end?* Trake wondered as he sank deeper into his hiding spot.

Trake fought with himself, hidden there in the bushes. He fought for clarity of vision, for control over his spasmed muscles, over the blanketing pain. And he fought for faith.

# Chapter 11

Hidden in the bush, the bone-deep cold, seamless pain and cramping hunger conspired to keep Trake from sleep. Every doze ended with the stabbing pain of the slightest movement or a dreamed image of a Wretched detection. Floating in delirium, in the half-light before dawn, he watched a large, armed man approach his cover. The man withdrew his member and urinated, soaking Trake's leggings with rapidly chilling, stinking defilement. Trake contemplated the event with surprising detachment. Was he victim or savior? Surely, his pants had soaked the majority of the offending liquid, saving Father this unthinkable indignity, but Father seemed not to care.

So how could these heathens get away with so much? Every dictum broken, all piety absent. Yet these creatures survived and even thrived.

It was a test, Trake's clouded mind concluded. That was the only answer. The Gods tested the resolve of the Chosen. They tested *his* resolve, confronting him with such ambiguities. His thoughts swam as he passed in and out of consciousness.

Then, through the haze, through the branches, silhouetted by the rising sun, the Humble Magician stood, his splendid robe fluttering and sparkling in the frigid breeze. He beckoned Trake without words. He locked eyes with Trake and smiled, a smile filled with encouragement and hope. The apparition leaned forward and, with uncharacteristic tenderness, placed his hand on Trake's fevered head. With the Magician's touch, everything became clear. One simple touch and Trake knew. The Directors had been wrong. Honored were not banned from Paradise. With proper testing and sufficient sacrifice, the Gods welcomed the Honored to the Encore. With that revelation came another. The Wretched were not invited; they never had been. The Directors had somehow misread the words of the Author. With profound relief, Trake slept the dreamless, unquestioning sleep of the truly pious.

He awoke with a certainty in his beliefs that he had lacked his entire life. Not only was he going to survive, he was going to thrive. Now he knew that the weakness of his body and the pains that still invaded were tests; obstacles to overcome, challenges to conquer. The arrows' poison could not kill him, the cold could not wither his spirit and hunger could not diminish his Strength. The Gods had spoken to him! He had obligations now and a sure knowledge that all would accept him as long as he did not squander his gifts, lose faith or question his path. The Gods had placed him in a unique and humbling position. From this he must not falter.

Through the bushes, Trake saw no movement. Charred pockmarks of consumed trees as well as a smoldering heap of bones and incinerated flesh dotted his view. Piles of excrement and puddles of urine mingled with the smoke of death to assault his nostrils. The Gods would not allow him to forget this scene, he knew. Yet as Trake inched from his cover and stiffly stood to survey the site, he was neither repelled nor enraged; neither surprised nor complacent. He stood resolute, for he knew he and the Wretched were acting out the Plan to perfection. He was to go to school, learn the ways of his enemy, then report back. The Chosen were indeed the *chosen*; no one had gotten that part wrong.

However, the Honored were to be honored—truly honored. They needed only to prove themselves, to test their resolve instead of just their skills. They needed to sacrifice in ways beyond those of the Blessed. They had to kill with full knowledge that those they killed would rot without redemption. They had to forego the comforts of soft pillows and soft flesh to eradicate those who threatened Father. And though they would have to sully themselves and Father in the process, they had to tread his skin to rid him of the menace and to prove themselves worthy.

Not all would make it. That was clear in Trake's new vision. Some would resist his revelations. He would have the Gods at his back, to propel him from the highest ropes. His words would carry the power of Truth, his arms the might of the Gods.

Even among the abominations around him, he stilled his mind with ease and found Father's Strength at his fingers. With his Strength, he reached out farther, father than he had dreamed possible and located the band of Wretched as they marched home. He picked up a stone and a stick and followed. These were all the weapons he would need to secure food, clothing and water. He was now an invincible force of one, destined to become one thousand, then ten thousand strong. He would become a prophet to unite all towers in their fight to save Father.

# Chapter 12

re you getting it yet?" Alcot sat across from a completely disheveled woman he hardly recognized, in his own living-grotto that was not his at all.

"I appreciate you dropping by to check on me, but I really don't need your interrogation. You are beginning to sound like one of our Deck Directors." Verbolana had her feet curled under her legs and was running her hand across the thick blonde hair that had sprouted across the back of her head.

"Vee," Alcot pleaded, "I am worried about you. You won't talk and you obviously aren't taking care of yourself. Won't you at least tell me what you've been up to?"

"Just looking back, like you told me to do," she mumbled as she picked at some dry skin on one of her fingers.

"Looks more like you're lost in the past, not reviewing and learning, which was my suggestion." Alcot sat forward, elbows on his knees.

"Like I said, I appreciate you dropping by." She finally looked up to meet his eyes. "I'll try to take better care of myself. Look." Then, without uttering a word, she transformed her hair and clothes to what she hoped was a more acceptable appearance.

"Cute," Alcot muttered. Then, with obvious anger, "I don't give a shit about how you look other than what it says about what you are going through. I care about where you are in your healing. I expect anger, loads and loads of anger."

"And who do I get angry at?" Verbolana demanded. "I understand, Alcot! I understand that none of this was my fault. I understand that we were all deceived, that anyone who thinks they know God's plan has been deceived or is the deceiver. I understand all that! What I don't understand is, what this is all about? You say I am supposed to find comfort here when everyone I have ever loved is suffering in the middle of all that deception. How is that supposed to comfort me?"

"The only thing most of us can figure is that God is giving us another chance here," Alcot explained. "My guess is that he is not as powerful as you might think. You can ask him, of course, but then you have to be willing to believe what he tells you." It was Alcot's turn to examine his fingers. "All I know is that the only chance we have to find happiness here is to heal whatever we can of our past and move on to what can truly be a fairly magnificent life."

"And I guess all I know is that I am not ready for that yet." She returned his stare with a snarl. She did not like admitting her deficiencies, and that seemed to be all she did around this man.

Alcot stood to leave. "I'll be back in a few days, if that's alright."

Verbolana followed his movements with surprise, not expecting to be dismissed quite so easily. She also realized she liked Alcot's interruptions more than she admitted, even to herself. Balling her courage, and with still a little sarcasm in her voice, she addressed her feelings. "So, is that it? I didn't give you what you want, so you are ready to leave?"

"I sensed you were annoyed with me and you wanted me gone." His body language changed as he turned to face her fully.

"I am annoyed with your interrogation," she responded. "But I do miss your company. And I could certainly use a little break from my *work*," she hissed the last word. "And I have to admit, you do bring a little comfort when you come by. What do you say you take off your Weaver mask and just sit with me?"

With stern eyes and a set jaw, Alcot responded, "Ms. Verbolana, that would be, well," and breaking into a smile, "most pleasant indeed."

Time was somewhat relevant to the citizens of Heaven, but not so much. Alcot stayed in his home that wasn't his longer than he had planned, and slowly, very slowly Verbolana started to talk. Her favorite spot for conversation turned out to be on a pile of cushions, pillows and comforters bundled in soft heaps in the center of Alcot's living grotto. With the lights dimmed and their bodies completely bared, Verbolana stared up at the domed earthen ceiling, following one root or another through its serpentine path as Alcot idly pleasured her with long light strokes of his hands, or feathers or anything else he could find or think up, across her flesh. Or he drew his tongue in lazy circles down her thighs or up her arms or occasionally deep inside her love muscle, as he called it. Their sex was so common and so protracted that she found herself talking. Talking about Wexi or Treena, Trake or the dreaded Deck Director became easier and easier. After a while, she felt Alcot probably knew them as well as she did.

Deep breaths came with this great slow sex. And deep breaths came with deep thoughtful searching. Precious melancholy came with the sex, usually after a particularly intense orgasm, and precious melancholy followed a particularly intense story of her friends or her home.

Then one day Verbolana broached an idea that had been brewing deep in her heart for a long time. "Alcot," she interrupted what had been an hour or two of cuddled silence, "I want to go back and make love to Trake."

After a few minutes of contemplation, Alcot agreed that such an exercise could be very healing. "You have grown a lot, though;

it might not be as easy as you think. The Chosen are very tied up around sex."

"He was almost in me during our last moments together. I don't think he will have any trouble if I handle it properly. I have been in his head for days upon days. He loves me. I will be patient."

"I have no doubt about any of that," Alcot agreed. "It is not you I was worried about being patient. Trake is a man, a man without proper training."

Thoughtful silence, this time heavier than ten blankets, enveloped Verbolana. She didn't need to hear any more from her current lover about her future lover.

With a simple wish, Verbolana felt herself snuggle down into her prone, recreated body. Sensations engulfed her now-mind. Immediately she wished away the wounds that burned her side. A deep cleansing breath brought her nerves under control.

Trake lay tight around her; his arms engulfing, his body pressing, just as it had been in the moments just before her death. His hard cock pushed firm and urgent, nuzzled into the crack of her ass. Over the past few months, Alcot had taught her to think this way, to use these words, and she liked it. She was no longer afraid; in fact, she felt an empowering confidence that in itself exhilarated her. With her ass, she pressed back into his urgent lust and wriggled a bit, this time feeling and appreciating her lover's firm belly and powerful warrior arms.

Talking quietly with God, she wished away the ferns and brambles that prickled her skin. Lying snuggled, she became aware of her surroundings. Remembering her previous trips, she wished away the sweaty stench that she hadn't noticed before a few days in Heaven. During these weeks spent with Alcot, in a paradise unimagined, she had learned the pleasures of bathing and the comforts of pillowed linens. Warm, inexhaustible water still amazed her. Despite herself, in the midst of her most cherished dream come true, she compared the feel of her two men. What was different? Alcot was larger; she felt that immediately. His arm was heavier on her side, his chest thicker at her back. Those differences were trivial, she realized; not what she sensed now. Their hands. She already felt a difference in Trake's hands. Verbolana thought about Alcot's hands; their thick fingers, short buried nails, the pads of his thumbs hard and strong. She had longed, deep in every fibered cell, when he had touched her, for Trake's fingers, long and lithe, strong yet delicate. She remembered wondering, Trake's hands with Alcot's knowledge, what pleasure they could bring. Then she imagined Trake's deep brown eyes with Alcot's sparkle, Trake's slim hips with Alcot's measured restraint and knowing power, Trake's chest, Trake's arms, Trake's lips, Trake's tongue.

With mammoth effort, she tore her mind back to her bed on Father's skin, sloughing away, as best she could, the comparisons. Alcot was a wonderful man. He deserved better. In her time of desperate need, he had given her everything, knowing full well her true desires. *Thank you, Alcot. And goodbye. I am where I need to be now. You are a wonderful man.*

Refocusing, Verbolana took stock. She had imagined long ago that she would need to take control here. Trake did not have her knowledge. How could he? He might even be timid or clumsy, she assumed. Or worse! The Gods' gifts of fear and guilt still steeped within his heart. He had not seen the truth as she had, and probably never would. A piece of her felt sorry for that and a piece of her was glad. She could bring him something special; she could fix him, even if it were just in this make-believe world.

She wiggled her ass a little more and coaxed him to wake. He did not respond. Feeling her feminine power, bold and confidant, slowly she raised her full-length smock. Then another idea struck her.

"God, I wish I were naked," she breathed. Her smock disappeared. Father's cool breath immediately dimpled her legs and belly as Trake's rough hands warmed her breasts. Her bare nipples responded pleasingly to his touch. The moment of pleasure stretched as she allowed warming waves to ripple through her body, lodging a curious numbness at the base of her skull. She marveled. *This is Trake,* her mind cooed. *My life's dream is now real. I want to stay here forever, in his arms.*

"God, let me enter his dreams before he awakes. Ease his transition." She lay still for a while. His hands began to roam her breasts, his fingers wide, her nipples puckering as each finger pressed and released. Shockwaves of delicious elegance rushed downward, heating and wetting her groin, a trembling in her legs. Through gritted teeth, an involuntary groan escaped her parted lips.

Trake stirred, then startled awake.

"It's all right," Verbolana cooed. She had rehearsed the scene a hundred times in her mind. "I want you close. You feel so good." She left it at that, waiting for his reaction. She felt him jerk his pelvis back, pull his arm free from beneath her. *Have I shocked him with my nakedness? Did I move too fast? Will he reject me after all this?*

She rolled to her back and exposed the length of her body. With boldness she did not at this moment feel, she met his eyes. His contorted face, was it revulsion? Horror? Fear? She could not tell. She watched his eyes harden as they suddenly pierced the calm love she tried desperately to exude.

"You need not reassure me," he asserted with unexpected composure. "If I want you, I will take you." Cold, gray metal crept into his eyes. "I am Honored; you will do as I say."

"Of course, my Honored sir," she reverted. "What is your pleasure?"

"Show me yourself," he commanded after a long appraising tour of her naked form. "Stand."

She obeyed slowly, as all her excited heat evaporated into Father's cool breath. Shame pierced her like a dozen arrows to her chest. Her emotions must have shown on her face.

"Do not frown at me," his next command. "Turn—slowly—yes, yes—more—all the way." Her eyes came back to his, as soft and calm as she could make them. She tried to smile, but all she felt now was violated. His rough, appraising eyes burned her skin, deflated her chest, soured her stomach.

"Now spread your legs. Auugh! What is *that*? Open *it*. Auugh! It is so ugly, like a Kah melon left drying in the sun. I thought it would be beautiful! Your body is so soft, pudgy."

The arrows that could come any moment from the slinking Wretched twisted in her heart as if they had already found their home. She could not help but think of Alcot: his gentle hands, his lazy, appreciative gaze, his murmurs of childish delight.

"Turn around again. Stop, bend over. Ah, yes, down on your knees," he commanded.

Verbolana heard his trousers shrugged off, felt him kneel behind her, one rough hand on the small of her back. When she heard him spit, she realized she could take no more.

"God, I wish this man would die," she squealed. She heard the arrows whoosh, felt his hand release its pressure, then heard Father's skin accept his weight. She did not look back. "God, I want to go home."

# Chapter 13

Vee, what did you expect? That is the only way he knows. You may not believe it, but he was doing the best he could." They sat across from each other on the pillows in Alcot's dank living room, Verbolana curled deep in the familiar position. She concentrated on a rivulet of water as it worked its way through the gnarled ceiling roots to rain down on the smooth stone floor. The water disappeared through the joints in stone. To keep her mind from exploding, she wondered where the water came from and where it went. Long moments passed. The dripping water could not hold back her thoughts. Next she pondered the faint earthen smells. How could any of this bring comfort? Alcot lived in a hole in the ground. Her anger surfaced and burst out her mouth.

"He is such a brute," her response too calm, eerie. "Ordering me like one of his Blessed companions, thinking he could take me like an animal. I could not deal with him. He feels no love, just lust for his own release. I could go back now and look again. I could dig deeper and find that he doesn't have even an idea about love. I feel so foolish. How could I have thought he would know of love?" Verbolana looked over at Alcot as if she had just heard his words. "If that was the best he could do, then I am glad I killed him."

"Vee, as I've explained before, you didn't kill anyone. You were in your own universe, as you are now. You can't affect what happens in the real lives of those on your home world. It's all fantasy." Verbolana heard the frustration in his voice. He was not as patient when they were out of bed.

"I am exiled," Verbolana continued. "Where do I go now? What do I do?" She did not expect or even want an answer, but Alcot had one.

"I could show you the city." Even through her anger, she heard his excitement.

"What city?"

"Vee, maybe I have been derelict in my duties, but you seemed like you needed to exorcise your demons before venturing out, but ..."

"But what, Alcot?" She thought this might be the first time she had used his name. If it were, he did not seem to notice.

"So far, you have not left your realm, as we call your personal universe. But God has given us so much more here. He has brought billions of people here from all over the galaxy. You can't believe the different cultures, the museums, the art. Each citizen has a realm, but not all choose to stay in them. In fact, from what I can tell, few stay in their realms all the time." He paused. "Outside this room is a city like you have never dreamed. Your realm is housed in a building and is grouped with other buildings that make up a neighborhood. All neighborhoods are set up with a central park where people gather and mingle. Even more parklands surround the neighborhoods. Then each neighborhood is connected to the others by an elaborate transportation system. Besides the neighborhoods, there are areas dedicated to sports, arts of every description, pleasure palaces, government and the like."

"Government?" Verbolana interrupted. "There are laws in Paradise? I thought you said I could have whatever I wanted. How can I have whatever I want when there are laws to restrain me?"

"A good question, and one everyone asks." He smiled. "You only have unlimited power within your own realm. Out in the city, you are subject to the will of the majority. In someone else's realm?" He paused again. "Oh, you will see." He fidgeted now. "The best way is for me to show you. He sat forward. "Do you want to see? You have been here long enough. Time is wasting. Let's get changed and be off."

"Changed?" Verbolana asked, a little indignant. "Is my smock dirty?"

"Your smock is fine, I guess," Alcot sighed. "It's just that, well, your look might cause a bit of a stir."

"I don't understand." She stood over him now. He still sat deep in his favorite couch, casually slumped, a mug of steaming tea at his lips. As usual, she felt stupid and vulnerable to his superior smugness. This new world confused her. She could not help but feel that Alcot was going to bless her with another startling slash of new and unwanted information. It was all he seemed to do.

She watched him with further annoyance as he extricated himself from the couch and placed his tea on the end table. Her heart froze as he sat forward and took her hands in his. *This can't be good*, she thought.

"Vee, the city is filled with the most wonderful sights you will ever see. God has allowed his people to flourish here. However, he has also allowed, or required, his people to maintain their roots. God only permits a select few to live here. He won't tell us how or why he picks whom he picks. He won't even tell us how many from a particular world. So, what that means is that most of the trillions of souls He created by His own hand have no afterlife." He paused for her reaction.

She sensed she was to say something. "Well, I knew the Honored wouldn't come, but the Wretched don't either? That's terrible. So many die. They were promised ..." She thought about those she had killed on that day a lifetime ago. She remembered the blood erupting, muscle and bone exposed, eyes frantic with surprise and fear.

"Your leaders told you those stories so it would be easier to kill the Wretched," Alcot stated. "Your leaders told you many things that are not true. God has many worlds; many people on many worlds. For whatever reason, he does not bring them all here. There are many theories; in fact, entire religions have sprouted up here to try to explain his choices. But not all the Blessed are here and not all Wretched or Honored are left behind. The only pattern I see is that God never brings children here, and he never brings the mentally impaired." Alcot's voice faded with each sentence, from the rote command of fact to the squalid sputterings of injustice. "And he almost never brings people from the same family or even from the same social group. We are, all of us, on our own." He could not look at her now. This Paradise with its sordid secrets had so many shocks.

The long silence, marked only by the playful splashing of a waterfall that shouldn't be, stretched into the growing sobs of a young woman and her endless memories. She dropped into Alcot's lap and held on to keep from convulsing. Eventually she found her voice, muffled through his thick sweater. "There's more, isn't there? We were talking about my smock — and my hair. Are the Wretched out there, ready to pounce? Are the ones I killed waiting for me? They were supposed to forget. The Blessed Amnesia was supposed to cure all."

Alcot started again, cautiously. "It is unlikely the ones who died that day will be here, since so few are brought. However, there will be Wretched, and they will remember. The worst news is that most of your neighborhood is made up of the Misguided. Your Cleansing is nothing more than unadulterated mass murder to them. The machines your people loosed on them killed billions. And those who were brought here after they died had front-row seats to what was to come. They watched their children and wives and mothers incinerated or smashed beneath crumbling rubble or left to starve. They watched your blimps rain poisoned arrows and cannon blasts on those who managed to survive. They do not—and few of them forgive."

"But Father needed protection," Verbolana mumbled.

"They don't see it that way. Look, Verbolana." He pulled her away from his shoulder and raised her chin with a firm hand. "You don't have to convince me. Look at me. I see your pain. I know they duped you. They have some compassion for the Blessed. Just don't go around looking like an Honored warrior ready to kill again."

She sat, absorbing it all. Betrayal upon betrayal upon betrayal. Spouts of new anger erupted from her soul. Her eyes burned through Alcot for bringing her such news. "What in the burning winds do they want of me? I am just a teacher of children!"

"A teacher with a whip and a sword," Alcot completed. "I don't mean to be cruel, but your hair and your tattoo mark you. But …" He waited until he had her attention again. "You can change your appearance easily enough."

"What do you mean?"

"Well, I'm not about to show you my given form, but I can tell you I didn't look anything like this when I first got here. My home world is, well, quite different from yours. Let's just say I also needed some changes to fit in around here." His easy confession melted a bit of her anger.

"You don't really look like this?"

"This is my chosen form, Vee. Outside, very few people run around in their God-given forms. Most people are more than happy to change the skin they were born in for something more pleasing. I can't say I follow the latest fashions, but I'm mostly up to date."

"You talk nonsense. I feel as though I am looking down the rings. What is 'fashion'?"

"Oh, let's just forget I put it that way. All you need to know is that you can change your appearance. Grow your hair, change your face, look younger or older, anything."

"What's wrong with my face?"

"Nothing, nothing." He sounded exasperated. "Hey, I've got an idea. Years ago, I had a machine—a tool, really—that helped me pick my current look. It's tucked away in one of the back rooms, I think. Let's break it out and see what we can come up with." Alcot stood and dragged Verbolana with him. They traipsed across the echoing living room, down a long hall and into a part of his house where she had not yet ventured.

The room Alcot picked resembled what she had always pictured a Wretched nest would look like. The earthen walls barely accommodated Alcot's height and looked damp and moldy. Alcot seemed not to notice. A low sleeping pad and some sparse blankets took up most of the room. A candle, then two flickered on with no apparent help. The meager light did not evaporate the gloom.

"What is this place?" Another piece of her anger fell to her curiosity.

"Historical artifact," he threw over his shoulder. From behind a freestanding screen, Alcot lugged out a gleaming ball attached to a tall, slender pedestal. He seemed as excited as an Honored before a bath. "Now, stand here for a minute. Let me remember how to use this thing. Oh, yeah, now hold still." He pushed a couple of buttons and stood back. A bright light washed the room, then extinguished.

"Okay, Okay," Alcot exclaimed. "What do you want to look like? You can sit down now, on the bed. Do you want me to start? I can give it some suggestions."

Verbolana was annoyed beyond words, lost again in a land of floor to ceiling Za webs. She slumped onto the bed, mute.

Alcot could not contain himself. "Okay, then I'll start. Give Verbolana a full head of hair." Verbolana's image appeared before her astonished eyes, standing on the stone floor just a few feet in front of her. She had a full head of straw-colored hair, much as it had been before she started her martial training. "Shoulder length." It grew. "Straight, not wavy. No, fuller, bangs to the eyebrows. Yeah." He looked at Verbolana expectantly. She sat frozen. "We could have done all this without the mach ... tool, but we're just getting started. Do you like what we've seen so far?"

"Fine." Alcot's dour descriptions of a few minutes ago still bounced inside Verbolana's head. She had derived some comfort knowing that Treena and Wexi would someday follow her. Now her exile was complete. Though she couldn't give up, she knew. Hopelessness and hopefulness battled. Alcot offered her a way out—but to what? More heartache? Unjust condemnation? Recrimination?

"Do you want to change anything?" he asked.

"No."

"Okay," Alcot responded, absorbed.

Verbolana watched the ropes hauling behind Alcot's eyes.

"Lose the smock," he stated flatly.

Verbolana blushed at her naked form as he appraised further. Verbolana appraised with him, trying to detach. She had grown used to mirrors in this time with Alcot, but it was still a bit of a guilty shock. The tower had some shiny metal left over from the old days, but to be caught looking at one's reflection meant the whip. Vanity begat ... Regardless, there was nowhere to stand naked on the deck of a tower. Naked was for the quiet hours where total darkness prevailed.

She was not unpleased. She likened herself to Wexi, not Treena. She was slim, with long legs and a short trunk, her neck graceful and her breasts high and firm. For a moment she longed for the heavy handfuls of breast that Treena could give. She shoved the memory down.

As Alcot spun the image, she noticed tight, lightly colored skin marred everywhere with the pink linear welts of the whip across her back and arms mostly, but down her legs as well. "Can we get rid of those?"

"Absolutely," Alcot mumbled, temporarily sobered. "Remove all scars and blemishes." They disappeared.

Verbolana ran her fingers down the back of her own arm. The scars were still there. With sudden rage she screamed, "On me! Alcot! Can you take them off of me?" It was as if a Za had jumped on her back.

"With your permission. Or you can ask for yourself. Say, 'God, please remove all of my scars and blemishes.'"

They were gone the moment she uttered the words. She felt immediately different as she ran her fingers down her new arms. Yet she felt somehow cheated, empty, more alone than ever. She thought again of Wexi and Treena, still trapped, deceived, marked; floundering in their illusions and lost to her forever. She faked a smile for Alcot. She was good at that, being Blessed. "Go on."

"Now, personally I like you this way, naked, but if we're going to go outside, most neighborhoods ask that you have at least something on. So ..." he thought for a moment. "Let's try a sundress, pink and flowered."

More startling than the reflection of herself naked, was the image of herself in soft pastels, adorned with Father's most cherished symbols. Her divided mind spun in fever, half dazzled by the tantalizing images, as Alcot scrolled through the gimmick's choices, half chanting rote prayers of protection and forgiveness. If the Gods were watching, if she were still in her Trials, she was condemned.

"This is the real genius of the tool," Alcot explained casually as Verbolana drowned in her fears. "Choices. Heaven is about choices. But who wants to sit around designing the perfect evening wear or swimsuit? And even if you did have the desire and talent to compete with designers from all over the galaxy, the choices of fabrics alone, 143 worlds' worth to choose from, not to mention what people have dreamed up here ..." He let his voice trail off; she got the point. And they hadn't even looked at casual wear yet.

With no recriminations from her Gods, and a thousand distractions later, they had a closet full of inspiration and one alluring compromise draped over their model. Alcot insisted she looked fabulous. Her hair was thick and lustrous, hanging in soft curls to the subtle rise of her butt cheeks. His favorite had been a very short, very low-cut, geometrically patterned shift that Verbolana had insistently vetoed. She could not imagine exposing herself to the Wretched with the breeze chilling her inner thighs, even when Alcot insisted the dress was quite conservative for Heavenly standards. Finally, she found a flowing full-length gown much like those described in stories of the Encore. She did a couple of twirls for him when he insisted, and he informed her they were ready for their adventure. Alcot took her by the arm and led her through his warren of a home to the door. Off to conquer new worlds, she felt none of the comfort he insisted this world was about.

# Chapter 14

Verbolana stopped ten feet outside the door of her realm, disoriented and lightheaded. She seemed to be floating in the open sky above her.

Alcot smiled. "Sorry, should have warned you. There was so much else going on. Your neighborhood just voted to lighten its gravity a little. Still catches me by surprise sometimes. Wait until we get to Voltif's. It's lighter than this."

Then, changing the subject, "What do you think? Your people are quite creative." As he waited for the sights to sink in, he added, "Each floor has its own theme."

"Where are we?" Verbolana asked.

"Not sure exactly, someplace in your home world's past, I'd guess. Check the flooring. I've never seen stone like this anywhere before. It seems as though you can see through a hundred layers; maybe you can. When I first came to see you, I wondered whether it were genuine or conjured."

Alcot's babble brushed past Verbolana's ears without soaking in, the alien sights took all her concentration. Tall confining walls stretched on either side, gently arcing as if she stood at the edge of the filters on her circular deck. A strip of blue sky accented with white-puffed clouds topped the walls and added to her confusion.

"I thought you said we were in a tower of some sort. How can there be a sky? Are we on the top deck?"

"It's all conjured," Alcot explained. "If one floor—one deck— agrees on a theme, they can make it look however they want." Alcot waved his hand. "With all the stone columns and carved wood doors and windows, I'd guess this is a recreation of some famous city street from your history."

"Everybody seems to be obsessed with confinement, with all these walls. It's strange, so much seclusion. Your world is like this too, with your caves. How do you live without your friends?"

"Most cultures prize privacy," he stated. "Maybe too much. I remember great loneliness in my first life. But here, you can have it either way, or both. You'll see. At Voltif's, the place is packed with his friends."

"What are all those things plastered on the walls?" Verbolana asked, feeling a little more comfortable as they continued on.

"Ah, it just goes to show. They don't want as much privacy as you might think. Look at this one. Must be a family living there." Plastered all around the door and walls were adolescent draw- ings; urban landscapes of children playing, lone trees, Mommy and Daddy standing by. There were other, more sophisticated pieces intermingled; a translucent seascape, lighted by a double- mooned greenish sky deep with heavy clouds, an elegant country home, complete with grazing animals, children frozen in mid- stride and framed by towering, green-laced mountains. Alcot seemed transfixed by a particularly vulgar scene of a dozen men, shirts off, glistening with sweat, actually plunging spiky weapons into Father's skin, raising great mounds of his moist brown flesh. Verbolana almost retched as she jerked her elbow free from Alcot's grasp.

"Who would display such filth? Wretched?" she demanded.

"Verbolana, you must understand. The way you were raised was quite different from almost every culture up here. Most people revere their Father for what he gave them, for his grounded strength, for his power. But your Father was aloof and separate. By necessity, of course, but nonetheless, others aren't wrong in the way they respect and treat Father. They are just different."

"This filth makes my back tingle."

"Your scars are gone, Vee." Alcot put his arm around her shoulders and hugged her to him. "It won't be easy, but you're going to have to let go—and the sooner the better. I know it seems I'm pushing you, but it won't get any easier if you wait. I know. I've seen it a hundred times."

"The scars are just under the surface, I can assure you." She bolstered her spirit, not exactly warming to his condescending advice. "Let's get to where you are taking me. I have no use for such heathen ways."

Alcot shrugged. "This way," and turned her down the make-believe street.

"What is this?" Verbolana asked in trepidation. A small room had appeared as two doors slid open.

"It's an elevator. This room works like the ropes in your tower, bringing people up and down to the different levels."

"Why, if we can wish for anything, do we travel this way? Can't we just ask to be at our destination? It would be much easier on my nerves."

"Another good question. You're getting the hang of this world." Alcot beamed. "Again, you can only have whatever you want when you're in your own realm. Out here, God listens to the majority and you'll find the majority is very conservative when it comes to their comfort. People come out to the city because they don't want the omnipotent power of a realm. They want familiar surroundings, and in this neighborhood, this is how the majority want to get from level to level in their buildings. Not all are like this, but many are. The elevator was a common conveyance in the cities of your home world before the Cleansing." He practically dragged her into the tight little room and announced, "ground floor." The doors whooshed closed, and the floor seemed to drop, throwing Verbolana into Alcot's arms again.

They were still smashed together when the doors opened and more amazement assaulted her eyes and ears. Like a skitterbug caught at sunrise, she froze, and watched a melee the likes of which she had never contemplated. The Director would have whipped everyone in sight for such behavior. Or worse, beheadings would not be out of the question for what she saw before her. Half naked and fully naked people dashed and danced everywhere. Thumping drums and peeling rhythms seemed to fixate and drive the limbs and torsos of all within sight. Oiled, bronzed bodies, faces fresh and bubbling—Verbolana had never seen such confusion or heard such noise. She felt Alcot's eyes on her.

"Should we make a run for it?" Alcot smiled at Verbolana as if to say, *Hey, I told you it would be different.*

His question came too late.

"Looky here." A raised male voice floated above the confusion. "We've got ourselves a ceremonial virgin." Eyes turned, and Alcot pushed another button. The doors closed.

"Thank you," was all Verbolana could manage. She felt the floor rise, then fall before the doors opened again.

"Sorry, I didn't realize what time it is. It's hard to keep track sometimes. Inside, it can be whatever time you want it to be, but out here the days and nights march on."

"Where are we?" Verbolana peeked her head out the open doors. She still heard the muffled beats and raucous laughter of whatever it was they had escaped from.

"Most residential buildings have dedicated the first few floors to commercial realms. We just went up one level. I think we can get out from here."

His words meant nothing to her, but she nodded her head in understanding. "Will they come up here?"

"I don't know, probably not." Alcot glanced out the elevator in both directions. "I don't think they're that motivated, but if they think you are an unrepented Chosen, they might."

"Why would they think that? We just spent the last few hours disguising me."

"The dress, I guess. Plus many of them know me. They know I'm a Weaver. I hadn't thought ahead." He stood for a moment. Hesitantly, he continued. "We can either go back and wait for morning, or you will need to change again. We need to get through your neighborhood park in order to get to the subway, and well, what you have on would have worked in the daytime, but in this neighborhood it will not work for evening wear."

"You want me — to dress — like them?" she faltered.

"We can go back to …"

"We will not! Just give me a moment." Verbolana stomped down the hall, her new hair bouncing with each step. She stopped and stood with her back still to Alcot. Images washed past her eyes: Treena waving her little goodbye as Verbolana rode the ropes to the battle blimp; Wexi's dying eyes; Trake's shock and dismay when she slapped him hard across the face; Alcot's amused superiority just about any time he spoke.

Then the collage of nakedness she had just encountered, the Godless self-indulgence of the Wretched and Misguided. What did I expect? They are the ones who need confronting. I have nothing to be ashamed of. I was the one who was lied to, not them. I will not let these people defeat me. I will match my pain against theirs any day! The battle raged in her head. She saw herself standing, defiant, with all the right words, toe to toe against their anger. For another day, she reassured herself. I will take them on another day, when I am stronger. She bucked up her shoulders and turned to face Alcot. With a determination she did not feel, she said, "How do we do this? I can't change here."

"Sure you can. Just ask God for that blue strapless number with the holes in the midriff. He'll know which one and you'll be in it right here and now. No one will see, anyway; I'm the only one here."

Verbolana did as instructed, yet again. Seamlessly, a gentle breeze dimpled her bared thighs and exposed midriff. She took in a giant gulp of stale air. "Let's find a way around those folks and get to your friend's place."

Alcot grinned and took her hands before giving her the once over. "Nice," was all he said before adding, "I think if we go down here and take a left, we should find …" That was about all she caught in any detail. They zigzagged through halls and down stairs, past a wall of glass encasing an opulent display of shimmering cups and plates, then past more glass that separated them from wildly colored chairs and tables, lamps and paintings. She caught a glimpse of herself in the mirrored surface and stopped to look. She was getting used to seeing herself. Alcot had lots of mirrors and at times even forced her to stand before them and appreciate what he saw. But that was private. This public display, what purpose did it have? He certainly could not expect her to act like the people she had just witnessed, yet why else would anyone dress like this? Titillation was not a public endeavor. Flesh had no place in open crowds. Desire was private, hidden in the darkness, or as in this world, at least behind walls. But this! Skin and curves on display for general consumption? She pulled away from her reflection with a gentle tug from Alcot, but her thoughts continued to whirl. *What if I see something I want more than you, Mr. Alcot? What then? Can you share as I was taught to share? It is not always easy.* The thought buoyed her. Maybe then she would finally have the upper hand.

Suddenly, they emerged into an open area filled with people, trees and wild contraptions she could not fathom. They ducked through trees, along walkways, across blankets of soft green plants, down more stairs and into something Alcot called the "subway." They jumped in a moving "car" and raced to the limit of her stomach through a maze of tunnels and open stations as Alcot kept up a constant commentary on the various neighbor-hoods they traveled through. Only one description perked her ears. It appeared at least one group of residents had as much difficulty accepting Paradise as Verbolana did. As they raced by the stop, Alcot pointed out an incredible array of posted signs. She had no time to read any of them, but the angry script and bold colors, along with Alcot's description of the contents, made Verbolana smile. Alcot explained, contrary to all evidence, that this entire neighborhood had rejected the notion that God was responsible for their creation, let alone this paltry excuse for Paradise, and they were going to hold out, in the face of this evil, for the true Creator.

"Not so farfetched," Verbolana commented. "That notion has occurred to me a hundred times today alone. In fact, I may want to visit that neighborhood next."

"Verbolana, that notion occurs to all of us. In fact, many people hold onto varying degrees of their religions. However, this one is a bit extreme. If you decide to go, be prepared to don a black hood, have rough men strip you and bind you from neck to ankle in a gauze-like wrapping, with only your sex exposed, and leave you to crawl from the subway to the Mahanda's temple in the center of the park. At least you'd be used to the whip applied by anyone passing on the way."

Verbolana sat and watched as a few more neighborhoods passed. Finally she responded. "You can be so cruel sometimes.

All you had to say was, 'Vee, I don't think you'd like it in there. They are mean people.'"

Alcot looked over at her. She was sobbing into her hands. "Sorry, I guess I've gotten a bit used to the idiocy. When you've been here long enough, nothing surprises you. It's just one of those things you talk about over a couple drinks with friends."

"Well, I'm not used to anything yet. I guess I'm just one of those things you talk to your drinking buddies about, too. Poor scared little skitterbug, afraid to step out of her own web. Is that what I have to look forward to? This place we're going, you gonna show me off? Show your friends your latest project?"

"Truthfully?" Alcot looked over, his eyes hard. It was the first time she had seen any steel there.

"Yes," she spat back. "Truthfully! If it isn't too much trouble."

"Oh, it will be trouble. But I don't mind. The way I see it, you've got nothing but trouble for as long as you choose to fight the way things are." He paused. "So, yes, I'm going to show you off. You're fresh and interesting and naïve. You're also beautiful. Not in any classic sense, but because you have not yet enhanced yourself." He sat staring ahead through two more neighborhood stations. Then he continued. "Why is it that women always think they want to hear the truth? It seems to be a universal curse from God. And you're probably going to try to respond with the truth—something I have no desire to hear." He tapped his fingers on the seat. "Let me know when you want to get out. All you need to do is catch another car and ask God to take you home."

Before Verbolana found a reply, Alcot announced their arrival at Voltif's neighborhood station. She did not move as he got out of the car. "So this is your fun. Do you ever weave for men? You say you are a Weaver because you enjoy meeting those who are new to all this, and then it turns out you have no patience or compassion. So what is the thrill, teaching some virgin about sex? Is that what this is all about? You pick women from my world because you know they'll be starved and vulnerable and 'fresh.' You are a sick, Honored!"

A small group gathered around the two as arriving cars piled up behind them. Verbolana was clogging up the works. "You asked me to be truthful. The way I see it, the only problem is that you have no experience with men. The only man you have ever had any meaningful contact with betrayed you, in your eyes. I am no different from him or any other man. I follow where my needs take me." Alcot looked around to see if he got any nods from the crowd, but there were no takers. "It's a human condition, really; women just have different needs."

"That is certainly true!" Verbolana shot back. "Women follow their needs for love and tenderness. They find enjoyment in giving more than in receiving. They look to bring out the best in their friends instead of turning them into some character in a gory story." She bowed her head for his onslaught.

"All true," his voice was gentler now. "Though you only picked the more noble of female traits. Even from what you said, though, you are the perfect counterpoint to me. God did not design males and females alike. How boring would that be? And I agree; I have been a brute. Maybe I have been weaving too long. Eighty-six years at anything is bound to jade a person, I guess."

"You've been weaving for eighty-six years?" The statement pulled her up by the harness. "How old are you?"

"I died when I was forty-two, by this calendar. I have been here for 194."

For reasons Verbolana could not explain, his revelation changed everything. As she stood she wondered, *Could a man that old be wrong about such basics? Maybe I'll give him the benefit of the doubt.*

# Chapter 15

Still stinging from her fight with Alcot, Verbolana bounced up the stairs of the subway, her stomach seeming to float, her head dizzied as her limbs flailed at what should have been familiar movements.

Alcot laughed. "Told you. The gravity thing can really throw you off. I guess it's one of the reasons God groups people the way he does. Voltif's home world is smaller than most. Without help from God, they'd have a hell of a time almost anywhere else in Heaven. As it is, they can't compete very well in any of the sports except the nil-grav ones."

Verbolana barely listened. They stood at the top of the stairs, and she was transfixed by more outrageous sights. In fact, she was not at all sure what she saw. She knew about trees from stories and her limited experience with Father, but this was far beyond any of those. She giggled, "Are those …?" She didn't have the words.

"Homes?" Alcot finished. "Yeah, I think there are twenty or so realms in each pod. From what Voltif says, this is how they live in their home world. Too many nasty critters on the ground. They grow and hunt everything they need right in the trees. Tap into them for water and everything. He says this one is a little bigger than those at home, but only by a little. Some of them get to be three thousand feet tall. This one's over four."

"But how …?"

"How do they get around? Yeah, the branches are quite far apart." Alcot finished. "In the old days, they did it like with your towers—ladders and ropes with intricate pulley systems, but now, well, see." He pointed to a square box sliding up the tree. "There's one! An elevator, just like in your building, only these are out-side."

As she looked closer, she saw what Alcot was referring to, small jewel-like cubes running up and down on the surface of the trunk. "Let's go. The party awaits," Alcot urged.

They took two steps before Verbolana screamed. A loud snapping sound, along with hidden movement, erupted from the shadowy shrubs. Alcot stopped, wary and alert. The crashing of branches continued, and a low echoing growl pumped Verbolana with the Strength. In front of them, out of the gloom, emerged a fanged face, twenty feet wide, eyes locked on hers. It rose, slowly, eyes still engaged, until Verbolana had to crook her neck to maintain her mesmerized stare.

"Told ya!" Alcot laughed. "They like to keep it real around here. Can't exactly say why. I guess they want everyone to know what they had to deal with on their home world. They aren't very advanced as a people. Maybe they're a little embarrassed. Anyone who enters this neighborhood, however, gains a new respect."

He watched as Verbolana's anger boiled again, her eyes still locked on the beast.

"Would have cheated you if I'd warned you. And cheated Vol-tif." He ducked back as a right cross, launched by Verbolana, brushed past his nose. "Careful! If you'd have connected, the first offense is one-year confinement in your realm. No exceptions, no appeal."

Alcot turned to the growling face, the joke over. "Scat!" With a menacing grin, the face retreated into the shadows. "Sorry, but this is Heaven. You can't be hurt here. Remember?"

A good part of Verbolana's anger evaporated into the explosive blow. With the withdrawal of the threat, she stood limp and giggling. "Your world ... what else does it have in store?" When he did not answer, she continued. "I guess after a few years here that would have been fun." Not ready to meet his eyes and not willing to give him any more entertainment, she stomped down the path that led to the unbelievable tree.

As they approached the base of the tree, its dimensions turned what was left of Verbolana's anger into awe. Easily as large as one of the decks on her home tower, the tree trunk climbed dizzily into the cloudless sky, its overhanging branches discernible only by the lack of stars above their heads. Patiently waiting, a line of glass cubes she now recognized as elevators stood in a row, doors open.

"I should probably warn you this time," Alcot stated cautiously. "The ride up can be quite a thrill, if you don't mind heights. Just remember, you can't be hurt here." He motioned for her to enter one of the nearly transparent cubes. The doors silently closed as he slipped in beside her. "Voltif Sartan," was all he said.

The cube quickly rose to speed, leaving the ground and Verbolana's fragile stomach behind. Her feet, though firmly planted on something, seemed to stand on nothing. Around her seemed nothing. Even Alcot backed off a few feet, seeming to float in nothing as well. Carefully looking behind her, nursing a heavy dose of vertigo, she noticed the trunk of the mammoth tree racing by. As her gaze followed out beyond the unlit forest and lurking predators, the adjacent neighborhood rolled into view. Before she could appreciate the gaily lit splendor of this alien sight, a neighborhood appeared to her right, then another to her left, each remarkable in its own unique way, with turrets and spires, sparkling glass and what appeared to be a circle of buildings formed from molten, flowing metal, frozen in place.

133

Faster than she could track, bizarre and dazzling visual treats tickled her imagination. As they passed the first set of gargantuan branches, which hid the entire city for a few moments, she had time to catch her breath. And before the next set of branches stole her view again, she was able to discern a pattern to the city's layout. Rowed circles of lighted neighborhoods, separated by dark expanses of parklands, lakes and dimly lit footpaths, lay before her as far as her eye could see in every direction, except to her left. There, sharply-cragged mountains scrolled beside her and stopped at the sprawling city at their base. The mountains appeared so close in the clear air that she felt she could run her fingers across them as they rose.

Mesmerized, the last remnants of her anger at Alcot melted into the spectacular vistas. With her anger gone, she began to appreciate Alcot's world-weary demeanor. Almost two hundred years of such unadulterated splendor could wear anyone out. Exhaustion had started to creep into her limbs after just a few minutes of the sensory overload. With a deep calming breath, Verbolana adjusted her shoulders, unclenched her fists and summoned the Strength in an attempt to appear as cool as her partner. She failed. Giddy with nerves and awe, she pressed herself against the front of the transparent enclosure and traced a vividly lit river and its surrounding parklands as it cut a dramatic swath through the city.

"There's the city center," Alcot pointed off to their right. "Follow the river to the larger set of circles. See, there's the stadium. It's an oblong ring, about the size of a standard neighborhood, holds four-hundred thousand or some such. And that one with the glass turrets rising up a thousand feet or so, that's the Parliament Building."

The next set of branches whisked by and Verbolana felt the cube had started to slow. She looked back to her left. Snow now covered the tops of the starlit peaks, with thick sheets of gleaming ice filling the crags. She anticipated the doors opening and prepared for a frigid blast. She need not have worried. The cube slid smoothly to a stop and the transparent doors whooshed open, giving her only enough of a brush of fresh air to dimple her bare thighs.

Without railings and high enough for the clouds, a landing had been carved out of the tree's thick bark. Alcot took her elbow and coaxed her out along a thin path of stone steps inlaid into furry green moss. If there had been even the slightest breeze, Heaven or not, Verbolana would have crawled on her hands and knees. As it was, even with Alcot to steady her, her head swam with vertigo. Below lay the patch-worked pattern of a city beyond dimension. Alcot turned her toward the mountains and her head cleared slightly with the anchoring view. What appeared to be solid ground stood only feet away and Verbolana rushed to rejoice on it.

A deep cleansing breath followed her first comfortable footing since leaving her realm, it seemed. Before her, a lighted path meandered through a field of short grass, then up and over a small hill. Small furry animals grazed peacefully around a gently bubbling spring, while an attractive couple smooched on a bench that overlooked the city a few feet off the path. Off in the shadows, a collection of wind chimes tinkled with the occasional basal boom of larger tubes.

"This way," Alcot indicated. "Quite a ride, huh?"

"Unbelievable," was all she chose to say, concentrating on the solid landscape around her, trying to forget she was so high up in a tree that she could not imagine the dimensions of any of this, much less the elevator ride.

"It's not far, just over this rise."

Moments later, Verbolana stood just outside the open door to Voltif's home. Alcot was already inside, beckoning her to enter.

135

How could this be? Thoughts layered faster than she could process.

It appeared an entirely new world lay before her, hanging thousands of feet above the world she was now being asked to leave. The vanishing point of sky and sea lay off in the distance, with the polished stones of a large deck at her feet. Gracefully curving stairs, leading to who knew what, framed a view of terraced whitewashed balconies that stair-stepped down toward the sea. A humid breeze of salt and tropical flowers brushed the hair from her face as elegantly sculpted partygoers chatted and laughed in various groups throughout the scene. With Alcot's help, Verbolana took a brave step into this impossible world, although her mind still did not accept that any of this could be real. With a minute to adjust, her head calmed enough to discern Voltif, that was his name, standing before her … Alcot's introduction … the man's smooth body draped against hers … his arms tight, hands roving … the woman at his arm next to hug her … tight, smooth, smelling of something wonderful.

Verbolana smiled at the greetings, noticed gestures, deep laughter. She laughed. More hugs around, promises to meet up, descending stairs, dazzling seas of blues and greens beyond any experience. Sharp green-laced mountains jutting, creating pools of aquamarine around them, pillowed sand, distant bronzed bodies, gaily-colored contraptions shading others, tall glasses and laughter, tables high with food. Could Father truly be so beautiful? She had not imagined this. Could people be so free?

"Let's take this path." Alcot guided her distracted stumblings, down into hushed, all-encompassing greenery, across a bridged creek and into a shaded clearing.

"Welcome," a hearty voice erupted. The nut-brown man was shirtless, with huge shoulders and chest, hairless and shiny as if oiled. His wide, white-toothed smile kept Verbolana from shrinking. He offered two tall, dripping glasses of green liquid with pinned fruit floating. She watched Alcot suck on one of the protrusions after thanking the man. She sucked a sweet tang across her tongue; calming, energizing, soothing. She would have added "frightening," but any fear she might have felt evaporated as she noticed her perceptions evolve. An altered focus coalesced behind her eyes, free from intimidation, she guessed. Wonderful, joint-loosening, giddy freedom supplanted her ever-present wariness. She took another sip and looked into Alcot's eyes. The world slowed its spin. She saw him anew, forgave him for their earlier quarrel, smiled, pulled him down to her face and kissed him hard.

"Thank you for sticking with me," she breathed when they disengaged. "I don't know what I'd do without you." When he just smiled, she continued, "Where are we going?"

"I saw some sails in the lagoon down there. I thought, since you've been so brave today, it is time for me to step up, too." He thanked the man again and headed them down the path. When out of earshot of the bartender, he continued, "Open spaces like this are not my favorite. And the open sea, well, it terrifies me. But when I watch you face one horror after another, it's a bit shaming to think that I still have demons after all these years. So, I guess it's time to go windsurfing."

He plunged down the path with Verbolana in tow. They did not stop until their toes hit the sand.

Verbolana took another sip and giggled. "This deck tickles my feet."

"It's called *sand*. It's finely-crushed rock, and yes, I see what you mean; it does tickle. Probably a bit to do with the drink, too." He took another large gulp, this time bypassing the straw.

She followed his lead and felt another soothing rush as she took a big gulp. She giggled. "I feel funny," and giggled again.

"Very nice, isn't it? I think it is probably Hepran, with maybe a little Artreanen Falce mixed in," Alcot surmised.

"Good guess." A beautifully browned young woman strolled toward them, naked but for a tiny string holding a patch across her sex. "If you got it from Granton up the path, it *is* Hepran and Galce, with a rather large dose of Grough, too. Perfect for windsurfing."

Verbolana took in the sight of this woman with a calm she had never before felt. The girl was delicious. Suddenly Verbolana realized that nakedness was completely appropriate for the outdoors. As the girl continued her approach, Vee's attitude continued to evolve. She was Vee's polar opposite in color, but her twin in body. Smooth rounded hips melded into a flat smooth belly, then up to two healthy handfuls of breast. Her hair was black, straight and long, all the way to her waist. Lust imploded the fears that had controlled Verbolana all her life.

"Can't surf in those clothes. Better change." The beauty gave them an easy smile, turned and sauntered back to a line of colorful boards pulled up on the beach. Verbolana devoured the girl's loose-limbed saunter, silky skin and tightly rounded tail.

"Finally found something you like?" Alcot noted. "Is it the drug or the girl ... or both?"

"What drug?" Verbolana tried to get upset, but she was just too happy. "Is there something in the drink?"

"Weren't you listening?" Alcot looked astonished.

"I never understand what you're saying. I'm not supposed to take drugs. It's forbidden unless you're sick."

"Who says?" Alcot asked. "Everything here is supplied by God himself."

"Maybe he doesn't watch everything." She hoped.

"Doesn't watch everything? *Everything* here is his doing, Verbolana." He spoke as if explaining to a child. "Have you ever wondered why everyone here speaks your language?"

"No," she stated as if she should care, but at the moment, nothing seemed to matter much.

"God translates every word, every nuance. He even manipulates your perception of my lip movements so there is no incongruity. He is everywhere, in everything, all knowing of what has been. The only thing he doesn't know or control is what will be."

Verbolana bypassed the straw and took a giant gulp of her drink, ignoring the implications that came to mind. "Can we try windsurfing now? It's hot and I'm ready to get out of these clothes."

# Chapter 16

Verbolana watched as Alcot fell off his board again and pounded the surf with his clenched fists. She adjusted her sail, changed her course and headed over to see if he needed help. The nut-brown girl had launched a board from the beach and was headed out to him, too. By the time Verbolana pulled up and dropped her sail into the emerald water, the girl had already arrived. With grace born from years at the ropes, Verbolana spun on the rocking board, bent and was soon perched on the side of her board, with her feet dangling in the luscious water. Alcot was furious.

"I don't need your help; I'll get it. I just had a few too many slugs of that drink." He thrashed himself back onto the board and sat heavily, breathing hard. "Plus, you girls are distracting me. Vee, you didn't have to pick the same outfit as Tarja here. You two make me think of much more than windsurfing."

At that, Tarja slipped off her board and snaked over to Alcot through what looked to Verbolana like liquid jewels. Then the tempting serpent grabbed the side of Alcot's board and rubbed her hardening nipples along his hairy legs, and stared up at him with pouting eyes. "I thought you hadn't noticed," she teased.

Verbolana sat fascinated. She had sexed Alcot many times now, but something like this had never occurred to her. What courage this girl must have, out here in the open, in the light of day, without covers and darkness to hide in.

"God, I wish I had a little more of that drink," she intoned. Adrenaline gushed through her muscles, leaving her immediately weak and shuddering. In her hand, God placed a half glass of the green juice. Without hesitation, she took two giant gulps as she watched this lovely creature bobbing, wet and sparkling, between Alcot's legs. Newfound courage, mixed with adrenaline, calmed her enough to command her muscles. Fighting every instinct, Verbolana set the glass on her board, then slid into the water. "God, I wish the water weren't so deep," she blurted aloud when she remembered she did not know how to swim. Then she remembered something else. Other worlds were not like hers. Heterosexuality was the norm, according to what Alcot said. She froze just as she was about to reach out to the girl from behind.

Apparently, Alcot had wished his swim trunks away while she was busy gaining her courage. He looked up from watching the girl's bobbing head. "Go ahead, she'll love it."

Verbolana flushed red, found out. "How do you know? I don't want to insult her," she mouthed at Alcot's smiling face.

"She is here for our pleasure. I know Voltif. Our host would have designed her for full service."

"Designed?" Verbolana mouthed back, not understanding.

"Sure. She's a recreate, probably a composite." He addressed the girl with casual command, "Tarja, where were you last week?"

The beauty pulled off and gazed up at him. Unmounted, she idly licked him while she thought. "I don't know. Hey, is your friend around? I could use some help; this thing is so big. Oh, there you are." She gazed back at Verbolana. "Hope you don't mind. He just looked so tasty."

Verbolana gathered more courage from the green stuff floating in her head, then stammered, "You look awfully tasty yourself. Do *you* mind?" She reached out and ran two hands down to cup both the girl's butt cheeks in the slippery water, Alcot's question fading into her lustful haze.

"Now we're talking," Tarja cooed.

It was all the encouragement Vee needed. She slid in tight to the girl's back, her hands traced up the smooth browned skin to cup this beauty's jutting mounds. She heard the girl catch her breath as each of Verbolana's fingers played across erect nipples.

Within minutes, Verbolana was wishing to God she could breathe underwater and that her tongue was just a little longer. After a few more minutes, all three were running across the beach, giggling, toward the girl's beach shack. With God at the helm, they spent until early the next morning exploring and drinking, eating and snuggling. When Verbolana finally dozed off, she could not remember a time when she had felt happier or freer.

White-laced curtains fluttered at the window and strobed the morning sun across Verbolana's eyes as she attempted to open them. *How do people live in such brightness*? was her first thought of the morning. She squinted around the messed hut and remembered. *Wow.* Vivid, full-frame images cycled across her brain. She selected an image, lay back and wallowed in the sensations for a moment, smiling. For the first time, she appreciated God's insistence on total recall. God!

Another full-color memory interrupted her reverie. Alcot's face, his casual arrogance evaporated, his instructional tone pounding into her, "God translates every word, every nuance. He even manipulates your perception of my lip movements so there is no incongruity with the translated words you hear in your head. He is everywhere, in everything, all knowing of what has been."

Her stomach heaved, her eyes bolted open. God saw everything, knew everything? She scrounged desperately for the crumpled sheet that lay across the crumpled bed and pulled it up over her nakedness. Still in a panic, she searched the hut for a taste of the serenity she had felt the night before. Nothing. Her mind continued to cycle. Alcot said not to worry—God is every-where—all is lost. She crawled to a window, dragging the sheet with her to cover her nakedness. Where was Tarja? Could she help? Her head turned as her eyes scoured the tiny room. Alcot slept in a corner of the wall-to-wall bed, but she couldn't bear to listen to his off-handed recriminations. He would laugh, or frown, in annoyance. She must expose herself again, to the power that controlled eternity, before her head crawled off her shoulders.

"God," on whimpered breath, she whispered, "I wish I had more of that green stuff." A glass appeared on the windowsill before her, a frosted invitation. She abandoned the sheet with both hands, grabbed the glass and drained it. The wash was almost instantaneous, though not soon enough. Relaxed now, Verbolana vowed to keep this stuff nearby from now on. She replaced the cup on the sill and crawled back to where the sheets were still warm from her body. She plunged down and buried her face, her backside exposed to God's eyes. She no longer cared.

Lying in chemical-induced bliss, she searched through her un-categorized memories. Snippets of the night before flitted behind her eyes. She focused on one of her many climactic moments. Tiny shards of moonlight dappled the white sheets. Alcot lay on his back, his dark skin made him almost invisible, which in turn made the frantic plunging of Tarja's hips almost comical. But soon the girl's feral screams and arched back threw all humor aside. Verbolana's hungry eyes gulped every image, her ears strained to assimilate every slap of skin, every groan of pleasure. She watch-ed Alcot's gleaming member disappear, reappear and disappear again; Tarja's wanton sex swallowing it to the hilt. She remem-bered Alcot slamming up; Tarja plunging down, impaling, screaming. Jealousy occurred to her as an abstract thought. Had it

144

occurred to her at the time or was this an insinuation of her now-mind? She could not tell, so she concluded it didn't matter. The euphoria created by green stuff did not allow for such a thought, so she delved back and watched as Tarja's beautiful handfuls bounced to the rhythm of the pounding; watched her sweet face contort, her mouth gape and gasp, until she fell panting off Alcot's perch. The girl fell to snuggle into Verbolana's open arms and Verbolana felt the glow of a thousand suns as her new treasure came to her welcoming embrace.

Alcot, though, was not finished, Verbolana remembered. Or perhaps he had read her mind, read her need. For, as the girl lay burrowed and almost sobbing in Vee's arms, Alcot positioned himself at Verbolana's feet and started sucking her toes, one at a time. As Tarja recovered, Alcot moved north, licking and nibbling his way up the two girls' calves and thighs.

Tarja, fully recovered now, mirrored her body on top of Verbolana's and coaxed their legs further open to allow for Alcot's advance. Fully immersed in sensation and no longer able to distinguish past from present, Verbolana's hands roamed across Tarja's smooth back and gently curving ass. Tarja pulled back slightly and caught Verbolana's eyes, then with the softest, most loving gaze, dropped her face to Verbolana's. They kissed, deep and long, their tongues drawing slow, powerful circles, their lips softly sliding. Verbolana spread their legs further as she felt Alcot reach his goal and start little tongue circles of his own. His tongue disappeared for little eternities as Verbolana felt Tarja's tongue push harder against hers, deep into her mouth. The building sensations stretched, the yearnings built to become intolerable and yet Alcot continued to disappear and reappear.

Engulfed in body warmth, completely freed from any semblance of worry or remorse, Verbolana envisioned herself a battle blimp, felt how the blimp itself must feel, floating free, fully loaded, waiting for the command to fire. The vision seemed incongruent to her, even at the time, she realized, but she had nothing else in her limited experience for comparison. It was the only real-world image that kept her grounded enough not to fall down the ropes or float away into the clouds. Then the order came. Her cannons blasted; her body spasmed as if in recoil. Violently she shook herself free of Tarja's mouth, afraid she would suffocate from her new demands for oxygen. Alcot's tongue quieted, but only for a moment. When her bucking subsided, he reengaged as Tarja smothered her arms tightly around her, cocooning Verbolana in her velvet grip. Again and again, Verbolana exploded, until she was a shivering, quaking mess.

Now it was her turn to sob, and the green stuff allowed her to let loose more than she could have imagined. She sobbed away the whip, the fearful eyes and scathing words of the Director, the squalid closeness of the deck ... and Trake.

Verbolana came back to her now-mind just enough to remember it was a dream. She was alone in bed, remembering. She dropped back and felt the body-rich heat and weight of her new lover on top of her. "God, make that Trake. A loving, caring, tender Trake. One who knows how to love a woman." Tarja was gone. Verbolana felt the prickle of beard at her chin, the soft skin turned to hardened muscle and Alcot's tongue turned to urgent stiffness. This new apparition plunged deep into her, with no preamble, no warning. But it was what Verbolana needed, to be filled and at the same time to engulf, to know with certainty that his desire for her was unmistakable, undiluted and unquenchable. He pulled out and plunged and groaned. A deep, soul-deep expression of appreciation? And love? The green stuff did not allow Verbolana's question to linger. She concluded it was love she felt. Plunging, hammering, filling love. Verbolana watched Trake's head rear back, his spine contort. She felt him drain into her with long spasmodic bursts. It was a moment she had never fully appreciated with Alcot, she realized. A vessel for his over-flowing love, a vehicle bringing forth his hidden expression. How liberating it was for him, for her.

Trake was now on his elbows above her, his eyes digging into her eyes. She watched his face change, his eyes shrink back. She remembered seeing this with Alcot and she waited, patiently, for him to mumble a little prayer as Alcot always did, then return to her. But Trake had no such prayer, she realized. And in horror she watched his eyes drift to her forehead as he gave one final gasp, then he rolled off her and flopped on the bed beside her, spent. She lay alone, confused, suddenly cold and abandoned—and somehow ashamed. Anger, even through the euphoric haze of drugs, came next. How could love be so wonderful and so brutal? How could a man be so loving one moment and so distant the next? Dizzied with drugs and confusion, she pulled the sheets back over herself and without looking, wished Trake away.

The curtained door flapped open sometime later as naked Tarja stepped in carrying a tray piled high with fruit, bread, and steam-ing drinks. "Good morning," she chirped, her voice so sweet Vee felt herself stirring again.

"Good morning, my love." Vee went with the words that popped out. Yet another liberation.

"Ah, you are too kind." Tarja always seemed uncensored. "I have brought the feast. I don't seem to be able to do what you do, wishing for things to appear. Maybe you can teach me."

"I am just learning myself," Verbolana confessed.

From the corner Alcot added, "You will never be able to do it. You are not like us. Now be quiet while I sleep." He buried his head back in his cushion.

Vee watched Tarja's face fall from Alcot's casual insult, then jumped up and with an arm around Tarja's shoulder, walked her back outside. "He can be such a lout sometimes. Let's eat on the beach."

Tarja recovered her pride and smiled back. "Men," was all she said.

An hour later Alcot emerged, tumbled and dragging. Vee and Tarja were in the middle of the lagoon, sailing. He waved, and Vee cut through the emerald water to pull within shouting distance. She was still angry with him and thought maybe this was the last time she would bother with him.

"I'm going up to see if Voltif is around," he yelled across the water.

"Fine, I'm going to stay here. You don't have to come back for me." He did not deserve further explanation.

Alcot raised his eyebrows at her. "Back on the juice?"

"Not yet." And she turned to sail off.

"You'll get your heart broken. Happens every time." He made a note to check on her in a week or so.

"Bound to happen a few times through eternity," she quipped.

"Oh, I can't believe I haven't told you," he yelled to her retreating form. "You don't have forever here. With the current Heavenly calendar, we each get 311 years, 85 days and some odd hours and minutes."

# Chapter 17

W hy do you think your Gods said these things?" Tarja lay naked in their big bed, her head pillowed on Vee's shoulder. Vee found her innocent wonder not the least bit threatening.

Verbolana looked around her new home while she took another long pull off her green drink through a great new invention, a straw. Over the last few weeks, she had become accustomed to this bright new world. The clarity of the sky and sea inspired her fearless explorations.

"I don't know." The drink still sparkled in her brain with each sip. "Whenever I look back, all I see are the faces of those I loved. Treena was so beautiful, or is so beautiful. She's still there." Verbolana drifted with the memory, heard Treena's soft words, felt her gentle fingers, watched a muffled giggle break on her face. "She's still there, and I can do nothing." Disconnected from the floating images, she continued, "Why … why, why? Such ugliness, so many lies." She did not expect an answer. Tarja snuggled deeper into her shoulder, pressed her body the length of Vee's. They lay as shadows traipsed across the floor and finally melded into their neighbors. Verbolana kept the straw to her lips, sucking at the slightest twinge of fear or melancholy.

There was an answer to it all, a grand reason, one she could surely find if she could quell the apprehension long enough. It was somewhere behind the joy, hidden in the forests of laughter.

For wasn't joy the sustenance of life? Wasn't joy, or the absence of it, the true motivator for all human activity? Fear, anger, jealousy, avarice, hunger, pain—all these indicated a lack of joy. They were all considered motivators for human action, but that was not deep enough. Comparing, Verbolana could hold up the template of how she felt at this moment to all the experiences of her life. With her perfect memory, she located and analyzed every moment that might have held an element of joy. There were not many. She excavated around each scene, before and after. Before, she some-times found anticipation, anxiety and the like, but afterward, she found resentment or jealousy, anger or betrayal and a longing to return to whatever had transported her to that joyous moment. She had always seen these luscious interludes as a respite from her dreary life. Now she saw them as an addition to her misery.

Verbolana sipped her drink and pulled Tarja closer. She felt Tarja's softness and strength, her willing burrowing, her empathy for the pain of questions and answers she would never even conceive. Vee opened her eyes and looked down. Ivory skin overlaid by toasted grain, dawn-kissed strands of hair mingling with midnight, raging anger smothered by unadulterated joy. She ran her hands down Tarja's perfect body, cupping and tracing. Joy was warm and smooth. Vee allowed the emotion to move her, felt its golden glow enter every cell of her body as the Strength could. She coaxed the girl on top of her and skidded her up, felt their nipples tweak in passing, then the girl's rough bush scour across her belly. She lowered one torpedic breast to her grazing teeth. She glanced up as Tarja's head arched back and Vee wallowed in the pure joy of giving joy. Eventually, she switched, hungry for Tarja's other breast. She felt Tarja grinding her sex rough across Vee's ribs, searching for some protrusion.

"God, I wish I had a cock," Verbolana intoned. Immediately she felt a swelling and stretching in her groin. She reached down, marveling at her new toy. Without delay, Verbolana guided her wanton friend down until fire met fire. Tarja needed no further coaxing or direction. Unquestioning, the girl slid down to fill her hungry void. Verbolana learned, in the best possible way, that filling was as blindingly joyous as being filled, joy for joy.

She allowed the girl to ride her for only a moment before she rolled her onto her back and felt an undeniable selfishness take over. She dipped one of her breasts into Tarja's waiting mouth as she accelerated her piston-like driving. New sensations overwhelmed her, though a hint of logical thought remained. Verbolana urged herself to slow, sensing the impending eruption. But logic did not rule this moment. She could not deny or delay God's design. A few more strokes and she exploded, spasmodically draining and filling, giving and receiving. Amazingly, the draining did not stop with the fluids. She felt her brain drain its urgency, and its passion as well. Suddenly, unexpectedly, she felt abandoned, lost and cheated.

From this new troubling void, somehow she remembered her partner. How could she ignore the one who had brought her here? But what should she do? She had nothing left. Her gifts had drained with the expulsion. Sorrow and guilt entered. She watched as Tarja opened her eyes and seemed to recognize her dilemma. Vee produced an apologetic smile, when all she wanted to do was curl away. She felt more naked than she had ever been, exposed to her selfish core by the scrutiny of her lover.

Tarja smiled back. "I have man in my design. They told me a little about my construction. I know your struggle, Vee. You can roll over and sleep if you'd like. I was filled more than you will ever know."

Verbolana saw no deception in her lover's eyes; heard no condescension in her voice. "But you ... I know. I am still a woman.

Part of me needs to stay connected, but I am so … helpless, so drained."

"Sleep, my lover. I am content and happy. I was designed to be content and happy. Unlike you, unfortunately."

Verbolana's last thought, before she dozed off, was of Trake. Were her eyes as distant as Trake's had been? She thought maybe they were.

Treena rustled, her warm body tight against Vee's side. Verbolana rolled her clouded head and felt her lover's breath hot at her ear. She could not catch the words. Urgency hung amid confusion. Verbolana strained her ears. The words came again. Nothing but a sense of frustration and fear. She turned and squinted, the darkness complete. She felt for her lover. Treena had disappeared. Vee's legs would not move. Her shoulders were pinned, too. It was not Treena, she realized. Trake? He had come back? From where? Why?

*You understand. You love me. You'll be flogged*, she breathed. The touch on her shoulder was still urgent, persistent. *Come to me, I forgive you. You did not know*, she breathed her from her soul.

"Vee, wake up," Alcot's hand moved to her shoulder and shook her harder. "You have to wake up. Voltif has changed everything. He sent for me. He was worried you wouldn't understand. Your friend is gone."

Confused, Verbolana's eyes peeped into the darkness. Alcot sat on the side of the bed in deep shadow, the meaning of his words still unclear. The unaccustomed weight of heavy blankets and the crackle of a flickering fire added to her muddle. She felt the sheets beside her. The bed was empty.

"As I said, she was a recreate. She does not fit the new storyline. Usually these set-ups come as a package and they include personnel."

"What do you mean?" Verbolana's whisper was not her own; defeat weighed each word. "I was happy." She could have gone on, *I was working it through, getting adjusted, learning to love in a completely new way, feeling stronger, exorcising my shame and my guilt ... and my sorrow.* She didn't bother; this was Alcot.

"I guess you could go back," Alcot hesitated. "I really shouldn't tell you this. As your Weaver, my duty is mixed. As I see it. I am supposed to orient you, get you on your feet, show you a little comfort. But it's also ... Well, I don't want you to get lost." He said it with such finality that Verbolana knew she was supposed to understand what he meant, but she didn't.

"But I *am* lost," she responded.

With his next comments, Verbolana knew Alcot had missed her point. His words flowed like the Director's sermon on the raised deck of her home. "You are not lost. You are here with me, a real and vital person. There is no doubt you have demons to battle, that you have not found comfort here, but life is not only about comfort. I know some disagree, but this is why I became a Weaver. A little comfort goes a long way. Too much comfort and you are lost."

"Can I get a new Weaver, then?" There was no hope in her question. She just wanted to get even a little.

"Don't be silly." He took her seriously; he was honor-bound to do so. "You don't need a new Weaver. I can get you through this."

"You confuse me, Alcot." Sleep drained from behind Verbolana's eyes and with it came the lethargy of defeat. She latched onto his contradiction. "You have said all along that 'comfort' is what everyone looks for here. You've said that 'comfort' is the drive that gives people purpose. Now you say it is poison."

"Yes."

"Which is it?" she bore in.

"Both, Vee," Alcot instructed. "Just as with anything, too much of any one thing is a problem. And here, where 'too much' appears with the utterance of a few words, it can be a real, immediate problem. It is what we call 'getting lost.'"

"Believe me," she came back after a moment. "Too much comfort is not a problem for me right now."

"It could be and you wouldn't even know it."

"I know how I feel without it." It was time to negotiate. This man could get her back to her beach hut. He had said as much. "You are my Weaver; take me back."

"You would have to do that for yourself."

"Tell me how," she locked on.

"Go back to your realm and ask for Voltif's set-up. It's not really done—stealing someone else's set-up, but you can." Defeat drained his voice.

"Now you're trying to shame me?" She jumped back, amazed at his attempted manipulation.

"No, not really, it's just that …"

She thought he sounded pathetic. "It's just that you don't want me to do it, so you're trying whatever you can to stop me!" Her anger was back at full swing. "Really, can I get a new Weaver?"

"Yes. Yes, you can, but that was not what I was doing. It is my job to show you how things work around here. Voltif's set-up took hundreds of Weaver hours to create. It isn't easy to develop a world so perfect. It takes a lot of research and just the right communication with God. Then for you to steal it with just a few words? Well, it's just not done."

"And do you think I care what your friends think of me? Alcot, you're lying." Verbolana knew, now, how to get what she needed. However painful it might be, she could sneak back through her neighborhood, get to her realm and return to her beach and her hut, Tarja and the green stuff. She felt safer confronting him. "What is really going on here?"

"I don't want you to get lost, that's all. If you go back to that beach, with that girl, you might never come back out."

Does he actually care about me? That would be a first. Treena cared about me, and Wexi, but nobody else. "Night soil, Alcot! What is in it for you? Tell me the truth."

"There you go again, wanting the truth. You want to do this again?"

"You know I do." Verbolana stared him down.

"It's because we keep score, and if you go in for more than a year, then I lose points." Alcot looked away. "Look, around here; it isn't easy to stand out. I know it sounds silly, maybe even callous, but it helps to motivate. Otherwise, there might not be any Weavers. Humans compete; that's just the way God made us. And God doesn't assign us—we volunteer. If there weren't competition, people might not be interested. And then where would you be?"

"Get out of here! You did your job. You woke me and warned me. Now leave." Her calm hid nothing, she knew. If her heart broke again, it might splatter across the room.

"Vee, come on, understand. It has nothing to do with you."

"Oh, I got that, like a fart in the dark. It was not me, yet I still get the stink."

"You don't have to go back to your realm." He stood up and paced across the room. "We can find you a place closer. There is usually a vacant realm or two in every neighborhood. People move in together. If you're gone for more than a year it gets released."

"Another of your little manipulations, huh?"

"Yes."

"Great. How do I do it?" she asked.

"Once you're out of Voltif's, just ask God if there's one available. He'll direct you."

"Fine, now leave."

# Chapter 18

Though Verbolana no longer watched, Trake loped through the tangled forest, his leathery feet barely grazed Father's skin. The day was warm, and the only real clothing he wore was the pair of cut-off trousers in which he had swung from the battle blimp a year or so earlier His shirtless torso hung heavy with the bounty of his recent raid, more rope and a long swath of Za cloth.

Even though he was a good hour's run from the Wretched camp, he could not leave a trail. At least not one that looked human. He had learned to mimic what he called a Vee, named after another graceful creature. Even with that, for the final three hundred yards to his hideout, he employed a more traditional Honored tactic. It had taken him more than a month and many dangerous sorties to steal enough rope to set up what were now seven, soon to be eight, swing stations through the trees. With a final bounding step, he lurched high into a tree, thick with suckers and parasitic growth. With the Strength flowing, he ran five steps straight up the side of the tree before he had to grab a limb. With practiced speed, he navigated through vines and hanging moss to his first concealed rope. Careful not to snag his bow, arrows or the coiled rope hooked around his shoulders, he swung without hesitation. Arcing low, then swinging back up, he landed high in the next tree, secured the rope and then grabbed another. The exhilaration tempted him to scream, but caution prevailed.

Soon Trake ducked into his cave and turned to watch. He knew no one had followed. However, it never paid to be anything less than thorough. The earthen smells he had learned to appreciate wafted to greet him.

"I will not compromise," he breathed, as his mind addressed the imagined masses. "*We* will not compromise. Every day we observe brings us new examples. The Wretched are wretched, the Chosen are chosen." His new mantra rang true with the imagined army that stood before him. "We will not succumb to their ways. We will stand resolute in the face of hunger, refusing the heathen bounty even if it means falling to an early death. We will stand naked against the thorns of Father and shiver from his cold breath if it means covering our bodies in the skins of Father's beasts." He stopped his tirade to swat at an insect that buzzed his ear. "We will annihilate the Wretched and those that suckle from their evil ways — the insects that infest their hair, the bugs that eat their waste, the vermin that, without the Wretched, would not exist."

Trake sucked in the adoration of the masses and turned to the dark cave. He loathed entering, so accustomed he had become to the sunlight and the warmth it brought. He remembered his first days, shivering and lost, the constant hunger, until he learned to eat from the bushes. He remembered his almost frantic joy when he learned that not all the Wretched clothing came from the dead of Father. They fashioned some from the hair of the animals, and he saw from the friendly nature of these animals that they gave their hair willingly! A gift from Father, no doubt. Similar to the gift of milk given by these same animals. Trake witnessed the relief apparent after they were milked of their burdens. And that milk hardened into chunks of fatty, pungent salvation that, once a taste was acquired, could not be equaled. The Directors had been wrong about this, too. The animals of Father were happy to help.

Trake spent many nights rewriting the Directors' words in his head. He longed for the skill to preserve these new lines. From one night to the next, he forgot. Already there had been many revelations he would not be able to pass on to future disciples. Already some of his earliest epiphanies had become self-evident, so obvious he now barely heard the contradicting lines of the Directors. He had seen the Wretched reading from papers as the Directors did. He had also seen them use sharpened tools to put new words down on paper and read them aloud.

And that is what led him to his current mission. He had already stolen almost everything he needed from the Wretched: clothing and bedding, a shoulder bag to carry his supplies, vegetable bowls and clay cooking pots, jugs to hold water and a bounty of grains and dried fruit and vegetables to keep him alive. He had even stolen fire.

Now Trake would steal a writer, one who would take his thoughts and put them on paper as the Author had done. Though he had not seen the Humble Magician since that night in the bush, he knew his Path. He knew he must record everything he saw, felt and thought. When he returned to the Chosen, he would be different. He was already different, and he must be able to trace this evolution in order to explain the changes to his people. Especially with the Gods as quiet as they had been lately. Even as the Truth burned in his heart, without the Gods to back him up, convincing the Directors of their folly could be his greatest battle.

So Trake sat in the flickering light of his cave and watched the smoke find its lazy way up to the domed ceiling and out the shaft he had dug from above for its escape. He thought about what he had seen today: the jubilant return of a large hunting party, each with a dripping, hacked part of animal on his shoulder; the whistled warnings and hushed disappearances as a battle blimp passed in the distance. Then there were the routine gatherings of the women as they searched for food and tidbits they could use for this project or that. His thoughts lingered across the images. Who would be the easiest to capture and bend to his will?

A female seemed the easiest prey, and during the time of gathering, they often wandered far into the fields, often alone. One female in particular had caught Trake's eye. He tried to convince himself it had nothing to do with Verbolana. After all, the girl didn't look much like Verbolana. She had dark hair that was long and straight. Her complexion was also dark, but smooth and firm like Verbolana's. He tried to convince himself that his choice had only to do with the fact that he had witnessed her writing and that she often strolled by herself. He wondered whether an older woman might be easier to capture, but realized that they seldom went off by themselves, and, he rationalized, an older woman might not have the resilience to survive the rigors of a life not supported by the whole community. It also occurred to him that, if older Wretched were anything like older Chosen, they would be too set in their thoughts. For certainly this would be his first convert.

That night Trake devised a plan. He thought about the girl's obvious strength and natural agility. He had watched her for a few weeks as she navigated the forest, swam in the nearby river, and when she knew she was alone, swung fallen branches in mock battle. She was quick and alert and knew the forest better than Trake did. He would have to use the Strength and every ounce of his newfound cunning to catch her unaware. He had procured all the bindings he would need, as well as a gag to muffle her screams.

Trake's biggest break was just the day before. As he stalked her, she stopped in a clearing with one huge tree in its center. He watched in confusion as she picked up stone after stone and threw them into the high branches of the tree. Trake snuck around to get a better look. Her target was an insect nest that hung from a stout branch. Insects swarmed out of the nest with each repeated blow and finally the entire nest fell from its perch, only to crack open and hang up in the branches below. In high spirits, the girl yelled at the swarm, "You have not outwitted me! I shall return tomorrow. Your home is ruined. Fly away to build a new one, and I shall climb and harvest what you have left!" Trake realized at that moment that he would harvest tomorrow as well.

Trake waited in a thicket thirty feet from the base of the tree. Behind him, coiled, lined and piled, were his tools for the day. His bow and arrows, along with his shoulder pack, sat back out of the way. His sword, however, was close by, a good tool for intimidation. The rope and gag were also essential, as well as the pile of rocks he had collected.

Hours dragged by with no sign of the girl. He busied his mind reviewing his plan. Let her get at least twenty feet into the tree. Then I'll summon the Strength, step from my cover, and hopefully hit her with the first stone. I can't let her scream, so I will have to knock her out and let her fall from the tree. If she dies from the rock or the fall, I will have to start all over.

Finally, he heard the faintest rustling, and the girl emerged from the forest. Up close, Trake caught a glimpse of her sparkling eyes and the swell of her youthful body. He would have to take extra care, he realized. *Maybe I will wait until she has climbed down before I pounce. I would be more assured of a clean capture that way. Yes, I will wait. I would hate to start over.*

So he did. The girl climbed the tree without incident, grabbed the nearly abandoned nest and headed down. With the added burden, she was not as agile and nearly slipped a few times. Trake summoned the Strength, and as the girl hung from the tree, one hand still on a low branch and one hand around the nest, he sprang.

The tackle ended with her flat on her back and Trake on top; the nest rolled off to the edge of the clearing. She was so surprised she barely got a squeak out before Trake shoved a wad of cloth in her mouth. She recovered quickly, however, and before he could secure the cloth around her head, he had his hands full of flailing limbs. Guarding his head from punches and clawing, he moved up to pin her arms under his knees, but that freed her legs and feet to pummel his back and head. Ducking, he absorbed the punishment as best he could and secured the gag around her twisting head. Then he pinned her arms to the ground with his forearms and slid down to control her lower torso. Her strength was no match, though her determination was another matter. As he slid down her body, his face came in range of her bucking head, and she delivered a mighty blow with her forehead that smashed his nose and caused his eyes to water. He wrenched his head back and, in doing so, lifted slightly from her body. She writhed below him like a giant serpent and managed to roll onto her side, free one arm, and hook it around his neck.

Trake almost laughed at her silly attempts to escape until she brought her face to his and, even with the gag deep in her mouth, latched onto his damaged nose with her teeth. This was too much. He sat up, pulled her with him, and pummeled her ribs with both fists. She released her grip only after Trake heard and felt one of her ribs crack. Quickly, before she could recover her breath, Trake grabbed one arm, shifted around, and savagely pulled it behind her back. Applying as much torque as possible to keep her from moving, he managed to grab her other arm and bring it back as well. He then propelled her forward onto her stomach and sat on her again. From around his shoulder, he uncoiled the rope, and within minutes, he had trussed her like one of the animals her people tortured and ate.

Without a word, Trake drew the girl's still struggling form up over his shoulder, stooped and collected his weapons, along with the excess rope, and was off through the brush.

The challenge now was to get away clean, he knew. If Trake had noticed one thing about these Wretched, it was that they looked out for each other, even their worker-type women. They would undoubtedly dispatch search parties as soon as the girls did not come home, and these Wretched were expert trackers. Trake would need to outwit them, so he had developed an elaborate plan. He doubted he could lose them in the brush. One broken branch or slight indent in the ground would scream of his passage. Therefore, he set off in the opposite direction of his cave. Continually summoning the Strength, even with his lopsided, writhing load, he loped gracefully to the river. There he unceremoniously dumped his prize onto the makeshift raft he had secreted in a thicket of overhanging bushes. As she thrashed and kicked, Trake secured her across the three short logs he had loosely lashed together. Then he tossed in his shoulder pack and weapons. Without delay, he pushed the raft into the current and walked it downstream until the sun dipped low on the horizon. Finally, near frozen from the seemingly endless trek, he spotted the ropes he had attached to a sturdy branch hanging over the water. After securing his writhing captive to one of the ropes, he collected the rest of his possessions, cut the logs free from one another and sent them floating downstream.

With new Strength summoned, Trake felt his faith push the cold stiffness of the last few hours from his muscles. Grabbing the second dangling rope, he pulled himself easily out of the river and into the high branches. As he teetered on a swaying branch, he noticed his precious cargo fighting against the current; the girl floundered to keep her head above water. Quickly he jerked at her rope and pulled her out of the water with one hand. Slipping and unsteady, he wrapped his other hand around a neighboring branch and with mammoth effort pulled his load higher into the tree. Now with both hands on the rope and somewhat secure in his perch, he hauled his jerking, choking captive up into the tree. Following his well-thought plan, within minutes he had all his ropes and weapons collected and slung over one shoulder while his suddenly subdued captive hung over the other.

Trake felt confident that this elaborate and taxing maneuver would be the key to his clean escape. He figured, especially this far downriver, the search party would only check the banks for footprints. By the time Trake had scampered through the trees and lowered the girl and himself to the ground, he was at least twenty-five feet from the bank. And finally, free from immediate danger, the Strength no longer buoyed his exhausted muscles. Shuddering with muscle fatigue and cold, he collapsed at the camp he set up the day before. After stretched moments of deep fatigue, Trake checked the girl's bonds, ate from his supplies and collapsed into a deep sleep.

Trake awoke in darkness, crunched against the girl, his thin blanket apparently insufficient to ward off the night chill. She moaned when he stirred and he realized she was shaking violently. It would not do for her to die after all his work. He drew the blanket from between them and threw it over her. Her clothing and the ropes that bound her were still wet from her river trip, as were his pants. The blanket would not help at this point. He needed to take drastic action. Stumbling around the dark camp, he located more rope and tied one of her feet securely to the nearest tree.

"Make a move to escape, and I will slice you open," he warned as he untrussed her hands and feet. With unsheathed sword,

Trake ordered her to sit up. When she complied, he stripped her clothing from her without permission or apology. He removed his own pants as well, and, pulling the blanket back over them, he crunched his body roughly against hers. Still gagged so she could not protest, after a minute or two, her body seemed to welcome the added heat and stopped struggling. Trake threw his sword arm around her and placed the blade on her stomach, between her breasts, to just under her chin. "Move and you die," was all he said.

Somewhere in the night, wild wonderful dreams attacked his sleep. He woke repeatedly to the complete darkness, his skin fused to the heat of another. And repeatedly he reminded himself this was a Wretched girl, not one of his suitable Blessed companions. In the dark and cold, with dream and reality fighting for dominance, his thoughts swam with heated desire. It had been so long since he had even thought of release, and now his needs rushed back with the power of a battle blimp. His erection was as hard as the steel in his sword.

What could it hurt, he thought in frustrated delusion. If I treat her like a pleasure boy, take her like a pleasure boy, what could it hurt? Surely, the Gods do not expect me to sacrifice all in this mission of theirs. Surely, the Gods need their prophet to feel human. Release is not an option for men; it is a reality. With one hand firm on his sword, he snaked his other arm free from under his sleeping captive. He spit on his hand and coated his straining organ with saliva, then back to his mouth and down to coat the entrance of her pleasure tunnel. She squirmed, and he moved his sword up under her chin and commanded, "Don't move."

He positioned his member and shoved. He did not enter. He shoved again, and felt her whole body tense. He repositioned himself and breathed into her ear, "Relax and things will go much easier." She was like a first-time pleasure boy, he thought, anxious and afraid.

Alarmingly, he felt her hand grasp his cock. Strength coursed through his body even without his summons. The tip of his sword moved under her chin and he felt her squirm as it sank half an inch. "Careful," he warned as the steel drew blood. Gently, slowly, he felt the slick head of his member slide to the gates of the forbidden. From the pressure he was already exerting, before he could pull back, he plunged deep into her, Za softness enveloped him, hot and liquid. He froze. This was not what the Gods allowed. He did not withdraw, however. He tried to pull out, yet found himself sinking deeper, his eyes rolling back, his hands clenching. With each slight movement, this new temptation grew slicker, and warmer, and slicker yet. Clinging to fleeting reason, he prayed, *Graceful Dancer, you have tricked me. You have pushed me beyond sanity to a place I did not ask to go. I see your deception now.* He pulled his hips back and plunged into her again, lunging his words with his frantic thrusts. *I see the danger; I understand the forbidden. Thank you for this insight. I have failed.* He was now deep into a pulsating rhythm. *But I will not fail again. Oh, Gods … oh, Gods … Ohhhhh. I will not fail again.*

# Chapter 19

Trake awoke naked, evidence of his sinful adventures crusted between his legs. His remembrances had not been a dream, he realized. Ashen faced, he looked toward the sky. *Graceful Dancer, thank you for this lesson. I see now that the Wretched women can be beguiling. Their men bow to temptation of which I had no idea. I will study this, and I will learn the ways this can defeat them. One must know of the sacrifice before it is truly a sacrifice. The woman will teach me and I will learn. I will learn so I can defeat the demon.*

Trake stood and pulled on his frigid pants, his piety restored. The woman had brought new challenges and new opportunities. His sword! He turned, jumped back and narrowly escaped the solid swing at his belly. "Stop!" he yelled. But she swung at the rope that held her foot, and with one swipe, she was free. Trake, however, had not lost a moment. He was bolting for his bow and arrows by the time she advanced, but it was too late. He had the bow, but could not bend to pull an arrow without leaving himself open.

"I said stop!" he repeated.

She tore the gag from her mouth. "And what if I had yelled stop last night?"

Trake circled, his bow on guard. "You tricked me. You saw my weakness."

"I tricked you!" she bellowed. "You kidnapped me. You had me trussed up like an animal. Then you gagged me, stole my clothes and raped me!"

"I have no desire for you!" he screamed back. "I have now tasted sin. You are the agent of the Gods and I will not take the blame. You have done this! You!"

"I will cut you to pieces!" she said as she took a wild swing, wincing with the pain of her busted rib. Trake watched and learned.

"You have neither the strength nor the skill to use that sword," he taunted.

"And you have no skill with your sword either, nor strength. You explode like a little schoolboy," she spat.

"Why, you blessed …" He lost his composure, foolishly advancing. She swiped again and split his bow in two, just above his hand. Amazed and angered, he switched what remained of his bow to use as a club. "You will make me a new bow, you vixen." He searched for the Strength, but found nothing.

"I will make you a eunuch before you die, that is *my* promise," she snarled and stabbed at his groin.

Trake blocked the feeble blow and circled watching her stance and waited for his opening as he wondered how she could make him an uncle. They were not related. He needed to keep her provoked, so he followed her lead.

"You cannot make me an uncle; I am an uncle many times over. My sister is a revered Breeder!" he blurted as he wondered how this was an insult.

"You are an idiot, soon to be a eunuch," she scoffed and took another low swipe.

Trake hunched his hips back and followed the arc of the blow with his blocking hand. He stepped in and continued the arc, adding his own force to the momentum of the blade. The girl had neither the strength nor the timing to recover. In an instant, he had trapped her arm tight to her body with his. In the next moment, he wrapped her tight with his free arm, and left her trapped with no room to maneuver. Once he had wrestled the blade free from her hand, he brought an elbow across in a vicious blow to her chin. She crumpled in his arms, out cold. He casually let her slide to the ground, where she landed in a loose heap.

"Who's your uncle now?"

Trake lost no time tying her back up, breaking camp and heading for his cave with her moaning over his shoulder. Once he had proper time, he had regained the Strength and made good time on the roundabout route to his cave. By mid-afternoon, he dumped her unceremoniously, still trussed, in her new home while he sat outside and gorged his hunger and wondered aloud about his new direction. "Graceful Dancer, the signs are still unclear to me. Was this a single test of my resolve or an opportunity for new revelation? Humble Magician, will this new knowledge help me conquer my foe or sap my strength for the battle?"

Over these many months spent alone, Trake had taken to speaking his questions aloud. He believed now that the Directors had been wrong about this also. If the Gods could truly read his mind, they would never have chosen him as a prophet. Too many errant thoughts cluttered his brain. More precisely, there were too many questions without answers.

"Humble Magician, talk to me as you did in the bush. I long for your guidance. The path to your glory seems suddenly overgrown with vines of ... " What, what did he want to say aloud to his Gods? *Temptation? Confusion? Pleasure?* What did he feel? Every emotion seemed blasphemous, but he could not blaspheme, for he was the prophet, and he was destined to lead with the Truth. Then it occurred to him. "Deception!" he shrieked aloud. "Vines of deception! The Directors are in conspiracy. They misquoted the Author on purpose. They have their own plan. Oh, thank you, Dancer. You have opened my eyes to the Truth. I have seen that the Directors have been wrong, but I only saw the threads, not the cloth."

He sat with this new concept for a moment, then looked up at the Heavens. "I see now. I must question everything, search out the patterns and explore the alternatives. You want me to find the Truths myself, don't you?" The Gods' silence answered his question. He smiled to himself and walked back into the cave, intent on more explorations.

\* \* \*

"I have released you from your bindings, Atasha. You may now cook for me, tend my fire and sew new clothes for me. You may not, however, leave this camp. If you do, I will hunt you down and kill you like your people kill the joys provided by Father." They walked from the cave, a deep morning chill clouding their breaths. Trake struggled with his emotions as they tied to his duty. Over the last couple of weeks the pleasure of his explorations had rattled his resolve. This woman, named after the comly daughter of the Graceful Dancer herself, was quite capable of delivering her own kind of Bliss and Contentment. But duty did not allow such indulgences. He must maintain his rigid authority.

Atasha locked eyes with her captor, but said nothing. Trake saw her anger and defiance. So like Verbolana, he thought for the umpteenth time; fiercely beautiful, yet vulnerable. "I have arranged a demonstration. A demonstration I will let you will survive … this time. I have noticed you eying my sword I casually leave lying around. Up until now your bindings have restricted your opportunities. So, now is your chance. Pick it up and attack me."

With doubt in her eyes, Atasha's intense gaze flitted back and forth from the sword to his face. He saw she wanted him dead and he had no delusions she would make it so if she could.

"What is the trick?" Atasha asked. "You would not give me such an opportunity if there were not a trick."

"Was there a trick last time?" Trake exclaimed with intentional arrogance. "I have defeated you once already — with ease, I might add. I want to demonstrate that the last time was not luck." He didn't add that he did not want her coming at him when he wasn't prepared.

"If I come at you, it will not be a time of your choosing." She sat on the log they used as a chair by the outside fire pit and wrapped her arms around herself for warmth before picking up a stick to stir the fire.

At least she was not a fool, he mused. However, his plan was not going as he wanted. "You're afraid I'll hurt you, is that it?" Maybe a little taunting would help.

"You have already hurt me in ways I did not think possible. You have also confirmed what the worst of my people insist upon. You, none of you, are worth our compassion or tolerance. You are worthy of only a quick death and the flames of the burial pyre."

Her ferocity and insolence were like ice, then fire, in his veins. Her complexities both fascinated and angered him. But, were all women so ridiculous? Why would anyone show compassion or tolerance to one's enemies? And why would she so readily admit her own pain? She must be riddling him, he concluded.

"Take the bow then; shoot me from a distance. Have you the courage for that?"

"I have no skill with a bow, or I would surely take you up on your offer. I live for the day my people catch up with you. I will watch the life drain from your eyes and then take up training to send as many of your kind as possible to follow you."

"Your passion for me is puzzling." Trake sat on the ground, resigned to the fact she would not attack. "I have done nothing the Gods have not directed. You are a captured enemy and a vehicle for my education. Beyond that, I am only directing you to do what women were designed to do."

"Kidnapping and rape are things your Gods direct you to do?"

"Of course," he responded with complete sincerity. "You think I find pleasure in consorting with the likes of you?"

"Most men think of me as quite a prize," she stated flatly. "I have always had my pick. I assumed that was why you picked me to kidnap."

"Hah! You thought wrong!" Trake's laugh was louder than needed. "Why would a woman be my first choice? I consort with you not from my own choice. The Gods direct me." He paused for a moment and looked off into the forest. "And this thing you do with your babymaker. That was at *your* direction. I would never have done that! Though it appears your men do. It sickens me, every time."

"Maybe I will make you sick to death then, the way you keep going back for more," she spat. Then, with curiosity, "You only take your women in the rear? That is where you were heading. And you say your Gods direct this?"

"Don't put your perversions onto my people. And don't pretend you have not heard the words of the Gods." He was up pacing now, too agitated to sit. "You ignore their teachings and I am here to find out why. You squander across Father, defile his joys, burn his skin, defecate across his face. Then you have the nerve to insult me with your assumptions. You know nothing of us, though you should. Just listen to the Gods and you will know us. Of course we don't take women like that. We don't take women at all! We live with the words of the Gods close to our hearts."

He saw what appeared to be true puzzlement in her eyes and stopped. Was it possible she had not heard the words of the Gods? No, it was a trick. Or some sort of self-deception these Wretched used for doing what they wanted in the full face of the truth. Everyone had heard the Truth; these heathen simply chose to ignore it for whatever reasons they had.

"The last Wretched who looked at me in that way is now nothing but ashes on Father's skin," Trake raged. "Claiming ignorance will not get you your Encore."

Dumbstruck, the girl continued to stare. Finally, "You speak so much nonsense that I don't know which of your idiotic remarks to rebuke first. You claim to know the words of the Gods, yet your people destroyed the paradise they built for us. For your own selfish reasons, you continue to kill those who would rebuild. How can you have deceived yourselves so?"

"Rebuild?" Trake screamed in shocked indignation. "Rebuild the abominations that were destroying Father? Of course we kill! There is no other way. *You* leave us no other way." He stomped back and forth in front of her in complete disbelief of her stupidity. Clouds of dust rose beneath his pounding feet. He stooped to pick up the water jug and the forgotten sword followed in a vicious attack to his back. The Strength alerted him just as the blade was about to dig into his flesh. Without thought he pivoted his hips and his lightning arms followed, subtly redirecting the flashing steel and simultaneously attacking Atasha's arm with such force that the sword flew from her hands. As he continued his pivot, he grabbed, wrenched and pulled at her arm, launching her forward and then around like a weight at the end of a whipping rope until she lost her feet and landed sprawled at his. "Very good," he almost laughed. "You rile me with your outrageous words to distract me from your true intentions. Very good. I had begun to think you actually believed that excrement you were spouting."

He watched her for a minute or two, sprawled in the dirt. When she finally met his eyes, he was shocked. They did not drop, waiver or blur in fear. They burned, dug and challenged further.

"Pick up the sword!" he commanded in frustration. She stood, brushed away the dirt, straightened herself and, without a word, walked over to the sword. "Pick it up, I say."

Atlana picked it up.

"Now come to me." His rage was undisguised. "Kneel before me." He pulled at his drawstring and dropped his pants around his ankles. "You seem still to question my power."

She did not look up. "You think you can distract and defeat me still. And you say I have no strength." He waited for his words to sink. "Take my sword," he commanded, "and place it between my legs." She did as he commanded. "This is your last chance. Take me in your mouth as one of my most skilled Blessed companions would and bring me pleasure. You nick me, you die."

# Chapter 20

You will write the words I say," Trake commanded yet again as he paced through the dirt, his foretuft slicked back behind his ears, greasy from weeks without bathing. He scratched absently at the welts that covered his arms.

"I will not!" Atasha shot back, sitting easy on the log by the smoldering fire. The sun was low and bugs were again coming out to play. "Your words are as fiendish as you are. I will not be a part of this!" She threw the precious quill and paper into the dust at her feet, stood and walked around the fire to bathe in the smoke. She was naked. Trake kept her that way during the day.

Through his irritation, Trake noticed her skin was flawless and sun-browned under the smudged dirt, though her long black hair was caked and ratted in the back from many hours of lying under him.

"You have no understanding of our people, yet you pass judgment. You have no knowledge of history, yet you claim to be an expert. Therefore, your conclusions can be nothing but rubbish!" She confronted him with fiery eyes.

"Yours is the history that is flawed. You say we destroyed your Paradise when there was no Paradise to begin with. The machines that kept your so-called Paradise alive were killing Father. How many billions languished at Father's generous hand? She could not support such abuse. Moreover, no one seemed to care. The Author spoke to all, told of the dangers, yet they ignored him.

There was no option but to destroy everything and start over. Do you think that was easy for the Author or his followers? They left everything behind, had to learn a whole new life, give up family, friends and every comfort they were accustomed to." Trake paused. What more did this girl not understand?

"You talk of sacrifice. Your people ran away to the safety of their towers, while you loosed the machines on everyone else. The horrors were unthinkable! I cannot even imagine the deaths because I cannot see the machines. However, I have seen the wreckage of some ... things they called harvesters with blades and forks and binding parts. Those are what you sent against us." She stopped, and when he did not respond, continued, "Other stories abound. Of domestic machines squirting acids and cleaning fluids or hacking babies in their sleep with kitchen tools. These machines were not designed to kill, and they did a sloppy, brutal job of it. Yet they managed to kill almost everyone. Only a few were able to hide long enough for the machines to finally destroy themselves and the cities they had built."

Trake had never heard these stories. He felt them bounce up against his battlements of defense; then he felt some of them sink in. He found, for some reason, he wanted to believe Atasha. She was so beautiful, standing naked before him. And the Directors had been wrong before. Was this the truth they had sent him to find? He could not tell. He would have to investigate further.

"Tell me about this Paradise as you know it." His voice was as soft as it had ever been with her.

"You know as well as I do," Atasha responded. "But maybe you do not know what came before Paradise." More silence; he was not about to admit any ignorance.

"The stories tell of great struggles, much like we, the Survivors, go through now, but with machines and evil living side by side. The stories tell of whole nations of people despising and envying their neighbors. These nations, many of which did not even speak the same language or look the same or have the same Gods, fought with machines and explosives and killed each other in great numbers with complete abandon. There was never enough food or comforts to go around, so they stole from their neighbors. Some tell of individuals who fought for things like the love of a woman or some toy a machine had just made. Cities battled for the use of water or crops or just to prove they were stronger. And nations fought for the power and glory of their Gods or the color of their skin or the shape of their eyes.

"All that changed, slowly of course, but it changed. The machines became so good at making people comfortable that people lost their desire to fight. I can only imagine what a constantly full stomach would do for me. On feast days, I get so lazy I can barely walk. I can just imagine being full all the time. And having the wind not reaching me, nor the snow of winter or the heat of summer." She was excited now. Her words rushed out. "Did you know the cities had covers from the weather? That is what they say. Covering the whole city! I have seen the rubble. It is truly amazing, how big their homes must have been. How safe they must have felt." She fell quiet suddenly, her eyes glazed, her hands clenched each other. "Not to fear death from the skies or from beasts that would eat you ... I cannot imagine."

"I have heard similar stories," Trake lied, and wondered why he needed to deceive a servant, and wondered at such a life. He imagined a full stomach and cover above his head. He thought about the bugs that had lived in his hair these last months. They would not live in such a Paradise, surely. Even he had heard stories of the water, piped to a private room, heated just so and sprinkled over you. Scented soaps and pillowed sheets for drying. The most unbelievable story he had heard was of a great room where pictures took up entire walls and the pictures seemed to move and tell stories.

Trake knew, in his own defense, that he must respond. "You speak of death and that is true. They did not fear death, either from another's hand, or from a wild beast or even the ravages of disease or time. They had learned to cheat the Gods, and that was one reason we destroyed them. They were abominations. The Gods have uses for us far beyond what we can understand. If we cheat death, we cheat the Gods." He looked at her with all the force of his will. "The Gods will have their way."

"And yet it is my understanding that you are not to step foot on the surface of what you call Father, but here you are, living in defiance of your Gods. Cheating death seems to be acceptable for you."

"The Gods have different plans for me."

"How convenient," she mumbled.

"What would you know?" he stated dismissively, even when her words stung. It surprised him that he cared what she thought. He decided to explain. "Surely if I had not received so many signs from the Gods, you would be right. Just like you, the Gods would not allow me to walk on Father's skin. Not only has Father given me permission; the Humble Magician has spoken to me personally. The Gods have directed me in everything I have done or will do. I am their servant."

"You have said this before, but I do not understand. How could a God direct you to kidnap me and treat me the way you have?"

"The Gods direct us to do many things that are not pleasant. Life is not pleasant; it is not meant to be. Our lives are a sacrifice to the restoration of balance. No pain is too great." When he saw that his answer did not satisfy her, he continued, "I have been given great powers. My defense of your attacks is only a small part of that. Father has given me Strength he has given no other, and the Magician has given me direction. He is tired of waiting for the Chosen to defeat and destroy the Wretched. They have charged me with the duty of developing a new plan. I would much rather be on my deck with my friends and my comforts. But I am here, consorting with the enemy, learning what must be learned, questioning what must be questioned. It is that simple."

"I see." She had turned away from him, letting the smoke bathe her back, hiding her thoughts. "Then you are still dedicated to killing us."

"Of course."

# Chapter 21

Trake slept snuggled tight at Atasha's back, his hand cupped around one perfect breast. He told himself this arrangement was for security purposes. If she moved to escape, he would know immediately.

On one particularly cold night, he felt her startle awake and he immediately came on guard.

"Did you hear something?" she whispered.

"No," he replied, but he had come to trust her forest senses. He reached down inside himself and asked Father for Strength. His sleepy brain struggled, finally connecting to his power and he instantly sensed an overwhelming presence. At the mouth of the cave, not fifteen feet from their small camp, was a life force so large it blocked the entire entrance. "What is that?" he whispered, as if Atasha could see what he sensed.

"What! What is it? I can't see anything," Atasha whispered.

"It's huge," Trake whispered back as he reached slowly for his sword. "I can't make it out exactly, but it is as large as the mouth of the cave and it seems to have a very long neck."

"A Vipeon!" Atasha exclaimed in horror.

"A Vipeon?" Trake stammered. "What are you talking about? There's no such thing."

"I wish," Atasha whispered back. "They don't have two heads like the one on your back, or wings, but they're real enough. He's undoubtedly already smelled us. Our only hope is that he's too big to get into the cave." She started a slow retreat, pushing Trake with her.

Trake focused his attention on the intruder. The thing was inching closer, in no apparent haste. "He knows we're here; I can feel his intention."

"Okay," she intoned doubtfully. "Where are your bow and arrows? I've heard of a lucky shot going down their throats. They don't like that, might make him back off. Beyond that, we don't have much of a chance. They have a soft spot right at the hinge of the jaw, on the underside, but they keep their snouts down when they attack. You'd have to get past the teeth and the claws."

Trake was up now, with sword at ready. "I can't believe this! The Gods will not allow me to die this way. It is a test. That is all it can be. I have not been saved for such a death!" The tremor in his voice changed his declaration to a whined plea.

"You and your Gods. This is not the time for prayer or laments. Kill that thing or die trying!"

"You say the underside of his neck?"

"That's suicide!" she hissed. "You'd have much better luck with the bow ... where is that damn thing?" She was on her knees, waving her hands across the pitch-black ground. She found it. "Here, here—take this. You need to wait for its roar. Then fire straight for the sound."

"You keep it. I've got a better idea." Trake pushed the bow back at Atasha. "He's coming in ... farther anyway." He pushed her deeper into the cave. "He's intelligent, too. He has a powerful presence."

"I don't know what that means, but yes, they are very smart. They are almost as effective as you, the Fiendish, at killing our kind."

"Why have I never seen one?" His amazement momentarily overpowered his urgency.

"You come by day, they come by night. Now quit the talk and shoot that thing!" She pushed the bow back into Trake's hands.

"No, I need you to shoot it. You need to find the ledge, climb up on it and wait for my signal."

"You coward! You know I can't shoot. I'll be exposed, with no escape." Now Atasha's voice shook as she pleaded. "Your Gods will save you with my sacrifice. Is that it? You figure that if the beast gets one, he won't bother with the other. Your Gods are cowards, too!"

"Shut up and do as you are told."

"Kiss my dirty hole!" And she threw the bow to the ground.

"Pick it up," Trake growled. "You have to trust me."

"Since when, you kidnapping, raping Fiend!"

"Since right now," he stammered. "I have a plan, but I need your help. And *I* need to trust you more than *you* need to trust me. I need you to distract him. Hurry, he's coming!" He bent, retrieved the bow and thrust it into her hands. "Go!"

Trake felt her move off as he refocused on the looming force in front of him. He shuffled to his right and felt the beast's head follow him. He needed time. He felt for a rock, a branch of firewood, anything. Nothing yet. He kept moving right, away from Atasha. He felt the beast's intention split. The thing was trying to keep track of both of them. Trake needed to make that as difficult as possible in this confined space. He kept moving right until he came to the wall. Switching his sword to his left hand, he fumbled across the wall, tearing with his fingers. Finally, he found a crack and dug in with his fingers. He felt the skin of his fingers rip as he pushed into the jagged stone, the Strength helping him dig but not toughening his skin. Once he gained purchase, he pulled. A sharp chunk reluctantly wrenched free of the wall.

"You ready?" he yelled across the space, his adrenaline amplifying what was supposed to be a hushed murmur.

No response.

"Atasha!"

Nothing. He realized she was probably unwilling to give up her position. "The thing knows where you are," he said, trying to calm his voice. "I need you up. Up on the ledge. I am going to throw this stone. Try to rile him. I need you to shoot. Take your best shot. Then I'm going to rush him."

"That's your plan?" Atasha finally answered. "It is shit."

"You'd prefer I call for a battle blimp?"

"Finally do something good?" she retorted.

Trake felt the beast focusing on the conversation. Judging distances and threats, Trake assumed. He felt the beast's attention refocus on him, then advance. With help from the Strength, he chucked the jagged stone hard and true. He heard the concussion on the animal's nose, felt him withdraw his energy for a moment and then blast forth with a roar of pain and outrage that sent Trake staggering back three steps until he hit the wall with a force that almost knocked him out. By the time he regained his senses, the beast was upon him. He felt for Atasha. She was picking herself off the ground, scrounging for the bow.

"Shoot, damn you! Ten feet left of my voice, ten feet from the ground." His command voice returned and rang across the enclosure. Trake switched his sword back to his right hand and prepared. He would have one chance and one chance only. "Seven feet … five feet … Now shoot!"

Trake heard the twang of the string and the glancing blow of the arrow as it ricocheted off impenetrable hide. At that moment he rushed, crouched low, under the beast's head. The animal's aura guided him almost as if he could see. Under the extended neck he thrust up into a spot where the aura was the strongest, figuring this was the soft spot. It was! The blade rammed deep, and the scream filled the room, bouncing from the walls, filling his ears with numbing pain. He pulled the sword and jumped deeper under the beast as a clawed foot sliced the air. The beast's head ducked and swung, searching for a bite of him. Trake scrunched deeper under the animal's belly, completely trapped. If his plan worked and the beast died, its falling weight would crush him. If his plan didn't work, he would be an early breakfast.

A feral scream erupted from the far end of the cave. Trake sensed Atasha rushing the beast headlong, a giant stone held above her head with both hands. The monster switched its attention. As it perceived this new threat, it turned its giant head to confront the audacious attack. Trake bolted forward like a smoke missile from one of his cannons, launched his sword and himself into the exposed neck yet again. The blade sunk to the guard, then deeper, until Trake realized his hands had followed his entire sword into the flesh. He let go of the handle and ran, knowing he would never be able to pull his blade free if he wanted to survive. He exited from under the massive body just as its legs collapsed and its head fell hard into the dry dirt at Trake's heels. Trake ran straight into Atasha and hugged her in relief and thanks.

"You saved my life!" Trake exclaimed.

"My baby needs a father, even if he is a shit."

# Chapter 22

Verbolana felt out of step without the constant rhythm of the waves against the sand playing in the background. She sat on a long wooden bench, as she caught her breath and wondered why she had done what she had done. It was hard to rationalize, even though it had only been a few hours earlier. *Why, again, Tarja, did I wish you away? Was my life on the beach really so awful? Is this any better?* She looked around at the meandering stone path, the reds, golds and yellows of the flowers, the shading trees thick against the sky and the towering buildings barely visible through the leaves. She did not even know where she was, or how long she had languished on the beach. She had just wished everything and everyone away and run out of her empty realm into the city in her Blessed smock. *Cloistered, I felt cloistered,* she reminded herself. *I can't live forever in a haze of drugs and kisses. There has to be more to this afterlife than lying on a beach with a head full of Za webs, every day the same as the one before. It is time to move! Remember, Verbolana, remember. You have wallowed long enough. Cried and ranted long enough. It's time to do!*

She glanced up through her stringy bangs and pulled at her hair, which now hung to her shoulders. She was sitting in some park, she realized, in the middle of an unfamiliar neighborhood. She took stock. She wasn't hungry; she had learned how to wish away that annoying need. She wasn't sad or angry, and that was good. She smiled when she remembered learning how to wish away her evacuations, all of them. That was sweet. She remembered Tarja's confusion around her decision. Tarja had wanted to continue defecating, in a freshly dug hole right there on the beach. She insisted her evacuations were some of the true joys of life. Crapping, fucking and getting stoned, and in that order. Windsurfing must have fit in there somewhere, but ...

A man plopped down beside her on the bench. She did not look up. The pebbles at her feet became very interesting.

"Beautiful day," he commented, apparently to himself.

"Aren't they all?" she finally snorted when the silence had stretched to breaking.

"Depends," he returned with a smiling voice.

"On what?" she hardened hers.

"Lots of things. Sounds like things ain't so beautiful to you."

"I'd rather not go into it." Verbolana continued to examine the pebbles, then her bare feet. She silently wished away her jagged toenails, reminding God never to let them get like that again.

"Suit yourself." He continued his easy banter. "Not from around here?"

"I don't even know where 'here' is." She tried to change her tone. The guy was just being friendly, and if she wanted to survive in the city, she knew she would need a few friends.

"Ah, well, you are in a Terran neighborhood. Mostly North American Pacific Coasters. We're an easy sort, friendly, not too bound up."

Verbolana finally looked up. The man smiled. "Name's Paul." He stuck out his hand. "We shake—hold hands and pump them up and down a little," he explained.

"Really?" She met his eyes for the first time, wondering if he were going to be like the men at Volif's, who wanted only to plough through her to plant their seed. "We don't. Where I'm from men and women don't touch."

"Bummer." His smile slipped a little as he pulled his hand back. "Hungry?"

"I haven't eaten in a very long time. I choose not to." She looked back down at her feet.

"Big bummer. I'm a chef." He waited for a sign of recognition. Nothing. "I cook ... food ... professionally."

"We had cooks. I never liked eating much, though. I found it very boring, just a necessity. Tarja liked to eat. She got me to taste a few things, but most of the time I didn't bother. Just wished my hunger away." Verbolana tried to smile as she looked back up to meet his eyes. She was rambling and saw the conversation was not going well. Paul had a nice smile, she noticed. For a man, he was quite good looking: even features; long wavy hair, brown with reddish streaks; nice eyes; good square shoulders.

"Oh, girl, you are in Heaven. You have no idea! I don't know where you came from, probably wouldn't know even if you told me, but there are worlds upon worlds of pleasure out there, just waiting for you. My place is just down the path here. Come on, let me cheer you up."

"I don't really want to eat."

"Because you have never had anything I have cooked. Listen, with 164 varieties of garlic, that alone would get you going if you knew what garlic was. But I have spent five or six decades now studying the cuisines of a hundred different worlds, and even though my place is called the Terran Café, it's not just comfort food we cook. Have you ever tasted Alterian gruel? I know it sounds terrible, but it's like no other gruel you've ever tasted!"

Verbolana stared at him blankly, though he didn't seem to notice. "I take the gruel, mix it with veal stock and use it for a sauce over wild bay scallops and Veturen sea spinach. Hard to beat." Then, with his best smile, "Sure you don't want to try it?"

"I have no idea what you just said, but it sounds disgusting. You eat things out of the sea?"

"We came from the sea and we eat from the sea," he responded, refusing to match her sour mood. "Shopping! How about shopping? That's universal for getting a woman out of a funk, isn't it?"

"You are speaking of a whole different world. I do not know scallops or spinach or shopping. Do they all come from the sea?"

"Shopping? From the sea? You fascinate me, girl. You really are from the far side of the galaxy! I promise you, shopping does not come from the sea. Would you like a new dress, or a pin for your hair or maybe some shoes? You have no shoes."

"I have seen shoes, never had much need for them," she returned, trying her best, but everything he wanted to talk about was beyond her knowledge. Then it hit her. She needed this man. She needed to learn! She had spent all of her lives sequestered. Of course, she wasn't going to know what this man was talking about. She was a child at the edge of the rings.

"If 'shopping' is getting a new dress, I have done that before. It was fun. Do you have a machine close by?" she ventured.

"A machine?" he wondered. "No, I wouldn't dream of using a machine. May I take your hand? I promise you'll love my way of shopping."

She was immediately suspicious again. "Does it involve sex? Most of the men I've met only want sex."

Paul laughed, deep and rich. "Well, you do come right to the point. And to be honest, the thought did cross my mind. You're a beautiful woman and I love having sex with beautiful women, but that's not what this is all about. You just looked like you needed some help. And helping people, for me, is as good as sex. If you decide you want to have sex later, we can talk about it. For now, I was just thinking a little shopping and maybe I could twist your mind around those bay scallops."

Verbolana took his hand, since he still offered it. It felt warm and strong and somehow honest, as she envisioned Trake's might be. "I'm sorry to be such a ... so suspicious. I did not grow up knowing men and it has been a bit of a shock."

"So you said. Men and women didn't even touch?" Paul stood and helped her to stand. They walked toward the tree-shrouded buildings. "Must have been tough to make babies. Is your civilization extremely advanced compared to this? I've heard of that."

"Hardly!" Verbolana exclaimed with her first laugh in a few days. "We were just very, well, protected." She picked her words carefully. "Very protecting, actually. We didn't have room for a lot of babies."

"Now you're the one speaking in riddles. I'm imagining all sorts of possibilities, but I sense you don't really want to talk about it."

The path opened onto a cobbled plaza sparkling with free-form fountains and a rainbow of awnings, umbrellas and gaily painted buildings. They walked directly toward one of the colorful displays.

"There're a couple shops I always like to check out." Paul changed the subject. "Almost every day they have something new."

Verbolana played along. "Uh-huh ..."

"Look, look, this is new." Paul pointed to one of the windows.

Wild colors assaulted Verbolana's eyes. They seemed almost to jump through the glass and embed in her brain. "It is beautiful," and she wanted to continue, *What is it?* but she hadn't the courage.

"I know the guy who does these canvases. Comes into my place all the time. I've got a few of his pieces at home." He pulled on her again. "Check this."

191

The next storefront held more indescribable objects that tickled Verbolana's brain, and before she knew it, Paul had swung her up into his exuberance. She giggled at his antics and marveled at his energy.

She noticed him looking at her, then at a shimmering strappy dress in the window. "Would you? I mean, you look fabulous with what you've got on. It's just that, well, I love to dress women, and this," he nodded back to the window, "this would look fantastic with your coloring and your face. I know it's gauche, but who designed you? Would I know them?"

Verbolana caught almost none of his prattle, though she did understand that he wanted her to try on the clothing displayed in the window. She looked down at her Blessed smock and back at the radiant drape. Her life experience had given her nothing to compare these colors to. Even her latest memories of the sun-kissed blues and greens of her lagoon or the blazing pinks at sunset did not help her. Effervescent bubbles grew in her chest, around her heart and she imagined them rise to burst forth on her face. *This might be ... this is ... my first true, unencumbered and undrugged smile.* She thought back further ... *ever? Maybe. It felt like the first.*

She shocked herself. "Sure, I'd love to try that on." Then she searched her mind and gut for a reaction. Where was the fear, the suspicion, the certain knowledge that she would pay with a lash or six? Was it gluttony or avarice to covet the kiss of such beauty on her skin? Of course it was. Could she dare contemplate owning such a marvel? *Yes, I can!* The pronouncement flitted across her brain. She did not convulse. Where had it all gone? The terror, the teachings, the righteous battles of will? *I had always questioned, so, when presented with the answers, answers that confirmed my questioning, why has it taken so long?* She looked back at her days on the beach with a wider vision. The sand, the hut and the forgivingly

192

altered sun. No one and nothing but Tarja and the green stuff. She could almost see the gentle leaching away of her angst, lying on the sand, the sun playing tag with the sea breeze, Tarja beside her, the light touch on her hand and the green stuff easing the journey, allowing for fearless, nonjudgmental examination.

Still holding her hand, Paul led her away from her reminiscing and through a door, into a place tight with walls and shelves and artificial bodies draped in magical fabrics. A discreet bell announced Verbolana's arrival. An announcement not lost on her.

"Angela, Angela!" Paul called upon entering. "Stop feeding your face and get up here. You've got paying customers."

Verbolana shook herself free of the last vestiges of her melancholy. It was time to live without fear and without that insipid green stuff. Alcot insisted this was a place to find comfort, that God designed this Heaven for comfort. *Is it courage I need?* she asked herself. *I have always had courage. I took the whip many times and stood tall. I am courageous, damn it! I always have been. So what is it I need? God, is it faith? Do I need faith? When all faith has been dashed, do you ask for more belief?*

**"Verbolana, I ask nothing of you. My hopes for you are happiness and fulfillment. That is why I built this place. To watch my finest design flourish."**

Verbolana's knees buckled and she sat heavily on the floor. "He's talking to me!" she muttered to the air around her, then looked up at Paul for support.

"Talk back," Paul smiled. Apparently he understood completely.

Another face appeared beside Paul's; a magnificent face, with luminescent charcoal skin, liquid brown eyes and hair spiked into a torch of yellow and red flames. "Wha's happenin'?" she whispered to Paul, concern on her face.

193

"God's talking to her. I think it's her first time. Just found her in the park."

Concern evolved to rapture on the woman's face. "Close you' eyes, hon.' Enjoy." Then, after meeting Verbolana's eyes, "Is nothin' to fear, sweetheart. Have courage."

Verbolana stared up, lost in disbelief. Courage? I have always been courageous, she repeated to herself. Or has that always been anger? Is anger what fuels me? And determination? Is that all it was? Anger, determination ...and stubborn will. She closed her eyes. *God, I am frightened. I dare not speak to you, and yet I must. You have all the power, and I am helpless before you.*

**"There is nothing you can say or do to displease me. You are magnificent. Every one of you is my pride. I have no needs you can fulfill and no expectations. My hope is that you will allow yourself to become authentically who you are ... deep, deep, deep inside."**

*And yet I struggle so desperately.* Even inside her head, she felt her words as a mumble. *And it is all because of you. Anger, always so close to the surface. You say you want us to be comfortable, to be happy, to be authentic — and then you hamstring us on worlds that allow none of that.*

**"I did not mean to imply there would be no struggle. Free will and self-awareness are blessings and curses, yet integral to your design. I have faith you will figure it out."**

*You have faith? In me?*

**"Yes."**

*God?*

**"Yes?"**

*Can I have some more of that green stuff?*

**"Of course."**

\* \* \*

With the Strength flowing, Trake slashed through the overgrown forest to clear a comfortable path even though every muscle pleaded for him to stop.

"Just stick to the story and you'll be fine," Atasha panted behind him, her swollen belly stealing the wind from her lungs.

"The *story* has more holes in it than a Za filter after a hail storm," Trake grunted as he chopped into a vine the size of his thigh. "If I was the loving, gentle person I am to portray, I would have helped you find your people long ago. I wouldn't have dragged you off to a forest cave and kept you there for a year."

"You were scared. You didn't know the Cheated would be so forgiving."

"I still don't know that." Trake took a massive swipe at a bush that offended him and might be troublesome to his toddling woman.

"If you appear truly repentant, they will forgive. Like I say, others have defected." She came up behind him and touched his shoulder. "And there's the baby. It is hard enough to survive in this world. Every child needs a father, even if he is a Fiendish. They will see that."

"Fiendish, ha!" He pushed the words out between ragged breaths. "I am neither fiendish nor repentant, you Wretched woman! I do this because the Gods will it. They demand I learn the ways of your people. They demand I burrow deep like the gradnat of the forest."

"Your ceaseless burrowing has born fruit, my prophet," she smiled, as she rubbed her hand across his back and pushed her protruding belly into him. "If you burrow into my people as you have into me, who knows what you will learn?"

"You joke and take liberties that ..."

"... that will be tolerated and appreciated," Atasha finished for him with a snicker. "The Gods demand it," she mimicked. "Otherwise your silly mission will fail."

"Augh, if I had you back on a tower ..."

"You would not be able to speak to me or touch me," she butted in again. "And regardless of your protests, you have become quite comfortable with our arrangement. As have I, my prophet." Tousling his shoulder-length hair, she let her hand trace down the tattooed Vipeon that covered Trake's back until she reached the drawstring pants she had made him from the hide of the Vipeon he had slain. "Your Gods only direct your mind, my love. I can feel your heart."

"Silly girl," he replied. "Sometimes I must play the part even with you. It is the burrowing you feel. And not the burrowing *you* refer to," he added quickly. "I follow the direction of the Gods, that is all." This was all he could admit, even to himself. The Gods watched him constantly these days. He felt their heated gazes like the summer sun, hot on his head, as they effortlessly read his thoughts. Their words, through his mouth to her hand, now filled many pages. She had even taught him the rudiments of the written language, and soon, he was confident, he would write on his own, away from her endless commentary and questions.

"And you must stop calling me 'prophet.' I have my part to play in this next scene, and you have yours. We must both start now."

"Agreed, my liege," she snickered.

Trake chopped at the next vine, amazed at how riled this woman could get him. Her quick brain and tongue brought shame to his plodding thoughts. He wondered and chopped, chopped and wondered. Questions of his worthiness, his competence and mostly his motives simmered deep below the surface. Buried in his heart, below any level the Gods could reach, he hoped, simmered the desire just to be. Just breathe. Just talk and laugh and let his heart flow. And to feel. At times, his losses weighed his feet to the ground and his arms hung heavy from his shoulders. His heart seemed to dangle like a full water basket dipped from the lake, stalled by not enough backs to haul it. Atasha was the problem. She sparkled with unguarded joy. She laughed freely, moved in grace, chatted in confident truths that were so obviously wrong and yet so well spoken. Would this girl go to her Encore when she was done here? He sincerely doubted it. Her blasphemies were too great, and that saddened him. His burdens seemed much heavier when he looked at her and felt her sparkle seep into him.

And now with his child growing in her. What did that add to his burden? He could not speak to her of these things, but he must teach this child the true lines of the Holy Drama. She would never understand, he assumed. But the boy, for the child was surely a boy, must be converted. He wondered how to do that. Urgency crowded his heart, raced in his blood and knotted his stomach. Of course, he must teach the child of the Gods, of Father and of the Cleansing, but what of all the rest? As the prophet, he knew his doctrine was still imprecise. The Gods and their Truths continued to reveal themselves. As new information became available, he knew he must remain fluid and receptive. For instance, were men and women supposed to be together? Of this, he wondered incessantly. Certainly, the Gods *designed* them to be together. And they were meant to create life. There was no question about this. The natural outcome could not be denied or avoided. He thought back to his earliest memories, seated in the learning circle, surrounded by boys and wondering, with his deviant heart, what the girls were learning. Secretly, he positioned himself so he faced a certain circle and caught a hint of exhilaration at the sight of a certain girl.

As he worked through these thoughts and chopped his way toward a Wretched encampment, Trake realized a freedom he had never known. Verbolana was a woman and the Gods could have no objections to this sort of union. Suddenly he knew as if he had known all his life that he could delve into his feelings without fear of retribution, allow his memories to surface and play across his mind, forbidden no longer. He took another giant slash with his sword and stepped into unfiltered sun. Surely a sign, he thought, after so many hours under the thick canopy. Unbridled memories jumped before his eyes as if a giant cat had been waiting for her moment to pounce.

Verbolana smiled a wicked, impish smile. "Welcome, Trake. You know I have loved you," the apparition cooed. "We have been kept apart, but no longer. Take Atasha as me. Love her, hold her and protect her. Find a way to keep her with you, even in the Encore."

Trake stopped short, his arm flexed for the next swipe. Tripping through a low snaggly vine, Atasha ploughed into Trake's back, then held onto him to keep her balance.

"Very good, my liege," she observed. "You have found the path at last. I knew I could count on you. My village is that way."

"Yes," Trake marveled. "This is the right path, I am sure of it," he mumbled and connected these latest revelations into a dramatic scene worthy of the ending of Act Two.

To emphasize the moment and build the suspense, his Strengthened perceptions felt and heard the signaling call of a Wretched lookout high in an overhead tree.

"We come in peace," Trake called into the forest. Then to Atasha, "Add your voice. They might not recognize you otherwise."

"I bring a great warrior, a Vipeon slayer. And I bring a new gift from Father. We must rejoice," she added.

Trake's constantly evolving skills honed in on the chatter that erupted through the trees as Atasha pushed at him from behind, invigorated by the thought of home. As they moved along the path, Trake wary and protective, Atasha in complete abandon, listened and learned. In his previous raids, he had not encountered the sophistication of the Wretched's hidden language. Like the Honored, they spoke of much importance through code and nuance. Trake went to school again, matched the intentions he felt with the twitterings he heard. By the time he had picked up a gathering of energies ahead, he felt he possessed a clear understanding of at least the rudiments of their signals.

Trake pulled himself away. His Strength caused him instinctively to raise his sword. Wretched warriors fanned out at the far edges of the clearing they now entered, bows raised, angry intent clear in their eyes. Atasha stepped around him, her arms outstretched. "I have come back to you, thanks to this brave man who has protected and cared for me. He comes in peace and repentance. He knows of the great Deception. He feels as much a victim as we."

In practiced measure, Trake lowered his weapon and laid it carefully on Father's skin. He then unhooked his bow and pack from the sling at his shoulder and laid those down as well. "I am sorry for the things I have done. My leaders deceived me, washed my brain with lies from the moment I was born. Atasha has taught me well and showed me the love of your people, as is obvious by her belly." He hoped for a moment of laughter, but there was none. "We have found you at last. *I* have found you at last and I have come home for the first time in my life." Though Atasha had taught him the speech, he found himself believing at least pieces of it.

A woman, old and wrinkled, broke through the circle of men. "Atasha, is that you? Speak to me child, so I can find you." She squinted hard across the field.

"Mother ... Yes, I am here!" Atasha blurted, though she dared not leave her position in front of Trake. "Come to me, Momma, I have someone for you to meet."

The old woman concentrated on the uneven ground in front of her. "Keep talking so I can find you," she requested, her voice frantic. The men lowered their weapons and watched the tearful reunion.

# Chapter 23

Gods, if this be your will, give me another cue, Trake pleaded.

Nothing but the sound of the wind whispering through the trees and the reek of excrement in the corner of the tent that imprisoned him. Trake hugged his knees harder and concentrated harder. Maybe there was a message in the dark wind, in the way the tent flap cracked against itself or in the growling and baying of the animals the Wretched had tamed. Trake could imagine the dialogue of his Gods, but he needed more than his imagination. He needed true guidance.

He could stand the cold and the beatings, the hunger and the multiplying welts of the Wretched parasites. But he could not tolerate not knowing. The Gods' silence crawled beneath his skin after two weeks without word, whirled in his brain and knotted his stomach. *Where is my mark? I need direction. This drama has turned to mystery and I do not know my lines. Prompt me, boo me, kill me off, but don't leave me here.*

Then to Atasha, How could I have let you talk me into such madness? I know better than this! I know men! Wretched or Chosen, they do not trust and they are not stupid. We should have taken our chances where we were. The Gods would not have abandoned us as they have done now. The Gods assigned me as both director and leading man, and I did not direct or lead. I wilted in fear during the climax, and now the villains have taken the stage.

Trake straightened. That is it! I am the director and the leading man. The Gods write the drama, but man acts it. To please the Gods, I must take heroic action. No wonder they no longer speak to me! My skills have disappointed them.

Trake stood slowly. His head spun with the exertion and his back would not straighten as he commanded. He called upon the Strength, but it did not come. He stood, waiting for his head to clear and his back to unknot. Anger filled him, a poor substitute for the Strength. He hobbled to the low slit that acted as a door and pushed his way through. He found himself immediately pushed backward to sit on the dirt. He stood again, this time straighter and more determined. "I will not be kept from Atasha," he announced. And with conviction he did not feel, added, "I have done nothing wrong."

He launched out the door, low and hard, tackling his guard before the man could adjust to the unexpected angle of attack. Without hesitation, he released his victim, brought his feet underneath himself and launched again, tucking and rolling and coming up to a defensive stance in one smooth motion. Poised for attack, Trake scanned the scene for any additional foe. None except the flattened guard struggling to his feet. Trake rushed, grabbed the man's dropped sword and backed away. *What now? These are now my people. I must prove myself and yet I must not hurt anyone.*

"Turn around," Trake commanded.

As the man turned, Trake rushed to his back, the sword brought around to his neck. "Give me your arm." When the man let an arm fall, Trake grabbed it and pulled it up behind his captive, giving him control and leverage. "Take me to Atasha," he commanded.

"Atasha is busy," the man said without moving. "You cannot see her now."

"Take me to her or die," Trake growled to his ear.

"There are things more important than life."

"Spare me your heroics," Trake returned and pulled the blade across the man's neck. Blood trickled down the sharp steel. "I will not be stopped. I will kill you and find another to take me to her."

"None will," he commented calmly. "The Gods would not be pleased."

"What do you know of the Gods and their pleasure? I am here on the Gods' behalf. Do not talk to me of the Gods." Trake gave the blade another tug, and the wound opened further.

"The Gods are merciful. They do not direct death, only defense. Your speech is your own, for your own benefit." The man proclaimed as if from rote. "Kill me and move on. My wives and children will be cared for. I die with them in my heart and Atasha in my heart."

Trake pushed the man forward and released his arm as he dropped the blade to his side. "You would die a fool!"

The man turned, relief clear in his eyes. "No man wishes to die." He stood at guard, still awaiting a fatal blow. "Will you go back into the tent now?"

"I will not!" Trake declared. "I will still find Atasha."

"Atasha's child was to be my child," the man spat.

Trake watched the man's eyes. He was about Trake's age and size. And handsome, Trake concluded. Maybe they could have been friends if not for … everything. "Atasha's child is *my* child. And I will see her and help her and love her, or you and your friends will kill me." Trake dropped the sword to the ground, picked a path through the underbrush and walked toward the noises he associated with the village. He heard the man pick up the sword and follow behind. Even without the Strength, he sensed the man behind him and prepared for an attack, so distracted he hardly noticed that the underbrush was not what it seemed. He realized that cleverly hidden, everywhere, were the dwellings of the Wretched. Now that he understood what he was seeing, other signs of habitation appeared: a fire pit cleverly covered with greenery, bushes cleared of their lower branches with fruit drying below. He saw eyes before he saw the people attached, so well-disguised they were in their earth-toned skin and tangled hair.

The path wove past a dozen huts and into a clearing. Five or six women squatted at flat stones, pounding nuts into large piles of meal. Trake felt their surprise and fear and then felt it ebb when they saw this Fiendish had an escort. He felt their intention return back to their work. A bird called high in the branches. Trake felt the message caught a hundred yards away and passed.

*I have pleased you, I see,* Trake commented to his Gods. *Your signs are not so subtle after all. As long as the Strength runs strong in my body, I will know I do your will. Thank you. I will not question again.*

Buoyed by this new message and confident he would find Atasha, he played with his regained Strength. He pushed it out, explored his new environs, collected information, pushed his limits. His first surprise was the size of this enclave. The boundaries seemed beyond his reach. The second surprise was harder to describe. He let his mind settle over those around him: laughing children running between the huts; women, bonded in a common chore, weaving at large standing frames; a circle of men cleaning and slicing an animal they had killed, deep in discussion. Others sat in their huts intent on some task or other; while still more wandered with what appeared to be aimless abandon. He compared what he felt with the energy signals of the Chosen. Since the Strength had first entered his life, he had grown accustomed to the furtive, guarded signals put off by all Chosen but the very youngest.

And those around him now? Childlike? No. His mind stepped back. Verbolana slipped through the opened door to stand before his scrutiny. Atasha snuck to her side and the two locked arms. Trake laughed aloud. "Why did I not see it before?" he breathed. "I guess I did, but, this is a whole world of ... calm? Ease? No, nothing that simple. But ... " He came to a split in the trail.

As if reading his mind, or at least the hesitancy in his step, the man behind him said, "Left here."

"You will help me? What of your Gods?" Trake asked in surprise.

"Our Gods are practical. If you will love her and protect her and bring her many children, the Gods will shine on you."

"She was to be your woman?" Trake wondered whether these men had truly conquered coveting.

"I have two mates; I will have others," he proclaimed flatly. "If you join us, you will have others as well. The Gods demand that we stay busy."

"You will let me join you?" Surprise upon surprise.

"We are also a practical people. Many men die at the hands of the Fiendish. We always need strong men. Some will object, but if you prove your worth, we will allow you to stay. Others have."

Trake stopped. "Others?"

"Some," he remarked. "Some have been very useful in our defenses."

Trake tucked that information away and continued to walk. It occurred to him the man could be walking him into a trap, but he had little to lose. Without an escort, they would no doubt block his passage, and there would likely be a scuffle. He needed to find Atasha immediately.

A feral scream in the distance jolted him. "What was that?" he inquired of his escort, though his senses already knew.

"That is your woman, I would guess," he replied with a chuckle.

Trake bolted down the path in the general direction of the scream. "You have no right!" he bawled. "She has done nothing. This is all my doing. I needed someone to write my words." His head pivoted as he tried to discern further clues. He did not have to wait long. Another scream shattered the muffled clamor of the camp. "Whoever tortures her will die!" Trake proclaimed. "You are animals, all of you!"

The man laughed as he jogged behind. "Your passion is only matched by your ignorance. If you want someone to blame for her torture, look only as far as that little man living between your legs. Kill him if you will, but the Gods will not be pleased."

Trake burst into a clearing and stopped, shifting from foot to foot, readying for his next move. From a thicket to his left, which he now recognized as a dwelling, came yet another drawn shriek. Trake jolted to his right and grabbed the guard's sword. Then with equal dexterity, he plunged into the bush that concealed Atasha. He almost fell through the entrance and regained his balance just before he plunged headlong between Atasha's spread thighs. Sword in hand, he swung out across the room in defense as his eyes adjusted.

"Hooo!" a woman's voice shot out. "Careful with that thing!"

Disoriented, Trake fumbled to stand beside his prone woman. There was no foe here, no hot irons or twisting ropes, just Atasha and her mother on the floor, both haggard and sweating.

"Since you are here, fetch some water. We are both in need of a drink." Atasha's nearly blind mother mopped her brow in preparation for the next contraction.

\* \* \*

Verbolana felt the familiar wash as she took the first sip. She glanced up at Paul and this new woman, cup in hand, and smiled as if caught in the quiet hours with Wexi. She took another swig and slammed the cup down hard on the floor. A little of the frothy liquid splashed around her fingers and the mottled tiles. She assumed she should be embarrassed or angry or scared, but she was none of these. *God, I think that's enough for today.*

**"Of course, my dear, any time."**

Verbolana somehow felt the presence leave, and an abstract notion struck her. She couldn't tell—man or woman. She had to ask, and with the green stuff for courage, she saw no reason not to. *God, are you man or woman?*

**"Whatever you'd like. I am not like you; you are unique as a person and as a species."**

*Okay, thanks … just had to ask.*

**"Everyone does."**

Verbolana felt God's presence retreat again and she was free to look around. She realized Paul was on the floor in front of her and was reaching out to hold her hands. She extended hers into his thin strong fingers and their eyes met. She fumbled in the embrace, not wanting to get his hands sticky from the spilled froth, but he held firm. *How sweet,* came her uninhibited thought. *To sit on the floor with me and hold my sticky hands. Is there any other man anywhere who would do this?* She thought not.

Paul was talking, she realized. "… not easy. Take another drink if you'd like. We're in no hurry." He looked up at Angela. "You in a hurry?"

"Darlin', I gave up dat hurry stuff 'bout a hunnerd years ago." Her smile broadened, showing perfect teeth and a little extra gloss to her eyes. "I 'member my firs-time. That *was* your firs-time, wasn't it? Well, I wish I had a drink after dat day. I didn't know I could drink. Never had. Oh, sure, I seen da master drink. An' his friends. But no good ever come from dat! An' then I get here, an' well, I learnt. In fact, God, please give me one of them she's got." A drink appeared in the woman's hand. "Cheers, girlie. Paul, can I git you one? Here." She handed Paul her drink. "God, make dat one more, please."

Paul fumbled with the drink thrust at him. "I've gotta go to work sometime today. Breakfast rush is half over by now. Frank's gonna have my hide."

"Frank's not gonna have nothin'. You da master o' dat shop and he know it. He been ridin' your tails for decades!" she scoffed. "And speakin' of 'master,' Master, ya bring me somethin'? You didn't come in here without somethin', did ya? Ya didn't, did ya?"

Verbolana watched as the two clinked glasses and held their glasses out to her. Puzzled, she picked her glass back up and held it forth. Clink, clink, the slosh landed on her leg. They didn't seem to notice.

"Drink, girl. You gotta drink now," Angela proclaimed. "You too, Paul. Fer havin' no worries, you sho' got lotsa worries."

"I got people counting on me," he came back defensively.

"Ah, let 'em miss ya!" She dismissed his complaint. "Drink. Your frien' here started it," as if she were an unwilling participant herself.

Paul took a big swig and relaxed. "We came in to look at some dresses," he announced as if it were news.

"Well, you can't do dat from da floor." She took another swig. "This's good; you make it, Paul?"

"Don't have a clue," he said, as he hauled himself up from the floor and put his hand out for Verbolana. When Verbolana was standing, he asked her, "What's in it?"

"Don't have a clue," she mimicked and smiled. "I've just lived on it for a year or so. Seems to help."

"Bet it does." Paul smiled back. "Been through my phases, too."

"We all has dem phases, darlin'," Angela interjected. "Now, darlin' — What's your name?" She put her free hand out and clasped both Paul's and Verbolana's, since they had not yet disengaged.

"Verbolana. My name is Verbolana."

"Pretty name, darlin'. Where you from?"

Verbolana looked at her, puzzled. The men on the beach had certainly asked her that question before, but she had always made something up or just been flippant about it. But here she was, in a neighborhood where, well, she didn't really know where, with people who she thought she might actually care what they thought. Panic tried to insinuate itself, but instead abstract questions bubbled. Did they know of her world? Had they heard the stories? Had those who called themselves the Cheated poisoned this world to her?

"Didn't mean to ask such a tough question." Angela apparently sensed her dilemma. "How long you been here?"

"I think about a year." She was surprised she could not even answer that question with certainty.

"Ah, well, dat explains it," Angela laughed back. "My firs' year … hell, my firs' five … ten years … jus' a blur. When I think back on what I did, how confused I was... See, I was a slave. I don' know if ya know wha' dat is; God sometimes has trouble translatin' dat to people who never know 'bout slaves, but I was owned by somebody who could do whatevah dey want with me. Ya know what I'm saying."

Verbolana nodded her understanding. With minor nuances that Verbolana didn't quite understand, but *felt*, God had translated the word as "Blessed."

"Well, I got up here an jus' wanted ta scream. My master had not been a nice man. I went back down an' I took his whip an' I strung him up an' I whipped an' whipped an' whipped dat man 'til there won't nothin' left. An' then I cried, right there on dat floor, in dat master's bedroom, I cried an' puked an' cried some more."

"Whoa, whoa girl!" Paul jumped in. "Give the girl here some breathing room. She doesn't need to hear all this right now."

"Paul, boy, I thin' she does," and gently she came to Verbolana's side and put her arm around her shoulder. "Give us a minute, Paul," she said, looking into Verbolana's eyes for confirmation. "Dis girl need ta have a little chat. Dat right?"

Verbolana looked up at the gorgeous woman and nodded. The green stuff, yet again allowed the unallowed.

"We be back before ya know it," Angela proclaimed softly and ushered Verbolana down an aisle of shimmering magnificence into the back of the store.

Fifteen minutes later, with red eyes and cheeks wished away, Angela and Verbolana reemerged. "You need ta talk, you jus' come back anytime, hear? We jus' got started. I didn't want ta keep Paul waitin' any longer, though. He's not a patient man when dere's a beautiful woman 'round." Then across the room to Paul, "Your girl here has a wonderful shape. I got plenty dat look good on her. Did ya know dis is her given form? Couldn't believe it myself. God just don't give out looks like hers every day. Paul, come here." She had picked a shimmering electric-green evening dress from one of the racks. "Look how dis works with her eyes an' hair. She a perfect size two. What ya think?"

Paul approached holding four or five dresses he had picked out. "Beautiful. I knew we'd come to the right place."

"Right place? You insult me. Dis da *only* place, you ingrate. An by da way," she exclaimed, smiling, "I axed you earlier an' you never told me. You brought me somethin'—didn't ya? Didn't ya?"

Without skipping a beat, Paul hung the dresses he had collected on the nearest rack, spun on his heel in a full circle, and with grand, flowing limbs produced two tiny brown nuggets from, apparently, the air around him. "For the two loveliest." He offered his conjuring first to Angela and then to Verbolana.

"Oh, tell me before I indulge, what is dere story?" Angela held the drop of decadence in the flat of her hand and examined it from every angle available.

"This little bit of magic comes from the world of Sartain, on the far side of the galaxy. You would think from the coloring and texture that it is chocolaty, but that would be far from correct. The flavor is more akin to the wind below a hummingbird's wing, melded with the effervescence of a waterfall's descent. It's refreshing and transporting, lingering sweetness with cleansing acidity. It is a recipe that, until recently, was lost with the defeat of a conquered people who hid the formula so efficiently they themselves could not even find it. Legends told of the concoction, but the stories merely littered their literature and could not be reproduced until a tenacious historian scoured back through the ages to find the *one village* that grew the *one ingredient* needed to complete the recipe."

Verbolana studied Angela, and as the woman put the nugget to her tongue, so did she. Both women's eyes widened and they looked at each other, needing to share the experience. Instinctively they reached for each other's hands, the flavors that intense. They rode the wave of sensation together, holding on for balance. As the crashing receded, their smiling faces broke, as deep fitful laughter erupted from each.

"Anythin'! Anythin' in da store is yours!" Angela shrieked. "Dat was indescribable." And then to Verbolana, "I make everythin' here myself." Her voice was still excited but had become a little conspiratorial. "I spent many years learnin', I think I told ya,

I was da chambermaid of a gran' lady from 1792 to 1817 when I died of da fever. I always loved her clothes, so I learnt."

Verbolana nodded as if in full understanding. "I never had that opportunity," she confided.

"Well, we can fix dat," Angela winked. "Paul here's very generous. An he got carte blanche here."

Of course, Paul overheard and when Verbolana looked up at him, he winked, too. With a sudden jolt, an old memory surfaced. She asked Paul, "Do you get points for this?"

"Honey, if I need points for this, I might as well quit right now." And now it was his turn to wink at Angela.

His words tumbled through Verbolana's brain, trying to line up in some order that made sense, but they never did. What did register, however, was his tone and spirit. She felt ease and pleasure here. She did not intend to walk away, no matter how many points he got for fixing a broken girl.

"We were looking at that little frock in the window, too. The one in blues and pinks." Paul motioned to the front of the store.

"Oh, dat. Well, yeah, it'll go great wit' her hair and color, but it won't do nothin' for her smokin' tattoo."

"Tattoo?" Paul frowned.

"Turn 'round, honey," Angela commanded. "He dint even notice we already switched ya outta dat thing ya came in." Then to Paul, "Check dis." With a flourish, she opened the back of Verbolana's dress to reveal the headless bird perched halfway down her back. Her shoulder-length blonde mop covered all but its body and legs.

"What were you girls doing back there?" Paul asked. And to Angela, "You certainly did a complete inspection."

"Oh, I'll just let your 'magination run awhile on dat one, you perv. But yeah, I take my job serious. Like I say, she got no enhancements, an she gonna be a blast to dress."

Shyly, but still with a head full of green stuff, Verbolana asked, "You keep talking about my 'given form.' What's the big deal?"

"Like I said, girl, ya don't have no enhancements," Angela explained.

"I grew my hair," Verbolana remembered.

Angela laughed, "Dat's it, but dat don't count. Ya don't need 'em!"

And Paul butted in, "Angela's a little touchy. She's been tweaking her look since she got here a few hundred years ago. Every time I come in she says, 'Whatcha think, whatcha think?' and I don't have an idea what she's talking about. Then she points out that her eyes are a tiny bit bigger or her lips are a little thinner, or some such." When he noticed Verbolana's quizzical stare he continued. "It's quite competitive here. Almost nobody sticks with their given form. It's a skill, though, to get just the right look. Some people are always tweaking. Just like I'm a chef and Angela is a dress designer, there are form designers. The trick is to get the look, keep up with fashion, seem unique, *and* not look like you've had a thing done. But, I tell ya, if you've got the look without tweaking, that's the bomb."

Verbolana suddenly felt exhausted. "I've heard a little about all this, but I had no idea everybody did it. Sorry I asked."

# Chapter 24

**A**uuuuuugh!" Atasha screamed in Trake's face. "This is all your fault! Get out of my sight. Auuuuugh. Get out of the way, I must walk. Ohhhh. Help me up, you idiot. Now stand back! Help me! I need to sit. Auuuugh! Where is my mother? I need my mother. Take this pain away. *Mother, take the pain!*"

Trake stumbled around the tent, trying to keep up with her. Atasha stood and sat and squatted, then stood and slapped him hard across the face. "You take some of this!" she shouted and then clutched his shoulders, sobbing into his chest. "The monster is ripping his way out. Auuuuugh!" She dropped and squatted, then grabbed Trake's hands for balance. Urine and feces squirted, staining the dirt floor and both of their feet. Trake held on, feeling more useless than an Honored in the commissary. He wanted the pain to stop; wanted all this to end. Silently he cursed the Gods for their part in this torture.

"I see a crown!" Nevera, Atasha's mother, screamed. She was down on all fours, head to the ground. "Stand up, Atasha. Boy — you imbecile — help her up!" He did. "Now, with the next pain, I want you to squat hard and push with everything you have left."

With quaking arms and knees, Atasha held onto Trake's shoulders again. Her elbows dug into his chest for support. "Come on, love, we're almost there," Trake cooed into her face.

"Shut the fuck up, you bastard!" she clenched between panted breaths. "*We* are not almost anywhere. This is *your* child. I will have nothing to do with it. You take it! Auuuugh!" She squatted and Trake watched her face contort with effort. But even as she pushed, she screamed, "When I get … this bastard out, *you* take it … take it *away* … where I can't see it."

"It's coming, darling," her mother squealed. She knelt now, reached in and yanked on the protruding head. Without warning, a gush of blood—and the Gods only knew what other fluids splattered across the floor—ran down Nevera's arms and coated Trake's feet. He jumped back, almost toppling Atasha.

"Stand in there, boy!" Nevera commanded. "I have your child …" she gave a mighty yank. "…your daughter… in my hands."

Trake looked down at the barely human mass in her hands, the face contorted, the head too long, the body smudged red with blood and white with crud. The fingers and the toes. Miniature and perfect. He fell in love, his heart ached, opened, burst, with love for his little girl's fingers … and toes.

Atasha craned her eyes over her still swollen belly. "Let me hold her. Is she all right? I haven't heard her scream. Is she all right?"

Nevera held the little girl up and gently blew into her face. Startled, the tiny creature sucked her first breath and let out a mighty wail. Atasha fell back into the dirt as Nevera brought the new life up onto her mother's chest, cord still attached.

* * *

Radiance emerged from Angela's shop after more than two hours of playful extravagances that ended with thankful hugs and kisses for Angela. Paul carried three hanging bags as Verbolana landed each foot as weightless as a swung landing from a hovering blimp. Left in a heap in the back room was her Blessed smock. Now covering her athletic exuberance was a body-tight black top with three-quarter sleeves shot through with gold threads. The effect was of deeply shadowed metal, embossed from beneath with the curves of feminine perfection. It laced up the back, leaving her tattoo exposed for all to see. Her hip-hugging Capri pants seemed to hang suspended from nothing, a good six inches below where the top left off and would have exposed the top of her curly blonde tuft if she had not recently wished her nether hair away.

"Where to now?" Verbolana asked, hoping to delay any ending to this perfectly blissful experience.

"Actually, I was supposed to be at the café an hour or so ago." Paul accelerated her to a brisker pace. "I think I said something about getting you a bite to eat. Are you up for it?"

"Maybe something like that little tidbit you gave us in the shop?" she suggested. If she'd thought about it, she would have realized this was the first time in her life she was excited about food.

"Oh, I shouldn't have started you there. I've got some amazing treats, but that one was the latest and greatest!" He forged ahead of her and spun, walking backward now, his admiring eyes washing over her.

Verbolana felt his gaze like the Strength from a hose, tracing her lines, caressing her curves, devouring her smooth white flesh. From almost outside herself, she felt her body respond. Her stride relaxed and lengthened, her lower back relaxed and her hips broke free. From the corner of her eye, she caught a couple watching the scene, her strut and Paul's backward antics. The girl giggled; the man turned and smiled. The golden glow in the back of her head burst to her face, and she gave the couple a dazzling smile.

"You forget," she refocused on Paul. "I am the one who comes from the desert. Angela may have been passing through, but I lived an entire life deprived. You can start at the beginning with me." She could not miss his appreciative grin. He spun back around and matched her stride.

The aroma of baking grains and roasting vegetables met them as they hurried around a corner.

"This is my place. You get a whiff?" Paul announced with obvious pride as they approached a storefront café with red-checkered tablecloths covering about a dozen tables with low-slung chairs strewn haphazardly between them. A gentle breeze ruffled the hunter-green awning that protected the first row of tables. A few patrons sat, sipping hot beverages from tiny thimbles; some perused large papers; some chatted. A man dressed in a white long-sleeved shirt and black pants stood in the background surveying the crowd. At guard, Verbolana concluded.

Paul excitedly pulled her through the tables directly to the man she soon learned was Alfredo. Paul introduced her to the man, who, until the introductions were over, stood stock still with hardly a whisper of recognition. Then, with great ceremony, he softly cupped her hand, raised it to his lips and kissed it. Before she could react, Paul whisked her inside the door.

"Hey, Paul, it's about fuckin' time!" A good-natured voice exploded before they could get five steps into the crowded room. "I thought maybe you'd fuckin' disappeared again and I was going to have to do the fuckin' lunch rush by myself, too." The jovial face looked up from an enclosure in the back.

Paul allowed Verbolana to catch up, then whispered conspiratorially, "He's from the East Coast, but people seem to love him anyway," by way of explanation.

"Oh, I see the problem, a new squeeze. My name's Frank, welcome to 'Fuckin' Franks and More,'" he yelled as he ducked his head out of the service window and came around to wait for them by the waiters' station. As Paul and Verbolana approached, he wiped his hands on a dirty towel tucked into his apron, and by

218

the time they reached him, his arms were spread wide and high. Verbolana froze in midstride as, thankfully, Paul took the lead, and was rewarded with a big bear hug.

"Now, don't fuckin' fall for this oaf too fast," Frank exploded as he disengaged from Paul. With lightning speed, Frank sidestepped Paul. "You gotta give the rest of us a chance." Frank pulled her to him and, along with a crushing hug, gave Verbolana an unexpected and unwanted wet, full-lipped kiss. She sputtered back and instinctively wiped her lips with the back of her hand.

"Whoa, partner!" Paul exclaimed. "I don't think she's quite ready for the full-court press." He turned to Verbolana. "Sorry, I should have warned you."

"Fuckin'-A!" Frank exclaimed in mock defensiveness. "Just trying to fuckin' move things along." And to Verbolana alone, "Paul here can be a bit fuckin' slow sometimes. Gets shy around the ladies."

Emboldened by the events of the day, Verbolana turned to Paul. "Really? I hadn't noticed." And then she pulled him close for the deepest, wettest, longest kiss she had ever given a man. Paul played along by running his hands down to cup her pert ass cheeks, then back up to push her chest tight to his.

"I stand *erected*," Frank exclaimed to the room and ducked back to his kitchen. "Now hobble your fuckin' ass behind the counter and get to work. And try not to drip into the food."

Paul sat Vee at the empty counter in front of his workstation and whisked into the kitchen.

"Order in!" One of the white-shirted waiters had come and gone.

Verbolana watched the men work, watched the waiters as they scurried back and forth. Then she watched the people outside, strolling as if without a care or anywhere to be. It just didn't make any sense.

Recreates? Were Paul and these other men recreates like Tarja? Why else would they work as Blessed servants? This is the last thing I need, to spend more time with recreates. But how? Alcot said recreates can only live inside someone's personal universe; that the city is only for what he called citizens. Her head clogged with the implications. Was she confused? The inside of a realm could look very real.

Verbolana retraced her steps. She had asked God to destroy her beach scene and had stood in her empty space with her thoughts just as empty. She could not think of what she might want. She had nothing, no idea what to ask for. For the first time she understood the value of a Weaver, as she stood there, confronted by her own lack of imagination. Then she had asked God for her Blessed smock and bolted out the door, down the elevator and out of the building. She was outside, in the city. She was sure of it. *So why, why are these men doing another's bidding? Dare I ask? How would they react?*

Wafting scents from the kitchen pulled Verbolana's attention back, and her first question became secondary. She found she was ravenously hungry. "What are you cooking?" She almost shouted her new excitement. Toning it down, she continued, "Your performance has roused your audience to ovation."

Paul smiled up through the smoke of his grill station. "That would be a first, but thanks. I'm just frying some maple-cured, wood-smoked bacon to a crisp. It's amazing. Real crispy bacon seems to be an American specialty. I can't tell you how many people get to Heaven and first thing they want is American crispy bacon." He babbled on as he flipped and stirred and poured. "The guy who ordered this comes every morning. He lives in a Terran neighborhood a few down that houses mainly Asians. He wants dark-brown hash browns, crispy bacon and scrambled eggs three or four times a week. That is his comfort zone, a big part of his Heaven." Some frantic movements and then, "Order up!" Paul came around the grill station and stood in front of Verbolana. "What can I get for you? The options are almost unlimited. If you can describe it, I can probably make it. For instance, I have 163 varieties of garlic, 82 types of bananas and 220 variations of potatoes. You name it, I can get it."

Verbolana pulled herself up. She did not like to admit to such ignorance; it would get the whip where she came from. "Milnox? Do you have Milnox?" It was all she could think of.

"Haven't heard of that one," Paul admitted.

Now that Verbolana had him down one step, she joked, "Good, 'cause I hated it anyway. Along with tapsu root and vetra greens. kah melon was my favorite and haulta fruit was okay. Brenut beans could be done well, but I'm here to taste what you're bringing to the table." Good, she had swung the rope back to him. "What was that you just prepared? That smelled good."

"Bacon and eggs with hash browns? Certainly not high cuisine, but, if you gotta start somewhere, it's as good a place as any." Their eyes touched, soft.

Verbolana pursed her lips in nervous response. "Let's start there," she concluded.

Paul hopped back to his station and started to work. "So, if you don't mind me asking, you said when we first met that where you come from men and women don't touch. Did you mean ever?"

"Yes." She did not elaborate. She had been waiting for the question. She knew from her experiences with Alcot and the men at Voltif's that this was an unusual arrangement. Everyone here seemed to be more like the Wretched. "It is a fundamental covenant of our religion."

"Interesting," Paul continued. "May I ask how you, ah, propagate the species?"

"We have Breeders," she answered as if it were still her reality. "They are the only ones asked to endure the indignity of childbirth" (and cross-sex relations, she didn't add). "The Wretched touch, but they are not the Chosen." She stopped her explanation there.

"And you still believe you are Chosen?" Alarm rang in his voice.

"It was once very simple. It is no longer." Then Verbolana honed in on his original question. She should have known, since he was a man. "But if you are asking if I still do not touch men, the answer is no—I think. The answer is I do touch men now. I just find it difficult at first."

"Well." Paul looked around to see whether anyone was following their conversation, but it was only Frank. "I was trying to be a little more subtle than that, but yes, that is what I'm asking. Even though I like dressing women, I also like undressing them."

"I don't know what that means," Verbolana sighed. "But since we're being blunt, can I ask you something?"

"Shoot," he said, as he walked a large plate of food over to her and took up the stool beside her.

"Why do you work like servants here, in a land where you can have anything?" Verbolana regretted the question as soon as it came out of her mouth. What if Paul snatched this glorious smelling food away in anger?

He laughed instead. "You *are* new, aren't you?"

She slammed her fork into her food. "Don't laugh at me. And no, I'm not new! I've just been busy ... adjusting."

"Sorry, sorry. It sounds like you have had a lot to adjust to." Instinctively he put his hand on her shoulder. "I didn't mean anything by it."

"Yes, you did," she said, then backed off. This guy was nicer than any she had met. Weighing her options, she mellowed. "But let's pretend I *am* new, and you tell me why you work."

"The simple answer is because I like to work. It gives me something to do. People like what I cook, and that feeds my ego. God didn't take our egos away when he brought us here, you know. Plus, I don't have the imagination to think up all the cool stuff I want. I could never have dreamed up that outfit you're wearing. I needed Angela to be able to do what I wanted, which at that moment was to see you in something truly fantastic. Fortunately, she wanted something from me too, so it all worked out."

Verbolana had taken a first tentative bite and now plowed across her plate.

"It's best to pick up the bacon," Paul threw in, loving her enthusiasm.

"This is the best food ... beyond anything I had ever imagined! The Orchards of Falmar could never have grown such fruit."

"No tree could have grown any of that," Paul commented. "Though I guess the little porkers might have had some fruit in their slop."

"Little porkers?" Verbolana asked in all innocence.

"The best," Paul responded with pride. "Raised on a farm in Norway, believe it or not. I tracked them down after one of the best meals I ever had; a four-star in the South of France."

"I'm not eating animals, am I?" Fork halfway to her mouth.

"You don't ...?"

Verbolana felt her stomach heave, sour and erupt. Chunks of food sloshed into the plate, across the counter and behind, splattering plates, glasses, anything in their way. She pushed away from the counter and ran, knocking into tables, chairs, waiters, newspapers. She ran out into the blinding sun, across the plaza and into the cool of the park.

Paul frantically followed at a discreet distance, wishing the mess he left gone as he went.

# Chapter 25

T rake's epiphanies were now commonplace, though Atasha was in no position to write them down. Little Atlana seemed constantly at her breast, even when they tried to sleep. The men of the Zartan clan tried to convince Trake that he did not need to stay with the pair day and night, but Trake could not be swayed. He saw the Gods, all of them, taking shape and form in tiny fingers and dimpled elbows. He also understood now why the Gods had not been speaking to him. There was no need for words or apparitions. The Gods had come, incarnate, to him. His only job was to protect and nurture this new life to full mature fruition, and all would be right.

And his lovely Atasha, mother to the Gods—what more could be said? He had never imagined, even contemplated imagining, the grace the Gods could bring to his woman. No matter how many times he explained to his new friends and no matter how many times they nodded in agreement, he knew they had no idea. For there was no experience they could have compared it to. Most of them had children, but none of them had experienced the divine. None of them could look into fatigued eyes and see the Encore; the Fruits of Bliss and Contentment, the Ponds of Abundance.

"Trake," Atasha pleaded, ten days into their new life, "Atlana is weak. My milk is thin and my blood is exhausted. I can no longer survive on the Fruits and Pearls of Father. I need his gifts to redden my blood and strengthen my spirit."

Trake sat beside her; a single candle threw heavy shadows across her face, smudged with fatigue. "Your spirit and blood are fine. Our child is fine. The Gods will see us through whatever our challenges may be. We must not spit in the face of Father when he has given us so much. If I must, I will leave your side to harvest the food we need."

"And you will make our new home from what? The clan has been generous only because you have been so attentive to one of their own. Soon they will expect you to join in the work and the first thing they will ask is that you build your own home. Every man must do that for every woman he gives a child to." She waited for his acknowledgement before she continued. "Your Father is also our Father, and we care for him in our own way. I know now that your convictions are strong and that you are well-intentioned. Nevertheless, you are wrong about some things. We cherish Father's gifts more than your people know. Go outside and look around. The forest where we live, is it the same as the forest where you placed your camp? It is not. Your forest struggles: Too many trees and not enough sunlight. Vines and underbrush strangle the ground, suck away the water before it can sink deep. Here, we clear the brush and small trees to make room for their big brothers. And yes, we use all we clear for our own purposes, so in that way our needs feed the needs of those that feed us. Leaving Father to heal himself will take forever. He needs help, and we are here to help." She stopped for a breath and to get back on track. "It is the same with the animals. Humans are a part of the balance. If we do not kill our share of Trints or Uxel, they will overrun themselves, just like the trees. There will be too many for them to thrive."

Trake stood shocked. In the year they had known each other, Atasha had never spoken her mind so forcefully. He was quite sure he did not like it. "How convenient!" he shot back, remembering those many months ago and how she had not believed him.

Not to be thrown from her reasoning, Atasha continued. "Yes, it is convenient, as long as we are not lazy or complacent. If we are to be fed, we must feed. If we are careless or greedy, we will starve. You are not the only people who live by important words."

"So you expect me to kill and eat flesh for you?"

"I expect you to step forward and care for what you have created. Ultimately, I must leave how you do that up to you. I am in no position to do for myself what I ask of you."

"I will care for you!" Insulted, Trake stomped out the door and into the dark woods, anxious to separate himself from such blasphemy.

Long before his thoughts could wrap around her words, Trake longed for the warmth of his wife and his bed. In part, he knew she was right. Somehow, he must find a way to provide for his family and fit in with these people. However, he was not ready to give up on one of the last sacraments he still held as Truth. Conflicted, he returned to his dark tent and molded to Atasha's tantalizing backside. Miraculously, both mother and baby were asleep.

Perspective was easier here, close to his family. Despite his dislike for Atasha's lectures on matters of faith, Trake realized the Gods may well have decided to speak through her.

*They must know how I much care for her and my new daughter. There is no disguising that. They know I will listen to her and I must not forget my mission. I am only partway there. My education must continue until the entire picture is clear. It appears that others have preceded me. I can assume they were on similar missions, and apparently they failed. I must not fail. The life of Father himself may hinge on my investigations and ability to sift truth from myth. The Chosen could not stand against so many. I must find another way. But I will not kill Father's gifts. That I cannot do.*

\* \* \*

Paul struggled behind Verbolana until he finally caught her at the bench where they had first met. "I am so sorry, I didn't know!" he blurted. "It wasn't your fault! I should have asked. I knew you were new and I didn't ask. I know better. There are lots of cultures that don't eat meat, even from my home world." He jabbered at the back of her head, following behind her like a naughty puppy.

Verbolana trudged on, not knowing where she was going. Away, she just had to get away.

"I cleaned up the mess," Paul continued, not knowing what line of reasoning might make her feel better. "It was all my fault. You did nothing wrong."

She turned on him, with tears running down her face. "I was having so much fun!" she sputtered. "I don't belong here. I never imagined … You were so nice. How could you?" The words regurgitated like the soured food. "It's Wretched!"

"I'm sorry," was all he could think to say. It wasn't like I killed your favorite cat, after all.

People walking nearby stared in displeasure at the rather raw public discourse. Paul nodded; he knew most of them.

"How can you be sorry? You slaughter Father's gifts for your own pleasure, knowing full well what you are doing."

"God does not have a problem with it," he blurted defensively.

"God, apparently, does not have a problem if you rape and strangle your bed partner. You can do whatever you want. I get it! But that doesn't make it right. Maybe God needs a God."

"Maybe he has one!" Paul shot back. "Look, I know this isn't what you need, a discussion of the moral implications of God. Can I just say I'm sorry and give you a big hug? That's what I want to do. I really did not mean to ruin our day."

"It goes against everything …" Verbolana sobbed and continued. "Everything I was taught."

Paul ventured forward and touched her hands. He was close now, and she did not back away. He ran his fingers a little up her arms, cupped them around her forearms and slowly brought his hands back down so they were palm to palm. Her fingers curled around his. "There are many teachings out there, a million books written by a million people, all claiming to know the word of God. Most sincerely believe. Then we get here …" Paul waited for her chin to come up, disengaged one hand and brought it up to wipe her tears with a soft brush of his fingers. "We get here, and everything is different." He waited for a weak smile to cross her lips. "I am not a monster. I am not … what did you say? Wretched. I was merely raised differently, with different customs, different beliefs."

"Don't you see?" Verbolana barely breathed the words. "That is the problem. That is my struggle. If they weren't the words of the Gods, then my people …" She took a big shuddering breath. "Then my people did some horrible things." *I did some horrible things,* she translated to herself.

"Verbolana, honey." Paul glimpsed a piece of the real issue and breathed easy. It wasn't about him anymore. "Life is messy. You heard Angela. Our world wasn't any better. I was lucky. I never served in the military and was raised in relative peace, but even I have regrets."

"And your people killed eighteen billion?" Her eyes raised, locked and took the offensive, anger stealing any sympathy.

"No," Paul conceded. "We killed a lot, but not that many."

But Paul didn't look away, and Verbolana felt him accept her anger, watched as he processed it, understood that he heard her. His wet hand came back to hers and he squeezed tight. "Can I ask what God said to you?" he continued after a long pause.

"He said he wants happiness and fulfillment for me."

"That's a tall order," Paul almost chuckled.

"Indeed," she conceded. "How can he even ask that after what he put us through?"

"Indeed," he responded.

"And he said something about free will. That it wasn't supposed to be easy." Verbolana sniffed and wiped her nose with the back of her hand. "What a shit!"

"You got that right. Unless he has a plan he isn't telling us about, his plan sucks."

"How do you do it?" she asked earnestly.

"Like I said, I was lucky. Raised with little religion by relatively happy people in a relatively happy land. I had vague ideas about seeing my kids and wife up here when all was said and done. And I still go back to visit sometimes. It's not the same, but ..." His eyes wandered to the overhanging trees and latched onto a bird singing in the branches. "We don't even know if that was reality. Sometimes I feel like a mote on the fingernail of some larger ... something ... soon to be brushed off to land in the dirt, to become indistinguishable from other specks of dirt." His eyes came back to hers and he chuckled in embarrassment. "And then I cook."

"How long have you been here?" He had brought her out of herself and she was grateful.

"Not long." The question brought his chuckle up short. "Fifty-something years. I try not to count."

"Seems like everyone struggles."

"Even those who are happy," he agreed. "Say," he said, lightening with sudden enthusiasm. "Do you wanna go do something? The river is just over there. We could jump in a canoe and take a little paddle!"

Verbolana suddenly laughed, relief obvious in her eyes. "Is that anything like windsurfing?"

"Oh, no; it's much less strenuous. You'll just sit and gaze adoringly into my eyes, while I, shirtless and sexy, will stroke us to where we need to go."

"I thought we were going to talk before we had sex."

"Ah, very good, you caught the innuendo," he snickered as he turned her and nudged her to a walk. "Mama didn't raise no fool."

"Mama didn't raise me at all."

"Shit, how can I step in it again so soon?" He shook his head. "I'll just keep my mouth shut for a while."

She turned and kissed him full on the lips, pulled back and whispered, "Open your mouth."

# Chapter 26

**M**olded to Atasha's side, their flesh singed together from mutual heat, Trake startled awake in absolute darkness. Atlana came to mind first, so he waited in exhausted patience for her next cry. Strength coursed through his body as a realization struck him. It was lack of sound that had wakened him. In a panic, he reached over Atasha, and immediately found his bundled gift. Atlana was warm, and his touch brought the slightest jolt with a hushed gurgle. She was fine.

What had awoken him? From outside his hut came murmurs and muffled rummaging drifting through the still night. He had not been the only one awoken, he concluded. Pulling away from his cocoon, he slipped from under the covers and rolled from his low sleeping mat onto the packed earth. In one fluid movement, he stood and collected himself. He had not lived with the Wretched for long, but he knew some things, and one was that they did not waste fuel by rising before first light. Something was wrong. He squelched his desire to bolt from the shelter and be the first to the defenses. Trake stood still and concentrated to summon more Strength. As his mind cleared, he calmed and images appeared almost immediately. Slinking forms with focused intention moved all around him. A number of these forms gathered a short distance away. Trake knew by the bundled energy of their fists that they were armed and intent on violence.

"What is it?" came Atasha's sleepy voice.

Trake dropped to her ear and breathed, "Stay perfectly quiet and put our child to your breast. Something is afoot."

Atasha hesitated for only a moment. "Vipeon," came her whispered conclusion.

Trake's heart froze, the still air screaming its answer. Not a bug chirped nor amphibian croaked. Every creature went to ground for a Vipeon. He kissed his love on the cheek and gently cupped the shoulder of his sleeping girl, sending her his love through a gentle hand. Then with the Strength of Father, he launched across the room, collected his sword, bow and quiver; and then slipped from their home.

Once outside Trake reevaluated the energy that converged around him. He did not even need the Strength to locate his new allies, they made such a racket. Frantic instructions were hurled back and forth as the frightened men tried to agree on a plan of attack. Men bolted with one idea in mind only to be called back for reassignment in favor of a newer plan.

And the Vipeon approached, Trake knew. Still in full stealth mode, the animal was a hundred yards from the closest hut and moving in steadily.

Trake pictured the beast slithering its heavy bulk across the forest floor, eyes focused, tongue anticipating an easy meal. Trake shuddered at the memory of his last encounter. He had never come so close to death and he had no desire to return. However, this threat could not be allowed to come close to his family. The Gods would not allow it. He would not allow it. And with the confusion around him, he knew he would get no help from these men. According to Atasha, none of them had ever successfully attacked a Vipeon, even en masse.

His mind made up, Trake sliced through the camp and picked the shortest distance to his prey. He felt, in each hut he passed, the huddled forms of women and children, all alerted to the danger and all praying for salvation. He felt the intensity of their love digging into the heads of their children, the frantic frustration of the question "Why?" forever unanswered. At that moment, Trake acknowledged his astonishment at the realization that *his* love was not unique, that others had feelings equal to his, that maybe his love was not singularly divine, but universally divine. He stored the thought as he moved, determined to write it down and examine it—if he lived through the next few minutes.

Surprisingly, by the time Trake arrived at the fringe huts, men had already lined up in defensive positions, bows drawn, listening for the slightest sign of the beast.

"He is fifty feet at ten degrees left of that large tree," Trake breathed to the first man he encountered, his command voice squelching any question. "He has stopped to take stock. He will attack shortly. It appears he has his eye on the second hut over. It is the only one still occupied. Can you get them out?"

"We can, but then the beast will simply move further into the camp," the man replied. "Those in that tent are old and have lived full lives."

"And they wish to die?" Trake shot back.

"My mother is in that tent!" the man hissed back. "I know who you are. Do not lecture me on death! You have brought plenty of your own."

"How about we not fight each other and fight this beast instead?" Trake suggested.

"I have every intention of doing what I can," the man stated as if he already were.

"Good," Trake continued. "He is on the move and we must set up fast!"

"I am in position," the man stated indignantly.

"I am going to kill this thing before it kills your mother. If you do not want to help, then don't." Trake moved off as strategies rushed through his mind. He sidled up to a thick tree; his mind probed the darkness ahead. The eyes of the beast appeared as cones of brightness, lancing through the jungle growth. It was close, but moving in the wrong direction for Trake to get a clear shot. Trake notched an arrow to his bow and stepped away from the tree. "You ugly stagehand, I'm over here!"

The cones of energy jolted and turned toward Trake.

"No, over here!" came a voice behind and to the left of him.

"No, over here!" another voice raised through the dark.

"Here, here, here!" Trake yelled, the new voices not fitting into his plan. The giant head was twenty-five feet away and jumped from one voice to another. As the cone came back to Trake, he fired. Off by an inch. Another voice, then another raised through the darkness. Trake notched, aimed and yelled. The animal rushed now, irritated by the shot to its eye. At ten feet, Trake loosed his second arrow, this one flying true, extinguishing one cone and prompting an ear-shattering roar. The beast stopped short, shook its head from side to side as it tried to rid itself of this new and unknown pain. Trake drew his sword and jumped forward, but his timing was ill conceived. In its wild gyrations, the snout of the monster slammed into Trake's shoulder and sent him flying into a stout bush that seemed to swallow him whole. Worse yet, the enraged Vipeon was looking for an outlet for its anger and whatever he had just bumped into seemed as good a victim as any. Fighting the clinging, tangling branches, Trake brought his sword up just as the hot putrid breath of the beast kissed his face.

*Thwack, thwack, thwack!* Arrows ricocheted off the tough hide as a chorus of voices rained through the night. The confused animal faltered and Trake struck. Clinched by the bush, he called upon not only the Strength but also the names Atasha, Atlana and, surprisingly, Verbolana. Still, the blow came up short and misguided. He held firm to the handle as the beast jerked back and forth. With all his might, Trake held the blade strong and felt it slide almost free before the creature's reaction drove it back in at a different angle. Reacting to the pain, the creature pulled back again, freeing the blade. Somehow Trake curled his feet beneath him and launched out of the bush.

More defenders arrived and it seemed as though fifty arrows bounced around Trake as he lay prone just beside the beast. He felt the earth jump as the beast swung its head and stomped its feet at each new threat. Rolling away from the danger, he crouched and took stock. The arrows were doing their job. The Vipeon seemed to have forgotten about him. Trake the Vipeon Slayer was about to do his magic again.

*Thwack!* Trake's right shoulder blazed with sudden pain, driving the breath from his lungs. He staggered and looked down to realize an errant marksman had driven an arrow straight through his shoulder. Worse, his quarry was moving off. Without further thought, he lunged forward, his heart guiding his hands up and in with blinding pain and a sick ripping sound from his shoulder. Blood showered him as he twisted his blade and poked deeper. A gurgling roar filled his ears as he dropped from consciousness.

\* \* \*

Verbolana lay propped in the bow of a small boat, deep in conjured pillows, as her new friend Paul paddled with apparent aimlessness down the wide river. The little bikini bottoms she had lived in with Tarja had aroused quite a stir when she had thought to conjure them as well. After many furtive glances around the park, Paul finally explained that this neighborhood did not allow women to "parade," as he said, "around topless." With a few wishes, she matched her bottoms with a pleasing top and reluctantly covered herself. She realized, with some surprise, that she enjoyed the way this man's eyes traveled across her, and with her top covered, his gaze was not nearly as intense.

So now, propped, cushioned, and properly covered, Verbolana closed her eyes to the glorious sun on her face and the sounds of lapping water. She took a long deep breath, released it, then took another, sinking deeper into the pillows. She almost spoke of this new comfort, but she held her thoughts. Silence was something they had not yet tried, and speaking, so far, had been filled with turmoil, only illustrating how different they were. In the last few minutes she had sensed how similar they were. Two souls, each searching for that perfect moment when comfort and ambition, satisfaction and questioning, sated bliss and desire were all in perfect balance.

Verbolana wanted to say, "The green stuff has worn off and I am not afraid," but she assumed he would not understand. She wanted to say, "I have never, in either of my lives, felt so relaxed," but he would probably read too much into it. She wanted to say, "Please pull to the shore and take me, there in the bushes," but she knew a man did not know how to love her in the way she needed. So she said nothing and took another deep cleansing breath. She released all her thoughts, constipated and blissful alike, to the Za-soft clouds that floated above. As questions and answers, fears and bundled courage seeped from her heart, up her neck and into her head, she released them too, without examination or guilt. Emptied and constantly emptying, she sunk still deeper into her cushions, hearing now, the birds in the rustling leaves on the distant shore. She released. Smelling the fresh, churned water from each powerful stroke, she released. Feeling the sun's cleansing warmth tickle across her exposed skin, she selected this sensation and sucked it in, felt its golden glow gathering in her belly until it created a glow of its own, filling outward to her groin and heart, then to her legs and arms, her feet and hands and eventually her head. She filled and breathed, filled and breathed, continuing to release any errant thoughts. Even the thought that told her she was filled, to the exclusion of anything else, with the golden glow of self-love— even that she released.

Verbolana awoke to floating words, "We're there." Somewhere outside herself she felt the bow below her mush into soft earth. Unaware she had fallen into sleep, she collected herself. Unexpected yet familiar energy flowed through her limbs. *The Strength! What is that doing there?* She panicked. *This is not battle.* She opened her eyes, confirming her safety. Paul sat smiling.

"Got a little nap in," he commented. "Nothing better than a little snooze in the sun."

To cover her concern, Verbolana replied with the practiced veil of her home world, "Nothing better." Then she practically launched out of the little boat with a movement intended merely to sit herself upright.

Paul jumped back in surprise. "Eager, are we?" he joked.

Continuing to cover, she said, "Yeah, let's see where you brought me." Inside she thought, *Does everyone have the Strength? Maybe he'll just laugh. But the Wretched didn't ... don't have the Strength and our trainers always stressed this was our secret. Will he think I'm a freak if I tell him? Or worse yet, will he lead me with his questions to the true nature of my skill? Will he shrink from the barbarism, from the blood that still stains my hands?* While thinking, she accepted Paul's hand for balance and jumped from the boat to the shore, propelling the startled Paul and the boat ten feet back into the river.

Verbolana turned to Paul's expletives. "Holy shit, girl, you must have jumped, well, I don't know, twenty feet! Let me get back." Manning the oars, he fumbled and splashed his way to shore. As the boat came within reach, she grabbed the bow and, this time with conscious restraint, grounded the craft without incident. Paul clambered ashore. "You ever play basketball? That was cool. Seen that kinda move in the zero-grav games, but outside of that ... well, you can jump, girl!"

"Where I come from, we learn how to jump," she said, trying to play it off. "Now," she looked around in mock fascination. "Where have you brought me?"

He did not answer, just grinned and motioned with his head and eyes for her to look around.

A shaded path of mossy stones greeted her, the air fresh and cool. Low flowers of blue and white sprinkled among sculpted scrubs of a violent red that made Verbolana shudder. Her enhanced senses picked out every bird and scampering critter within fifty feet. People strolled in the near distance, their energy signals docile, almost lifeless, to her eyes. She followed one set of signals, felt them conversing in hushed easy tones. She watched as their signals changed, each with its own level of intensity, to focus on something before them. Whatever they had found gave off no aura, and fearing Paul's reaction to her internal experimentation, she pulled herself back and focused on him. "It's beautiful, but what am I looking for?"

"Look beyond the trees," he suggested. "Walk in some."

With Paul tagging behind, she took a few steps to the path and followed it into the park. Among the trees, she noticed a spot of water. Well, she decided, not a spot, but a fall of water, in midair, with no stream to feed it and no pond to collect it. She walked on for a different angle, but the water sprouted from the air, fell three or four feet, and disappeared back into nothing. She noticed a small plaque under the fall. "From Nothing to Nothing" was all it said.

"How did they do that?" she asked in true amazement. "And why?"

"The 'why' is up to you, Verbolana, but the 'how' is easy. Just conceive and ask."

"Oh," was all she said, still perplexed. They walked on.

Paul stopped a few yards further down the path. "I particularly like this one," nodding his head toward large floating iridescent bubbles, apparently sprouting from the ground, rising a few feet, then bursting. They seemed to follow no pattern, sometimes coming in clusters, sometimes by themselves. The sign read "Epiphany."

Verbolana made no comment. Paul urged her forward.

"Then there's this one," he said after they walked a few more yards.

"Where?" Verbolana saw nothing.

"Up there, in the tree." Paul pointed to a densely leafed branch with a bird's nest half hidden. A mother bird held one end of a worm; the beak of her baby tugged endlessly on the other. The caption read "Release."

"Who is supposed to release?" Verbolana asked.

"That's always the question," Paul smiled.

They spent a few hours walking and talking; with Verbolana finally relaxed enough to enjoy the sun, sky and company of a nice man. They parted, after an awkward kiss, with the promise to get together soon. Paul reminded her she had left the dresses behind and assured her he would keep them safe for her return.

# Chapter 27

The hushed night lay thick and humid across his shoulders, stooping his back, forcing his blackened gaze down toward the ground. Clouded images approached. Jeweled moccasins and embroidered leggings moved wavering in and out of focus. Hands stretched into the tunnel of his vision with an offering. Trake accepted the offered package—the gift—without comment. His hands trembled as he fumbled with the stiff wrapping, anticipation building in all those who watched. Atasha sat beside him on the dais, he realized, slightly lower, separate, nursing the little one. They had not been there a moment ago. He felt her gaze and the admiration in her eyes. The fumbling continued; there seemed endless layers to this gift, all wanting to close back around his hands. Frustration crept into his brain, along with other thoughts, incompetence, undeserving, a charlatan, a Director spouting words he had just thought up instead of reading from the script. The last layer. Through the sinewy material he fought until he caught the slightest glimpse.

"Vipeon!" he screamed. The bloodied, shrunken head came to life in his hands, squirting blood, snapping, lurching, growing. Verbolana screamed beside him, dropping their child and pulling a Talsartt from her gown. Atlana squirmed and squealed on the ground as the head grew a body, legs and claws. Slashing across his chest, the first claw raked gaping flesh and blood until organs hung loose. Trake saw in his death the Talsartt come down,

243

chopping through bone and teeth of the beast as well as his own hands, which still held the jaw of the beast. Pumping hoses of blood, his stumped wrists poured gagging blood down the beast's throat. Wild eyes and flailing claws dissolved, the teeth squared and came together, snarling lips softened, plumped, accepted his draining arm? No; his hands cradled Verbolana's head as his hips jerked in spasmodic release. Atasha stood beside them, watching, smiling, draped in Za linen — perfect, angelic.

Guilt rocked him in realization, stealing his final pleasure. Atlana cried somewhere, refusing Atasha's perfect breast.

Atasha's voice came not from her smiling lips. "You dream, love. You will tear the stitches if you continue. Lie still."

Trake fought through the layers of pain, his desperate eyes orienting to the dark. Atasha's face beamed down at him. "I am so proud of you. No one believed me when I told them you had killed a Vipeon. Now the stories will spread across our land. You are a hero! Your advice will be sought from every corner."

While Trake reeled from the lurid, bewildering images, Atasha's praise bounced from his ears. He shifted his head to escape her smiling eyes. Blackening pain shot through his shoulder as queasiness jumped from his stomach and lodged in his throat.

"Auugh!" came his involuntary response. "Where am I?"

"It will take some time to heal; that is for sure. But you will heal, and all is well with us. The entire clan is here to support us. Your valor has ensured our prosperity. The skin from that one Vipeon will house us for many years to come. And its meat dries even now. It will be shared throughout the village, but we will be a part of every kill for this season and more." She stopped. Trake felt her eyes on him again. Greedy eyes, he recognized even through his fever. Coveting eyes. He had killed the Vipeon to protect his family, not out of greed or desire for status. Would he partake in this newfound bounty? Would he allow *her* to?

"I can see your concern and I hear your unasked questions, but you demand too much of me right now. I am muddled with sleep and pain. I cannot hear the Gods ..."

"My love, I ask nothing of you. You are my hero. I will sit at your feet and keep them clean. I will have baby after baby, if that is your wish and never ask another thing of you."

Unprepared for battle, Trake conceded, "I'm sorry. I misread your eyes," knowing he had not. But it was a small lie, not worth confronting. He closed his eyes to hide his disappointment. He knew it was too much to ask of her, to give up this new wealth. And the Vipeon had not come from Father, he was sure of that. The Vipeon, all of them, deserved only death since that was all they brought. Wasting their carcasses, it followed, would be a sin. Would the Gods ask for one more sacrifice, then? Just the *thought* of animal flesh coating his tongue revolted him. Blood and tissue, built on the blood and tissue of innocent men and women. He would be eating them, really.

Trake opened his eyes to avoid one terror, only to confront Atasha's eyes, probing still. He turned away and felt his entire life tilt. The balance of power could pivot on the next moments. She knew she had lied — and she knew he knew. He could tell all this from her veiled gaze. And he knew, in that instant, that if he allowed this lie to stand, that he had forever altered their love and their relationship. His love for her now colored his love for his Gods. She had taken precedent, and he did not have the will to take it back. Living in righteous belief was a cold and lonely place. Body warmth, moist lips, smooth skin, easy conversation — even if it hid the cold truths of the Gods — this was true divinity. Or if not true, at least real, tangible, fulfilling.

Trake looked back at Atasha, locked eyes with his love and without words, forgave her for her lie, forgave her for her greed, forgave her for her search for status among her people. With his good arm, he pulled her close and mashed her soft yielding lips against his strong yearning lips and probed with light delicate flicks into her trap. Her tongue lay back, docile yet responsive, inviting with its submissiveness, the ultimate dichotomy.

\* \* \*

A few hundred yards down the path, barely out of Paul's sight, Verbolana felt her blood thickening to Milnox stew.

Emptiness awaited, she realized. Home, friends, purpose? There was nothing. Earlier in the day, only hours really, out of anger and frustration she had destroyed her only life. Then the park bench and Paul, and a blissful realization that somehow she could belong.

But now what? Paul had a life. Verbolana could not latch onto the first person she met, could she? Alcot had said this was a land of choices, and she realized that so far she had made none, really. She had globbed — globbed onto Alcot — globbed onto Tarja. Was she now to glob onto Paul? No, he was too nice a person for that.

So what now? Aimlessly, Verbolana strolled down the trail, taking time to enjoy the scene resplendent with Father's wonders. Others passed, some in hurried posture, eyes focused, faces grim; while more often they ambled along as Verbolana now did, enjoying the sun low in the trees, shadowing and coloring the scattered blossoms that seemed so universally pleasing. Wordlessly, sights stole into her mind, nipped at her sudden blues. She kicked her feet across the age-smoothed stones, playfully imagining she had come here when she was a little girl, wondering who she might have become with such freedom. Towering red-leafed trees dropped a leaf or two in her path and she bent to retrieve one. She marveled at Father's work and wondered, as she had for years, hopefully below God's reach, if Father were not the truest God.

A sign, incongruous to her thoughts, stopped her. Momentarily taken aback, she stood for a moment, to concentrate.

> *With Every Breath and Every Step,*
> *You Make a Choice.*
> *Those Who Surrender to Allah May Enter.*
> *All Others Must Fend for Themselves.*

"Doesn't look like you belong." A voice jolted her from behind.

Verbolana turned to a sweating, beautifully formed woman wearing a short, tight top and skimpy flared bottom. She danced in place as if the stones were heated.

"What does that mean?" Verbolana asked innocently.

"What it means is you're not welcome," the woman spat between breaths. "It means that God, in his infinite wisdom, allows disease to reign under his very nose. It means, even with evidence staring them in the face, that some people were born with a sickness only a second death can cure."

"I thought we all had perfect health."

"You must not be from around here." The woman kept her feet dancing, with sweat dripping from her chin. "I'm a Jew," she announced with finality. When she got no response, she continued, "These people have killed my people for generations. Then they get up here, fuck their forty virgins and spit in our faces!"

Verbolana finally caught the depth of the woman's anger. Feeling somehow responsible, she asked, "Is that how you died? They killed you?"

"I lived in one of the towers," the woman explained.

Verbolana rocked back as if she had been punched in the face. "Then you are Chosen?"

247

"Honey, everybody up here thought they were Chosen, even those fuckers in there. But only the demented or deluded think that now." The woman nodded to the path that led past the sign. She turned and started down a smaller path. "We might not like it, but we were all wrong. Just take my advice and find a different way to get to wherever you're going." And then she disappeared around a bend.

To the empty space the woman had left behind, Verbolana muttered, "I was a warrior. I killed for my Gods. Maybe I would be welcomed there." She took another look at the sign, and then strolled in the direction the woman had taken, tried her best to regain her light mood, only to be confronted by questions with questions she thought she had left behind.

Lost in a cloud of thought, Verbolana picked one trail after another, sometimes surfaced to awareness in the middle of a crowded plaza or, like now, atop a sturdy stone bridge staring at the passing water. So many people with so many ideas, problems and solutions. Her mind kept migrating back to Paul and his little café. And Frank. What a strange character he was! She envisioned what Frank's face would be if she ever stepped foot in there again: anger, disgust, without a bother toward sympathy. She could never go back, she knew. She was fragile enough without his condemnation. And Paul; underneath it all he seemed fragile, too. Desperate to please, hungry beyond his food. Then there was Tarja. She already missed Tarja.

*Why can't I go back?* she wondered as her mind craved silence. *I could step slowly into this world. Go back to fortify. Sip and lie in peace. Why did I think I had to do it all at once? Why did I destroy such a beautiful friend?* The thought shocked her. An unnamed fear suddenly gripped her belly. *Where did she go? God, where did she go?*

"Tarja?" God asked. "She never existed. I would not burden you with such horrors here. Real human life cannot be created here, be assured of that."

*But where is she?*

"She was scattered back to the universe from which she was made. She felt no pain or anguish when she disappeared. She lives in your memory and the memories of all who met her, that is all."

Verbolana settled with the thought. *God, I need help. I do not wish to burden others with my pain, but it all still wells so easily. Is there a place I can go to explore and learn with others who are also searching?*

"Everyone here searches, Verbolana. But yes, there is a whole community of those who take a very active role in their searches. They have built a wonderful home in the city center. It is called Paradise University."

*Can you show me how to get there?*

"Of course."

And she instantly knew.

*Thank you.*

"My pleasure."

Verbolana watched the river, deciding, though there was really so little to decide about. As the river passed under her, she thanked Paul and blew him a kiss to the water.

With the sun low on the horizon, Verbolana's mind reached back to her tower, back to another life also with few real choices. She pictured Treena as she finished her evening meal sitting beside a new friend, probably Cendra or Tallet. They would share a private joke, giggle with heads together as they finished their last few bites of Tantrot mush. Then the two would shuffle off to stand in yet another line to fetch dinner for their Honored charges. Simple and easy compared to here. Her heart reached out as she turned to follow the directions God had given her for the university, allowing a memory burned by His hand to blossom behind her eyes.

Treena sat on the bare deck, looked up and smiled casually at her approach then went back to work darning a sleeping sock she had inherited from a distant cousin. The hole in the heel bothered her and she was determined to fix it before another night shuffled by. Verbolana bent to kiss her forehead, and then sat beside her to watch. "Find comfort where you can, Treena." She changed the memory. "God takes nothing from our pathetic existence. We cannot help him and he refuses to help us. So live, my darling. Live, laugh and love with anyone who will give it back. And care not for anyone who would tell you differently."

Verbolana checked her landmarks. She still had a long way to go to reach the university. She thought about the subway, but concluded there were no shortcuts. It would take her just as long as it took her to get there, and exploring along the way seemed appropriate. She would contemplate and file every sight and sound for future review. Ignorance was something she could no longer excuse. She was here, cheated and deceived like everyone else, yet unique in every experience and every thought. If for no one else, she would be happy for herself. The teacher would teach herself.

By the time Verbolana reached the campus, the sun was back in the sky. On her seemingly endless walk, she had wished away the pain in her feet and legs many times and asked for her eyes not to shut from exhaustion. Yet, in honor of Paul, she had decided not to wish away her hunger or the weakness it brought. Traveling by her nose, she crossed tree-lined avenues and cut between magnificent structures of a hundred different styles and configurations. She dashed up the final steps and presented herself to a man sitting at a high counter.

"I have no money," she declared.

"You need no money here. Education and everything that goes with it are free here," he answered matter-of-factly.

"I don't eat animals," she declared again and expected some horrid reaction.

"That line over there," was all he said as he pointed to his left.

# Chapter 28

Trake lived. He remembered that he had confessed to Verbolana how he did not want to die before he had lived. He lived now, pillowed through the long cold nights with his pleasure girl, behind walls of privacy where she tended to his every desire. Atasha was true to her word ... the word that still covered the lie. She worshipped him, pleasured him, cleaned and fed him. Wealth and status seemed to diminish the urgency of his mission. No new lessons presented themselves, so he waited in luxurious repose, counseling himself to practice patience.

During the short days when leaves dried and fell, Trake resumed his martial training on the pounded ground outside his newly enlarged hut. Healing came slowly, so to urge things along, he started with gentle movements, designed to loosen his tight muscles and stretch scar tissue so it did not heal bunched or frozen. As his movements increased in their vitality and his fluidity improved, he started to draw a crowd, though he still grimaced from the pain.

First, youngest boys of the clan gathered, and a few others as they happened by. Then some of the old men made a habit of stopping to watch, and eventually the young bucks took up their activities within sight so they could watch without commitment. Since Trake worked his routines without weapons, he was not sure if they even understood what they saw. Most of the movements could have as easily been interpreted as dance, and Trake took comfort in this. Though he now lived as a Cheated, he could not forget that those around him were sworn enemies of the Chosen. Even if he no longer believed they were in any way "chosen," they still deserved a loyalty that went beyond their beliefs.

As he worked, Trake noticed that the youngest had started to copy his movements, first from sitting, then the bolder stood, still self-conscious, to mimic his hands and arms. Before many days had passed, Trake had the boys in lines and made minor adjustments to their positions. He realized he enjoyed being back in command and smiled to think these youngsters were more willing and adept than the adult Blessed he had struggled with.

Dark days of rain, sometimes frozen, halted the lessons. On those days, Trake retreated back into his hut and into his thoughts. Cloistered with Atasha and Atlana in their gloomy hut, he reclined there for hours, his mind darkened as well, and questioned the evolution of his beliefs. He searched for the missing pieces that had at last brought him happiness and ease. Where were the Truths? Could his new devotions to mother and child, comfort and indulgence, be the true path? No matter how right it felt, there were times when nagging images of angry Gods soured his stomach and rattled his nerves.

Was he really expected to understand the notions of the Gods? Was that not their providence alone? Could they expect him to continue his sacrifice in the face of ultimate gratification? Of course they could expect it, but would they understand his failings, if indeed that is what they were? After all, he reasoned, they made mistakes as well. They allowed the Directors to falsify their words, they allowed the truly pious to live entire lives in deception. How could they demand him, and only him, to see through the fog?

"You ask too much. I am not divine. I am flesh and bone, and by nature inferior in understanding!" Trake moaned to the gloom.

Atasha glanced up from her endless feeding of their daughter. His eyes were closed, so she said nothing.

"I am not your leading man. I too have failed." Silence. Then he said, "Maybe I just need time. Time to adjust ... to feel ... to learn these new sensations. Do not give up on me. That's it. I am human; I am frail. I am supposed to be this way. It is supposed to take me time to adjust, to let things settle and steep." He was acutely aware of Atasha's presence. He realized he meant some of these words for her. Words he could not speak to her directly but he must coin in code, directed at someone else. She would not listen otherwise, and he wanted desperately to avoid any confrontation.

As Trake pretended to doze, he floated on the stream of his thoughts, let them take him where they may. He wondered, suddenly, in his gloom, when he had become so weak. He looked back across his days. His life on the tower had been so simple; solid beliefs with proscribed actions. He was strong and confident; he knew his place and could visualize his future. He had cared for Erox and his other friends, but that caring had never diminished him. It was different here with Atasha. In order to be more of a man, it seemed he had to be less of a man. He had to share power and decisions in a way that sucked at his ego, punctured and drained his Strength, devoured his every belief, masticated it and spit it back at him, forever altered.

Trake wondered if all men who loved women felt this way. He doubted it. Men of the clan still strutted undiminished and many of them had many women. They stood forth proud and strong, gave their women little quarter. He saw the hollow look in the eyes of the women, broken from the strength and pressure of their men. Could he have that if he wanted it? Would he want it if he had it? He could not imagine what one of these women would be like when the lights were off. Most likely placid and yielding, lacking in any real vitality. How diminishing would that be? And then he saw the truth. These men, the strutting ones, were already diminished, already frail and damaged. They would never feel the sacrifice of self because they had been sacrificed long before, in some other way.

*I must give in to my love, watch and learn where it takes me. I must not be passive, but conscious in my sacrifices. To live in Strength, I must risk everything, challenge the lies and face whatever conflict arises with courage. There is no middle ground.*

Trake's eyes shot open and he bolted upright, startling Atasha so that Atlana broke from her nipple, gasped and exploded into a gurgling wail.

"Trake!" startled Atasha exclaimed. "What is it?"

"There is something eating at me," Trake proclaimed with his courage balled into fists, his words clipped and harsh as if in anger. "I love you more than I could have imagined a year ago." He watched Atasha's eyes freeze and withdraw. She looked down, fumbling to help her girl back to the breast.

"And this eats at you?" Atasha's voice was injured.

Trake felt her manipulation immediately and it fed into the anger he now recognized was there. "It is not my love that eats at me. Please, this is difficult for me; just listen to me."

Atasha nodded, her eyes suddenly fierce and stony, boring into him. Trake felt her willing him to stop.

"It is not a big deal, just a small pebble in our path." Trake purposely softened his voice, removed his hidden anger. "You said a few weeks ago that I was your hero; that you would not ask anything of me. Yet I do not feel heroic, and I feel that you have asked much of me." He stopped for breath and emphasis. "I killed the Vipeon; not for riches or glory and not for the acceptance of your people, but because the creature threatened my family. I accepted the riches and the glory because you asked it of me ... not in so many words, but silently, with your eyes and your touch and your attentions. I feel …" He hesitated, his courage wilting before the fire in her eyes. "I feel like we must discuss these things, not just let them run on without comment. You know I am torn by this; that it runs contrary to my beliefs. My love for you and our girl is …"

"How dare you blame our love for this! I give you a child … It is your duty to provide. I did not ask you to run from our home and confront that monster. How can you make me to blame for your choices? Are you now going to tell me you have not enjoyed your newfound fame? You have lapped up the attention like a Tarlot finding a stream in a drought."

"I do not blame you, and I do not deny my pleasure. I love nothing better than pleasing you. That is part of the problem. I love you to the exclusion of my Gods."

"I have never asked you …"

"I do not say you have. This is something I have brought upon myself, something I must work through. I just bring it up now to let you know I am troubled, that I am struggling."

"It doesn't sound that way to me," Atasha continued. "It sounds as though you blame our love; that you blame me for your dilemma." She looked up; and her tears and set jaw seemed to contradict each other.

Trake softened further when he saw her tears. "I don't know how to do this. I don't know where I end and you begin. I want to please you, but I want to be true to myself. Why is that so difficult?"

"Why do you think it should not be difficult?" she shot back. "Do you think I do not sacrifice for you? Do you think your struggle is somehow unique? The only thing unique about your struggle is that you try to blame it all on me!"

"And you take no responsibility for any of this?" Trake exploded. "You deny you have ignored my struggle for your own gain?"

257

"I deny nothing!" she proclaimed. "I have a child at my breast. I will do whatever it takes to protect her. I thought, with time, you would come to a similar conviction. I see I was wrong. You are selfishly holding to your perverted comforts. Comforts that do not include your family."

"How can you say that?" He stood and paced the floor in front of her. "Everything I do is for you and her and our love."

"You question and threaten our love to protect it?" Atasha asked, accusingly.

Trake stomped before her. "Yes ... that is exactly what I am doing!" Confused more than he had ever been in his life, he stomped from the room.

* * *

A thing called "Terran Pizza" brought Paul to the front of Verbolana's full-color memory. She was surrounded by new friends; and music and strobe lights pounded with a popular beat. But even with all those distractions, pain or embarrassment could be just a slipped thought away. Chunked vomit lay forever sprayed across dark blue granite and white dishes. Well, not forever, she reminded herself. Time marched on while new insults piled on top of old ones.

Verbolana looked around. This wasn't a bad place, the setting anyway. The Last Dance Saloon at the Palladium had sounded like fun. She concentrated on her pizza. She wasn't hungry, but she definitely needed a drink, and not this Ultianna Ale that foamed before her.

*God, give me some green stuff,* while avoiding the memories that evoked.

Across the long skinny table, Natek, her new best friend, noticed the switch and yelled through the throb, "Going to the hard stuff already? We've still got thirty-eight minutes."

Verbolana glanced up at the countdown clock that hung on the wall of the private room they had all pitched in to rent for the evening. No wonder Paul's memory had surfaced so easily. Anything to escape the melancholy that could so easily slip in here.

"It's my first," Verbolana reminded her sexy new friend.

"Buck up," Natek shot back. "It's all for the best."

Verbolana did her best to smile at the stupid, ridiculous, arrogant, diminishing platitude. *"It's all for the best." Where does such nonsense come from?* Her mind endlessly chewed on her thoughts as she looked around. Obviously, Adrette, their honoree, had spent her last time at the university. Verbolana couldn't see a speck of hair in the whole crowd, or an eye for that matter, with everyone hiding behind darkened eyewear. She remembered the fuss her tattoo had caused when she had first revealed her scalp; the endless explanations and steadfast refusal to remove what everyone around her considered gauche and unseemly. But then some, like Natek, had seen it as rebellious, and that had done the trick.

Somebody from one of the booths jumped up on a table. "A toast!" he yelled at the top of his voice. "Life is eternal to those who continue to learn. Contrary to the clock counting down on the wall," he added.

"Here, here!" somebody yelled. "Here, to Adrette!" another voice joined.

The entire room burst forth in choirs of hail greetings and traditional song. Fortunately, Natek had briefed Verbolana. The rowdy songs counted the clock down to twenty minutes.

A few people hoisted Adrette onto the table of the alcove as everyone crowded around. Verbolana stood and wished to God she were three inches taller so she could see past the men who crammed in front of her. God obliged. Adrette started an address

Verbolana knew she had been working on for at least since Verbolana had known her.

"I have been to a thousand of these parties, and they all go pretty much the same way. We've heard the speeches of how great I am, and I thank all of you for those. We've had the toasts to life eternal and to the suckiness of God's plan, or lack thereof. I have tried to come up with something different that would leave you with a lasting impression of who I am, but I have not succeeded in this. For I know that three-hundred and eleven years is too long to remember anything, yet God insists we do so. Three-hundred and eleven years is too long to believe in anything, yet God insists we do that also. And three-hundred and eleven years is too long to believe it will ever end; yet here we are." She turned to look at the clock. "Nineteen minutes left. I prepared a speech that could fill that time and if I thought it would help, I could talk for another fifteen years. But God will have his due. So I will stop now, leaving you with no great words, no touching poems or philosophical fables. My only hope is that I have touched lives in a positive and comforting way; that I have learned all I can learn and felt all I can feel. And, as you have no doubt seen at a hundred such occasions, I will now revert to my given form in the hopes that you can all love me, at least for this moment, as I once was and still truly am."

With that, the Adrette Verbolana had only recently come to know transformed from a perky imp-faced peer into a frumpy, rather large woman with thinning silver hair, wrinkled sallow skin and pendulous untethered breasts. Feeling somewhat ashamed, Verbolana's first concern was to wonder whether the table would hold the new weight. But she shook herself free of the thought and crowded forward for a chance to give her newest friend a hug and kiss. She never got the chance. Those who had known Adrette longer monopolized her time as the last minutes flew. Before Verbolana could wangle her way to the front of the crowd, Adrette had vanished, simply evaporated while a statuesque man who appeared to be no more than thirty gave her a tearful hug.

Shock and muffled grief clutched every heart, or so Verbolana imagined. She admitted, though, that she really had no idea what the others felt. They had been through this how many times? A hundred? A thousand? People here disappeared. No matter where they were or what they were doing. The fact that they knew it was coming and they knew exactly when; maybe mattered a bit. The fact that they lived a life longer than any human on a natural world maybe just made it all the harder.

All Verbolana knew was that she felt awful. Empty, hollow and lost. She wanted more green stuff. She wanted to go back to her realm, return to her little beach and crawl into Tarja's arms. She wanted to fill her brain with Za webs and suckle at Tarja's breast until her time here was up. And she wanted none of that at the same time. She wanted to scream and fight and rave. She wanted to dance to exhaustion and fuck into oblivion. She wanted someone to hold her, so she searched for Natek. It seemed only a minute ago she had been sitting across the table. Then the table had disappeared, along with the chairs, to give everyone easier access to the honoree, and Verbolana had lost track.

From the corner of her eye, she caught a hand waving near the exit. Natek already had her back turned by the time Verbolana focused, with her arm around someone's broad shoulder.

"Looks like she ditched you," a male voice observed. "Was kinda hoping that would happen. Natek's a little flighty for my tastes."

Verbolana had seen him around. Tall, handsome, bald, just like everyone else. Eyes hidden. Maybe her class in Vutrean world sculpting or centurial philosophies.

"You've been watching?" Verbolana asked, a little suspicious.

"Pretty girl, the tattoo, yeah, I been watching. Want another drink?" His voice was smooth, practiced. She pictured Adrette changing and realized this cherub-faced, sweet kid by the name of Darown might be two-hundred and eighty years old. Though she doubted it. His were the only eyes in the room with tears in them. The sight welled her heart, and without warning, she burrowed into his broad chest. He immediately engulfed her. They stood, pulled tight, until the room emptied.

"Been through this before?" Verbolana groped.

"Some," he answered without commitment.

"It's my first," Verbolana admitted.

"Really?" Darown looked down at her tear-stained face. "It doesn't get any easier if you let yourself care. And if you don't care, what's the point? Of course *I* don't have a choice, 'cause I care, whether I want to or not."

They moved toward the door, arms still clinging. Decision time, she knew. But there was really no decision.

He asked, "Do you want to come over to my place? Or go somewhere?" He shifted slightly to his far foot, maybe preparing to bolt.

"I don't want to be alone," Verbolana responded truthfully.

"Not a rousing endorsement, but you gotta know … If you come home with me and we get into bed, I'll care."

"And that's a bad thing?" she asked.

"Depends."

Verbolana sensed a melancholy deeper than current events could explain. Something more permanent. "I would like to know a man who cares," she responded despite her trepidations.

262

# Chapter 29

*H*ow could I have been so stupid? Trake lamented as he spun in a tight circle and released his leg, and sent the heel of his foot crashing into the padded trunk of the Wata tree he used for practice. *Finally, I had everything I desired, and I ruined it.* He pulled his foot back, planted it in the squishy ground and continued his spin. *Now I walk on twigs and branches in my own home, afraid to rouse the ire of a woman all I want to do is love.* He smashed a perfectly arched back fist into the tree, pivoted his hips further, and then came around with an eye-level roundhouse. Simulating a head grab, he brought his two hands down to meet his rising knee. "Die!" he yelled aloud at the moment of imagined impact and then stepped back into a defensive stance.

"The shout is designed to focus your intentions and strength into the point of attack. It can be used during any of these strikes. However, I prefer to save it for the death blow."

The line of students nodded their understanding and smiled through chattering teeth. "Alright, Grevtan, stand and approach. Remember the things you cannot control. The ground is slick, the roots make the footing uneven and the rain will blur your eyes. Also, keep in mind that each strike must be successful before you attempt the next. It is never advisable to get too close to an opponent if he is not already injured."

But Grevtan was his star pupil. Tall and lanky, the whipping movements came naturally to him. For now Trake concentrated on standing fighting with him, knowing that ground fighting would be his real challenge. The boy, maybe fifteen, with piercing green eyes and flawless brown skin, executed the moves with only minor corrections needed.

Slowly, Trake worked through the rest of the boys, as dialogue went round and round in his head. *Surely you understand how difficult this is for me. What you ask of me goes against everything I believe. You are the most important things in the world to me, and I do not wish to upset you. I love you. Yes, Vipeon are evil, and this one, when it attacked the village, deserved to die. And yes, I see how your people care for the land. Thinning the forest seems to help and I see where thinning a herd might do the same. And I see that your people, my people now, are not mindless procreators as I was taught. However, you are not all right. The Chosen have a place in the truth. They bring discipline and single-minded purpose. Why would the Gods have given us the Strength if we were not worthy?* Trake's imagined discussion stopped there, but his mind continued. Was this all the Chosen had to offer? They came from the sky, murdered thousands and flew back to their towers. Discipline and single-minded purpose; was that it? And the Strength?

Giggles erupted from the boys around him. He focused on his troupe. A line of young girls passed their makeshift training grounds, apparently on their way to the river. Trake watched and shuddered. Such easy, natural communication. Tears welled behind his eyes as his rage erupted, devouring, filling, replacing. Verbolana's eyes reached him across the mired deck, knocked him back a foot or two and fluttered away, leaving his heart pumping and pained. Glued to her face, he watched as her Blessed mask softened, her gaze now on a child in her lap, safe. Trake knew, as he knew nothing else, that the softening was for him. He drank it like a tonic, his eyes now elsewhere, lest they catch him.

Trake's rage could not compete with the soft eyes that seared his memory. However, it wasn't just the eyes. The neck, the line of her jaw, her lips and ears and delicate hidden shoulders that held such strength. And further down, the swelling of her feminine form, her breasts and hips stirred him even now in memory. *It is not right; it never was right. It is not just me. I see it in these boys. Gods, what have you done?* Trake shrunk as other memories surfaced. He had always wondered what was wrong. Painfully, he sorted through the images that crowded his brain. The hollow eyes of his Blessed companions. Were their smiles forced? Were the moans of passion learned? Acid erupted in his gut as he pulled himself away from the visions. The girls were off to the creek. The boys around him looked up for their next instruction. Trake staggered at their gaze, stepped back, rocking as if from one blow after another.

He turned and ran, with bile choking his breath, fear stuttering each step, until he arrived at his hut. Throwing open the flap, he dumped himself on the floor, startling Atasha so that she clutched Atlana from her little bed and bolted to the farthest corner. Trake lay prone in the dirt, willing the vomit down and his heart to still. *Safe.* This was his place of safety. He belonged to this place. The Gods would not take this place away from him; he would not allow it. They had taken so much already; taken everything. With strength of will, he came to his hands and knees. He crawled across the floor, conscious of his wife's eyes following him. Around the fire pit he crawled, to the thin planks in the corner that held their plates, utensils and stored food. From the shelf he grabbed a long dark rope of dried Drak meat. His teeth tore into the stringy mass as he chewed with all his might, letting the rough texture scour the collected bile from his mouth.

\* \* \*

"When he said he would 'care,' I really had no idea what he meant," Verbolana confided to Natek after not seeing her in more than a month. "I guess what he meant was that he would attach himself to every movement I made. Problem was, he was so nice. I really liked a lot of things about him."

Natek crinkled her freckled nose to the sun, her eyes hidden behind purple bangs and the omnipresent tinted glasses. Verbolana wasn't even sure whether she were listening or counting birds or what she was doing.

"He probably thought you'd know. It's kind of a buzz word, code for being overly protective," Natek finally answered. "Are those birds always in the same place? Seems as though somebody could have done a better job in designing that."

"What do I need protection from?" Verbolana asked, trying to keep her on track.

"Vee … you don't mind if I call you Vee, do you? He wasn't trying to protect you; he was trying to protect himself." Natek gave an embarrassed giggle to the birds. Finally she looked back at Verbolana and removed her shades. "Love is hard up here, as you are finding out; too many temptations, too many years. If you love, you're going to get hurt. If you don't, life can be pretty hollow."

"Yeah, that's pretty much what he said, but why can't I love lots of people? I've got room in my heart for lots of friends."

"Oh, I'm sure you've got plenty of room, and you can and will love lots of people. But people worry about losing something that makes them feel so good. Everyone tries to protect what they've got. Seems to be in our nature, no matter how much we've got. Sharing actually seems to be even harder here, at least for some people."

"Are you trying to tell me that you're good at sharing?" Verbolana asked, searching her friend's vulnerable face.

"I try," Natek responded. "I doubt that you are good at it, though, really. You just haven't found anyone worth protecting yet."

"Why do you say that?" Verbolana scooted around on the bench so she could confront Natek better.

"You haven't been here long enough. You haven't been through all the heartache," Natek stated with finality.

"I don't think you know what I'm capable of!" Verbolana shot back, angered.

"Maybe; time will tell. Doesn't really matter to me."

"Even if we get together?" Verbolana dared.

"It's still just your problem. I won't get hurt." Natek shrugged. "Do you want to fuck?"

"Yeah, kinda." Verbolana's heart pumped faster. She thought this girl was very cute and had been working up to this moment for weeks before being sidetracked by Darown.

"Okay. Then let's do something tonight. You ready for a challenge?"

"Uh, yeah, I guess. What do you have in mind?" Verbolana was suddenly afraid she had stepped into the center ring with only one rope dangling.

"You'll see. Meet me at the student union at about twenty-six hours and we'll go from there." A small smile spread across Natek's lovely face. "I'll give you a clue, just to build anticipation. We're going to the Palladium ... below."

"Below," Verbolana started. "Are you sure?"

"Sure as hell." Natek turned on her heel and walked off. Verbolana stood in shock, watching Natek's lithe shape and bare midriff, wondering if the pursuit was worth the prize.

At twenty-six hours, Verbolana sat alone at a table in the center of the crowded student union, giggling at the antics of the boys she watched. For the last hour, they had been plucking galaxies from the night-sky display that rotated overhead and tossing them back and forth to each other. And they were getting pretty good at it. They had figured out how to pick the center-weighted ones and toss them underhand with a flick of the wrist. They were now sailing them all the way across the quad in huge banking arcs that just skimmed some of the lower stars in the display before floating back down. It was also funny to watch the discarded galaxies, for, if left alone for any length of time, they floated back to retake their original positions.

Definitely better than waiting in an empty realm, Verbolana concluded, though she wondered when Natek would show up. They were going "below," as many called it, so she had dressed in her latest clubbing outfit, barely legal for the university grounds. *Skin, skin, skin,* she lamented. It seemed to be the universal and timeless attraction, even here in Heaven. Verbolana had adapted, and now sat in what felt like mere patches of iridescent gauze covering only the barest of essentials. Everyone said, "Why not? You have perfect skin," and of course she thanked them and countered that they did, too. To a one they said, "Ah, but yours is perfectly flawed. Either your designer was the master of masters, or you are still natural. Either way, you are perfection beyond perfection." So she sat, overdressed to the limit, having lingered since twenty-three hours, having to explain herself to a number of passing friends. She had shared her plans for the evening with the first few, but after a few nervously showed their disgust or horror or whatever it was, she decided not to mention it again.

Finally, at twenty-six forty, Verbolana spotted Natek sauntering toward her with three strangers in tow. "Wow!" was all that came to mind. In a world of excess and designed perfection, it was hard to turn heads, but these four managed. Verbolana stood and moved away from the table with instant interest, waiting for the introductions. Hungry for companionship and acceptance, she melted into Natek's embrace and lingered at her neck, stealing a moment of comfort. The frontal bump, slide and breath to neck were the latest greeting ritual with the university set. Moments normally reserved for private darkness were public and bright here, so Verbolana had adapted yet again. Natek introduced Tru, a strikingly exotic girl with Za-white nested hair and deep umber skin, and Dron and Tels, two boys with rippled, shirtless chests and skin-tight, bulging pants. Verbolana, now "Vee" again, felt cold appraisals flowing though the new group. Dron seemed friendly, Verbolana concluded, but both Tels and Tru seemed withdrawn and labored with the niceties, which added to Verbolana's anxiety.

Without further loitering, Natek announced that time was suddenly important and they must hurry. As they walked, Vee sidled up to Natek and whispered, "Am I dressed all right? I didn't know what to wear."

Natek laughed, "Ah, the universal question. Well, let me assure you, it won't matter one little bit, since you're going to lose it all anyway."

"Really?" Vee responded.

"Shocked?" Natek inquired with no apparent interest in her answer.

"Not at all," Verbolana shot back, trying to raise Natek's opinion of her just a little. "I spent my first year here wearing nothing more than a string around my waist with a little patch of cloth attached."

"And a head full of green stuff. Yeah, you told me. Well, where we're going, that little patch will definitely get in the way." They had arrived at the subway and Natek ordered up a large car for all of them to fit. As soon as it morphed, Natek and one of the boys jumped in the front, and left Vee to pile in the back with Tru and Dron.

"Been to the Palladium before? Natek says you're new." It was Dron trying to make nice.

"I've been to the Palladium many times, but never below. The rest of my friends think I'm crazy," Vee answered truthfully. She didn't see where she had anything to lose since she didn't care what these other three thought.

"Could be," he shrugged.

"Could be, my ass!" Tru broke in. "There's nothing crazy about going below. Nothing but a bunch of prudes running around this world. Pleasure is what counts. What else is there?"

"I enjoy lots of things." Vee tried to match the girl's intensity, but didn't know if she believed her own words. "I went to the zero-grav raceway the other day and drove what they call a winged thrasher. That was exciting." When her words fell flat, she realized this group had probably done everything Vee had done, only a hundred times to her one.

"I have a feeling you're going to *be* a winged thrasher before this night is through," came the comment from the boy in the front seat.

"Vee, don't be so nervous," Natek threw over her shoulder between sucks on Tels's painted nipple. "It's all about breaking down barriers and letting Eros flow. Comfort and pleasure aren't always compatible. Sometimes you just gotta jump in with both feet and go for the ride. Tonight is that night. You can't get hurt, remember? But you can't go back either."

"And that's supposed to help me get over my nervousness?"

"It's more to convince you that you don't have much of a choice. You don't seem very happy, so you might as well shake things up."

"I'm getting happier." Vee resented criticism of something she was working on so hard.

"Whatever you say," and Natek slid over to work on Tels's other nipple. "You can get out any time," she slurped.

"Who said anything about getting out?" Verbolana whined. "What's wrong with being a little nervous when you're trying something new? Isn't that part of the thrill?"

"Yeah, I guess we're just jealous." Sarcasm dripped from Tru's voice.

"Fuck me!" Vee had had enough of this girl's attitude.

"I plan to," Tru whispered back to her ear. "But only after you have fucked *me* raw."

Sandwiched as she was, Vee had nowhere to look to hide her dismay. The subway sights had long since lost their appeal. She laid her head back, closed her eyes and awaited the approach, as everyone called it.

After long minutes, Verbolana felt the car slow. She opened her eyes as the last neighborhood slid by. The car climbed from the tunnel and before them appeared a moonlit panorama of the East Mountains, sharp and snowcapped, slicing the heavens so their peaks could live among the stars. Gigantic, thrusting, evergreen trees framed the mountain vista on three sides and, as the car proceeded, slowly stole the mountains from sight. Trees loomed all around now, so thick and dark they seemed to block the car's path. Close to each side, eyes appeared in the darkness, soft and frightened, disappearing with a flutter of wings or a rustling of brush. Tunnels, just large enough for the car to pass through, appeared in tree after tree until the car emerged from the forest and the mountains presented themselves again.

Tru leaned across Vee, apparently ignoring her existence, and commented to Dron, "I can't believe we have to go through this every time. They should build a bypass or something."

"What always amazes me is that there is no track up here, and there's one down in the subway," Dron returned. "Why in hell can't people see how silly that is? Obviously, God doesn't need track to work the subway, so why is it there?"

No one bothered to respond. They had all heard his complaint before.

"I love the approach," Vee admitted, countering Tru's pessimism. "I never tire of the trees or the views of the Wilds, and the underwater gardens are magnificent."

"Augh, the Wilds," Dron groaned. "If God didn't want us to see the rest of his precious planet, why did he give us this little teaser?"

"I couldn't care less," shot Tels from the front seat. "Who would want to go out there anyway, naked against a savage world?"

"How does that work, anyway?" Vee elicited groans from the rest of the car with her question.

Natek took pity and answered, "If you go outside the city, you're on your own. God doesn't allow any of his gifts outside the city, not even clothes or enhancements. If I went out, I would die within moments of old age. Doesn't sound like much fun to me," she concluded.

"It's like spitting in the face of the Old Man, the way I see it. And if it wasn't for the Old Man, I'd be dust." A surprising comment from the cynical Tru.

"Doesn't anybody wonder about what he doesn't want us to see?" Vee continued her questioning.

"Nobody in this car—except you maybe," Tru said, more to form.

Beside them now flowed a wide, turbulent river. Verbolana wondered what fairy tale the designers had taken this landscape from, with its moonlit rapids and graceful tree-lined bends. As the car lifted up into the sky, the scene took on new magnificence. In the distance, dwarfed by the rising mountains, sat the moon-drenched Palladium, sparkling from its million cut-glass windows and gold-shingled roof. Only the trees surrounding this pleasure palace gave it true perspective. What just moments ago had seemed towering and impossibly large now appeared as but mere blades of grass at the feet of a mighty prairie bull. God wanted his children to have fun. With this view, it was the only conclusion possible.

With a sudden rush of downward speed, the view was lost and Verbolana's focus changed. Rushing toward her lay a deep bend in the river. With crashing force, the car slammed into the river with … a miraculous lack of impact. A protective bubble formed as they slipped below the surface.

The moonlit bubbles from their entry engulfed and rose as if they had plunged into an ocean of sparkling wine. Ominous pounding music erupted as the car dove into total darkness. Only the slight motion of the car gave them any reference. They felt the car turn, and ahead, hanging, the balletic grace of a thousand jellyfish greeted their arrival to the first display. Each hanging mass of colored luminescence pulsated to the beat, which had evolved into orchestrated flight. The car floated to a near stop, seeming to hang like one of the fish around them.

"Let's move it. This drives me fucking crazy!" Tru blurted, breaking Vee's spell.

"You know the drill," Natek moaned from the front. "Gotta pay your dues to the arts."

"Is Tels paying his dues now?" Tru asked, not giving the slightest attention to the splendor around her. She leaned forward and spied over the front seat. "Lick that thing, Tels!" she routed. Then looking back at Vee and Dron, "Now, *that* would make this slowpoke trip worthwhile." She sat back, spread her perfect, smooth legs and yanked at her short skirt. "Any takers?" she tempted, running her fingers deep into her exposed hairless sex.

"The jellyfish stings less," Vee proclaimed with a little giggle.

Dron, however, seemed to enjoy Tru's antics, for after a little rustling he pulled his growing appreciation from his pants, matched Tru's strokes with his.

So surrounded, Vee threw her head back and concentrated on the retreating jellyfish.

"What did you bring her for?" Tru complained to Natek. "She's just in the way."

Natek responded as if Vee were not there, "She'll loosen up; I'll make sure of it."

Vee closed her eyes. She imagined the jellyfish behind her, pulsating to the beat of her anger, their stingers dangling with her exposed humiliation. *Bitches, nasty jaded bitches. Why did I agree to come along?* She searched for an answer, but only found anger and loneliness. *Does everyone become mean over the years?* She looked back and only saw Paul as different. And she had vomited all over him, left him standing. *In a hundred years, will I look back on these memories and cringe at my naiveté? Buck up and stand proud!* she commanded herself. *You have nothing to apologize for, not to these people anyway. Let them wallow in their boredom and pity.* With that, Verbolana made up her mind. In solitary fascination, she watched the accumulated displays of a hundred worlds and tens of thousands of years pass by while all around her groans of self-pleasuring reminded her of the intrinsic loneliness that seemed inevitable for all humans.

Eventually the magical displays ended and the car rose dripping from the river. The protective bubble evaporated as they climbed high into green forest.

"Some say this forest covers half the continent to the east and north," Dron commented to the group. "That blows my mind. I was quite an outdoorsman before I got here, and I gotta say, this view calls me a bit."

"How would anyone know anything about this forest?" Tru spat. "No one in their right mind would go out into that."

"I don't know about being in their right mind, but people do go out there. And they come back. I've even heard of people being born out there. Don't you read the papers?" Dron countered.

274

"And you believe everything you read?" Natek's head popped up from behind the front seat.

Vee wondered aloud, "If this car were to fall, would God save us?" After a moment's pause, she continued the thought. "We're floating above what, for all of you, would be certain death. Kinda gives you pause, doesn't it?" Casually, she jumped around in her seat, and the car jolted violently. Alarmed explosions came from each rider. Despite herself, Verbolana grinned. Suddenly she jumped into Tru's lap and pushed her with her hips. "Scoot over, I want to sit on this side." The car dipped deeply, eliciting another round of groans. "All that would happen to me is I would lose my clothes and have to walk home." She hopped onto her knees, faced backward and peered over the side. "Hey, look at that big fucking animal! Wonder if it's a meat eater." Verbolana pointed to the savanna spread out below them. "Oh, crap, check this out!" she squealed. "There's another animal, long and lean, hiding in the grass. Stalking, I'm sure. Oh, yeah, look, watch. Guys, you're missing it!" Verbolana jumped up and down, manic with pent-up aggression and revenge.

Natek grabbed onto the back of her seat. "Verbolana, stop rocking this damn car! We get the point! You win!"

Enjoying the moment, Verbolana ignored her one-time friend and suddenly realized what she was about to witness. "Hey, stupid, look up!" she screamed at the hairy beast. "You got trouble coming!" She frantically waved her arms in an attempt to gain the creature's attention. Unconcerned about her own precarious position, she rocked the car even more, but nothing seemed to work. The beast, intent on its feeding, heard or saw nothing.

Only yards away now, the wily predator readied to pounce. Verbolana, for the first time, realized there were other cars in a line before and after theirs. Voices erupted from across the line, some rooting for the grass eater and some rooting for carnage. The

275

latter won as the graceful, fanged aggressor leaped and sunk its teeth deep into the other creature's neck. Screams of panic and pain bounced against the trees and across the savanna. Blood flew below as groans of disgust or fascination danced between the cars. As if drawn by invisible strings, and Verbolana's diminishing antics, her jaded compatriots peeked over to watch death in all its bloody glory, then popped back into their seats as the car moved them out of sight.

Quiet and brooding, the carload finally pulled into the Palladium station. Verbolana waited her turn to depart, and to her surprise, Dron offered his hand to steady her exit. Something had changed. Somehow, she had become part of the group.

# Chapter 30

Trake sat like a stuffed drazle in his airy hut, its sides raised to let in the first puffs of spring. By midmorning, the breeze blew, sun-warmed and perfumed with a flower Trake could not yet name. Atlana lay on their sleeping pad, her head raised to her father, blown bubbles dribbling down her chin. Beyond her, Atasha lay asleep in the corner, her angelic face half covered by her thick locks, her shirt still half opened from feeding, reminding Trake of the surprisingly sweet milk he sampled whenever he got the chance.

Outside a few boys loitered nearby, hoping for more words of instruction from the Vipeon Slayer. They worked the moves they already knew and argued over who did them best. Trake breathed the energized air deep and drank the sight of his contented family into his soul. Though questions still haunted him from time to time, and he still struggled with putting meaning to his life, things had calmed. Now he longed for things more pedestrian. He longed for companionship and camaraderie. Children and young men accepted him, but only, he insisted, for what he could give them. He saw this was the way with children, all primarily selfish. They were hungry for knowledge and acceptance, but only if it eased their way among each other. They were eager to please, but only if, in the pleasing, there was something in it for them.

No, Trake longed for true male companionship. Both longed for it and feared it. When he was able to filter his thoughts properly, he remembered back to his evenings with Choldt and the other Honored warriors, as they repeated tales of ancient battles or postulated on those to come. As he whiled away evenings in his hut, he often heard the raised laughter of men and pictured them sitting around a banked communal campfire trading stories, as he once had done. The few times he had attempted to join them, troubled silence and lowered eyes were all that greeted him. He understood and accepted that he was an outsider. He could not even imagine how it would have been if the tables were turned. A Wretched would not have lived a minute among the Chosen and Trake now understood why. Lies were fragile things and questions were dangerous. A clenched fist on a lashing whip was essential to the remolding of the soul.

"How can I explain to these men that I have rejected my former life, that I was the one who was deceived, that anger burns in me for the lies that burrow behind my eyes?" he had once asked Atasha.

Trake remembered her stroking his hair, pulling his face to meet hers. "No amount of explaining will convince these men, nor should it. Only I have witnessed your struggle, and only I will understand. Your weakness is strength to me, your woman, but it would be seen as weakness to the men. They would snicker behind your back if they saw your tears, and yet they fear and shy from your Strength. Men do not trust change in this way, because in order to change one must first admit having been wrong. And for a man to admit he was wrong brings into question the things he must do to survive and protect his family. You have changed, but only because you were forced to do so. Even I know this, and even I question your sincerity. The fact that you changed once means you could change again. Self-preservation flies in the face of sacrifice for the greater good. You came to your new beliefs through selfishness, and selflessness is not what is needed to ensure our survival."

"Are you trying to tell me that standing before the Vipeon was a selfish act? That creature was nowhere near me or my family. I could have stood back and let it eat its fill, and then watched it slither back to wherever it came from."

"Why then did you fight it?" Atasha asked, her head bowed to avoid his eyes.

"Because I could," he stammered after a few moments' thought. "Apparently, I was the only one who could. You told me none of your people had ever killed one. I could not allow such a creature free rein to plunder our village." It was only a half-truth, he realized, but he was not going to allow his wife to whittle his bravery into a mere statue of himself.

But Atasha was more perceptive than he gave her credit for. Without effort, she finished this thought. "Thinking that, on this trip or the next, the Vipeon would find his way to your child or your wife." She paused for a moment before continuing. "I am not saying you were wrong or that I do not appreciate your valor and protection. I am simply suggesting that under different circumstances your reaction would be different. You were not raised to sacrifice all for the whole and therefore you will always be an outsider to these men."

"Are you telling me that these men who judge me are not the same as I am? That is absurd. Every man, when entering into battle, weighs the risks and the benefits. Even if the benefit is some abstraction like the greater glory of his Gods or the survival of his clan, there is some benefit to him if he survives. And every man longs to survive."

"Your lack of understanding is exactly my point. You will never see beyond yourself. My people do." Atasha looked up at him with a sad smile.

"As surely as I have seen through the myths of my people, I see through this myth as well," Trake insisted. "You cannot tell me you can see into the heart of a man. You have been told these lies by someone you trust and everyone you know has repeated the lies, no doubt. But these concepts are not true. They are romantic and noble, but they are also just as self-serving as the lies the Directors told to me. In some way, this gives me great peace, to hear you spout such nonsense. It tells me I am not the only one who can be so deceived. I know you will not believe me, for you cannot see into the hearts of those around you. And they, surely, will not open enough to let you in, for that would be an unforgivable blasphemy. So I will have to sit in my own selfish pond and splash the Truth across my head so it soaks slowly into my heart."

They both sat in stunned silence, Trake with a smile; Atasha with a worried frown; both incredulous that the other could be so wrong and wishing they could somehow bridge their differences. Finally, with the strength of victory, Trake stood, crossed the room and brought Atasha to him in a gentle, knowing hug. He felt her melt to him and knew that, for her own reasons, she would press this issue no further; and for his own reasons he would do the same. He did hope, however, that over time she would think about this conversation and realize he was right. Would that be too much to ask, to share the vulnerability of deception?

And he had been right; the conversation never came up again. Though Trake knew he was right in his assessment, this knowledge brought him no closer to breaking into the male allegiance that surrounded him.

While still in his lazy remembrance, the boys playing outside caught his attention by their altered movements. Suddenly silent, they peered through the overhanging branches to the blue-gray cloudless sky. Trake heard birds twittering and noticed Atasha rustling. Something was wrong. The twittering birds were Nightgrot, not up at this time of day. He snatched Atlana from her pad and slunk to Atasha's side.

"Your people approach overhead. Stay still! They search for movement," she whispered, just waking.

Trake knew well what the Fiendish searched for. He imagined Choldt in the wheelhouse surveying the ground below, breathing orders as they ran silent.

"It must be a ship from my tower. How often do they fly over?" Trake asked as he moved toward the edge of the hut to get a look.

"Quiet and get down!" Atasha hissed.

"They cannot hear us while they travel," Trake said. "The wind of passage whistles too loudly for them to hear voices, or anything short of a felled tree, for that matter. But you're right about movement." Through the trees, he caught a heart-freezing glimpse of a single blimp floating low and fast across the sky. "And if they were a little lower, or more directly overhead, I can't imagine they couldn't see the netting or a hut or two." His mind clamped on the sight of raining arrows and swinging Honored as they erupted from the belly of a dozen hovering blimps. Aloud he thought, "This would be a difficult place to attack without landing a large force. There's no room to swing, and the tree branches would deflect many of the arrows. They would probably stand off and pummel us with cannon fire. But even at that, with the shrapnel they use, most of it would not get through the branches either."

"What would stop them from landing and marching on us?" Atasha asked, undoubtedly with her own visions running through her head.

"Setting foot on Father is strictly forbidden, though I don't know what the Generals or Directors would think if they knew such a large settlement existed here. I suspect the rules could change rather quickly if they saw the need." Horror burst before Trake's eyes. Choldt approached in full Strength, blood dripping from his blade, eyes locking on his old friend. Trake realized, in that moment, how Wretched he had become. There was no discussion of the wrongs in the world, the deceptions and lies told on both sides. There was only swinging steel and flowing blood, and endings. Empty revolting endings, whichever the outcome.

Trake moved slowly away from the sight to stand between his family and the floating juggernaut. "We must prepare."

"We are as prepared as ever," Atasha mumbled.

"The Vipeon Slayer has not even begun."

* * *

Verbolana awoke snuggled into a warm body her perfect memory informed her was not Natek. In panic, she asked God to let her fall back asleep.

Sometime later, she awoke alone in a big cool bed, covers thrown and pulled as if from a great wind. She uncrumpled a corner and covered her nakedness. However, Tru had apparently heard her rumblings and came to investigate.

She started in immediately. "Natek told me you had been raised around women, so I was amazed how well you wielded a cock." When she got no response, she continued. "You're not embarrassed are you? How could you be? I've never seen a first-timer take to it so well. Usually we have to work on a newcomer a bit before we start the initiation, but you were gung-ho."

"I think it was the drugs," Vee offered.

"Don't give me that. We all take the drugs," Tru teased. "You were a natural. Maybe that's it. Starved? You are naturally a cock lover and you've been starved up till now. The look on your face

... you could *not* have faked that. When you had all five cocks ... I was watching. You were in Heaven."

In an attempt to change the subject, Vee asked, "Does it really work?" She arranged the sheets, drawing out the question, hoping to divert. "Asking God to make it feel like the first time?"

"Sure it works. Kinda. I mean, you still remember you've done it before, so you know what to do, and everything isn't so alien. But yeah, the thrill of the first time is still there. I like it better, actually. See, I don't like all the anxious energy of not knowing, but I love the thrill."

Verbolana concluded this was a different girl than she had first met on campus, and she was intrigued as to what had happened. Plus, she wanted to keep the focus away from herself. "Seems like you had a good time."

"I love being naked with my friends. I can't even comprehend those who don't. I mean, why not? The tingle of hands on my skin, the electric shock of lips on my nipples or lips or butt hole. The filling warmth of velvet steel plunging into me. I mean, how can it get any better?" She fell down on the bed, cradling her head onto Vee's shoulder. "I get a little cranky when I don't have it."

"Why don't you just stay there, then?" Vee wondered aloud.

"I don't have the money. And I need new people. I need the rush of seeing your face. And later, someone else's face," she stated as if everyone had the same need.

"What is that thing with money?" Vee asked, surprised the subject had come up.

"I don't know," Tru stated flatly. When Vee craned her neck to give her friend a questioning glare, Tru continued, "I really don't. Why should anything cost money or points or whatever they want to call it? This is Heaven, but the same things still fascinate people. I met a guy once who tried to explain it, said it had something to do with giving people purpose, but when I put his cock in my mouth, all discussion seemed to end. He really couldn't come up with a justification after that." She lay for a minute, apparently lost in a memory. "That's why I hang out at the university. Everything is free there and most people don't worry about money."

"So what happened last night?" Vee wanted to know. "Did that cost money? I've been to the Palladium a bunch of times and never paid anything. I was never even asked."

"Yeah, everything there costs money. One of the guys paid. He's a big shot in something or other. I think he might even be in government."

"A Director?" Vee shrieked at the thought of the only government she knew.

"I don't know what they call themselves," Tru mumbled, bored. "Guys who negotiate the weather and gravity and stuff. And the rules for the public areas. Never really paid much attention." She turned her head and licked Vee's exposed nipple. When it stiffened, she gave it another lick and ran her hand down Vee's side.

"Stop it!" Vee exclaimed, trying to concentrate. When Tru flinched in response, Verbolana softened her tone. "We were talking about money; and I still don't understand."

She was too late. Tru had launched herself out of bed and was padding out of the room. "Let yourself out," she muttered.

# Chapter 31

It surprised Trake to realize all he lacked was courage and determination. He was the Vipeon Slayer, courageous and determined. However, he needed a different courage for the mission he now undertook.

Head high, stride strong, armed with every weapon he owned, Trake walked straight into the center of the evening circle. In the firelight, he watched his new allies bristle and posture as they glanced around to see who would take on this new threat.

Trake gave them no time to organize. "You are woefully ill prepared," he started. "The battle blimps will one day find you, huddled here below your nets. They will find a way to destroy you." His Strength-filled voice pierced through the night air and galvanized even the strongest in the circle. "I am not your friend and I see now that I never will be. I have wasted too much time in the hopes that someday I would be. Let there be no doubt, however, that I am your ally. I live with a woman of your clan and my child is half yours. I am Fiendish; yes. In your eyes I always will be. So think of me as Fiendish, if it makes you comfortable. I am Fiendish, so I am selfish and undeserving of your trust. I am also your only hope for the survival of your clan!" Trake pulled his sword from its scabbard, and then reached down for his dagger in the sheath on his calf. "Come at me, two, five, ten. I do not care. Stand back and shoot at me with your bows. How many of you will die before I die? I will wade through you like a shallow creek and bathe in your blood!"

Ten or twelve among the sixty who sat around stood in anger and drew weapons. Many shouted, but one voice rose above the others. "As a true Fiendish, you are ready to kill for no reason and we are ready to die for those around us. Take my life first. I will chink your armor so the next or the next can defeat you!" The man, large and menacing, stepped through the crowd to stand before Trake. "You are right. You are an outsider, and we do not trust you. Go back to your jungle cave and take your woman and half-breed daughter. We have no need for you here!"

"That is where you are wrong!" Trake challenged. "You need me and every Honored warrior you have shunned."

Three other men, weapons drawn, made their way to stand in the clearing before the fire. "I say remove yourself or you will surely die," another threatened.

"I would happily withdraw," Trake responded calmly. "Or I would happily die or kill each of you, if I thought it would protect my woman and my child. But none of that would help." He came to guard before the three. "My lot has been thrown with yours, like it or not. And I will not sit idle while my family is in danger. Soon even your children will be more prepared than you are."

"Enough!" the man cried as he approached with a vicious two-handed swipe.

Trake stepped back without missing a word and let the blow arc to the ground before him. "Your children drink new knowledge like the earth below the first winter rains. But I cannot wait for them to grow enough to help me defend you." Another strike sliced the air behind him. At the last moment Trake raised his sword to meet the new threat, spun and redirected the blow down and away. "It is only a matter of time before the Fiendish find us. As much as you wish to think it, I am no longer one of them. They will cut me down first when they get the chance." Another blow. This time he countered with a feint, a step and a flick of his dagger. "I am not the most skilled of my people." Two came at him from opposing sides. Trake stopped talking to focus. With Strength, he stepped into the arc of one sword, locked the man's arm, and using the momentum, pulled the man's body around him. The second assailant jabbed air until he made contact with Trake's new shield, the first man's side. The crude sword tore a ragged hole in the man's shirt and a small gash in his side.

"Enough!" Trake commanded. "I need you men. And I do not need you to die here tonight. If these are the bravest among you," he proclaimed to the crowd, "then you are my new sergeants." He hoped this announcement would give each man a graceful exit, and he bowed in apology to each. "Training will start tomorrow at first light, here," he said and walked out of the firelight.

* * *

Verbolana, face raised to the sun, sat on her favorite green university bench and soaked in the tranquility. As always, fifty-nine birds chirped and squabbled in the branches above. The temperature was a perfect sixty-nine point seven degrees. Smiling, unblemished faces bobbed on top of perfect bodies, carting books as badges representing who and what they were. With fifteen minutes before her weaving class, she closed her mind to the bliss and reviewed her most challenging assignment. The class was simply called "Self-101."

*It sounds repulsive, but I can see the benefit, I guess. But the Deck Director, the one who whipped us when we were children, why did I have to pick him for this assignment? He was nothing more than a brute.* She dropped her head to her hands and sat drooped. *I must carve from this life a place of comfort. I must decide what I believe and*

287

*who I want to be and make it so. And if this is one of the ways, then I must do it.*

She sat with her back straight. She did not know whether to cry or laugh. She was taking charge of her life; that was for sure. And it would take time; that was equally obvious. But so far, the journey left a lot to be desired. In fact, it was horrible. Lonely nights and busy days, with friends appearing and vanishing as if only a cloud had ever existed.

Carve deep, they said. Peel and examine, and peel again. Dig out the roots of every thought, every belief; and see what nourishes them. Hollow-eyed, she squinted at the sun. "I don't want to do this anymore," she mumbled to the sky. "I want to go home. They say you can't do that, especially from here, but I want to." Verbolana felt the shadow of a passerby brush her legs and she looked over at the face that had created it. A couple, arms around each other, caught her look and smiled back.

"Just do it." The man's voice could not have been softer, more empathetic. They kept walking without looking back.

Verbolana felt she should have been embarrassed, being overheard like that, but she wasn't. Everyone here struggled. God's curses were universal. Every class discussed it, every song touched it and every eye mirrored it.

*I don't need to step into the mind of that stinking Deck Director right now. I don't need to sit through another class on weaving. I need to go home. I need to touch the deck and smell Milnox and snuggle into the back of a real friend.*

Without warning Verbolana stood and knocked into a young man piled high with books. With mumbled apologies, she gathered her own books and launched toward her realm. Things were never simple, but the biggest hurdle was behind her. She knew what she wanted. Now, as she walked, she had to figure out how best to get it. Should she bring her friends here, or should she go to them? They would be lost here, while she would be lost there. Maybe she could join two Za webs by going back, getting into the head of the Deck Director and reconnecting with her friends. Maybe she could weave a special little world and invite everyone there. Weave her friends a little, to keep them from becoming too confused; that should be doable. Maybe she could invite them to the Encore, give them what they expect.

*That's it*, she thought. *I never enjoyed the Encore when I was there. We all have a clear picture of what it is like. It's a perfect idea!*

Verbolana almost skipped back to her realm in anticipation, her heart so full it caught her breath and exploded warmth up her neck and through her cheeks. As she entered her door, with specific additions, she asked God to build the Encore he had stolen from her dreams that first day in Heaven.

Dappled sunlight played across her head while tiny white and yellow flowers appeared at her bare feet, sending a riot of fragrances deep into her nose, filling her face. She filled her lungs, held her breath and then released, relaxing into a home she had never known. All they had promised was here, she was sure, except the Blessed Amnesia. She wondered why she had waited so long, why she had struggled, rejected and questioned. Everything for contented eternity awaited: Za-spun clouds suspended in the clearest skies of her dreams; carpeted hills stretched to distant unnamed mountains; majestic broad-leafed trees dotted the landscape, adding depth and texture, their branches hanging to breaking with magical fruit, offering every sensation imaginable. The Ponds of Contentment were, no doubt, just over the rise.

Then Wexi approached, beautiful lost Wexi, draped in the same flowing Za cloth that now covered Verbolana, her hair ablaze with sunlight, the stains of a thousand fruit juices coloring not only her robes, but smudged across her lips and cheeks. She smiled and held out her hands in welcome. Verbolana remembered the stories, and, as they embraced and kissed, she slurped her first taste of this sweetest of lives. Tingles of flavor brushed deeply across her tongue. She felt what she now knew as a drug venture lightly through her brain. She relaxed further, drinking deep the kiss and all the sensations it brought. Omnipresent, unacknowledged tension drained from Verbolana's neck and shoulders, from around her eyes and cheeks, her lower back and clenched buttocks. She held tight to Wexi, remembering their last encounter, letting herself fall into this new reality. Wexi was here, safe and happy.

Wexi pulled away, her face clear of the slightest worry, her eyes sparkling, her hands like flutterbugs, holding the promise of magic. "Treena awaits. I'll take you to her. The Ponds of Contentment are too much for her to abandon just yet."

"Yes, that is my Treena," Verbolana confirmed. "Like a purring dawn cat she must be."

Indeed, over the gentle rise lay the Ponds, deep blue and tepid to the toe. Treena floated, suspended in the viscous water, her generous bosom and wide flat hips breaking the surface, creating riot in Verbolana's head.

Without hesitation, Verbolana waded in, tension draining further with every step. Even the desire brought on by the sight of her long-lost friend melted into the magical waters. Treena smiled at her approach, her full, pink lips gaping slightly in invitation, her floating brown hair haloing her clear pink cheeks, undulating with the tiny waves Verbolana brought. Verbolana knelt at her side and laid her head on Treena's shoulder, the knee-deep water buoying them into a relaxed embrace as her clothes dissolved into the water.

"You have missed me?" Was it a question, a statement, a probe? Verbolana was not sure.

"I have missed you," Vee confirmed. "And now, at your side, with Wexi here too, everything is perfect." Her chest heaved while a cleansing sigh escaped her lips. Had she been holding her breath for … forever? It felt like it. Wexi sidled up to her back and the three floated. The sun did not move and neither did they. They did not speak or question or even want. They lay and soaked each other in and smiled and sighed.

Sometime later—an hour, a day, a year—Verbolana stirred. Wexi broke back a fraction as Vee slithered free. "I want to romp," she stated and stood, as if all this were an everyday thing.

Wexi paddled free and stood next to her, magically drying and draping.

Treena looked up confused. "Stay."

"Let's romp across those hills, to the trees. Let's pick from a tree and sample." With a silent prayer from Verbolana, Treena rose, and they raced across pillowed greens, tagging and dodging, tackling and rolling, instinctively learning playful games they had never known as children on the crowded deck of the tower.

So many trees waited, with fruit of every color, size and shape; muted reds, electric greens, even the blues and yellows of a candle's lick. From the stories, they knew each tree held different treats. Some tingled in the mouth; others watered or puckered. But it wasn't just the mouth that benefited. The swallowing, the warming or cooling in the stomach, then the tiny fingers reached out, tickled like a sprinkled breeze or smoothly scraped like sharpened steel. Sensations only dreamed of and prophesized, longed for with the knowledge that something better awaited, something miraculous and divine.

The girls giggled with each touch, laughed and compared, described to each other with words so lacking. Verbolana recognized some of the sensations; the green stuff came to mind, and other things she had experienced since. A skitterbug of disappointment burrowed into the base of her skull. She laughed and dismissed it, contacted loving eyes to dissolve it.

Verbolana watched Treena with her new teacher, Wexi, tasting some peeled flesh, vibrant green with tiny black seeds. "Crush the seeds with your teeth," Wexi coaxed. "Feel that!" She exploded with laughter. "It feels like … like dropping from the ropes and falling to the hands of the Graceful Dancer. I feel it in my head and my heart, and between my legs. Lick me there."

The two dropped to the ground with no further prompting needed. "Which one did you bite?" Vee demanded. "Give me some!" She picked the wet fruit from where it had fallen onto the grass, felt it warm on her tongue and melt its way down her throat, where it burst like liquid sunlight in her stomach. She sat from the load, giggling as the searching fingers of the drug traced through her body. She lay back and watched her friends. Her hands, as if separate, smoothed and plucked her own body. Then, not satisfied, with woven inspiration, other hands replaced her hands. Treena and Wexi vanished. She offered Trake a bite of the fruit that still clung between her lips. He bent to her, flashing teeth from a broad smile, biting with the slightest brush of teeth to lips. This was a Blessed Trake, a different man, soft and knowing in the eyes and lips, but still hard and muscled everywhere else. She realized she had woven this Trake a thousand times in her mind, but never had the courage to bring him forth.

He dipped his face to hers. Leading with his teeth, he bit the flesh of the offered fruit and brushed his lips across hers before pulling back to savor. He chewed, popped each seed with great show, telling the story of each explosion with his eyes.

Now accustomed to, and anticipating, his manly swelling, Verbolana juiced. His perfectly crushing weight burst her ripeness and sent rivulets down her inner thighs, wetting her retightened butt cheeks.

But this Trake knew her anticipation, her need. He read the hunger and wanted it to grow. They kissed again, Trake held back just enough to force Vee's tongue to come looking. They battled; a parry, a thrust, a feint, as Trake's hands traced upwards, smoothed, cupped, brushed, combed. Verbolana felt his cock, full and straining, perched at her gates. She pushed down with her pelvis. When that did not impale her, she reached deep, grabbed his cheeks and pulled him to her.

Trake was too strong. Without the slightest effort, he kept the head of his cock just at her heated lips, with mouth agape, as she struggled to drive him in. Ignoring her, his hands still entangled in her blonde hair, he slid his body roughly down her, scrubbing her flesh and perked nipples with his brilloed chest. His hands snaked from her hair to cup her aching breasts. Teeth and lips attacked her protruding nipples as one hand continued down between her thighs, usurping his cock with skilled fingers. He slid slightly off her, to the side, widened her legs and unwrapped her wanton package.

Though his intentions were true, Verbolana could stand no more. From the back of her eyes to her curled toes, she needed him to fill her, ram her with his hot desire. She needed to receive *his* frantic need. A mumbled prayer brought him back on top of her. With full force, he drove to slick bumping in a single thrust. His grunt and unfocused eyes brought her unparalleled comfort. He withdrew and thrust again, this time locking his eyes on her and smiling in hungered surrender.

Forever, this could last forever.

# Chapter 32

Trake walked through the darkened camp, knowing he had accomplished only the simplest part of his mission—show them a few tricks, appeal to their fears and they would respond. He sent his Strength forward, searching for the distinctive energy signatures of the Honored. He had no idea where to find his next new allies; had no idea if they even gathered in the evenings. He needn't have worried. Within a few steps, he located a group of six of them not far off. He veered through clustered tents and arrived at a communal fire just as things appeared to be breaking up. To a man, they turned with suspicion, a number of hands suddenly resting on the hilts of their weapons.

"Please relax," Trake responded jauntily as he closed on the circle. "I was hoping to have a word with you."

The men exchanged glances, and from their flickering eyes he knew they had not lost the skill of sign and body language. His command voice took over.

"Excellent; I see your skills have not languished. And I am sorry I have not engaged you earlier. I had my reasons; so if you would all be so kind as to take a seat, I will explain." Freeing his hands from his own weapons in a sign of trust, he motioned them to sit back down. No one moved to sit. On the contrary, they fanned out to face him, Strength butting Strength.

"I understand your distrust." Trake dropped his hands down, this time clasping them in front of him, away from his weapons.

He realized for the first time that he had no idea where to go from here. He had no idea of these men's loyalties. Were they still loyal to the Chosen and merely hiding among the enemy? Alternatively, had they converted, out of necessity or conviction, to the ways of the Cheated? All he knew was that his plan did not allow for delayed action. His mission was vital and urgent. He would simply have to overwhelm them with his conviction. Fortunately, he was the Vipeon Slayer.

"How should we proceed?" Trake decided to hand the dangling rope to them. "I need your help and I am here to ask for it. We can fight or kiss; it is up to you."

"You think we don't know who you are? We see you and your Breeder. We hear you are training the children." A small, corded man stepped forward, removing a knitted cap to reveal his freshly shaved skull and long frontal braid. The colors of his tattoo showed him to be of equal rank to Trake.

"I can guarantee you do not know who I am or why I am here." Trake shot back. "The Gods have not abandoned us, and I have not abandoned them." The declaration stirred the other men, but not this one.

"Tell me how this can be so. I may hide my hair from these fools, but I cannot hide my soul from the Gods. Our mission is clear," the man proclaimed. "When the time is right, we will strike from within. Either you are with us, or you will die." Trake felt the man's Strength pushing him back. He countered with his steeled determination and strong footing.

"Hear him out, Gartat," pleaded someone to Trake's left. "He *is* Honored."

"He is not a Breeder, and yet he procreates; he says he is loyal to the Gods, yet he not only teaches Wretched young in the ways of the Honored, but he kills their enemies. You, Vipeon Slayer, have forsaken the Gods. Repent or die!" Gartat drew his sword and advanced with his Strength exploding like a sheet of lightning.

Trake responded with his own lightning, drawing and coming to guard. "This is not the way it must be!" He circled as the rest dropped back to give them battle room. "I have spoken to the Gods. There is a new way." There was no pleading in his voice; no panic or fear. His conviction spoke as his Strength grew. All noticed and Gartat took pause. Trake pounced, his Strength now a weapon of its own. Gartat fell back, stumbling into the rocks that surrounded the fire. Trake saw him stumble and shot his free hand out, grabbed Gartat's flailing arm and pulled him to safety.

Amazed shock obvious on his face, Gartat stammered, "Thank you," and stood, straightened his clothes and sheathed his sword.

Trake stepped back as if a training exercise had just ended; apologized to Gartat in the traditional Honored salute. He continued, taking this new Strength as confirmation from the Gods. "As I say, the Gods have a new way. As Honored, you have been called upon to bring this new way to fruition." Trake made contact with every eye as he spoke and drilled them with this new, directed Strength. No one would deny his words. Even he could no longer deny them. "Honored and Wretched must learn the new way. Both have been right and both have been wrong. There is Truth that lies between the two, and the Gods have charged us to lead the two to the middle. Unfortunately, to accomplish this we must use the tip of the sword and the sting of the arrow."

"Can you tell us this new way?" Another man stood forward, dark and brooding, thick with age and abundant food. "Unlike Gartat, the rest of us have floundered. I, for one, see the disparities. For instance, the Wretched do not poison their arrows as we were told they did. Was this a mistake of our Generals or, dare I say, a lie of the Directors? I cannot determine, though I have wondered."

Trake could tell the man wanted to continue but dared not. "There have been many mistakes. I do not wish to call them lies, for I do not know all the motivations. But one thing is very clear: the Wretched are also the Cheated, and the Chosen are also the Fiendish. We must sit at the same table, sometime soon, and eat from the same pot, all foods being the gifts of Father."

Heads nodded. Trake invited all to sit again and threw his arm around Gartat in true appreciation and honor.

\* \* \*

"Trake cannot stay," Treena insisted. "I don't know how he got here, but if the Magician sees him, and I can't understand how he hasn't seen him already, he will eject all of us."

"Why is an Honored here anyway?" Wexi wanted to know. "How can he be so important?"

Verbolana muttered some words and watched as the two girls' eyes glazed and clicked into a new reality.

"Why is Trake the only Honored here? Don't you find that odd?" Treena looked over her shoulder to make sure he couldn't hear her. He sat a few yards off at the base of a large tree, twirling a yellow blossom between his fingers. "And why is he around us all the time? Doesn't he want to be with his men friends? I have never seen anything like it."

"He seems to be quite attracted to you, Vee," Wexi declared. "That's sick."

Verbolana blew hard to keep her composure and muttered another wish to God. She was ready to start over for the umpteenth time. *I guess I could have used a few more classes in Weaving,* she groused to herself. *There's got to be a way to get these girls to accept Trake without changing them completely.*

"I'm dizzy," Wexi complained. "It feels like I'm forgetting something." She sat down hard on the soft grass and gazed off at the mists as another Blessed arrived on his sled. Or was it a Blessed? Verbolana could no longer keep track of how her weaved Encore might have changed.

"I have to go," she announced without preamble. Before her friends reacted, she offered up a silent prayer and stood in her empty realm. She crumpled to the cold hard deck, spilling her heart and eyes to the floor. Nothing remained inside her, no hope, no longing, no sorrow or regret, just cavernous space without seam or corner.

God did not permit hollowness, however. Sometime later, she stirred with resignation, boredom, acceptance. She was not sure what got her off the floor and through the door. She found herself in a barely familiar hall running for an elevator. She clothed herself when she reached the sliding doors and bolted into the real sun with real grass below her feet as soon as she was able.

*Control.* The only freedom is in the lack of control. *Where have I heard this? How do I know it? Paul, Paul must have taught me this.* She grabbed onto the thought and held tight. Insanity was her only other option, and she had learned in one of her classes that God didn't even allow that! She ran, out of the park, past the circling buildings, across a bridge that spanned a river with a name she had never bothered to learn.

*This is your home!* she screamed at herself. *You have no choice! You must learn to live here. Fantasy always ends and you are left with nothing. Paul, I must find Paul. He has made this place work for him. He has found purpose and meaning. I must search out the mundane, learn to live within the rules and let things unfold as they will. Paul knows comfort; he lives in the mundane and ekes out his measure of happiness. What more do I need? I come from a life—a world—of sacrifice. Why can I not accept the sacrifices of this place for what they are and move on?*

Verbolana's breath came ragged now, her legs ached from disuse, but she would not wish the pains away. She ran harder, breathed harder, ached more, and reveled in it. She searched for the sun to get an idea of the time. It seemed to be midmorning. She bolted into another neighborhood that seemed familiar. She retraced her steps from what she now realized was one of the best days she had spent since her arrival here. She found the sculpture gardens and the river where Paul and she had floated. She smiled with relief when she finally collapsed on the park bench where she had first met him. Fighting for breath, she wiped at the sweat that ran freely down her face. She did not ask God to whisk it away or to clean up her clothes or to freshen her hair. She sat giggling and stomping her feet in glee, excited about her new path. She hardly noticed the glances or smirks from the beautiful people who passed. How could they know, when she had just learned, that the answer was within her grasp? Random chance, sweat and dirty clothes, broken hearts and wiping after a shit. That was life; that was the key. She could not wait to tell Paul, though she knew he already knew.

And as she sat, the sweat dried. As her stink rose, her confidence faded. Paul had balance, she remembered. He didn't ignore God's gifts; he used them as tools. He did not forge his own knives or build his own tables, and he probably did not wash his own clothes. She swore at her foolishness and asked God to wash away the dried sweat and fix her hair. She slipped into one of the dresses he had bought those many months ago and chose a pair of shoes to match. She allowed her stomach to growl, though, and did not wish away her aching feet.

And she sat, hair combed, in a new dress, face frozen in an expectant grin, as she watched from the corner of her eye for his arrival. The sun moved through the trees, and the warmth of the day rose. *Was it too much to ask, this recreation of our chance encoun-*

*ter? Apparently so. Can I face walking into his shop after all this time? Frank will have a field day. Paul has undoubtedly moved on. Will he even remember me? I'll have to play it casual and light, accept the ribbing gratefully and give it back with vigor.* She stood. There was nothing else to do, nowhere else to turn.

With a purposeful gait, Verbolana strode through the park. As she emerged, she remembered Angela and almost stopped. *There will be time,* she reminded herself. *First things first. Open your eyes and your heart. Stay bold.* She was tempted to call upon the Strength, but she realized that would be silly and counterproductive. *You are free because you are vulnerable.* She thought maybe this would become her new mantra. *You are free because you are vulnerable,* she repeated and smiled. *Dazzle him with your humility, amaze him with your mistakes and shock him with your reverence to his guidance. Even Frank,* she pondered, *even Frank has a path that seems to work. Wow, I wasn't expecting that!*

Her dialogue continued. *There must be something with those people, the people from his planet, that makes it easier. I could ask him … I will ask him.*

She passed Angela's and approached the corner. Around the bend and she was there. Suck it up and let loose. Flow Vee, flow. Be humble yet strong, apologetic and confident, contrite but not morose. You disappeared from his life without even a glance back as far as he is concerned. Expect some anger and accept it as yours.

# Chapter 33

Trake stood in the first rays of the sun, the shadows deep and rich against the faces lined before him. The six Cheated who had attacked him the night before stood tall at the head of the lines, even Salkat with his stitched side. His new Honored friends, as instructed, stood intermingled with their new allies.

"I have a problem," Trake shouted once he had everyone's attention. "The Cheated and the Honored now stand together. And yet no one here has been cheated, and no one here need be honored. Everyone here, in this first battle of a new war, must be respected. These titles we give ourselves and each other do not speak of respect. One speaks of a cowering victim, while the other speaks of an arrogant brute. This new army will tolerate neither of these! You are Survivors, all of you. Survivors are strong, cunning and resourceful. You are willing and able to adapt to changes dictated by your circumstances. You have no shame. No shame, I say! You have already proven yourselves to whatever Gods you pray to. And you might be surprised to learn that everyone here prays to the same Gods. We might have given different voices to these Gods; that is the only difference."

Trake paced before his troops and let their mumbled questions die down. When he returned to the center of the formation, with a cross-armed draw, he smoothly pulled his favored weapons from their sheaths and held them at salute.

"The dagger and the sword—you must learn to wield both as if they were extensions of your arms. If the rules change, the enemy will no longer swing into battle. They will swing to land, and then they will cut through us like a Vipeon to dinner!" Trake's voice carried across the lines of ragged warriors, each man, he saw, with his own fears, his own motivations. Trake made eye contact with those Honored he could see, wondered about them even after their pledges of loyalty the night before. Would they fight against their own? "In close fighting, success comes from trickery, from survival. Kill the man in front of you or lie in the mud of your own blood, of no use to your family. Success lies in keen observation and bold, decisive movement. Hear the music and dance to the rhythms. Even in practice, like today, feel your natural beat. Some of you will glide and spin, arms graceful, feet sure and light. Some will pound Father with a bass beat, your strength of action will stem from solid weighted feet and a twisting backbone. Learn which you are and live from this moment in your new persona. Release the envy you feel for the strength of those around you. Yes, we all have it. We all long for what we do not have and devalue what the Gods gave us. Know that in this battle we need all."

He paced now, calling on the Strength to carry his message. "Even the weakest among us, the few who have neither grace nor brute strength, even these men have great value here. I know, for I am one of you. The sword has always felt alien to my hand. My feet neither glide nor plant with any natural grace. I plod and trip, have trouble finding my balance, and have no clear sense of the music in my opponent's head. Yet, with all these handicaps, I killed a Vipeon. I feel no shame in what I lack. I feel pride!"

He stood now, centered before the group, and threw his arms high as if to halve a moon and drag it, like dripping fruit, to the ground. "The Gods have given me nothing. I steal and I sneak; I mimic without an original thought. I let imaginary battles rage through my head when I should be watching my daughter, and when I sex a woman, I feel and exploit her movements, bend her to my will, defeat her, conquer her. I take every opportunity to hone and perfect my ability to kill. I am a warrior, without skill, but with unshakable determination. I glory in death as a celebration of my own life."

He brought his weapons down and sheathed them with great ceremony. "Enough speeches. Rows count off. You there, you are number one. Okay. Even-numbered rows, turn to the man on your right. Apologize and honor his death." The ritualized salute he had taught them rang through the forest.

"First position," he ordered. And it went from there. He migrated through the ranks, correcting, answering well-conceived questions and punishing, with the sting of a well-placed swagger stick, incompetence or stupidity.

Watching his new charges flounder further bolstered his confidence in his new path. If the Gods had wanted these people destroyed, they would have perished a hundred years ago. They were clumsy, unskilled and easily distracted, almost to a man. Trake was convinced that if the forests were not crowded with game and berries, starvation would have taken them before the Honored had their chance to do so. Also, he watched his Honored. Though they knew the movements, total indoctrination could be slow with them. They had all come from different decks and two from different towers. He would continually have to prove himself to them before he started on his real work. He must bring them around, but up until now he had not bothered even to get to know them. They had not been priorities.

"Hargot, come forward," Trake commanded.

The man broke from his line and hurried to stand at attention before Trake. He was five inches and thirty pounds Trake's superior as well as five years his senior. "Summon the Strength," Trake breathed, "and let's give these morons a little show."

"The Strength is not easy with me," Hargot breathed back.

"I see." Trake was not disappointed. "Bring what you can and we will spar," Trake ordered. He turned to his students. "Attention, all! Hargot and I will demonstrate the movements you are practicing and where they lead. Never forget your desired results. Visualize, as you move, the sequence to its completion. See it as one flowing river. Later we will add branches to that river and branches upon branches so no matter how your opponent disrupts your flow, you have another comfortable, practiced direction to move and conquer. Hargot will now attack me with the first movements we are practicing. I will counter with the proscribed blocks and then let things flow from there. Hargot, proceed, and give no quarter." They faced each other and apologized for the other's defeat.

Trake allowed and guided the battle for maximum grace and showmanship. He realized after the first two strikes that Hargot had no access to the Strength and therefore no hope of victory. He relaxed and played, remembering the joys of training while always keeping in mind his goal. All must continue to be impressed, Honored and Wretched alike. He must leave no doubt that he was the dominant male of this clan. He must breed confidence and respect while at the same time clearing any fantasies that any of them would ever challenge him for dominance.

So Trake did not play long. Hargot lunged with a lancing blow that was apparently his favorite. It was the perfect opportunity for the whole congregation to go to school on his mistakes. Trake parried, stopped short his blade, and lunged, slicing an inch into Hargot's rippled belly. Hargot fell back horrified; his sword dropped, blood ran freely from between his fingers. Trake stepped back, saluted and apologized.

"I think you can all see this would have been a death blow!" Trake shouted to the crowd, the Strength amplifying his voice. He reached down, picked up Hargot's discarded sword, and handed it to him. "You are dismissed. Have that looked at," he said to Hargot. "Now, it is important that you understand this. Each move we practice cannot stand alone. Each sequence does not exist in a vacuum. All the exercises, all the techniques, all the sequences build on and flow into one another. Never say, never even think, 'This technique doesn't work. My opponent is never going to come at me like that,' or 'I can never master that.' For as much as all of those statements may be true, it does not make your learning of them invalid." He stopped to let their confusion grow.

Trake walked from one end of the rows to the other and then back to the center before he continued. "Take the battle I just had with Hargot. I hope you noticed our builds were completely different. Hargot is a large-muscled, tall man. I am small and rather puny beside him. Some of the moves you will learn were designed for men with large muscles; some were designed for small men. The large man will seldom master a perfect spin and jab, whereas the small man will seldom carry the strength to execute a crushing overhead chop. This all may seem obvious, but I cannot tell you how often I have heard the grumblings. The big man does not want to learn to spin, and the small man knows in his heart that he will never use a two-handed overhead attack. You will learn them *all*, not because you will use them all in battle, but because, as you *learn* them, you will *feel* their vulnerabilities. There is no perfect attack. There is a defense and a countermove to every technique and every nuance to every technique. It will be your job to master the art behind the art."

He stopped again. Even the birds in the trees seemed to quiet. Trake leveled his ferocious gaze and contacted every eye he was able. "And now we must choose. For I must have complete devotion from those of you who go forward from here. Who among you will continue in training, and who will support those who do? Who is going to hunt and skin, mine and forge, and who is going to come with me to certain death?"

\* \* \*

Verbolana put on her best smile as she entered the Terran Café. She nodded to the waiters and greeted them by name, for once grateful for her perfect memory. "Frank!" she yelled out from across the room. "You old son of a bitch, how have you been?" Terran jargon flowed from her mouth with a little help. "You seen our old friend?"

Frank looked up from his cutting board. "Well, look what the cat drug in!" Then to one of the patrons sitting at the counter, "Better watch out; last time this broad was in, washed the whole place with her puke." The man jolted his head to see who could have done such a thing.

"Yeah," Verbolana shot back. "Amazing what two-hundred-year-old sausage can do to a gal!" At that point, Paul stuck his head around the hood. She could not read his eyes. He gave her a weak smile and she knew she was in for a rough time. Without hesitation, though, she gave him her most apologetic smile and sat a couple seats down from the only other patron at the counter. "Hey, stranger, I kinda took a wrong turn a few months ago. Hope you're not too mad."

"Mad? You don't owe me anything." Paul's voice was breezy and remote.

"Yeah? Maybe, but I *want* to owe you something." Her eyes drilled into him with sincerity as soon as he looked up.

"Yeah?" he questioned. "What do you want to owe me?" He gave her another weak smile.

"Well, at least an explanation."

"At least," he agreed.

"I think you owe him a blow job," Frank threw in.

"Damn it, Frank, stay out of this!" Paul shot across the grill.

"Well, she does! At the very least," he continued to the amused patron.

"Look," Verbolana admitted. "I know I messed up. But you knew I was a wreck when you found me in the park. I'm doing the best I can, and I came in to apologize. It's not something I am good at."

"You want something to eat?" Paul asked to ease her way.

"Still can't pay." Verbolana gratefully accepted the diversion.

"Ah, what's money?" Paul shrugged and came around the grill to stand in front of her. When he was closer, he confided, "You know, it hurt, you disappearing like that. I don't mind helping folks, and I don't mind not getting thanked, but I thought we connected. I like you; and I don't like getting stomped on."

"I don't imagine you do. About all I can say is that I will try not to do it again. That's the only way an apology makes any sense. I am sorry, and I will try to not do it again," she repeated.

"I guess that's about the best I can ask for, then, other than that blow job." Paul's joke fell flat.

"So what about that food?" Verbolana tried to fill the gap.

"Ah, yes, I assume you are still not eating animals."

"Please, please, don't even ask. I can feel my stomach heave just at the thought."

"Oatmeal and raisins it will be, then. Milk and brown sugar?" he asked.

"Just no dead animals," she reiterated and did her best to laugh. The idea that he, and apparently all those around her, did eat dead animals was something she was going to struggle with.

Paul shuffled back into the kitchen and started furious activity. As he worked he babbled, "These are steel-cut organic oats that I have toasted slightly. It gives them a nice nutty flavor most people really like." He paused for a moment while he rattled some pots. "The milk comes from the south of Spain, a little farm where the cows are all range-fed. I get summer milk." He looked up to make sure she was listening. "It makes a difference. The grass is dry, so it doesn't dilute the flavor. This particular farm produces a soft, rind-washed cheese that will knock your socks off. That's how I found it—the milk."

Vee tried her best to listen, but she didn't have a clue what he was talking about. All she knew was the smells he produced back there smelled a lot like the roasted Milnox she still craved. She watched him intently as he moved about the kitchen and, though she tried not to, compared him to Trake, both with their sure movements and focused intent. "That smells awfully good. It brings back memories of home."

"Is that a good thing?" Paul asked.

"Yes, this memory is. It's funny how comforting a food can be."

"Bingo!" Paul shouted. "That's why I do what I do. I don't think there is anything as comforting as food ..."

"Except of course that blow job," Frank threw in from across the kitchen.

They all snickered this time and Verbolana began truly to relax. She gazed out the window at patrons sitting at the outside tables with their papers and coffee cups and beyond them, strolling citizens in their stylish clothes and perfect smiles.

"I need to find a job," she blurted without thought.

"Don't be looking here," Frank reacted with similar surprise. "I have a waiting list a few years long."

"I wasn't—I didn't—I just realized it," Verbolana stammered. Then she saw the implications. "That's not why I came here. It just occurred to me. That might be what is missing in my life. That *is* what drew me back here. You two have something—something

310

real to hold onto. I need that, but don't worry, Frank, I need to find my own something."

Paul came around with a steaming bowl of mush, accompanied by other smaller bowls filled with a variety of shapes and textures. He placed the platter in front of her with a flourish and caught her eyes. "I'm glad you came back. Real connection is hard to find in this place. Can you stick around a while this time?"

Verbolana smiled with relief and gratitude. "I'm going to try. I don't know if I am any more stable than the last time you saw me, but at least I think I know what I am looking for. At least part of it."

"Good enough." Paul smiled back. "Okay, this is brown sugar, sweet and full on the tongue." He pointed to one of the ramekins. "And these are raisins. Not just any raisins, though. They make most raisins from table grapes, sweet but very low in acid. I found a little place in the Napa Valley that makes them from fully ripened Chardonnay grapes. They are sweeter, but the acidity counterbalances the added sweetness and gives them a much fuller mouth. Somebody found these by accident in '05. They had a bumper crop and didn't pick everything, just left them hanging on the vine."

Paul continued to explain each condiment as Verbolana plucked, prodded and tasted. The unfamiliar babble flooded her with comfort and distraction. One hundred and forty-three worlds of knowledge awaited if she wanted. She was a teacher with nothing to teach, she realized, and she shuddered at the memory of the switch and the whippings. She kicked herself and refocused on Paul's monologue. It was too late. One memory after another assaulted her humor until she almost dipped her head into the slop before her.

"Paul, I need help. I need to heal my past before I can move on. I keep running and crying and skirting the issues. I need to face, full front, who I was before I have a chance of figuring out who I want to be. Can you help me?"

"I can try." He pulled a stool and sat across from her. "Eat and talk. Tell me about your life, who you were and who you wanted to be. Everyone has a dream. I believe everyone, no matter who life forces them to be, has a tiny child hidden somewhere deep inside who knows who he or she should be. That is why some struggle so desperately. Their child screams at the injustice as their adult copes with the realities of life." He waited for her to take a few more bites and chew on his words. "You have a chance here, if you can dig deep enough and face, with courage and tenacity, what you find; you have a chance to have it all."

"And you would help me?" Verbolana dropped her spoon and her eyes as they filled with tears.

"I would be honored," Paul whispered.

# Chapter 34

have heard of your speeches; the whole camp is buzzing with them." Atasha stirred a large pot over the fire on their dirt floor. "You said nothing to disprove my point of a week ago. Fiendish are self-centered brutes. Everyone is saying so."

"And yet they follow." Trake reclined on their sleeping pad. Atlana was asleep on his bare chest, her heat scorching his skin.

"Can you not at least play the game?" Atasha requested.

"There is no time for games," Trake responded easily. "And you forget; I have missions greater than myself. Don't think I have forgotten. Myths, all myths, must be broken. Fiendish and Deceived, Chosen and Wretched, however you wish to call them; all must learn to live together. It is the only real hope for our daughter."

Trake put one strong hand on his daughter's back and squeezed her to him, the warmth of their skins branding his heart. "We must represent the Gods with their true words. We must expose all falsehoods, and all men and all women must flounder through their own quagmires to find the Truth. Simple platitudes cannot stand the scrutiny. We must dismantle even the most complex dogmas to glean the Truth from what is merely convenient. Or, better yet, throw all that out. Start from here," he pointed to the sleeping form on his chest. "Start from this. Start from the moment you first open your eyes in the morning, still snuggled tight to my chest. Start there, before the worries and questions of the day pollute our minds. We can write a new script that comes from a warmed heart instead of a cold hand. We can anchor our thoughts in love and build outward from there."

Atasha stirred the pot, stunned and confused. "You talk to the men of giving death and the inevitability of dying, and you talk to me of the power of love and the need to change what is. Which is it?"

"Both," Trake asserted without hesitation. "If we wish for change, we must survive. And, whether you see it or not, I am giving Fiendish and Deceived common ground. When we are ready, I will welcome a Fiendish attack. Fear is a wonderful motivation for change; I should know. Respect is the only way to get another to listen. Don't you see? We must do battle, but we must battle as equals. We must fear and respect each other if we are to have any hope of living together."

"Only a man would say something like that," Atasha lamented.

"Then only a man would be right," Trake asserted. "There is no middle ground here. Things are too far gone for that. We can chip away at our cemented beliefs for the next century or two, or we can blast it with the cannon fire of enlightenment and raw strength!"

Quiet enveloped the hut; both seemed uncomfortable with a conflict that stemmed from mutual caring. Atasha's eyes wandered around in her head, sorting, while Trake's blazed in staunch determination straight through the top of the hut.

"I wish it didn't need to be this way," Trake conceded, softening his voice. "But the more I learn of nature, the more I see I am right. Brutality is a part of who we are. To ignore simple facts is simply wrong."

"You compare us to mindless animals? Instinct is not what drives us. Intellect is our salvation. If you start thinking like an animal, soon you will start acting like one."

Trake sat with his thoughts for a moment. "Tell me of the Vipeon. When it attacks the village, does it simply eat its fill and leave, or does it take a little something home with it for the little ones?" Trake knew the answer to this, but then he asked, "Or is it driven by fear? Does it see us as a threat that must be destroyed?"

"I don't know what a Vipeon thinks. I just know we are not animals and that there must be a better way than going to war!"

Atlana squirmed on Trake's chest, and then settled when the harsh words faded.

Trake understood Atasha's anger. He let it soak into him and mingle with his own. Resentment and anger, frustration and hopelessness were the tools of an Honored warrior. Righteousness was his only salvation. Righteousness and the blind privilege that came with it.

"At our base, we are animals, bent on self-preservation. You fear conflict because you see yourself, or me or Atlana dead on the ground. You see your survival in question."

"I fear conflict, or more precisely war, because death is no solution for the living. Death begets death, nothing more."

Trake let her hot words steep and then let them cool on his tongue before he spoke. "You contradict yourself. A few days ago you marveled at the selfless sacrifice of your people and now you minimize that same sacrifice as useless."

"There is a difference between protecting the clan and spoiling for a fight. Do not question my loyalty or dedication to my people. Fighting is necessary and noble in self-defense. It is brutish and selfish in any other context. I respect and cherish your skills, Trake, and I hope you never have to use them again."

"I guess we disagree on what is meant by 'self-defense.' It is not always a passive proposition. Sometimes a preemptive strike is more valuable than lying in wait. And don't think for a moment the Chosen feel any differently. They feel they act in self-defense, both for themselves and for the greater good of Father. Like I say, no one looks to die; everyone has a cause."

"And there are no brutes?" Atasha spat.

"Of course there are brutes!" Trake responded in exasperation, trying to track her wandering thoughts.

Shyly, Atasha asked, "Are you one? That is what they say. You are a brute, who looks for other brutes to play with."

"The only difference between a brute and a holy warrior is his cause. That is always the trick. We must always have the right haircut, lest we be misunderstood." Trake concluded.

"And the man across the sword from you?"

"I can only assume he feels the same," Trake conceded.

\* \* \*

Verbolana closed her fingers around Paul's as they emerged from the subway station into the brilliant sun of the university campus. The cobbled avenue and majestic three- and four-story buildings soothed her with their beauty and solidity.

"I can tell you how many birds are in that tree over there." Verbolana pointed to the bench where she had sat a few months earlier.

"This is where you were hiding out? What were you studying?" Paul asked as he swung their hands to the rhythm of their stride.

"Weaving, psychology and stuff like that," she answered, trying to stuff a sudden nervousness around their mission. "I'm not sure I want to show you my world. I'm afraid it is going to shock you."

316

"I have no doubt about that; but then a lot of things shock me," Paul admitted. "Doesn't sound like a very nice place, but that wasn't your fault. You can't help where you're *from*, just who you *become*."

"I don't want you looking at me there."

"Don't worry; you can control where we go and what we see. It's really pretty cool, these rooms they have. They are all set up for exploration. You can go as broad or as deep as you wish. We can even go to my planet first if you want. I could give you the full tour, all the wars and greed and fumbles we made. Might make you feel better when we look at all the mistakes people made on your planet."

"That sounds like a great idea. You wouldn't mind?"

"Got all day and then some," Paul laughed, his brown eyes sparkling with mischief.

They walked for a while in silence as Verbolana wondered. She couldn't help trying to peer into the future. Was Paul someone she could stay with, settle down with? Would he want her more than just for the novelty? She remembered Alcot and his attitudes. What a jerk! But maybe that was just the way it went here. He was right about one thing, though: three hundred years looked like a very long time.

"Here we are, the library," Paul announced.

The freeform glass structure was the strangest building Verbolana had ever seen. From a distance she had noticed its vaulting snakelike spires, but up close it was even more bizarre. She remembered her trips to the Palladium and the underwater displays. They had said it was a jellyfish, the thing she remembered, but this one was on its back, with the dangling tentacles reaching up.

"They say it is symbolic of the search for knowledge. I am proud to say that a man named Chihuly designed and built this place. He was from my home world, from my country," Paul beamed.

"It is magnificent, but it makes me a bit dizzy. Looks like a lot of climbing, or are there elevators?"

"As a matter of fact, this building is quite unique in that way, too. We will be teleporting," Paul announced. "Ever done it?"

When she shook her head no, he continued. "Isn't as fun as it sounds. Kinda like in your realm when you ask God to take something away or change a scene. You ask, and you are there, no big deal; but it is one of the only public buildings where you can do that. In a bunch of neighborhoods you can, too. All it takes is a majority vote, but the people from my world are too set in their past. Most people are that way, as evidenced by the subway system. Even that is a compromise, though, with some people who would still like us carried around on animals. You'll see soon. We can go to all sorts of planets if you'd like. Ready?" Paul walked ahead and pulled her along.

They entered the stark, molded glass lobby, and immediately a wall of words popped before their eyes. "This freaks a lot of people out, too." Paul giggled as he watched Vee's reaction. "It's a directory of departments and ongoing research projects, stuff like that. We don't need any of this," he said and, with a hand, brushed it away. "Do you want to look around before we go to a room?"

"Sure," Verbolana would have said almost anything to avoid their ultimate mission. "What's over that way?"

"Augh, cafeteria. Worst food on the planet! They've tried to please everyone and ended up pleasing no one. Over here, however, is the book repository." He took her hand again and led her through double glass doors as tall as the trees outside. The view was as she had imagined her tower would appear from the outside, except every floor and every wall was a different color of glass. And each floor held rows upon rows of books and people and more books.

"We had five volumes of the same book on our deck," Verbolana muttered. "Do the colors of the floors mean anything?"

Paul waved his hand, and another directory appeared before their eyes. It was a busy place and most of those passing dodged around the apparition, but some walked right through it, either not noticing or not caring. "The colors and patterns signify different planets and then different cultures on each planet."

"I'm guessing my planet doesn't take up much space," Verbolana suggested.

"Let's see. What do you call your planet?"

"Father?" Verbolana guessed.

"God will know what you mean. Just ask."

"God, show me the floor for Father."

The directory scrolled down and highlighted fifteen levels of maroon floor, broken up with a dizzying array of patterns. Verbolana looked at Paul in puzzlement. "Is that a lot?"

"God, show me the floors for Terra," Paul demanded. The directory took another spinning trip and landed on eight floors of highlighted red. "I'd say you might have underestimated your people."

Verbolana crinkled her nose and tapped her leg nervously with her hand, trying to stem her trepidation and give herself courage. "Can we go there?" she managed.

"Sure, God, take us to Father, level eight." They stood before shelves at least twenty feet tall. "Scroll shelves down," Paul commanded. Noiselessly the bottom shelf disappeared below the floor as shelf after shelf slid past them. "Stop, scroll left." Now the shelves of books slid by sideways as Verbolana tried to catch a few of the titles.

"I'd say your people were quite prolific. I've got an idea. God, show us the last book published on Father." With a blink, the titles changed, along with the patterns in the shelves and floor. "Instead of moving the books, God actually moved us that time," Paul explained. "Here it is. Does this look familiar?"

"No." Verbolana glanced at the book and then to the shelves. "But this one does." She picked a beautifully bound volume from the shelf and leafed through it. Something was different. She flipped back to the title page. "Holy Drama, Director's Cut," she read aloud. "Huh?"

"These are cataloged by date of publication at this point. It appears there were quite a few books published after the one you have," Paul commented. "And then there are all these. God, what are these?"

**"Unpublished Manuscripts,"** came the answer.

"It appears your people continue to write." Paul sauntered down the row and picked an unbound stack of papers at random. "Tunneling and Ventilation," he read aloud.

Verbolana pulled herself from her studies and furrowed her brow at Paul. "What are you looking at? Must have been written a thousand years ago."

"Maybe, but it would be misfiled if it was. God, when was this book written?"

**"Completed century 82, year 852, day 475."**

"That mean anything to you?" Paul asked with no real interest.

Verbolana gently placed the Holy Drama back on the shelf and walked over to Paul. Her hand clasped his shoulder for support. "The Wretched are writing books? That's impossible."

# Chapter 35

Stand tall! Now drop and pivot at the hips. Bring your arms around only after your hips initiate the movement. All true power originates in the hips."

Then to the next student, Trake demanded, "Absorb that overhead blow with your legs. Your weapon needs to stay at a forty-five-degree angle to the strike so the strike will glance off to the side. Watch." He took the man's place and instructed his new opponent to strike again. He first demonstrated the wrong way, letting his sword collapse under the attack, then the correct way, which moved him smoothly into a counterattack. "Work on your leg strength. They must become like coiled steel."

Trake stepped back to make a quick count; twelve rows of eight. They would soon outgrow their practice grounds. Every man who had dropped out so far had been replaced by two, and still they came from the forest. The slightest hope began to grow. With his current numbers, and a few more months of training, Trake decided they might be able to repel one blimp's worth of Blessed Militia. Clearly, this was only a beginning. They had many months, if not years, ahead of them, but they had not spotted a blimp since that one the month previous, so there was hope.

From the path to the main village, Trake sensed a new group of men approaching, their energy signals strong. Trake watched as Salkat, his new sergeant, approached with obvious deference and started a hushed conversation. Trake pretended not to notice and continued his instruction. He had wondered when the truly powerful would arrive. He was sure he need wonder no more from looking at the clothes, the postures and the men themselves. As each of Trake's students recognized the new arrivals, they stopped practice, dropped their weapons to their sides and stood as if embarrassed. Soon, even the former Honored looked around and wondered what was afoot.

Trake wandered over to the group with casual purpose. "You seem to be of some interest to my men. I am Trake. And you are?"

Salkat stammered, "Sir, this is General Bartoldt. And these are Generals from neighboring clans."

Trake bowed in what he hoped was a universal sign of respect. "I was unaware of a military hierarchy. I hope I have not offended anyone."

"Each Militia is free to train as it wishes," General Bartoldt responded. "Joint maneuvers are infrequent. We are, however, interested in your training methods. You are the man they call the Vipeon Slayer?"

"I have been lucky enough to survive two such attacks," Trake admitted.

"They say you are Fiendish," Bartoldt continued.

"I was born an Honored warrior," Trake countered. "Though I no longer believe in such distinctions."

"May I ask what precipitated this change of heart?" the General inquired.

"Love," Trake responded without hesitation or embarrassment. "And a clear understanding that I was deceived."

"Deceived?" The General laughed. "What was your rank?"

"Deck Commander and Blimp Captain, sir."

"And you felt you deserved something more than deception?" the General scoffed.

"Of course," Trake responded in confusion.

"Son, every war is fought on deception. Men do not fight and die for the abstractions that fuel most wars. Every soldier needs a higher cause. However, I am not here to discuss propaganda with you. I am here to evaluate your skills and offer you a position if it seems appropriate."

"I'm sorry, sir. I am confused. What kind of position? Where?"

"We can discuss that if and when it becomes appropriate. In the meantime, we have brought you a little challenge."

"I don't need… " Trake stopped short. From around a bend in the path, a Strength signature appeared without warning. Before he could analyze how this could be, a man in full battle gear stepped from hiding and approached, his intent obvious. Trake retreated to the open field as his students instinctively fell back to form a semicircle.

The man, large and imposing, with the military haircut of an unrepented Honored and the colors of a Master Instructor, drew his swords as he entered the clearing and said, "I apologize for your death and will honor your life."

Trake brought every modicum of Strength to the fore, drew his swords, and then asked, "Is this truly necessary?" When he received no answer, he replied, "I apologize for your death and will honor your life." Silently he prayed, *Gods, cradle me in your hands while you reveal the path to victory. My swords are but your servants.*

The man approached in classic style. As if without a care, he kept up a running commentary as the battle progressed, "He has good Strength. His moves are clear and confidant and his style is appropriate for his body."

And as Trake attacked, defended and attacked again, he carried on his own internal commentary: *This man is arrogant and rude … his defenses are impenetrable … he is really pissing me off …*

They battled. Trake soon learned what it felt like to be played with; every thrust was easily countered, every block transformed into an elegant attack. Trake felt his Strength shrinking, softening when he needed it the most. He concentrated, tried to regain his confidence. Nothing. The man had no rhythm to play off of, no pattern to exploit, no weaknesses. He did not spin, Trake noticed. He stayed engaged, pressed with almost gentle persistence at every move. There was no retreat, yet no obvious aggression. Trake's opponent was on balance as well as on point at every moment.

As Trake felt himself shrink further, flounder, his mind flitted to Atasha, then Atlana. He advanced with a sudden flurry as he rallied his Strength and pressed a blocked thrust into an attack that nearly sliced the man's ear. Trake felt his Strength surge further as he knocked the man off balance and into the man's first retreat. But his opponent countered with his first spin and Trake felt his pressing attack suddenly transform into a headlong plunge that sent him sprawling forward. Heated steel brushed the back of Trake's neck as he fought for balance.

"He is trainable," the man commented as he calmly stepped back, pulling his attack at the moment Trake would have lost his head. "But let's leave him here for now. His skills are good enough for this Militia, but nothing special."

* * *

"How is that possible?" Verbolana wondered to Paul's concerned face as she leafed through one of the volumes they had borrowed. "The Wretched don't write; they can barely speak! They live as nomads in wild little villages and suck off of Father."

Paul eyes mirrored her concern. "I can't follow everything you say, but why are you so surprised? Even the most primitive cultures have writings. These Wretched shouldn't be expected to be so different." They sat at a table in the cafeteria with a warming drink Paul had suggested.

"I guess not, and I doubt this will be the last surprise. That is what I came here for, after all." Verbolana looked at Paul sheepishly. "I guess I just wasn't prepared yet. With this drink in me, maybe I'll be all right. Sure we shouldn't have something a little stronger?"

"We could if you want, but I wouldn't recommend it. Best to hit this stuff with a clear head, or at least that's what my mom would say." Paul laughed as a memory flashed across his eyes. "Ready?"

"Yeah, let's hit it." Verbolana tried her best to match his idioms.

When they reached the lobby again, Paul requested, "God, we'd like a history room." The scene changed. In front of them stood a table and a few chairs. The walls were indistinct, black, shadowed. "Directory," Paul requested. As in the other rooms, a directory appeared. This time, rows of spinning planets displayed short descriptions after each. "Do you want to sit?"

"I'm too nervous," Verbolana responded and dropped back into silence.

"Okay, my place or yours?"

"Your place." She tried to match his lightness.

"My place it is, then. God, please show Terra." The walls came alive. A peaceful planet, with brilliant blues, swirling whites and muted greens, hung before them, spinning in slow motion. "Historical Catalog." Another directory appeared. Paul scanned it. "World War Two, D Day, observation mode."

Paul and Verbolana stood in midair, two hundred feet or so above a rolling gray sea. Before them, the sky held a smoky glow where it appeared the sun was about to rise. Blinding flashes of light and deafening explosions erupted all around them, followed by high-pitched whistles and more explosions. Directly below their feet tiny craft crammed with bobbing helmeted heads moved toward a thin line of beach.

"This was a crucial day in one of our many wars."

Paul brought up a new directory, and together they read the gruesome statistics of deaths and injuries, cataloged by nation, sex and age. They watched as new, smaller explosions hit the water and boats as the boats neared land. With a few instructions, Paul moved their vantage point closer as the battle progressed. Soon Verbolana felt the percussion of the mortars and heard the whizzing of bullets below her feet. Soon screams of pain and horror reached them, suspended safe above the battle. She remembered these sounds from her own battle and her stomach soured around the tea that had been meant to soothe. She wished her stomach calm.

"Do we have to watch this?" she whined.

"Of course not. I just thought I'd show you how brutal my people could be. God, stop playback." The walls went black again. "You see? Death and destruction are nothing new to the human race. We seem particularly good at it."

"Can you show me something of your religion?" Verbolana queried.

"Religions," Paul corrected.

"You had more than one?" Verbolana seemed confused.

"Thousands, probably. Maybe over the years, tens of thousands."

"How did you keep them all straight?" she wanted to know.

"We didn't."

"How did you choose?"

"Most of us didn't get that option either. Usually our parents picked our religion and then crammed it down our throats, or sometimes the community where you lived used social pressure. In some situations, the government chose. Actually, when I think about it, it was mostly either the community or the government. Parents pretty much just followed along and tried to protect you from those other forces. I think it is safe to say that the authorities thought the form of worship was too big a choice for the individual to make. God's wrath was too large and wide, and maybe they were afraid of being caught in the crossfire. Or maybe," he thought for a minute, "the government just didn't care about the individual and wanted to impose its will. Faith is a very personal thing—but religion?—I guess religion has always been extremely political. The idea of God has always been a great motivator, and since religions are not based on logic, they must be delivered with an iron hand."

"Interesting. My religion seemed very logical, extremely logical."

"Yeah? I don't think I can say that about many of the religions I knew of on Terra, in fact, none of them. They were all anti-logical as far as I can tell. And I don't mean illogical, but anti-logical. Because most of them follow logical paths of thinking in order to make sense of non-logical issues. That to me is anti-logical. Now that I think about it, it's amazing how so many Terran religions got so much of it right but ended up being so incredibly wrong."

"Where it appears my religion started from a logical base and also got almost everything incredibly wrong," Verbolana said. "Can you show me what you are talking about on your world?"

"Sure. God, take us to the birth of Christ."

Heat and stench assaulted them; the humidity of urine-soaked hay and animals too close added to the confined squalor. Verbolana instinctively jumped closer to Paul and grabbed his arm, then reminded herself this was only a recreation.

In front of them a woman squatted almost to the packed earth, her legs spread, her dress hiked to her hips. She gave a feral scream and the man in front of her flinched. "I can see its head!" he screamed back. "Push that miserable thing out before you collapse!" The woman squatted deeper and grunted. A splash of urine and feces hit the ground below her. "Move over, Mary, you've fouled another spot!" The man yanked her and she stumbled forward, squatted again, while Paul and Verbolana watched her neck and back spasm in pained effort.

The man reached forward, grabbed and pulled between her legs. Another gush of fluids splattered the dirt, this time blood and a variety of clear and cloudy glop. "I got him, I got him, by God, we got a boy! Come here. Lie down! I gotta bed for you over here!" The man ushered his exhausted mate to a pile of hay he had prepared, trailing the cord and bloody mucus through the dirt.

"Actually they got this part pretty much right," Paul commented as they watched unseen. "Of course, none of the stories mentioned the horse shit, Mary's toothless smile, or the fact that both his parents were of mixed blood with very dark complexions."

"Who are these people?" Verbolana demanded.

"The baby, there, was one of the messengers God sent our world to help us out," Paul explained. "Countless religions and sects eventually formed around this kid's teachings."

"Why are we watching this—this grossness?" Verbolana complained. "I think I might be sick."

"I don't know," Paul admitted. "I guess 'cause this is where his story starts. This is where the myth of his life takes on form and compassion. Look at Joseph. He is a filthy, crude goat herder. Turns out he is very fond of the drink when he can afford it, and Mary here wasn't known to turn a drink down either when she was offered one."

"And?" Verbolana was still confused.

"And," Paul continued with some annoyance, "there was no royal reception to his birth, no great star in the sky, no idyllic manger. In fact, no virgin birth. If we were to go back nine months, we'd witness Joseph here banging her up royally."

"Paul!"

"Sorry, but I get a little worked up over this shit. I can't tell you how many millions of people died because of myths like this. Campfire stories that justified entire nations doing battle."

"I thought you said he was sent by God to help."

"He was!" Paul bellowed. "We can walk through his teaching if you'd like; hear the words from his own mouth. Then skip forward to the campfires where the witnesses to his teachings told and retold their stories. We could watch the exaggerations bloom and the outright lies begin. Or we could sneak into the squalid rooms of the lonely and rejected men who decided to write these or their own stories down. Each had his own agenda, his own twist. Then we could skip forward to those who choose which stories would live on and which would be burned or destroyed — where self-aggrandizement, greed and politics took over."

Paul stopped for a breath and to calm himself. "Then the real idiocy began. Scholars, many of them with good intentions, yet still ego-driven, studied these tainted texts word-by-word, searching for deeper and deeper meanings. You see, with these original stories, many of them contradicted each other. So, taken out of context, almost any belief could be justified. The gist of it is that God sent this messenger to give us some broad-brush words to guide us, when what we wanted were definitive answers. When we couldn't find those answers, we made them up!"

"Can we go now?" Verbolana had seen enough.

Mary screamed again, and Joseph pulled on the cord that protruded from between her legs.

"Sure," Paul agreed. "One more thing. God, how many messengers have you sent my home world?"

**"Eight hundred and fifty-two."**

"Are you going to send any more?"

**"It is unlikely."**

# Chapter 36

Who were those men?" Trake asked of Salkat after the men left.

"General Bartoldt commands an army of two thousand or more to the east of us. He visits every once in a while to make sure we stay in our place." Salkat spat in rage.

"I don't understand. There are larger settlements to the east?"

"Of course! We would not live under the blimps if we had a choice," Salkat answered as if insulted by the question.

"Genera Bartoldt keeps you here?"

"Keeps us here to keep the blimps busy," Salkat spat again. "They claim they are building for an offensive, but they have been building for many years now as we act the decoy. You did not know of this?"

"There were rumors, but nothing solid. Our commanders never let us fly more than a day's journey from the tower."

"We know that, but don't you have men on the ground? Reconnaissance?"

"That has never been permitted either," Trake confessed.

"That explains why your people have not found this camp. We assumed the other Honored were lying, as I guess you could be."

Trake stood back. "Do not call them my people! They are no longer my people. We must stop all thinking like that. Now tell me about the people to the east."

"They have great wealth," was Salkats first revelation. "Homes and farms, livestock in great pens. Beyond the horizon of the furthest reach of the blimps, life is good. But the land is crowded, so they pushed us out. I don't think they will ever attack the towers. They have no reason to do so."

"But—but—," Trake blurted, stalling for his brain to catch up. "The Chosen do travel between towers."

"The flight paths are well known. Much land is safe. I cannot believe you did not know this." Salkat shook his head. "No wonder the General feels no hurry. That Honored he had with him must know all of this. They must know that they are still safe."

"And he keeps his army not for attack, but for defense ... from you," Trake concluded.

"The bastard!" Salkat made his own conclusion.

\* \* \*

Paul asked, "Where do you wish to go? How far back?"

They stood in an empty room, God awaiting their command. "I don't know. Before the Cleansing, I guess."

"Do you know where?"

Verbolana thought. "There was a city to the north of the tower. They attacked it quite often. We could start there," she suggested.

"Good enough. God, take us to the city just north of the tower Verbolana was raised in, before the Cleansing. Whatever that was," Paul added under his breath.

The room transformed. The air was as still as a moment before, but the view was something Verbolana could not reference. For 360 degrees below lay a vividly colored landscape like nothing she had ever seen or even imagined. Even the neighborhoods of Heaven seemed pale. Bright blues and greens contrasted with muted maroons and beiges. Verbolana realized they saw the rooftops of a thousand, no ten thousand buildings. Above her was … opaque, bright yet indistinct … the dome, she realized. She had read her students stories of the dome. The great separator; the facilitator of evil. It seemed so benign; so passive to be such a thing of evil.

Paul seemed to have no trouble orienting himself. "Do you want to go down into the city?"

"That's the dome," Verbolana whispered.

"Yes."

"It is important," Verbolana explained. "It separated the people from Father. It alienated them from the world around them."

"Were people left outside?" Paul took a stab. That would have been terrible if the planet were hostile.

"No—no, everyone was inside." She knew she did not make sense to Paul, but she didn't want to be distracted. "Let's go down. God, take us to ground level."

Buildings towered around them, blocking all but a hint of the dome. People bustled everywhere, all intent on a destination and all talking, as if to the air. The flow made Verbolana itch, standing still as she was, feeling their focused intentions and knowing she was an impediment.

"Where could they all be going in such a hurry?" Verbolana wondered aloud.

"Busy days," Paul lamented. "I know what it's like. I still get that way sometimes. Too many things to do and not enough time."

"In Heaven? Too much time as far as I am concerned. What do we do now?"

Paul thought. "Maybe a library?" he suggested.

"A library within a library? For someone who didn't even know one existed, it is pretty strange. But why not? Seems to be the way." Verbolana laughed at her former ignorance.

"God, take us to the main library," Paul commanded, assuming any evolved society would have a library. A spacious lobby with open-air gardens, statues and free-hanging paintings surrounded them. A rushing stream fell from the ceiling, cascaded over and around mossy boulders and eventually fell into a churning, fern-lined pond.

The roar put off by the angry water surprised and confused Verbolana. From her experience, water had always been docile. But here, the volume, the diamond sparkle and the rising mist served to drive conscious thought from her mind. She ventured closer to the unexpected power as if magnetized. The thumping base of the colliding waters pounded her chest, compressed her heart.

She closed her eyes and forgot Paul, forgot … everything. She surrendered to the power. *Father,* she rocked back with the percussions. *Father, I have lived, existed, away from your majesty; filtered, protected and separated. I do not know you, yet I worshipped you. I do not love you, yet I was devoted to you. I have noticed only your bitter fingers, the cold of winter and heat of summer, and I have ignored your caress in the spring and fall. Please forgive me and those who kept you from me.*

Verbolana opened her eyes. Paul stood at her side, watching, patient yet unmoved. "It's beautiful," was all she divulged.

"Yes," he took a guess. "The power of nature is probably some-thing these people crave, insolated as they are, with their dome and buildings and manicured lawns."

"Is it that obvious?" Verbolana dropped her chin and eyes.

Paul burst out with unfiltered laughter. "Yes, it is that ob-vious!" He took her arms and turned her to him, then raised her chin. Her eyes stayed demure. "Don't hide from me, my love. Open, blossom, drink." He turned them both back to face the water. "Feel that power. It speaks to all of us. That's why it is here. Suck the air into your nose. Feel it cleanse and energize."

They stood together and inhaled the mist-freshened air. "I will learn about your world, but I see so much already. That day when I found you crumpled in the park ... were some of your tears for the birds in the branches above, for the spots of sunlight dancing across the cobbles?" Excited, he continued. "There is something you should know about me. I do not spend every day cooped up in that kitchen. My real joy is exploration, traveling to the farm where chickens lay the best eggs, where cows eat the perfect mixture of grasses and grains, where the ocean's waves deposited salt a thousand years ago and that is now harvested for my table. Nature—real places under real skies, where random events still exercise their colliding wills."

Verbolana looked at him, missing most of his meaning. "Yes, yes!" His babbling had pulled her from where he had insisted she go. "I will have to come back here or go with you on an adventure. But right now I need to know how all this came to be. Can we trace back to before this city, before the dome?"

"Sure. I am not a historian, but I'm sure we can work something out. Do you have any reference points? Any place to start?"

"All I know are the stories. Stories of how people hid inside the domes while machines raped and sucked up everything else."

"Well," Paul thought for a minute. "Let's bail out of here. Let's go outside the dome and then just start rewinding."

"Okay."

"God, take us above the dome." They stood in midair, the dome below them. "Higher." Still all they saw was the dome. "Higher, higher. To the north twenty miles." They still floated above the dome, though they saw the edge, off in the distance.

"Big place," was Paul's only comment. "God take us to the edge of the dome. Now down." He pointed to a mass of buildings outside the dome. "Verbolana, see that?" She looked, but they meant nothing to her. "All those pipes and stacks—must be a power plant, or water. But I don't see any water, so it's probably power. God, follow the edge. Yeah, see that; it's got to be water. See that huge pipeline? It probably heads to the mountains. Yeah, look; through the haze. Mountains, over there."

"This means something to you?" Verbolana floated by his side. She was growing accustomed to the sensation of weightlessness.

"Yeah, everybody needs power and water. And it's obvious where the food comes from. Look across there." He pointed at square after square of different colors off into the distance. "Wonder what ...? God, move us closer to the fields."

Then, as if they were pulled down a giant slide, they saw the landscape rush under them. Verbolana clutched Paul's arm and screamed. "Whoa, sorry, got carried away," Paul said. "Slow down, God." The scene stabilized as they approached more slowly. "No people in the vehicles," Paul observed. "That's cool, pretty advanced."

"It was all machines," Verbolana commented as if by rote.

"Cool," Paul intoned.

"How is that cool? The machines destroyed."

"Well, it's cool because if the machines were manned, I'm guessing it would be a pretty rotten life out there. Look at the sky, dirty and gray, and everything so flat and cultivated. There isn't a stream or a tree or anything out there."

"Oh." Verbolana grunted. "You'll have to translate all this when we get out of here. I don't really understand most of what I see here."

"Sure, but I'm sure I'm going to see it from a different perspective, so ask questions as we go. We're not in any hurry here." When he got no response he continued, "As a chef, I hate this shit. Look at those fields, all lined up one against the other. Exactly the kind of shit I avoid. Wheat grown on a north-facing hillside, watered by spring rain, dried by a gentle summer sun; it makes a

336

huge difference. Look at those animals penned down there, tromping around in their own shit, eating from troughs. Meat's gonna taste like shit."

"The people ate meat, too?"

"Looks like it; maybe they just drank milk; I don't know. You ready? I've seen enough."

"Sure. Where are we going?" Overwhelmed, Verbolana had forgotten their plan.

"Let's just stay where we are and shoot back in time. God, scroll back in time … a year every second. Let's see where that gets us."

The scene changed very little for the first minute or two. Fields held different crops; machines changed in appearance and location; the skies cleared slightly. After about five minutes, they noticed machines scurrying across the dome more frequently, equipment was dismantled and eventually disappeared along the edge, fields reverted to grassland, streams and roads appeared. Somewhere during the seventh or eighth minute, the dome developed an edge along the far horizon and they watched as second after second it retreated, until the entire city was revealed. Then they noticed smaller domes within the city. And people! They noticed people for the first time outside the city, moving in vehicles, running machinery, walking in the fields.

"God, please stop," Paul commanded. "This seems to be a fairly pivotal point," he observed. "God, what is the date?"

**"In reference to what?"**

"The Cleansing," Verbolana shot in.

**"318 B.C."**

"How do they broadcast—communicate news?" Paul asked.

**"Direct access."**

"Then please show us the global news of the day."

An announcer droned between Verbolana's ears as images filled her sight. A smoking mountain appeared, cultivated fields at its foot running halfway up its side.

The narrator spoke as the video ran: "And in Calbassis, watch continues. Day five, and all but the Civil Guard and fire crews have been evacuated. Earthquakes continue to tell the story of rising magma and the eventual eruption. Authorities now expect the west face to explode at any minute. Good news for the city of Ountrup, which sits at the base of the east slope. For further coverage, please request Baroux National News."

A new voice and a new scene filled her vision. Running, dodging figures in a burning cityscape. "Civil unrest continues in Chatram. Local authorities have imposed a sunset to dawn curfew, but nothing seems to stem the violence. The kidnapping and murder of a Tragot national last week have sparked tension that has been building since last year's boycott of Tragot fruit. Chatramian citizens are demanding the international living wage be extended to Festerian workers living in Tragot. Tragotian merchants ..."

"Change to local news," Paul requested.

"... immigration laws do not seem to be the answer." A young man with unnaturally pale skin and hair leaned forward at a table, his hands clasped, and his eyes fierce. "Until Morivans have equal rights and equal access to health care, travel, universities and the like, things are not going to get any better."

Another face and another voice, this time a young woman with dark skin and hair. "The only solution is to close our borders. Those who are here can stay, but we can no longer allow the continual flow of immigrants to invade our land. We do not have the resources ..."

"God, show us local arts and entertainment."

Engulfing music and the backs of heads filled their views. Across a lavish hall they saw others sitting in rapt attention, dressed in beautiful gowns. Below, performers in gay costumes danced to the music, apparently telling a story with their movements.

"Augh! What are we doing?" Verbolana screamed. "This is driving me crazy!"

"Like I said," Paul soothed. "I've never done this before. With my planet, I always had an inkling as to what I wanted to see or where I wanted to go. I'm shooting blind here and you're certainly no help."

"Isn't there a directory like before?"

"I'm sure there is, but let's have a seat. We might be here for a long time. God, give us a couch." Paul dropped into the new offering and beckoned Verbolana to join him. After she curled into his shoulder, he continued, "God, show us a directory of everything recorded on or about this planet." A scrollable listing appeared. Paul reviewed the choices for a few minutes before deciding there were too many. "Show just histories." The list changed but was still daunting. "Just historical overviews." The list shrank to less than a hundred offerings. "Seems to be a popular planet to write about. Show only multimedia presentations." The list narrowed to five.

Paul frowned. "I recognize one of these names. He's from Terra. Maybe we should look at one of the other ones."

"From your home world?" Verbolana perked. "Let's look at that one. You'll probably be able to relate to him."

"I doubt it, but I am curious. I knew this guy, Josef Goebbels, had somehow landed in Heaven. He has complete control over two neighborhoods not far from mine, but I didn't know he was branching out. Probably wants to take over the whole fucking city."

"Doesn't sound like you like him very much." Verbolana raised her head to catch his eye.

"He was one of the leaders of the biggest massacre in my home world's history. I watched a lot of young men march off to war and never come back because of that man and a few others. And I felt guilty because I was too old to fight. I was quite upset when I heard he had made it up here. I took it as absolute proof that God doesn't give a rat's ass who he lets in."

"Then why don't we pick someone else?" Verbolana concluded.

"No, no, this has my curiosity now. God, show us 'The Final Solution Done Right' by Josef Goebbels."

A strikingly handsome man with blonde hair, chiseled cheeks and full military regalia stood before them, a lone hazy planet circled slowly in the background.

"Good day," the figure began after a warming smile. "It is my pleasure to talk to you today about one of my favorite subjects: The grand design of God himself and those who have the insight and courage to follow his ... "

"God, stop!" Paul called out. "This is absurd! I've seen a thousand pictures of this fucker. God, is that really Josef Goebbels, one of the high command of Nazi Germany?"

**"Yes."**

Paul pushed back in the couch and stared at the blackened ceiling. "I guess it figures. Couldn't expect him to be any different." Then, looking down at Verbolana, he continued, "The guy was a rat-faced motherfucker; black hair, squirrelly body with a limp. Oh well. God, continue."

"... direction." With the clicking heels of his knee-high boots, Goebbels took three steps to the left as the spinning planet grew. "Choices, especially those directed by God, are not always easy. And yet, the very nature of our survival as the dominant species of our home world sometimes, oftentimes, relies on those most difficult of choices." Slowly the spinning globe dissolved into pictures of people in obvious distress; children, mothers, hollowed cheeks, dirt-stained and raggedy. The images ran, one into the next, to the strains of mournful violins and oboes. Goebbels watched as well and shook his head in disgust and pity. "These people suffer because others have stolen food from their mouths, roofs from their heads. They sit in the cold, unjustly deprived of dignity because no one has the courage or strength to stand up for them." The images continued, one piled on the next until the weight muddled Verbolana's straining heart.

"Such suffering is inexcusable," Goebbels continued. "And it is brought on by what I call 'devilution.' — the evolution of the devil and his ways." He brought his hands from behind his back and leaned into his audience as if to grab each of those on the couch by the ears. "This imposter who sits and watches us knows nothing of God. He is the devil and he is having his way with you."

"Stop!" Paul shouted. "This is insane! The man is a master manipulator. I cannot watch this. God, shut this man off!"

# Chapter 37

Trake tore through the crisp skin and into the soft flesh of a Sarat leg. Grease coated his cheeks and dripped from his hand. Staring into the flickering fire, lost in thought, he wiped his lips with the back of his hand. Chewing the savory meat, he contemplated the revelations that continued to bombard his already decimated beliefs.

"Well, I can't say for sure; only what I've been told, but yes, the cities are inhabited," Salkat reported. Trake looked up from the flames and pulled his fur cloak tighter. For confirmation, he looked at the men who sat around the fire. Some nodded; others just looked down, the burden of the unexplored truth bearing too much close scrutiny. "We've had a few visitors who claim they've been there. One said he was born in a city just to the north of us. Told stories of his life living underground. Didn't sound like much of a life to me, but then he didn't think much of our life either, under the guns of the blimps. Guess everybody gets used to what they're dealt and fears what's unfamiliar."

"That's undoubtedly Barstat," Trake concluded. "We pummel that city regularly. Can't be much there."

"I wouldn't be so sure," Salkat retorted. "This guy said they live way underground where the blimps can't get them."

Trake frowned with this new thought. "How would they live? What would they eat?"

"Don't know exactly," Salkat admitted. "The guy said they had rebuilt some of the machines, that water still came out of the pipes and that they had light whenever they needed. He said there were plenty of small animals around. Pets gone wild, I think."

"Rebuilt machines!" one of the others exclaimed. "That cannot be permitted!"

Salkat retorted, "I'd take all the machines I could get my hands on. Problem is, they defend their stuff to the death. This guy told stories of repeated attacks from folks like us. They send the machines after them; drive them out."

"Those must be the people we fight," Trake guessed. "The losers."

"Yeah, that's why we haven't gone up there. It's not worth the fight; we get it from both sides." Salkat stirred the fire with a long stick, bringing an artificial brightness to his face.

"You can only play with those you were born with," another threw in.

"Not the way I see it." Trake let the anger from such an easy defeat show clearly in his voice. "Seems more like the saying should be 'if you want to play, you gotta step up.'"

"It's just an old saying." Salkat defended his colleague. "But it's more true than not."

"Maybe so, but it speaks of defeat before the battle is even engaged," Trake insisted. "I don't care about their machines as much as finding a way to align ourselves. Seems like we are the buffer for many very comfortable people. Seems like we need to shake things up a bit if we're going to survive. I keep thinking that things are going to change. Eventually the Chosen Generals will wake up to this new world. Maybe they already know, and they just haven't told their rank and file." That revelation stopped him for a moment before he continued. "Either way, we must prepare."

The statement garnered a few nods around the fire. "So," Trake continued before his men fell into the gloom that waited, "What's the plan?"

"Dig in and defend," somebody threw in. "That's what we've always done. And it's worked so far." Then the man got brave. "This is news only to you. The rest of us have known these things forever. You're the only who says the situation has changed."

One of Trake's Honored defended the unknown voice. "No use throwing ourselves on our own swords. The Directors will never authorize a ground assault, and that is the only real danger we face."

"The Directors will do whatever they need to do," Trake insisted. "Look at what they've done already."

"What? What have they done?" came another voice from the dark. "They defend themselves just like we have talked about doing, just like the farmers to the east and just like those who live in the cities have done." When there was only silence around the fire, the voice continued tentatively. "Just because you have chosen to sleep with women does not mean the Directors are evil, or wrong or even misguided. The Gods speak to different people in different ways. That is what I think." The voice fell as its surety faded. Then it reemerged. "The Gods ask that we glory in our own survival. That is all."

"And that is exactly my point!" Trake jumped at the words. "Survival trumps all. Survival is what the Directors focus on. And when they perceive a new threat, they will adapt. The voices of the Gods will change. And when they do change, we will find ourselves caught in the middle, human shields for those who already enjoy more safety than any of us have ever known!"

* * *

345

They sat in an empty room again, the walls enveloping them in their blackened forever. After a long few moments, Paul apologized. "I'm sorry. I thought I could handle that guy's shit, or maybe I thought he'd changed. He persuaded an entire nation of sixty million people that their suffering was due to others and the great conspiracies of everyone around them. Maybe not that unusual, but the destruction and devastation it brought to our entire planet was phenomenal."

"So how does he tie that into what he was saying?" Verbolana asked innocently. "Maybe he *has* changed."

"No, no, I don't even want to go there. I saw the writing on the wall and it was in blood. Let's just pick someone else and get on with this."

"Okay," Verbolana agreed. "I'm sorry this is upsetting you so. I thought it was just going to be me who got upset on this trip."

Paul brought up the directory, picked a name at random and started the next program.

*"Welcome to the Kingdoms of God,"* a lovely female voice called out to a star-filled room. As if traveling at great speed, the stars rushed past their couch until the blurring voyage settled on one that grew bigger until it filled their view. With a swish of speed, their vantage point veered from the enveloping sun and raced past one swirling planet after another until it honed in on one. The onslaught of this planet slowed, then stopped with the same hazy globe hovering about where it had been with Goebbels.

"Oh, my God!" Paul blurted, then sat up and leaned forward for a better look. "Is that you?"

Verbolana also jolted as her double, in full battle gear, complete with Talsartt and gleaming tattoo, strolled before them.

Paul laughed. "The program must have picked you up from the room. I've heard of that in games and stuff, but usually you have to ask. Wow, check you out! Quite a warrior!"

346

The image suddenly blurred into action, took up the Talsartt and made large graceful figure-eights while she danced from one elegant position to the next. Then the image morphed into a shirtless Honored male. Without a break, the Talsartt disappeared, only to be replaced by a two-handed broadsword as the man's hair sprouted and rough clothing grew across his body. Before they could adjust to the new character with his awkward slashes, he evolved into a new man with waving fists, his clothes smoothed into buttoned refinement. The twisted face of this new character mouthed silent venom as his hands raised in shaking emphasis. Again morphing, his hands dropped, his face relaxed and his clothes flowed into robes of concealing folds.

"A Director," Verbolana whispered, as if the figure that now stood before them could hear her.

But the Director did not stay long either. His benign face and soft body continued to transform and to Verbolana's surprise, settled in the shape of a rather attractive woman; tall, with long black hair and mottled shirt and pants. An obviously well-trained, solid body with square shoulders and sinewy arms stood proud before them and eyed the Talsartt that had reappeared in her hand.

"An interesting weapon for an interesting and unique battle, the battle for a beleaguered planet holding tenuously to its ability to support human life," the narrator explained. "At least that is what one side to this conflict contends." A woven harness grew around her waist and chest as a rope grew from the air around her. She casually grabbed the rope as it accepted her weight and lifted her. The bottom of a hovering battle blimp appeared, and as the woman gained height, she spun in the harness and brought the Talsartt around for a sweeping pass at a Wretched warrior who had materialized in thin air below her. The Talsartt swung freely through flesh and bone to splatter blood off into the blackness.

"A typical story of the haves and have-nots, you might think; but things are not so clear-cut on Father," the narrator continued. "Layers of intrigue and deception await in this the unfolding drama. In fact," the narrator emphasized with another swipe of the weapon, now at an archer, his bow drawn to fire, "Their entire culture is built around drama, complete with a bevy of Gods who write and choreograph these ongoing acts. But what is truly unique about this world and this conflict lies in two facts. The first fact is that, beyond creation, God has never set foot on this planet and has not sent any helpers; and the second fact is that, due to the catastrophes brought on by man, all of mankind has actually de-evolved."

While the woman talked, she had floated down to the unseen floor and now stood before them in flowing iridescent robes. Her generous bosom, hourglass waist and smooth tapered legs peeked from the folds of the translucent gown. "Not without the force of a thousand suns would any woman give up such beauty." She pulled the collar of her gown back to reveal a single strand of shimmering blue and green stones. "Not ten thousand suns.

"Yet some on this planet asserted that such luxuries were too easily reaped, and at the same time at too high a price. Do I have your attention? Will you stick with me through the set design and rehearsals so I can tell this story properly? Yes? Well, let's get started."

The woman's clothing changed again to tight, roughly sewn furs as the scene around her solidified into a stone-ringed fire with a collection of dark-skinned hairy humans huddled close around a warming fire. "As with most of our worlds, God created mankind from a carefully orchestrated evolution, with a later forced migration that populated this world with humans uniquely adapted to their environments, yet remarkably similar in overall makeup."

The scene changed to fire after fire as the woman changed in appearance and clothing, depending on the climate and circumstances encountered. "Again, as with most worlds, each settled area developed its own language, customs and Gods, all evolving from necessity to help them survive." Crude drawings of exaggerated faces, flowing bodies and warrior deities floated through the sky as the woman's garb and features flowed from race to race and eon to eon until she stood proudly in flowing white beside a broad-shouldered man in full leather armor, complete with helmet, sword, belted dagger and shield.

The woman stroked the man's shoulder and bulging arm as she spoke. "The human condition is set from its earliest evolutionary strain or from God himself. That we still do not know. And though the vast majority of individual humans are content with their share of food, sex and shelter, there are always those who crave more. From the smallest gatherings to the largest nations, those with the need for more make themselves known." She leaned into the man with pursed lips. "With voice, fists or bombs; these few who crave more inevitably convince others to follow. The people of Father are no different, nor has the propaganda been different. Deities must be appeased, races must be homogenized, nations protected and wrongs righted." In response to her speech, the warrior beside her lunged forward with a ferocious scream and jabbing sword. Verbolana jolted back in spite of herself.

Another montage of images erupted before Verbolana could settle. She hung tighter to Paul as great armies with lances and swords clashed across green landscapes. Smoke and confusion covered the battlefield before the percussion of explosions filled the room, bloody bodies flying, limp with death. As the smoke cleared, buildings burned. A frantic woman with clutched infant ran coughing, dodging the dead strewn across the pavement.

"Innocent?" The standing warrior dissolved as the running woman froze, head turned toward the couch, desperation clear on her face. The narrator now wore a beautiful ball gown, her long hair piled elegantly on her head before it fell in tight curls down across her bared shoulders. "How can we know? Did this woman vote in the last election? Did she stand mute when the bullies of the street grabbed another victim? Or was she a whisperer? Did she fill a man with her wanton desire ... for this dress maybe, or these shoes?" She swished and swirled in her gown as the woman behind her moved again, this time her motion slowed so that the building that exploded beside her came to pieces with bright oranges and yellows, enveloping her and her child before she could turn her head to the new disturbance. Verbolana watched an inkling of the coming doom flit across her eyes.

"Stop!" Verbolana shrieked. The playback froze, the woman's eyes just visible through the cocooning fireball. "Turn it off!" Verbolana screamed again. The room went black except for a slight indistinct glow.

"Why is everything about death?" she demanded to the room. "Is there no discussion about the accomplishment?" Paul sat mute. "When did we learn to fly? How were those buildings fed with water? Who designed the dress and the shoes? Does no one care about these things?"

Reluctantly, Paul stepped in once the silence enveloped them. "Death is the ultimate drama of life, I guess. It pinpoints, with great focus, our frailties and stupidity." He thought for a moment, then continued, "Looking back through history, it is so easy, with the advantage of hindsight, to see the mistakes, to maintain proper perspective and to assign blame or credit. I guess it makes it all a little easier, when we shrug our shoulders at the future, to know that those who went before us were so incredibly stupid."

Verbolana groaned. "So the stage is set. My people started out no differently than yours or many others. I guess that is comforting, but I can't take much more of this! Is it possible to skip ahead?"

Paul muttered something, and a new index appeared. "Looks like it is broken up into chapters. We were just viewing the preamble. This thing goes on forever. God, how long is this whole presentation?"

**"Eighteen hours, twelve minutes."**

"Holy crap!" Paul exclaimed. "We'll be here forever. God, how long to finish the preamble?"

**"Ten minutes."**

"Verbolana, can't you buck up for a few more minutes? As much as I like you, and as much as I want to know where you come from, eighteen hours is a bit much."

"Ten minutes?" Verbolana responded. "I guess. I certainly couldn't stand eighteen hours of this!"

They sat in the blackened room, silent. Finally Verbolana muttered, "God, continue the preamble."

The woman and baby disappeared into the fireball, which continued to enlarge, only to stop inches from Verbolana and Paul's noses, the heat enough to make the two grateful when it receded.

The gowned narrator stood unaffected, tinkering with the beads of her dress. She looked directly into Verbolana's eyes. "This is where Father's history starts to diverge from that of so many other worlds." A farmhouse appeared in the distance, rows of crops ran off out of the picture, with penned animals to the right. A large green-leafed tree stood solidly in the foreground. Three children scampered around the base of the tree, while another swung on suspended ropes. A fresh breeze reached Verbolana's face and washed the last horror from her skin.

The narrator spoke: "Please keep in mind that this planet is one of God's oldest creations. With God's assistance, every other world he created in this era was more technologically advanced by this point in its evolution. Medical sciences, mathematics, engineering, agriculture. In fact, all the sciences suffered on Father because of the retarded development of such concepts as the zero, the wheel, the lever, calendaring, the arch and many others. Most cultures received these concepts through divine inspiration, but not the children of Father. In addition, compared to many worlds, the climate was mild, so inventions born through necessity came slowly as well. These facts become extremely important at this point in the children's development."

A woman in simple clothes and swollen belly stepped from the farmhouse and watched the children playing for a long while, as the narrator also watched. Verbolana drank in the scene, remembering that at this point in history Father did not need protection. Verbolana drank in a peace she had never known and snuggled deeper into Paul's shoulder.

The woman finally called her children to their noon meal, and as the narrator took up her next point, Verbolana watched the children tagging and dodging toward the house, in no particular hurry. "What took centuries to develop on other worlds took eons on Father. This gave them time. For thousands of years more than their contemporaries, they languished around campfires and waterholes telling stories and gazing at the stars. And for thousands more years they plodded to develop organized agriculture, roads for trade and abstractions such as currency and national boundaries. They had time. Time to talk and love and think. And time to develop solid philosophies of tolerance and acceptance so that, by the time the technology of killing became easy, Father's children had pretty much lost the taste for it."

Their view picked up a man leading some sort of animal to the front of the house and tying its lead to a rail. As he climbed the steps, his audience soared down so by the time the man closed his front door, Verbolana and Paul were at his back. They followed him through the house. Upholstered furniture filled one room, its walls lined with books. The next room contained wooden chairs with a long table between. Finally he entered a bright open room so large that the table where the mother and children sat hardly filled a corner. Silently the man strode to what Verbolana now recognized as a sink and thoroughly washed his hands. Drying them, he finally spoke, "Creek's running a bit high; opened the gates at the north forty. Thought I'd flush the Marlot pond while I had the chance. Everything fine here?"

"Noticed a little mold in the granary. Been spreading the Milnox out on the racks to give them a little more sun, but other than that ..." she nodded her head at their three offspring, "life is glorious."

"Let's give thanks," the man said as he sat at the head of the table. Verbolana crinkled her forehead at the unfamiliar words the group chorused.

*"Gods of peace, watch over our land,*
*Gods of rain, please take my hand,*
*Gods of health, bless everyone to see*
*That love and happiness is all we need."*

Verbolana watched with moistening eyes. She sniffed her nose and wiped at her cheeks. "These are my people," she whispered to Paul. "Father is so kind and they barely notice. What I would have given ..."

"As already shown," the narrator continued. "All this is not to say these people didn't still have their squabbles and indiscretions. It is merely to point out that they did not suffer the wholesale killings and genocide other worlds experienced. And therefore, when the homogenizing influences of effortless travel came to this world, those technologies were more given to bringing people together than to annihilating or alienating them."

A globe free of haze appeared behind the narrator. Great cloud masses dissolved and reformed with the lazy spin. Verbolana tracked one particularly well-organized spiraling mass from one rotation to the next as the narrator continued. "As any astute student has already learned, God has yet to answer whether He chose or created planets with an advantageous orbit and rotation on which to create his little toys. Still, the fact remains that every planet inhabited with humans is not only a proper distance from its sun, but also has a rotation and tilt that allows for similar length of days as well as seasonal changes."

The globe stopped spinning and as the clouds dissolved, the globe started coming apart at the seams, flattening to stretch in only two dimensions behind the woman, who was now dressed in a heavy skirt and jacket, her hair gray, with her body somewhat deflated.

Paul laughed aloud. "Must be getting into the heavy stuff now. A professor is a professor on any world, I guess."

Verbolana frowned at him, but the woman gained their attention before she spoke. "As you will note, the tropical zone is approximately eighteen degrees from the equator on Father. I have shaded this section in green. As I start the map in motion, note that the first humans appear and flourish within this shaded area."

The woman now had a long pointer in her hand and as light pink dots appeared, she pointed them out. "As these areas grow darker, it indicates population density. As wide blue shadings appear, they indicate general paths of migration, and as the pink shadings change to different colors, this indicates the evolution of different races. We will move at thousand-year clips for a while so you can see the migration and refinement of races, roads and settlement boundaries. You will note that as populations move out of the tropics and develop into different races, the concentrations of people are more formally defined. And, as the blue zones shrink into specific routes and roads, the temperate areas for twenty degrees above and below the line of the tropics develop their forms and quality of transportation exponentially. We call this the 'brown grass phenomenon.' Where weather is less hospitable and growing seasons are more defined, populations needed to band together and organize more carefully to survive."

They all watched as more colored smudges and blue lines appeared. "We will slow now to a five-hundred-year clip." They watched a little longer as their aged professor traced lines and spots of interest. "And, as development speeds up on the planet, we will slow down to hundred-year clips. Note how the temperate zone continues to connect as the tropic zone tends to languish in this development."

As new darker bluish green lines appeared, the professor informed them, "We will now slow to hundred-year clips and in a moment slow to fifty-year jumps. Note the straighter routes developing. These indicate rail transportation and in a moment … Yes, there." She traced a line across the map. "The first formal air route."

They watched for another minute until the map was a jumbled mess of different colors. "Keep your eyes peeled now. We will slow to twenty-year clips. Watch as rather rapidly surfaced roads disappear as rail and air routes increase. Also note as only a very few years pass, the cities, first in the temperate zone, start to change color to indicate race migration. And please read into that religious and cultural migration as well."

The woman's pointer was busy now, flitting from one area to the next, and as only a few minutes passed, great concentrations of population colors deepened and mixed. "We must stop here. The great migrations have begun. Here the real fascination of this world begins to unfold. As I stated previously, ethnic and cultural animosities were greatly reduced on Father because of their slow, unassisted development. Also, without the traditional conflicts, which on other worlds killed millions upon millions of each generation, the population of Father grew and melded much more quickly."

Above the map, a great blimp materialized and floated effortlessly across the scene, while an equally impressive ocean liner floated below in the opposite direction. In between the two, a snaking train whizzed through midair at great speed. "Civilized, efficient and cheap travel developed with these enormous floating liners, which could carry up to five thousand travelers in great comfort and style. Rail and ocean travel continued as well, so with these three modes working together, anyone who wanted to travel was on the move. As leisure time grew with the mechanization of agriculture and industry, travel and the arts became priorities with almost all people." Her pointer returned to the map. "Watch now as the population almost completely abandons the rural areas and concentrates in the ever-growing cities. And note that as the density of the cities increases, various racial and cultural colors blend into a medium brown."

They watched as very little changed for a few minutes. Then, as if with a giant eraser, the entire map was wiped clean of colors, leaving only tiny specks here and there.

"The Great Cleansing." The woman's attire had switched back to her original garb—Verbolana's double, complete with mostly shaved skull and tattoo. "The largest genocide of any world to date. More than eighteen billion individuals died in a single day, with another five hundred million in the next weeks. All performed by the most diabolical conspiracy between a small group of malcontents and an army of domestic, farm and industrial machines. One of the most homogeneous, civilized and peaceful populations destroyed in the name of ecology."

Verbolana's double took a giant swipe with her Talsartt. "But the story does not end here. Join us to see how a decimated beleaguered few are rebuilding a world while still constantly harassed from the sky by the descendants of the Great Conspiracy."

The woman turned and walked into the engulfing blackness.

"Wow!" Paul sighed. "She really left us hanging. What happened?"

Verbolana sat up, still wondering why the woman had doubled her. "According to her, my ancestors murdered an entire world of peace-loving families for their own hidden selfish reasons. At least that's how she made it seem. Of course, she didn't go into any of the real reasons. She obviously has her own agenda and political bias."

"I hate to say it, Verbolana, but she certainly got my curiosity up. What say we take a little break and then watch the last two chapters: 'Cleansing Father' and 'The De-Evolution of the Deceived and the Deceivers.'"

"Sure," Verbolana groaned. "I guess we can't stop now."

# Chapter 38

Trake, your place is here." Atasha worked quickly over the low cooking fire. "You can't do any good there. Like you have said, we are the ones caught in the middle. No one is going to jeopardize their position for us."

"I'm tired," Trake lamented. "First I had to convince the men. And now you? I know I am right. That should be all there is to it."

"Should be? Since when is anything ever the way it 'should be?' What 'is' is that you have responsibilities here, to me, to your daughter and to this clan. Your adventuring can serve no purpose beyond your selfish desire to travel and quench your curiosity." Atasha flipped the meat that sizzled just above the coals.

"You are provided for." Trake latched onto one piece of her argument, hoping to defeat her with logic. "The clan remembers. They bring us what we need."

"And what of your daughter?"

"What about my daughter?" Trake was lost. "I won't be gone forever. I am going to trade, that is all. At least that is all they will see, a trader, bringing meat in trade for what? What do you want, Atasha? A new pot for the fire, soft cloth for the baby?"

"Don't try to bribe me with trinkets. It's you; I want *you*. Here!" Panicked love shuddered through her voice. "You are trying to prove your selfless devotion to me and the clan, and you are doing the exact opposite. We need you here, all of us."

"What we need is a defensible position!" Trake shot back. "My Lieutenants can handle the training for now. The recruits need endless repetition at this point."

"Why are you the only one who sees the threat? If the men required so much convincing, maybe they were right to begin with." Atasha flipped the meat onto one of their only plates. With a longer stick, she rutted through the coals and extracted three small root vegetables and pushed them onto the plate as well. "How can you be so sure your Generals will abandon their ways, laws they have followed for more than a hundred years?"

"The Gods speak to me. They test me and challenge my thinking. They have prepared me for this mission, so I must obey." Trake paced with his speech, five steps, turn, and five steps back.

"Maybe you and Atlana should go with me. I can protect you, and we would be more convincing. A family traveling together could not be seen as sinister."

"Now you are talking plain foolishness," Atasha scoffed. "You would throw your daughter to the mercy of the wild road to face those who would push us under the cannons of the Fiendish? Don't you remember why we joined the clan in the first place? Vipeon by night and blimps by day. You talk of protecting us, and then you suggest throwing us into the path of the very storm you wish to avoid? Have you gone insane?"

"At this point, I am convinced we would be better off on our own than we are here sitting in the center of the bull's-eye. If we are free to move and react on our own, I can protect us. I would put myself up against any other sword in this land."

"At this point we are as safe as we will ever be. You are training your army and we are building defenses. Winter will come soon, so the blimps will slow their missions. They have not seen us, even though they have flown over us a dozen times. We have no reason to panic or even worry beyond our borders. We have game and a bountiful harvest."

"We are fodder for the cannons of the Chosen and a decoy for those comfortable on their farms," Trake complained.

"Is that it? You are resentful and jealous?" Atasha blurted. "You would rather die than live with shame because others have it better?" She peeled the charred skin from the vegetables and mashed the centers onto the plate. She then cut the meat into bite-sized pieces and handed the juicy plate to Trake. "Do we mean so little to you that you must focus on what you don't have instead of what you do have?"

"*Think so little of you?* What madness are you spouting now?" Trake refused the plate, as if accepting it would mean he accepted her accusation. "We live in dirt and smoke from the only heat we have stings our eyes, while others live in comfort and safety. Is it so strange that I should want more for my family?"

Atasha offered the plate again, and with his countering words, he was now in a position to accept, as if the plate was her apology. "Is the price for this comfort and safety worth it? And how do you know what these others have? All you have are stories."

"That's all I have had all my life—stories," Trake said to the plate lingering just under his nose. "I want to see for myself. I must know how others live."

"We are not enough," Atasha concluded. "Will we be enough when your son arrives?"

Trake looked up from his plate, searched her eyes. "Are you telling me...?"

"That your constant pollinations have yielded more fruit? Yes, I feel your son growing in me."

\* \* \*

"Truth layered with fiction," Paul lamented. "It is this way with all history, I fear." He looked down at the top of Verbolana's head. She still lay snuggled to his shoulder, the room now black.

"There was no proclamation." Verbolana's voice was a tiny squeak. "They didn't even know. They didn't have a chance!"

"Do you think it would have made a difference?" Paul's eyes teared for her pain.

"So many babies!"

"Yes."

"Would I have listened? Would I have even noticed?" Verbolana searched her feelings.

"Life carries as many distractions as truths, maybe more," Paul rationalized for her.

"But how could they die without the choice? The Directors said they all had a choice."

"Great men lie," Paul stated with finality. "Your world is no different. The greater the challenges, the greater the lies. Most truth is not compelling enough. Fiction is what moves people."

"How much is a billion?" Verbolana wondered aloud.

"I don't know, a thousand million, I think. But it hardly matters." Paul was stunned, too, but he knew that showing it would not help Verbolana. "You were duped, they were duped, but it was probably all unavoidable. People don't listen when their stomachs are full and their children are happy."

"But the Prince, the Author, he was so conniving," she muttered. "All the lies. The towers. We were never told how they were built. We were told they were built by the Righteous, as a testament and monument to their commitment, not by trickery and deceit by the very machines that facilitated evil!

"And the Leading Man," Verbolana exhaled in disgust. "To kill your own sister and then turn on your cousins, just to prove your commitment to your great-great-grandfather. What kind of barbarism is that? The men I was raised to worship were murdering fanatics!" Rage and confusion choked her until her eyes fixed on another insult that tore words from her throat. "And the invocation of the towers, the grand challenge. Brilliant lies conceived by brutal men. The whole world watched to see if their city would win, to see if the most creative minds of their city would be anointed. What diabolical mind came up with that idea? That one blast of energy killed nine-tenths of the world's population in one blow."

Silence filled the empty room. Finally Paul commented, "Certainly explains where the homosexual concept came from. It was a great way to control the population of the towers, but I don't think I would ever have thought an idea like that could work. But since the Leading Man and his cronies controlled the guest lists, they could pack them with their friends—friends who needed no convincing. From there, all they needed to do was create the dogma. And it was a dogma each one of them had lived with all their lives."

"The narrator called it a 'grand experiment,' but I saw nothing grand about any of it," Verbolana continued her mumbling.

"She was probably referring to the scale. The scale was certainly grand—meaning big, expansive. But I'm not sure. We could go back and ask her. The program is interactive, has a clone of her actually attached to the presentation. I think she used 'grand' as 'bold' or 'ingenious.'

"Verbolana, you have to get over the idea that what your world went through was unique or uniquely brutal. The scale *was* certainly grand, but only because the scale of the problem was equally grand. Your people simply made it further than most worlds did before reaching the tipping point the Prince feared. I'm sure, though, that if we went into her comparative analyses, we would find that your world is neither the most brutal nor its people the most conniving. It may even be praised for finding such an elegant solution."

"Elegant solution!" Verbolana spat. She sat up and stared at Paul, with a new fire burning in her eyes. She slapped his hand from her shoulder. "How can you even breathe something like that?"

"Because there is an inherent and inevitable rub in God's design. God does not allow his children to cheat death. Not for long, anyway. And people always try. God understands that the desire must be there, but the reality must never be reached, for then the ultimate motivator would be lost."

"How do you know what God understands?" Verbolana spat.

"Ask him," was Paul's simple answer.

Verbolana sat mute, boring lasers through his eyes. The jangling, familiar excitement of resentment and fear battled with the soothing, seductive flow of acceptance. Little pieces of stillness, like logs floating atop a raging river, insinuated themselves into her heart. She heard, for the first time, an elegant solution of her own; one that might, just might, allow her some peace.

She sat back down, away from Paul's encroaching arm and threw her eyes into the surrounding blackness. Images of her own making swirled before her eyes, her own "direct access" to her perfect memory. She saw the whip, both received and administered; saw the ropes dangling, the giant blimp hovering. And the faces. With flawless recollection and zoom capabilities, she sat in review. Random faces on random days. She searched and found it all—joy, confusion, fear and envy. She saw pride and suspicion, bewilderment and certainty. And she found love behind the masks. In everyone, if she looked long enough. A sudden, unrepressed sparkle; a soft sideways glance; a gentle touch on a shoulder or hidden brush of a hand. "I was not a deviant," she mumbled to the darkness.

Trake crossed the frame of an investigated moment. Verbolana perked, focused, zoomed. He walked with friends, strutting and laughing, with little regard for the day circles they invaded on their way to wherever they felt like going. In mid-laughter, his head back, eyes wide. His eyes brushed hers where she sat those many years ago.

"What was that?" Verbolana exclaimed and sat up, oblivious of Paul now. She froze the image, rewound, played it back, froze, zoomed, burrowed. She watched Trake's arrogance dissolve with the eye contact, his pleasure soured as his longing welled. With the next heartbeat it was gone; the hard mask of arrogant resentment returned. Validation enveloped her heart and pumped through her body like a healing tonic.

Body-rich with fortifying love, she evoked, "God, show me Trake, what he is doing right now."

Flickering images filled the room. Nothing looked familiar. Dark shadows danced and layered across darker shapes. Trake moved into her frame as recognition grew. He was squatted in some sort of small enclosure. Verbolana scanned to her left. A small fire burned on the floor, the only light mingling with loitering smoke. Trake moved and brought her attention back. His head was down, his hands busy at a low table. Another shadow moved, allowing light to fall on the subject of Trake's attention. Shock and confusion knocked her back against the couch. Trake was swaddling a baby.

# Chapter 39

He looks like a good man," Paul contended. "Strong, forceful, resolute, yet still compassionate and tender. Can't ask for much more."

"No, no, you can't," Verbolana agreed. "It hurts, though, to see him giving another woman what he could not give me. Then, part of me is happy for him. He has learned so much. I am proud, too! I knew … I always knew he had it in him, that he was different."

"And yet, my guess is that he isn't different," Paul contended. "Trake hid, like all people hide. Circumstances dictate outward behavior, but it is a mistake to think that repression, brainwashing or a complete lack of opportunity actually diminishes who we are inside. I am still amazed at how some people can emerge from the most horrible surroundings to become saints. Sure, some are damaged beyond repair by outward circumstances, but who's to say that those people weren't damaged at birth and actually flourished with their lot in life?"

Verbolana sat with that for a moment. *Unique, yet uniquely similar. Were all so blessed?* She closed her eyes and asked God for a review of what she had just seen. Trake reappeared before her, as did the woman and small child. In the golden glow of the dying fire, Verbolana observed anew. This time she watched Atasha, Trake's so-called "Wretched" woman. Her passion was obvious in her words, fighting for Trake to stay with her, but there was more. Her eyes, the quick jabbing movements as she cooked, her jaw, working the words before and after she spoke. Verbolana saw anger—and confusion—and fear. She also sensed an intense protectiveness that would have struck Verbolana as sinful a year or so ago. Yes, it was all there in this woman. A woman who should have been stupid and pathetic, if the stories were true, was instead as deep and rich as anyone Verbolana had known.

Verbolana pulled back and looked at Paul. She felt his eyes searching hers, looking for a sign of how she felt. She obliged him. "I feel good, peaceful." Then, as his eyes smiled, "I think I have seen enough for today, though. I need some time to absorb all of this. Will you take me home?"

He laughed. "And where would that be? Home?"

Verbolana smiled at the joke that was hardly a joke. She searched Paul's eyes for any kind of rancor or derision. Apparently, he was not uncomfortable or displeased with what he had seen. She felt a deep sense of relief. She had bared her secrets and her most intimate failures to this man and he had not shied away. He had not judged or incriminated her with jealousy. He had seen and felt her pain and simply acknowledged her human struggle.

"I want to see your home, Paul. I want you to take me to your home and lay me on your bed and hold me."

He smiled, and without another word, they rose together, departed the world of retrospect and, arm in arm, strolled to the subway.

\* \* \*

Trake lay on the bank of the river, well upstream from the village; Atasha snuggled tight to his shoulder, Atlana fussing on his chest. "How do you think this is going to change anything? A man is born to protect." Filtered sun dropped through the thinning branches, dancing his vision. A cooling breeze rustled the remaining leaves, releasing a few fluttering ships of deep maroon and dusty yellow to drift slowly to the ground. "I will wait, see you through your swelling and welcome my son to the world. But then I will go. I owe it to you and the little ones."

Atasha snuggled deeper, nuzzling his ear and pressing her still-full breasts into his side. A sneaky hand played across his thigh and straightened his thickening cock against his belly. "We have all winter then. And today. Are you ready for a swim?"

"I'm ready to watch you."

"I would love your eyes on me." She stood, pulling his member with her a bit as she stood. Playfully she stood over his head as she bent to retrieve Atlana, which gave him a tantalizing view up her long skirt.

Giggling, Atasha stepped back off him and laid Atlana on the animal skin they had brought for lounging. Trake watched as she evolved easily from temptress to mother and then back again once their daughter was asleep. Catching his eye, she danced to the water's edge, dropping articles of clothing along the way. Naked and pimpling from the cold water, she stood in the shallows, splashing and smoothing water across her full form. Glistening now, she turned back to Trake with an evil grin, and coaxed him by fondling and plucking a finger across her puckered nipples. Trake responded by sitting up and pulling his thick straight monster from his pants. "My appreciation is obvious," he said, locking eyes with her and slowly stroking. "Come to your pleasure."

"Ah, I think not," she teased. "This time you must come to me. Kneel at my altar and pray to your most precious God."

With a jolt, Trake moved to his left, rolled and instinctively tucked his rapidly shrinking cock back into his pants. The Strength poured into him as he looked back to where he had rested only a moment before. An arrow protruded from the fur he had used for a cushion. "Atasha," he screamed and jumped to a full run. He watched her playful face try to catch up with his frantic movements. The arrow that pierced her chest convinced her that something had gone terribly wrong. She looked down in surprise, then back at Trake, an apology in her eyes. She crumpled into the water without a sound. Another arrow followed, and whizzed past Trake's ear. He batted at it like a bug, and splashed through the water to Atasha. She had rolled face down into the water, bobbing, relaxed. Trake snatched her up with one arm as if she were a straw doll and headed for shore and his other arm waved in defense of the next arrow. Two flew before he reached shore and he batted both away with a lightning hand.

He reached the laid-out skin, dropped his love as gently as possible, retrieved his sword and drew it all in one continuous motion. "Come out from the bushes, you Wretched coward! I will slice you to worm food!"

"Might as well," came a casual booming voice. "My arrows are obviously too slow." And out strolled the Master Instructor, General Bartoldt's stooge.

"You?" Trake bellowed, as he advanced to put himself between this Fiend and his family. "What are you doing here?"

"I should ask you the same thing," the man answered with a calm that shivered Trake's skin more than the frigid water that still clung to him. "You train the enemy to fight your own, and you wonder why I am here? Think of me as the long arm of the Directors."

He raised his sword in a mock salute. "And I apologize for your death."

Trake looked back at his crumpled, beautiful wife. "You *will*, before you die, apologize for my wife's death!"

"And your daughter's?" the man asked.

Trake jolted around. "Auuuuugh!" In a blind rage he rushed the man, astounded that he had not noticed the quills buried deep in his daughter's belly. The man stepped and laughed. "So different from the height of a blimp, isn't it? How many children have you killed?" He stopped to ward off a staccato of blows before continuing. "I can hear the order now: 'Target the breeders and the children. Father must be spared.'" He laughed again. "Eh, Blimp Commander?"

Somehow, Trake pulled his mind back from the edge of his sword. There was no blood on it, and he needed blood! He needed torn flesh, bulging eyes and screams of panicked pain! He needed to watch life drain into the dirt with the certain knowledge that Father would reject this man for his blasphemies. He dared not look back. Vengeance was now his life, his only focus. And this man had all the skill. Calm. Trake needed calm. Instead he vomited. Still in his stance, head up, at guard, his projected disgust flew past his raised sword and onto the feet of his terror.

The man jumped, and Trake swung, spontaneously and decisively. Blood. And flesh. Trake pulled back and evaluated just in time to meet a flurried counter-attack. He blocked, blocked, spun, sliced and ran to regroup. Nothing. The man stood with only the previous flesh wound on his right forearm. "Your deck loves to spin, I see. It is a waste on the trained," the Master instructed.

Trake's mind galvanized beyond his opponent. Limp and lifeless lay everything he lived for. Dizzy with a new wave of grief, he dropped his sword point to the ground for support. His head slumped, arms quaking, knees weak. He welcomed death. He felt the Master's obliging intent approach, swinging wide and low. Trake collapsed to his knees, scraping his sword point through the dirt in an attempt to remain upright. He fell forward, feeling the whoosh of the blade slide past his back. His blade pulled free of the dirt just as he collapsed, and from somewhere he found the incentive to lash out, driving his blade up and in. Before he succumbed to the full force of his grief, he felt his blade sink home, deep and satisfying. Though he knew, beyond any words or thought he had ever had, that he would never be satisfied again.

# Chapter 40

O rder in!" Verbolana called as she hung a ticket on the wheel and spun it to face the kitchen. "Fire twenty-three."

"I'd fire you if I could," Frank spouted from his grill station.

"And lose my regulars?" Vee shot back. "I don't think so." She spun back to her tables, her short skirt following her hips with a swish and a settle. She surveyed the room with its red checkerboard tablecloths and gay, abstract wall hangings. Her room now, her home turf. Everyone seemed content. She needed to give the couple at table forty-two a few more seconds with the menu; the folks at fifty, by the window, would need to be cleared just after, but since they always had dessert she didn't need to prepare their bill yet.

Everything was in order and under control. That felt good. Great, actually. She smiled and took a deep, cleansing breath—as if she needed it. No butterflies, she noticed, no trembling angst, no anticipated confrontations. *Peace, so this is what peace feels like.* Idly, she twirled her finger through her long high ponytail, waiting with absolutely no agenda.

She glanced back at Paul, his expert fingers flicked the edge of a knife through a multitude of sauces layered on a plate, creating an intricate web of colors and flavors. Without a wasted step, he reached into an under-counter refrigerator, pulled out a baking dish, and carefully scooped a pre-cut square of layered delight onto the plate. Verbolana recognized the dish, of course. They had named it after her, Verbolana's Dream. Who would have thought her planet offered so many treats? Paul had started with the staples she had grown to hate that now gave her such comfort, Kah melon and roasted Milnox. Then he had dragged Verbolana through fifteen centuries and the six major continents of Father in search of accompaniments. Verbolana had not only learned of the astonishing array of flavors and colors of her world, she had also learned about the people who enjoyed them. Real people. Honest, loving, genuine people. And diverse cultures and languages, religions and beliefs, all insinuating into her like water sucked into a damp sponge. By the time she returned to Paul's kitchen, she was determined to create something sweet from all of the places she had visited. From her basket of memories, she picked vibrant berries, fragrant spices, tangy fruit and sweeteners from every latitude for Paul to distill and craft into a home world comfort that could only exist in Heaven.

"Order up," Paul called.

Though the dessert was not for one of her tables, she sidled over to the window to make sure Paul had done justice to her people. She smiled at the plate, then at Paul. She saw the Ka and Milnox layer cake suspended in a Za web of woven cultures. She saw each face, each smile of those who had given, without hesitation, to the fabric of her world. This time she needed her cleansing breath, for tears welled up behind her eyes. All she needed to do was step back and watch her world spin backward through space and project through the centuries. Gone were those simple times when a smile meant nothing more than contentment, when hands grew and created all they needed and took pride in the simple accomplishment of survival. Yet she also saw the wasted death of a child from drinking contaminated water and the lean years when the weather conspired to steal the grains from the ground. So she did not mourn when she witnessed her friends' irrepressible desires to better their lots, their headlong stumblings to make safe what could never be safe, to steal pain and death from a God who apparently cherished both. She watched them invent and improve everything until their hands no longer touched the soil, though the grains they grew sprouted with plentiful abandon. She watched as survival became a right and pride a cherished commodity. She watched as machines and people cross-pollinated, washing the distinct colors from fruit and human skin alike. Lost were the myriad of flavors and of Gods, all designed to distinguish one experience from the next. Progress and safety, everyone called it.

With the luxury of fast-forward review and the ability to look into the heart of anyone she wished, she watched and mourned for it all. God set the stage, but he did not write the play. He hadn't the ability, Verbolana was convinced. The joy of a child's unconditional smile and the pathos of that same child's death seventy years later cannot be written, it can only be felt. At that moment, Verbolana felt sorry for God. There was no way he could feel what he had given her the ability to feel.

Something brushed Verbolana's bare arm, and she pulled herself back to the moment. Ricardo, one of the other waiters, wanted his dessert. Verbolana looked up and smiled, then looked back into the kitchen at Paul.

"Remember the rule," Paul said without looking up. He had obviously watched her eyes drifting.

"That's a man's rule," Verbolana concluded. "A woman can live with and feel both the past and the present. I can feel both the pride and the anguish and still have room for you, and Frank, and everyone in this room."

A voice drifted across sizzling meat on the grill. "Don't include me in your sick little fantasies," Frank shot, breaking the spell and sending Verbolana to take her next order.

# Chapter 41

W hat, our little place?" Paul responded in amusement. "No, that didn't help. It's called advance planning and boatloads of cash." They sat at an open-air table with a breathtaking view. White tablecloths, crystal glassware and low candles added to the feel of total opulence. Verbolana marveled at the line of five wine glasses above each place setting of four forks and three spoons, along with an extra knife above a larger dish she had learned they called a charger.

"I reserved this table the day the ballot came out, a year and a half ago from today," Paul added.

"Well, I can see why you asked me to dress up. Everyone is so beautiful here. But why such a secret for so long?" Verbolana's eyes sparkled in the candlelight, her long hair piled high, allowing her cheekbones and graceful neck their full statement.

"Well, to be honest, I didn't know you'd still be around," Paul stammered.

"Oh." Verbolana's easy smile fell for a brief moment before she caught it. "I keep forgetting the rules. This place can be so cruel."

"Indeed, but let's forget all that. We're here now, together, about to witness history, and still madly in love. Right?"

Verbolana smothered Paul's hand with hers, looked into his eyes, then across the city to the Parliament Building, the center of so much attention these days. "More right than you will ever know, my love." She waited for her words to accumulate the proper weight before she changed the subject. "Now tell me what's going on. You know I don't follow politics."

Paul, too, took his time before he answered. Instead, he breathed in the still night air, sat back and smiled. "Well, politics are not always as boring as they may seem. Some people live and die over this shit. What we have going here is that some people want to redesign the Parliament Building."

"And that isn't boring?" Verbolana quibbled.

"Not if you dig deep enough," Paul responded without offense. "See, the current building has stood for more than four thousand years. Civilizations grow and change a lot in four thousand years. People on my world, for instance, were barely throwing rocks at each other back then, and now they imagine colonizing other planets." He paused before changing tracks. "Each neighborhood sends a representative here to hash out everything from the lengths of the days to behavioral codes in the subways. You can't believe, with so many worlds and so many cultures represented, how contentious things can get."

In spite of herself, Verbolana yawned. "I'm sure that's all very interesting, but what does that have to do with the building? They all get together and yell at each other. I can imagine that easily, but who cares what the building looks like?"

"It's not so much what it looks like as how it functions," Paul insisted. "Let me give you a for instance. When they built this building, many cultures on many worlds were enamored with indoor plumbing. Hot baths and steam rooms were the epitome of comfort and luxury. So for those four thousand years, most of the coalition building and power brokering has gone on in segregated bathhouses. There are many, like most from my world, who feel it is imperative to change that system."

Verbolana raised her eyebrows and nodded her head up. Paul followed her gestures. A waiter stood a little off from the table.

"Ah," Paul acknowledged.

The waiter approached carrying a bottle of wine nestled in a silver cradle. "May I pour?" he asked with great ceremony.

Verbolana giggled with embarrassment, then commented, "A little different from our place."

The waiter smiled. "Don't think I don't know where you two are from. I've been to your place a few times over the years. Very comfortable, with great food." He looked over his shoulder before continuing. "Pomp and circumstance don't make a great restaurant. Fortunately the food here is pretty good, too."

"I'm sure it will be," Verbolana agreed. "I've been looking forward to it for—hours."

"I was told this was a surprise," the waiter continued with easy comfort. "Any special occasion we should know about, other than the vote, of course?"

"Nothing that I'm aware of," Verbolana said, looking at Paul.

"Just the vote," Paul commented offhandedly. "And of course, dinner with the most beautiful woman on the planet."

"Ah, well, that is always a special occasion." The waiter bowed as he poured a taste for Paul. "I hope this is to your satisfaction."

Paul swirled the huge glass, held it up to the light, sniffed and finally tasted the lightly golden liquid. "Wonderful!" Paul commented. "Barrel fermented?"

"Indeed, on the lees for six months in French oak, twenty-five percent Malolactic fermentation. The grapes are from the 1972 harvest. All gravity produced, never seen a pump or a filter. We aged it for two years in oak and then three in the bottle. Napa Valley of course, Carneros region."

"Did you make it, or is it original?" Paul wondered.

"The sommelier here has quite a background. In '72, Carneros wasn't even planted much. And there weren't any wineries using gravity flow; they were enamored with their pumps. No, Jorge, our sommelier, rewrote things a bit. He had these Chardonnay vineyards planted in '62, I think, and just waited for the perfect year. In the meantime, he built the ideal winery and got the top people from the last three centuries to make the wine. He did the same thing for the cabernet, the pinot, all the wines under our label."

"Really, I'd love a tour sometime." Paul seemed fascinated.

"No problem, any time," the waiter said with enthusiasm. "His commercial realm is just off the restaurant's foyer. We take people in all the time. It is quite fascinating. Once we got the world up and running, we just left it alone and picked the best vintages."

"I gotta say," Paul continued, "I'd be bummed if my favorite inn wasn't still there. I have visited the real-time Napa Valley many times for my own list, and there's this place just north of St. Helena called ..."

"Ah, boys," Verbolana interrupted, clinking the side of her glass with her fingernail.

"Oh, of course," the waiter apologized. Then to Paul, "Is the wine to your satisfaction?"

"Very much." Paul swirled and drained the small taste in his glass.

The waiter filled their glasses, and as he did, he addressed Verbolana. "Since this was a surprise, you may not be aware of the format here. The chef will orchestrate the meal. There are no menus and the courses come at a leisurely pace. You have your table for the evening, so feel free to linger, get up and walk through the gardens, anything you like. We even invite you to come back and watch the kitchen at work." He took a breath after delivering his standard spiel. "Paul has informed us that you were raised vegetarian and that you are just beginning to eat meat. The chef considered this when planning your meal. My name is Jonathan. I am here at your pleasure."

"Wow!" Verbolana responded. "Very nice." Then to Paul, "You really know how to treat a girl."

"And you're just figuring that out?" Paul responded in mock disappointment.

"Ah," Jonathan intoned. "Looks like something is happening in the square." He motioned to the scene below.

From such a distance, it was hard for Verbolana to discern exactly what was happening, but there seemed to be some commotion among the crowds that lingered in the large plaza. Random shouts filtered through the still air. Others joined. The pitch and volume evolved into competing, organized chants.

"They'd better be careful," Paul fretted. "God will only take so much acrimony. Somebody's gonna get sent home in a minute."

"What's that?" Verbolana asked.

"God reads intentions as much as actions. He's judge and jury. If there's only the slightest contact at a moment like this, people will start disappearing back to their realms."

"What are they chanting?"

Paul strained his ears. "Can't tell exactly, but the culmination of a year-long vote is only minutes away. Everybody down there is getting a bit excited."

"You didn't finish explaining about the bathhouses," Verbolana reminded him.

"Where did I leave off?" Paul wondered. "Oh, yeah, well, the long and short of that one is that the men are tired of being shut out. Terra and the other patriarchal worlds are in the minority and are not allowed into the real power centers as long as the bathhouses are segregated. If the bathhouses are allowed to stay, my people insist they be desegregated."

"There are worlds where women are in charge?"

"Oh yeah," Paul exclaimed. "The vast majority of worlds evolved with women in leadership roles. It caught me by surprise, too, coming from a world where men ruled almost everything. But it makes sense when you think about it. Women are just more ..."

"Concerned, compassionate?"

"Catty, contentious," Paul finished. "Don't get too full of yourself, but yeah, women have a direct connection to 'family,' and if a society encourages that connection to broaden into a connection with larger families, women develop into tremendous leaders."

"We could have used a little more of that on my world," Verbolana lamented.

"Actually I think you did, before the Cleansing, anyway," Paul countered. "At the very beginning of our research I saw an index of eras or something, and they were divided by women's names."

"Really? I guess we were truly evolved!" Verbolana joked.

"Yeah," Paul agreed, missing the irony.

Silence fell as Verbolana retreated into thought. Discussion of her world seldom came up without a certain amount of pain, but this time, nothing. Paul mentioned the Cleansing and she did not shudder. She even countered with a lame joke.

Gently, she took her own cue and turned another page in her memory. She saw Treena's sleepy morning smile, her eyes still swollen with sleep. They kissed good morning and Treena closed her eyes again. Verbolana rolled to Wexi and they shared a conspiratorial snicker. Wexi, it appeared, loved her training time with Vee, unencumbered by Treena's forceful presence. They hugged quickly before starting to dress under the covers.

Verbolana searched her memory further and found him, this time at one of the long dining tables, laughing too loudly. Rewriting history, she strode boldly up behind him, pulled him roughly by his collar and as he came back, planted a big wet kiss on his cheek.

Instantly she fled back to safety and Paul's attentive eyes. "Where you been?" he asked.

Sudden fear enveloped her until she looked deeply enough into Paul's eyes. "Counting my blessings," she realized.

"You know, none of this matters." Paul swept his arm across the panorama. "The view, the table, the meal. I don't have to count my blessings. They are all sitting right here, bundled up into the most beautiful package ever wrapped." Verbolana noticed tears welling in his eyes as she marveled at his depth. How could one man, one person, be so fun and so steady, so tender while so strong, so vulnerable with so few faults?

"You amaze me, Paul. You drag me along by my hair, safe in your wake, to places inside myself I could have never gone alone. The past two years have been so improbable for me. I am happy and content, yet hungry for tomorrow. This place does matter. This view, this table, this meal would have been impossible for me without you. And not the planning and money it took to get here. I'm talking about the emotional freedom. Until this very moment, I have never been as 'me' as I am right now. The safety you provide me is what amazes me. And it appears to be all just for me."

Paul grinned. "Well, that's where you're wrong." Then he became serious, "You throw all these compliments my way and I realize how undeserving I am. Vee, I am a selfish, conniving, arrogant man. Do you think I brought you here without an agenda? Hardly!" He waved violently for the waiter. "Bring dessert," he commanded. "We have things we must do."

Confused and frightened by the sudden turn of mood, Verbolana's stomach soured. "What's wrong, Paul? Did I say something? Are you offended?"

Frantic movement surrounded them as two elaborate bowls arrived before them. Paul grabbed one of his forks, clattering silver across the table, and started digging into Verbolana's mound of creamy whatever. After only a moment's search, he pulled a gleaming ring from the mess.

"You see, I am selfish and arrogant. I do not have the courage you accuse me of. I am weak and pathetic and do not want to face this life any more without the knowledge that you are by my side, for as long as God allows."

"A ring?" Verbolana responded in disbelief. "How can this be?" She looked up into Paul's eyes. "What of the rules?"

"Fuck the rules. God has no rules. It's just people who make the rules. I told you I was arrogant. I believe we can rewrite the rules." He dropped to one knee beside the table, pulled the ring from the fork and held it up to Verbolana's frightened gaze. "Verbolana, will you marry me?"

# Chapter 42

t's too bad Frank wasn't there," Verbolana ventured, her piled, curled and primped hair finally set free to fly in the wind.

They took two more tight turns in what Paul called a "convertible sports car" before he answered. "Oh, don't worry about that." He paused to take another tight turn on the Napa Valley's famed Silverado Trail. "Our friendship is primarily circumstantial. Frank is a very unhappy person and he doesn't have the courage even to try to be happy. You, on the other hand, are a runaway train, determined to be happy. I teeter. Frank loved that about me. My struggle fascinated him. And my constant failures reinforced his worldview. When I found true happiness with you, he lost interest. I became a constant reminder of what could be for his life. I became an abomination, a freak."

"Where did he go? I still feel guilty. I really liked him."

"And he liked you." The rear wheels skidded and Verbolana felt the car floating toward the far edge of the road. Paul jerked the steering wheel back in the opposite direction and the car shot forward again. "Hey, I'm just learning here. Never driven a Porsche before. The rear ends are a bit tricky!"

"Good thing there aren't any more of these things on this road. What happens if we smash into something?"

"Nothing. God won't let us get hurt." Paul grunted around another turn. "So hold on, and let's see how fast this thing will go!" He punched with his right foot and the car leaped forward into a straight stretch of road. Verbolana felt pinned to the molded seat; her heart raced, not quite believing in her safety. Symmetrical rows of gnarly, black, dormant vines blurred into the vibrant yellows and greens of a plant they called mustard. One of the vintners they'd invited to the reception had explained that this cover crop would soon be plowed under and the vines would explode with spring growth.

Anticipating an upcoming turn, Paul removed his foot from one pedal and punched down on the one to the left. Verbolana shot forward against her restraint as the car set up a tremendous screeching somewhere behind her. Drifting again, Paul yanked the wheel back and forth, as he switched pedals again. The car ploughed sideways down the road, feeling as if at any moment it might give up its purchase and just start rolling. It slid sideways into the turn and jolted violently off the road and up a gentle slope into the weeds and bushes. Thrown from side to side over the rough ground, Paul and Verbolana watched a sturdy oak approach. Verbolana screamed and Paul howled. Metal crumpled, the tree screeched and the car stopped dead, its occupants cushioned in an invisible pillow.

"Yahoo!" Paul screamed. "That was fantastic! Let's do it again!"

"Let's not," Verbolana muttered, her entire body rattling like the deck in a heavy wind.

"God, I wish we were back on the road," Paul shouted, still high with exhilaration. The broken car sat on the road. "Very funny!" Paul yelled at the sky. "God, very funny, would you please fix the car?" The car sat idling, in perfect repair.

"Can we take it a little easy this time?" Verbolana whimpered. Then she offered, "I find our conversation so much more stimulating than this car thing."

"Good try," Paul laughed. "But okay, I'll slow down. We're almost at the inn anyway. And just in time for their afternoon wine. You're going to love this place. We have a little cottage down almost in the vineyards."

"You've been here before, then?" Verbolana asked.

"Yeah, I told you."

"You didn't tell me with who," Verbolana clarified.

"Ah, a little jealous?" Paul snickered as he put the car back in gear and started off.

"Well, isn't that what we just did, committed ourselves to each other?"

"Sure, I've got no secrets. But do you really want to know all the fine details of my past?"

"I guess not," Verbolana admitted. "I guess this whole thing has me a little confused. Everything we are doing here goes directly against my upbringing. And no matter how hard I try, I can still feel the switch at my back every now and then."

"It's hard to shut out the past, that's for sure," Paul sympathized. "I've only been married a few times, but I'm struggling here a bit myself. Love is always a bit of a rollercoaster—a trip down the ropes for you."

"You've been married before?" An edge came to her voice.

"Well, yeah. I was married on Terran for thirty-two years. So you can imagine that when I got to Heaven I was pretty lonely. I married a gal within a couple years and stayed with her for almost twenty years."

"And?" Verbolana persisted.

"And after that broke up, I took a break for a long time. Like I say, love can hurt. Anyway, eventually I met someone I really liked again and tied the knot for the third time. Life is long up here," he defended. "Lots of people have long-term relationships with eight or ten partners."

"I never knew any of this." Verbolana felt a bit lost, disconnected.

"We've mostly been working on you when we aren't having a blast. Is this going to be a problem for you?"

"No, no, I don't think so." She stared out at the passing vines, all lined and orderly, so unlike her thoughts. She continued haltingly, "The past is the past. It makes you who you are. And I love who you are."

"Are you trying to convince me or yourself?" Paul asked, not really wanting to hear the answer.

Irritation bubbled. "I'm not trying to convince anyone. I just stood before all our friends and a bunch of strangers and proclaimed my love. This changes nothing. I guess what it does point to is how selfish I have been. To find that I don't know the most basic parts of your life is shocking to me. I am ashamed."

Paul made a sharp left on Lodi Lane, shot across a tiny bridge, and announced, "We have arrived, just in time for more wine and food. You're going to love this place! They will make you feel right at home." He cranked a right turn up a tree-lined driveway to the sight of a three-story stone-and-wood building hiding behind hundred-year-old olive trees. Paul sighed in satisfaction. "This is just the beginning, Vee. The beginning of a whole new life. Drop off here, all your baggage. Fill suitcases with all the garbage you have collected and chuck them on the sidewalk. I have stuff to leave behind, too; we all do. And though God may not allow us to forget, with discipline, we can ignore. From this moment, right now, we can build. Not rebuild or remember or re-anything. We can craft, for our own comfort, anything we wish. And to help us do just that, in a few days I will take you to a magical place called Sedona Arizona. There are a few people I want you to meet, people who will guide us on this new journey." He pulled to the front of the inn where a man in blue jeans and pullover shirt waited. When they came to a stop, he rushed to open Verbolana's door.

"Welcome to the inn, I am your innkeeper, Jim. Can we get your bags for you?"

Verbolana climbed out of the low-slung vehicle with a helping hand from the innkeeper. "No, no thank you," she stammered, with her full, elegant, low-cut wedding gown falling around her ankles. She brushed her hands down her sides and shook the dress free of folds before meeting the innkeeper's eyes. "We have nothing with us. You'll have to take us as we are."

The innkeeper appraised her, not catching any of the private joke. Without hesitation, he met her eyes and said, "That is our specialty."

* * *

"Your Earth is powerful," Verbolana announced to the cold air and strange man sitting beside her. They had been "honeymooning" on Paul's home world for what seemed like a very long time now, exploring the hidden strengths of another of God's creations. She closed her eyes to the brightening skyline, the approaching sun preparing to erupt over the barren red-rock mountains of Sedona. She felt lifted by invisible hands, floating, yet tethered with a force that burned to the center of the planet. She released thought, matched the spin of the vortex around her with the vortex within. Strength built on Strength. She felt the spinning energies settle. She found herself in the eye of an energetic storm.

"Release your thoughts," the voice of her guide reminded her. "Release all expectations. Feel your consciousness beaming through the top of your head, swirling, marrying the energies that surround you. Build a globe with the mingled forces. Live in the globe, be in the globe," the voice droned. "Here and now. There is only here and now." *And the bitter tang of the cactus button you had me eat an hour ago,* popped a thought that she calmly imagined as written words behind her eyes. She jumbled and packed the letters of the hallucination into a tiny ball, and then released it to the winds above her head.

"Grow the globe," the voice came back. "Build it with love." The words struck Verbolana, rocked the rock she sat on. *Love,* she exclaimed. *Father's Strength for "love?" Selfish, blasphemous, hedonistic love. Father's Strength is for Father's love, not mine.*

"Feel your heart." The voice seemed to sense her turmoil. "Release and feel ... your heart."

Verbolana could not help but follow his words. She allowed her mind to wander to her core, felt the spinning connection to Father. But this time, instead of following the vortex down to connect with Father's love, she allowed her mind to travel up to her own heart, found it glowing; hot, red coals in the night. Then, as a spectator, she watched the crinkling fire grow, felt its heat. She saw this loving force as a thick mist, filling her body, her limbs, her head. Now filling the space around her, the body of her guide, the air of the crystal dawn, then permeating down into the solid rock. She watched and felt the globe of her intention expand further. She felt Paul's presence a few hundred yards away on his own journey, and filled him with this special love. She flooded further, through empty space, filling deer and coyote, grasshopper and worms. Her mind reached the burgeoning town of Sedona, waking to the same dawn. She filled every house, every store and café with the imagined mist of her love.

Suddenly, through closed lids, the sun burst with immeasurable power across her face, its power undeniable, its love washing Verbolana's puny mist away with a single stroke.

"Here and now," the voice returned. "Without judgment, feel the power ... the furnace of the universe. Wash yourself in the fire and never doubt the powers that are greater than yourself. You do not control, you do not dictate, you float, here and now, in a universe beyond any control."

Anger erupted volcanic. *This man knows nothing!* Her lava-hot thoughts emerged. *If that were true, if the universe really were beyond any control, I could accept that. But it's not true. God is there and he is a worthless piece of shit. He does nothing, helps no one. He sits back and laughs at his own creation. If this man knew, if this great philosopher of Earth knew, he would be raging now, not meditating on nothing, not teaching others to be complacent.* The thought convulsed from her gut and regurgitated up, extinguished her glowing heart, jumbled her brain, before it spewed out the top of her head. Her eyes jolted open to the needle-sharp rays of the sun. She shook the thought free, the anger, the resentment. Aloud she lamented, "Where did that come from? I've been doing so well!"

Aldous, her startled guide, settled back. "What happened? I felt your energy. You were really traveling."

"I don't know," Verbolana searched. "Obviously I've got some resentment still. Something you said — I had quite a reaction."

"I see," he responded. "Is it something you want to look into?"

"Not here and now, Mr. Huxley."

*  *  *

"This is quite a climb," Verbolana commented through ragged breaths.

"We could take the bus," Paul suggested. "It's not too late."

"No," Verbolana concluded. "It's helping me clear the cobwebs. That opium stuff is strong. I can still feel it like sludge in my body two days later."

"Yeah," Paul agreed. "But it sure was fun. Not something I'd like to do all the time, but I had some pretty wild dreams."

"Some of those weren't dreams," Verbolana admitted meekly. "Are you okay with everything that happened?"

"All right?" Paul exclaimed. "I've just never had the balls to go there by myself, and none of the other women I have been with seemed to have any interest. When I wasn't living the dream with you, I was dreaming the dream with the drugs. You have no idea how happy you made me!"

"But we're married," Verbolana said.

"Married, to me, means mutual consent, not mutual deprivation. It has always been my fantasy that a true partnership would free me to be who I truly am, not who my partner needs me to be." He grabbed Verbolana's hand. "I think I may have had my prayers answered."

"Then we can go back to Phuket sometime?"

"Vee, we can live in Phuket as far as I'm concerned. But there are still a few places I want to visit with you. This place and a few others."

They heard another bus lumbering up the dusty road. They moved to the cliff side to let the bus pass. Road dust clouded into their faces.

"I wish we didn't have to put up with all this dust," Verbolana lamented. Then a thought struck her. "Can we switch times? Go up before this place was ruins, while people still lived here?"

"Well, sure." Paul thought for a minute. "But we'd create quite a stir. If we want to observe without mucking things up, we'd have to be invisible."

"Invisible," Verbolana exclaimed. "Yeah, let's be invisible!"

Paul had a little chat with God and suddenly the road they stood on morphed into a rocky, thin trail. Vertigo wavered both of them as they adjusted to the idea that one misstep would plunge them a thousand feet to the river below. By the time they made it to the top, they were exhausted. They enjoyed the view, watched the natives for a while, and left Machu Picchu after a few hours.

\* \* \*

"Do you think we can do this?" Verbolana questioned, lying naked on the low mats. The room, comfortably warm, hung with an array of scrolls, all depicting lovers in various moments of rapture.

Paul lay beside her, as naked as she was. "Well, yeah," he responded. "I don't know if I want to, but I think we can."

"Bet ya!" Verbolana laughed.

"What, you think I've got no self-control?" Paul smiled back.

"You or me?" Verbolana added. "I think I'll have just as hard a time as you. I'm already feeling horny."

"Good thing," Paul shot back good-naturedly. "This is still our honeymoon, you know."

"Is it normal on your planet to have a year-long honeymoon?"

"Normal? What's normal about any of this?" Paul questioned. "Normal for this world would be a couple of rolls in the hay and back to our separate lives. We are breaking all the rules, young lady."

"Well, then," Verbolana concluded. "Let's break some more. Ready?"

"Ready as I'll ever be," Paul laughed again. "You do the honors."

Verbolana unfroze their instructor to continue his babble, "... heightened. The first step, as with any meditation, is the breath. The breath ..."

"Can we get through this introductory stuff?" Verbolana complained as she froze the robed monk again. "I know how to breathe."

"No, no," Paul insisted. "This is different, I think. Maybe just subtly, but they're going to have a different take on it. Everybody else has."

"I guess you're right," Verbolana sighed. "We just had one application for meditation on my home world, martial." She thought for a minute. "Maybe that's why ours is so much stronger."

"Stronger?" Paul questioned. "You think yours is stronger? Since I've been back here with you I've felt some pretty wild stuff."

"Oh, Paul," Verbolana complained. "I haven't seen anything that even comes close. We keep hearing stories, but when we investigate, the realities are downright mundane compared to what I could do right here, now."

"You keep saying stuff like that," Paul confronted. "But you won't show me. I'm beginning to think yours are just as mythic as theirs."

"So I'm going to have to prove myself to you. I thought we were beyond that."

"Hey, you need stuff proven to you. I'm no different. How can I know what you're talking about unless you show me?"

"Ask God for the Strength. He'll give it to you," Verbolana suggested.

"That's different. Then it would just be God doing it. I want to see you do it for yourself."

"How do you know I wouldn't be asking God for it?"

"Because I trust you," came Paul's simple explanation.

"All right," Verbolana conceded. "When we're done here I'll give you a demonstration. Sure it won't hurt your ego?"

"No, I'm not sure it won't hurt my ego; but we gotta do it. And hell with this Tantric stuff, I want to see it right now!"

"No way," Verbolana blurted. "I'd probably use it to fuck your brains out. I am way too horny for that right now!"

"Ohhhhh," Paul teased. "That could be fun. But all right, we can finish here. Unfreeze that guy, and let's get on with it."

A couple hours later, Verbolana circled in the same room, a stocky man in full armor with blade raised, followed her movements. She was naked, her sex still dripping from Paul's last gift.

"Are you sure this is a good idea?" Paul cautioned. "I know you can't get hurt, but doesn't this put you at an extreme disadvantage? We asked for the national champion of Japan. They were the best, probably still are."

"How else can I prove it?"

"You could at least have similar armor," Paul insisted.

"It would just get in the way," she commented. "Anyway," she stood tall and shook her shoulders playfully, her breasts giving a little jiggle, "Don't you think this might be a little distracting?"

"Probably pissing this guy all to hell. These were macho dudes. Taunting him like that can't be good."

"On the contrary," Verbolana observed. "I have already won. All his energies are redirected."

The Asian tornado advanced, swung, and with one fluid motion, brought the blade back for another and another swipe. Verbolana danced around the blade, ducked and before retreating, slapped the man hard across the face. "God, I wish I could feel the pain. That probably really hurt my hand. I hit the chin strap of his helmet." Her hand immediately buzzed with pain.

"What are you doing?" Paul exclaimed.

"Don't worry," Verbolana responded. "He won't cut me."

The warrior advanced with crazed eyes. "Heeeyyyaaaa!" he screamed as he swung at where Verbolana had been. *Better than the Wretched*, she mused. *But not as good as any of my instructors.* She slipped in and drew the man's short sword before retreating to more frustrated growls and ill-timed strikes.

"To be honest, if this were a real man, in a real fight, I doubt I could do this," Verbolana admitted. "I know I can't be killed, so I am taking chances I normally wouldn't." She danced some more before asking, "Do I have to kill this guy for you to get the idea?"

"No," Paul answered with awe. "You can stop any time. I get the idea." Then, after the man disappeared, he continued, "I wonder how your people developed such skills. And without God's help."

"I don't have a clue," Verbolana said, barely breathing hard. "I guess we could go back and trace it down if you want. I don't really want to go back, though."

"Boy, if I'd had those skills I never would have become a chef," Paul concluded. "I'd have become a sports legend."

"What's that?" Verbolana asked.

"A legend?" Paul asked. "It's a ..."

"No, I know what a legend is. What are sports?"

"Sports," Paul spouted. "I've never taken you to any games! We've been together for, what, two and a half years now, and I've never taken you to see nil-grav soccer? Man, have I been distracted!"

# Chapter 43

Before we leave, I'd like to see where you were raised. You never talk about your life here."

They stood at a little viewing notch cut in the jungle, the roar of the Falls De Iguasu filled their ears. A group of young tourists jabbering in some guttural language crowded beside them, jostling for the best camera angle. Paul pulled her up the well-worn path for more privacy. "Without God's curse I would have forgotten I ever lived on this planet."

"You never go back to visit?" Verbolana persisted.

"I've been back some, once for quite a while," Paul's voice almost drowned in the roar of distant water. "But at some point you move on. For me, that point came a long time ago."

"Has it changed much, your home?"

"Verbolana, can we just drop it?" His plea was barely audible.

"No, Paul, we can't." Anger, never far from the surface, steeled her eyes. "You have brought such comfort to my life." She softened. "I need to know how you got to where you are, what life experiences built upon each other to craft such a wonderful man. Paul," she almost pleaded, "I want to be wonderful. I want to be free and happy — and at ease." She stopped to see if he were listening, if he understood. She couldn't tell. He studied the rocks in the path. "Paul, I remember a couple of months ago, you said I never ask about you and that has stuck with me, nagged at me." She stopped again for effect. "And then I realized you were full of crap. I *do* ask.

You just don't answer. It takes two to have a conversation, and any time there's an opening to talk about you, then you steer the conversation back to me. I never really noticed before, probably because I needed to talk about me, but relationships evolve. Our life can't revolve around me," she insisted. "It's too one-sided, and that becomes diminishing for me. 'Poor Vee, we gotta fix her, but I've never needed any fixing, I'm pretty much perfect.'"

"Perfect!" Paul connected with the words instead of the emotion. "Hah, hardly perfect." He tried to twirl her back to the path. "We don't have to fight. The only thing 'perfect' around here is this day — and you're ruining it."

"And there are thousands of more perfect days ahead of us. That is if we don't fuck them up," Verbolana persisted, using the vernacular of his world.

"Are you threatening me?" Paul became immediately defensive. "Are you blackmailing me with your love?"

Verbolana softened again. "What are you talking about?" Frustration was evident in her voice. "I'm just saying that our life together can't be one-sided. I love you and I want to know you."

Paul kicked at the dirt in the path. He glanced up to meet her eyes, then back to the dirt. "I haven't been one-hundred percent honest with you. I told you once that I was raised in a tranquil land by easy parents. That's all true, but not the first time I was here." He looked back up into her eyes. "I have had two complete lives on this world. It's called rebirthing."

She felt his eyes searching hers, looking for some reaction, but she had none. She didn't understand. "You were lost?" remembering Alcot's condemnation.

"So lost," Paul admitted.

Verbolana breathed easy. "Is that all? I don't care about things like that. This world and its rules mean nothing to me. I just want to know you better, learn your secrets to success."

"None of who you see as 'Paul' came from this world, not really," Paul declared. "If you want to see me, know me, then we have to go back to the Café. That's where I became Paul. You would not even recognize me here."

"And you are afraid for me to see you here," Verbolana concluded.

"Yes." Paul raised his eyes to hers, sudden anger pushing her back. "Satisfied?" he spat.

"Yes—no—I didn't mean to make you angry," Verbolana apologized. "What can be so horrible?"

"You just can't let it go," Paul growled. The camera-clicking tourists caught up with them and mumbled to each other as they passed. Verbolana caught a couple sets of male eyes checking hers, making sure she was okay. She faked a smile and they moved on.

"I just can't imagine," she explained.

"No, you can't," Paul agreed. "You think yours is the only screwed-up world. I've been trying to tell you all along that you are not so unique, but your arrogance won't let you hear it. You are the victim of all victims. Your Gods cheated you more than any other Gods, on any other worlds. That is where your comfort is right now, and I have accepted that. More than accepted," Paul admitted, "I need that from you. Don't you see? The pieces have to fit together. You supply one piece; I supply the other. You heal me as I heal you."

They stood silently, searching each other's eyes. Verbolana saw love, compassion. She also saw a certain desperation. "I just don't know where you're coming from. What healing do you need?"

"You are already giving it to me. Why do you have to know more?"

"Because I do." It was so simple and clear in her mind. There was nothing Paul could have been or done that could lessen what he had already given her, except, she realized, if he couldn't allow himself to be vulnerable.

Somehow, Paul sensed her conclusion. "In my first life, if I were on your world, I would have been a Deck Director."

* * *

"Can we cut off the smell?" Paul pleaded. "I'm gonna pass out."

"No," Verbolana responded, also in obvious distress. "I want to experience everything." They stood in complete blackness as another wail filled the room.

"Loooooorrrrdddd, what do I do?" a man's voice bounced through the darkness.

"Get down between my legs!" a woman's voice commanded. "Feel around." Then after some shuffling, "Get in there, see if you can feel the head. Lord sakes, you didn't mind rutting around down there nine months ago. See if you can pull it open. Ohhhh, it's killing me! Get it out!"

"I can't see anything. We need a midwife!" More shuffling and grunting. "I wish we could at least open a window."

"Wish for whatever you want. Just get this child out of me!"

Verbolana connected with the Strength, trying desperately to gain her bearings. She felt the closed room, two bodies fumbling on the ground, their intentions focused. To her surprise, she felt other, smaller signatures lying haphazardly across the floor, one she almost stepped on. Past the walls of the tiny room, she felt others, many others, most with the unfocused energy of the sleeping. Another scream filled the room. What appeared to be a child's energy jolted on the floor, rolled a foot or so across the dirt, and clung to another child, who clung back.

"I think I feel something. Bear down! Yes, thank the Lord! Push!"

Verbolana watched with her mind as a new energy signature joined the room. Its wail followed shortly after.

"There you go," Paul commented at her side. "Satisfied?"

"Hardly," Verbolana exclaimed.

"Born to squalor in the year of the Black Death, 1665. We're in the slums of London," Paul explained. "Not a worse place to be on this planet, in this year. Couldn't even afford candles," he added.

"Can we move on to dawn? I want to see."

"You don't," Paul persisted in his disapproval.

"I do," Verbolana insisted.

Hazy light filtered through a few miserable cracks in the walls. Besides that, it was as dark as ever. "No windows?" Verbolana wondered aloud.

"Boarded up," came Paul's flat commentary. "My brother's infected." He pointed to a bundle of rags in a corner. "He'll die in a few days. My sister next." His finger traced through the gloom to another pile. "We weren't allowed outside. There's a guard at the door. Shit and peed in the corner. Well, I just shit and peed anywhere. Sucked my mother to death before the summer was over. We couldn't get any food," he continued. "We didn't have any money to bribe the guards."

"But ..." Verbolana stammered.

"But nothing," Paul interrupted. "But nothing. The only thing that saved my father, sister and me was the fire. When the slums started to burn, the guards took off. My father finally busted through the door. They had left it locked." Bitterness returned. "Of course I don't remember any of this. Just blinding hunger and vague feelings of heat and bitter cold. My father told the stories the rest of his life. Once I got to Heaven, I went back and looked. Fun, huh?"

"Hardly," Verbolana sympathized. "How did you become a Deck Director?"

"My father's trials did not end with his escape from London. There were thousands, tens of thousands in the same boat. More than a hundred thousand died that summer, but about a million lived in London at the time. And once my father escaped with us, there was no going back. There was nothing to go back to. The city fathers blamed the whole epidemic on the slums, and they weren't about to let anyone rebuild them. They fenced off about two hundred blocks of slums after it burned and rebuilt it for the rich.

"It was a pitiful home," Paul continued. "But at least it was something. Fortunately for us, many people had died out in the country, too. When the rains stopped that next spring, farmers needed help with planting. My father found refuge in the basement of a church and, along with fifty or so others, he ventured out during the day to work in the fields. Left us to strangers. My first truly coherent memories are of that place. Hunger finally abated enough to let me feel something else."

They still stood, hand in hand, over the crumpled figures, flies coming to life after a cold night of rest. "Can we go now?"

Verbolana wiped at her eyes with the back of her free hand. "Terrible. I didn't know anyone could live like this."

"Half this world, my world, three centuries later, doesn't have it a whole lot better. It's a disease called AIDS now. God always gives us something," Paul snarled.

"How did you survive?" Verbolana implored. "I don't understand."

"God's miracle of creation. The body eats itself after a while. They say there's a clarity that comes. I don't know. All I can remember is clouds." He stopped, stared at the dirt floor. "I remember, after getting to the church, must have been a year or two later, my sister and I made up a game. We picked at the scabs of the sleeping until they bled. Maybe kept us alive. I gained quite an appetite for blood."

"Stop!" Verbolana screamed.

"I'm not trying to be melodramatic," Paul mumbled. "I'm re-membering. This was your idea. I didn't want to come back here."

Verbolana sucked up a little composure and, seeing Paul was in real pain, decided they needed to move on. "How did you get to be a Deck Director?"

Startled, Paul looked through the gloom to find her eyes. "You still want to see?"

"I want to see you in something happier than this. You can't leave me with only this."

Paul laughed, wicked and snarling. "Happy? You want to see happy? Maybe we can skip ahead a few years to my little excursion across the Atlantic, sequestered in the black airless hold of a wallowing ship for three months, sloshing around in our own waves of shit, piss and vomit. Maybe we can jump further to the lessons of the Good Book at the hands of newly converted fanatics."

He disengaged their fingers and placed her hands at her sides. "Vee, it took me a century or two to leave this shit behind, and with God's curse it is always still there, just a slip of the mind away. You go! You and your endless curiosity. Delve into my deepest corners."

He took a few steps through the stinkhole that would soon be his mother's and two brothers' funeral pyre. "God, show me the door." A door appeared. "I'll wait for you at our bench; don't be long." He pulled the door open. As light flooded in, Verbolana recognized the hall outside her realm and remembered they had set up this world in her space.

"Happy honeymoon," Paul proclaimed with false joviality as the door shut.

# Chapter 44

Verbolana stood mute, stunned. Her stomach turned. Acid dumped and she noticed, as if from a distance, her fingers quaking. She looked around at the gloom and suddenly felt lost.

"What am I doing?" she muttered aloud. "I can't lose him." But her feet would not move to follow him.

"I have to know," her clogged brain concluded. The decision prompted a picture of Paul, waiting on the bench in the park, his head buried in his hands. Puzzled, she looked back to the days before their wedding. They had closed the Café. Paul explained something about the neighborhood council and how they did not allow empty commercial space and how Paul didn't want to be hamstrung to a timetable. He wanted their honeymoon to last as long as it lasted, without encumbrances.

"Why do I need to know?" Verbolana demanded of herself. "I don't." The words dragged from her mind into the stagnant air. "I don't need to know." Then, "But I do! Why?" the questions and answers raged until, "Centuries? It took Paul centuries? What does that mean?"

Realization struck her between the eyes. "God, where's the door?" Without hesitation, without even a glance back, she bolted into the hall to the elevator. The ride to the ground was the longest of her life. The doors whooshed and she sprinted, catching Paul before he got halfway through her neighborhood's park.

"I have been such a fool!" she blurted as she grabbed his shoulder and spun him into a smashing hug.

"How long?" Verbolana asked. "How long do you have?" Verbolana pulled away so they could be eye to eye.

"Here?" Paul clarified. "Twenty-two years."

"Twenty-two years?" Verbolana didn't know whether to be relieved or horrified. She knew she was angry. "Isn't that something I needed to know? When were you planning to tell me?"

"Never," Paul declared.

"Never!"

"Well, I guess it was in the back of my mind that I'd tell you if we made it to fifteen years," he gulped. "But I didn't see that as likely."

Verbolana pushed his arms off her and slapped him hard across the face. Without a sense of movement, she was alone again in the stinking hovel of Paul's birth. Without question or recrimination she stood, her happy life as vanished as the world around her. Numbed and whirling with emotion and ungraspable thoughts, she collapsed there, in the middle of the floor, flies buzzing her ears and eyes, acid stench filling her nose and insinuating into her brain.

Somewhere in the distance, before long, a frantic knocking came at the door. God allowed Paul's voice to carry through. "Verbolana, I'm sorry, I'm so sorry. Please let me in."

Verbolana hadn't the strength or will to respond. Cheated. Cheats and lies. That was all her life had ever been and all it would ever be. She felt shuffling around her and startled in reaction before she remembered her company could not see or feel her. Regardless, she hunched in a corner before burying her head in her arms.

Wallowing in Paul's betrayal, his constant hammering at the door only increased her misery. She sat for as long as she could in clouded anger, long after Paul's knocking had stopped. Movement around her pulled her head up and her eyes open. Paul's father struggled to sit. Through the sequestered darkness, she watched his antics, almost funny if separated from the situation. He was obviously stiff from his few hours of sleep on the hard ground, and he was trying to rise without waking the infant sleeping on his chest. He elbowed the ground, shuffled his hips, rolled and finally made it to knees and elbows, the whole time clutching the naked child with both hands. He rested there a bit, while Verbolana observed further. The man was clearly exhausted by his efforts. His breath came ragged and his bony back caved from the tiny weight of his load. Verbolana sat, struck with wonder. *How could this be? Surely this man and this woman. How could they live like this otherwise? They must have wires — some invisible strings of strength to help them move. Paul said they have no food. How can that be? They must be different, molded by circumstance into, what? Something less than human. How else could they survive?* She watched the man gather himself, then push off with his elbows. The baby squawked once, then quieted. Other bundles of rags jolted, and Verbolana felt another set of eyes opening, though no further movement followed. *Different,* she concluded. *How else could a child lie awake on the ground without bounding into activity?* She watched the man struggle across the ground on his knees to his wife's side and lay the baby to the woman's deflated breast, which apparently had not been put away from the night before. *Yes, these people are different,* she assured herself. *They were born to this, knew no different, expected no more.* The man straightened and looking around, decided on a new errand. He shuffled, still on his knees, to his wife's head. With gentle effort and a little coaxing, he moved his wife a foot or so deeper into the corner of the shack. Plodding through the dirt, he made his way to her feet. With broken fingernails, he clawed at the packed dust, trying to raise a large enough pile to cover the fly-buzzing stain that marked his son's birth.

Verbolana was dumbfounded. *What are you doing? Look around you. You live in your own excrement. What is one more stain in this shithole?* With nothing else to do, nowhere else to go, she sat with her reaction. What did she care? The man could bury anything he wanted, didn't matter. But a puzzling anger returned. She dismissed it, but there was nowhere to turn.

Verbolana looked back. The man had finished his futile chore and had crawled to one of the living piles. He appeared to be rubbing Paul's sister's head.

"It'll be over soon," she heard him whisper. "The devil's work will soon end and God will prevail. You'll see. God has a plan for us all. A glorious plan. A wondrous land where His love shines warmth like the sun and the streets are paved with gold. You'll see, everything will be all right."

"I'm afraid." A weak voice drifted to Verbolana's ears. "Why have they done this? When will they let us out?"

Verbolana screamed, "This is it! You're there! Welcome to my Heaven!" They didn't hear, so she continued, "Look, I'll show you!" She thought for a minute, then changed the scene. The family was on the beach, windsurfers in the distance. Sunlight fluttered their eyes.

"Verbolana, you came back!" Tarja's voice was at her back.

"Shut up; you don't exist!" Verbolana raged. The family sat stunned, looking around in horror. "This is Heaven," Verbolana proclaimed. "Enjoy!" She conjured up a table, laden with fruit and meats. "Come on, get up! Dig in! What are you waiting for?" She jumped up and ran to Paul's father. "You idiot." She pulled at his shoulders, ripping his fragile frame to its feet. "Here are your dreams. Go to them. You're right: God is great. He will provide. Everything will be all right."

Paul's father slumped back to the sand, crazed eyes greeting her. "Augh!" she screamed and ran from the scene. She bounded up the stairs of her long-lost beach shack and threw herself on the crumpled white sheets. "Green stuff!" she shouted. "God, give me green stuff!"

* * *

The knocking came again, with Paul's voice resigned to failure. And it wasn't that she couldn't remember; she remembered everything. It was that she just didn't care. "Come in," she muttered.

Paul's face appeared at the door to her little hut. Sheepishly, he commented, "Nice place you've got here."

She looked up from the big bed, Tarja still curled at her shoulder and layered down her side. "She doesn't lie to me," she commented in detached explanation.

"I see," Paul returned. "Have you forgiven me?"

"For what? Oh, that? What's to forgive?"

"Vee," he pleaded. "We have to talk."

"I saved your family," she offered. Then she giggled, "They're outside."

"And you're loaded," Paul realized. "Back on the 'green stuff,' as you call it."

"Fuck you," she answered benignly.

"Vee," he pleaded. "What are you looking for?"

She examined the question fearlessly. "Truth," she concluded.

"There is truth all around you."

"Is that what you call it?" Verbolana laughed again. "Seems like something else to me."

"Vee, are you talking about my betrayal or something bigger?"

"Betrayal?" She rolled the word around on her tongue. "Look at yourself out there." She pointed to the sunny beach and the

409

table of endless food. "There is not a fly in this whole land. You will thrive out there. You can shit in the sand and bury it every day until God burns in hell. You just might grow to be a great man."

"Verbolana, you can run round and round every tree on the beach and you're going to come away with the same conclusions. Either God created humans and their circumstances with divine genius or with fatal flaws. Or you can get to where I am; that both are true, and I am exhausted trying to figure out which is which. Faith and letting go are required — regardless of where you end up. You have faith in divine genius and you let go of the inequities you see all around you. Or you embrace our fatal flaws and have faith that your efforts to improve those same inequities will be to the good of humanity as a whole. Or you can fall into selfish resignation, as I have, letting go of all but your own happiness, and have faith in God's actual words that tell you this is what he intends."

"And those who don't make it, those who can never find happiness, what of them?" Tarja rustled at Verbolana's shoulder and perked her ears for Paul's response.

"They're fucked."

# Chapter 45

P aul, I love you." Verbolana snuggled deeper into his shoulder, the astounding display before them glazing her ageless face to porcelain flawlessness. "Do you think God created this?"

"You never give up, do you?" Paul idly responded. "Ask him if you want," he suggested after a stretched silence.

"No," Verbolana mumbled. "Seen enough?"

"Of the nebulae? Yeah, but not of the way it shines in your eyes." He turned from the recreation to nuzzle his love's ear. "I will never get enough of this lovely lobe."

"I'm glad we reopened the Café." Verbolana's thoughts took another leap. That was the way, these days, bouncing from one memory to another. "I'll keep it going." It was a promise she made often these days.

"My legacy lives in you, my dear, not a place. I read somewhere, 'the best things in life are not things.' That about sums it up. The Café gave me great pleasure, but only because of the people, you and Frank." He reflected for a moment, leaving the words hanging. "I'm glad Frank came back. And the regulars." His thoughts seemed to be bouncing, too. He leaned forward and gave Verbolana a long soft kiss. "I didn't get a chance to age much in my first life, so I don't know for sure, but this just seems so unnatural, to be marching off to my death in perfect health with my only sin being that I have lived long enough, in God's eyes anyway."

Verbolana pulled him back for another kiss. "I just don't know how I will survive. I want to hold on and go with you. I already feel so empty."

"I'm almost tempted not to go to the bar tomorrow. If I thought it would be good for you, I would stay right here, floating in this nebulae, your naked skin against mine, with me deep inside you, until I vanished."

"We could do that," Verbolana agreed eagerly. "Maybe I could hide you inside me."

"No, I've known people who have done it. It isn't good for the one left behind." He pulled back from Verbolana slightly. "You've got a lot of years still. Your greatest honor to me would be to live, to continue to flourish. Say goodbye, keep me in your heart and forge ahead. You have the tools."

"A head full of memories and a heart full of emptiness? Those are some dynamic tools."

"You have a heart full of compassion; no matter how hard I have tried to pooh-pooh it. And a head full of questions. Those are the tools of greatness," Paul persisted. "My only fear is that you'll forget to have fun; for that is another tool. You have gained such joy these last years. I would hate to see you give that up."

"The joy came from you." Verbolana averted her eyes as tears spilled down her face.

Playfully, Paul licked at her face, gathering her sorrow to savor. "You do me such honor, shedding tears so freely. Feel free to honor me in that way whenever you feel the urge. Remember, though, the tears are for me, not for yourself. You need no regret. Regret would not honor me. And remember, it's all about me."

She punched him hard on the shoulder. She laughed and waited. God did not react. "You can be such a shit. Can't you see I am in mourning?"

"Suck it up," he blurted, suddenly energized. "I'm the one with less than twenty hours to live. Think I wanna be with a sad puss? I wanna fuck."

With that he grabbed her blouse and ripped at the fabric. Her breasts jumped free, as startled as her face. "Always wanted to do that," he exclaimed. "God, give us some green stuff." Two drinks appeared on the table at the edge of the couch.

"Paul, I don't …"

"… want to disappoint you," Paul finished. "Have a sip or two. This is my time. You'll have plenty of time to pine. What, 287 years?"

"It isn't …" she faltered.

"… my place to refuse you anything," Paul finished for her. Then, still mimicking, "Here, watch me take two big gulps, you stud." Paul handed her the glass and, dutifully, she took her prescribed slugs. A cool freeze played across her brain and she smiled at his antics. "You can always pull me out. That's what the tears were for. You're right, not for you but for me. I'll turn that around."

"Why don't you try turning this around?" He had jumped from the couch and was undoing his pants. He presented himself as he took his own sips from the glass he had pilfered from her hand.

"Always know how to get a girl in the mood."

"It's a talent." He laughed. "But this thing is real. Didn't ask God for any help."

"You will before I'm done with you." She sat forward and grasped his shaft. "You'll be calling his name while begging for more."

"You look absolutely lovely tonight. A little different from the first time I saw you." Paul appraised her as they stood waiting their turn in the crowded subway.

"Tears then, tears now," Verbolana observed. "Seems like I haven't changed much at all."

"Hah!" Paul exploded. "Do you remember? You were pathetic. Like a lost puppy. Sad eyes, pouting lips." He made his best impression. "Look at you now. You're a magnificent creature, ready for a brave new world." Before she could react, he diverted her further. "Ever read that book? By Huxley? You sat on a cliff with him on our honeymoon. Then you never read any of his stuff. The time might be right for that. Here and now, baby. Let's stick to the here and now."

"Got more green stuff?"

"You bet. God ..."

"I was just kidding," Verbolana interrupted.

"I wasn't. Verbolana, you won't be able to do this alone. And Frank won't be any help. None of our friends will, I'm guessing. They're all gonna wanna forget. Sure, they'll mourn in their own way, but reaching out to you—I think that will be too hard for most of them. I've seen it a hundred times. They'll just want to fuck their brains out. Weddings and funerals bring out the fucking." A car arrived to offer further distraction and Paul took full advantage. "God, give us some green stuff," he blurted as soon as he sat. "We gotta name this stuff." He held his glass up for clinking. "Drink, you gotta drink!"

"Paul," she pleaded. "I don't want to hide."

"Drink," he insisted. "Don't you remember? It's not about you. This night is all about me."

"Yeah," she resigned herself to it and took a big gulp.

"Now, isn't that better?" he said, as if talking to a young girl.

"Don't push it, buddy." But the green stuff stole the force from her words, so she laughed instead. "We could call it Paul. I could call out, 'God, give me a cup of Paul.'"

"Good, good," Paul thought aloud. "I was thinking of something different, though. How about forgiveness?"

"God, give me a little forgiveness? Will he know what I'm talking about?" Verbolana wondered.

"Sure. People make up names for stuff all the time. God knows your intentions. He can't give you real forgiveness, anyway."

Just then the car slowed and started its climb to the surface. The Palladium was only a short ride away. Verbolana gulped what was left in her cup and before her emotions could get the better of her called out, "God, another cup of forgiveness."

Paul smiled. "That's the spirit, Vee. Now let's enjoy the ride as if it were our last." Giant, deeply shadowed trees greeted them as usual. "These trees weren't here when I first got here," Paul informed her. "None of this was. I remember the whole thing, the years of planning, the endless votes and all who bet on the outcome. For God would not hear the petition until we had worked out all the details. And he demanded a five-sixths majority. Of course, we had nothing to lose. He had never even entertained a petition before. It was all so much fun. And when it finally opened, oh my God, it was packed wall to wall for the next fifty years."

"Who worked out the initial ground rules with God?" Verbolana wanted to keep the conversation going. They were now sliding down into the river, and she felt panic bubbling through the forgiveness.

"There were three of them, all from different planets and different times. They came from three of the more advanced planets, Cofnifi, Alterna and Pulternya. Two women and a gent. Each was a brilliant designer, but they were also devoted hedonists. If my world had been asked to participate, we wouldn't have had a clue as to what to do. The United States was in the middle of our most brutal war, a civil war while we were getting tons of new citizens, they had lived such atrocious lives, most of 'em didn't know pleasure from pain."

"Worse than your life?" Verbolana found that hard to believe.

"As bad, certainly," Paul confirmed. "Disease got most of 'em ... Wow, check that out; it's new." A blast of rainbow, swirling flame approached the car in slow motion. Bubbles of exploding gases ignited and undulated through the water heavy with current. Words appeared, swirled and vanished. Faces superimposed on rural landscapes, bypassing conscious thought. "This is familiar," Paul stammered. "That was—and that." He tried to collect and piece together the disparate images until, "I know that voice. It's your voice." He looked across in amazement at Verbolana. "What the ...? How could you?"

"Keep watching," Verbolana urged. Images assaulted, thoughts and emotions collected, melded, shaped, until, burned into his retina and singed into his chest, the message congealed. Love and admiration, respect and gratitude—and warm remembrance.

"Vee, how could you have?"

"Don't focus on the how, my love. Focus on the why. It's all about you, baby. And the love of a thousand people you have touched. I know you know that food is not just food, that food is home and comfort and peace. And I know you know that those things are hard to find, no matter what world we might find ourselves on. What I don't think you realize is the power your simple life has had on so many others. Prepare yourself, baby, for the party of your life."

As the car climbed from the river, a great wail echoed in their ears. The car rose higher into the trees as what they could now discern as a human wave of sound surrounded them. The trees' shielding broke, and the Wilds lay at their feet. Whoops and hollers greeted them from below.

"What the ...?" Paul peeked over the side of the car. "Who are all these people?"

"Friends, come to see you off."

416

"But, this is outrageous! They could die out there. They're all naked to the world. Get them in!" Paul welled with panic.

"They put up guards, and only those young enough ventured out. But they wanted to tell you something. How, without the comfort you provided, they would all still be naked in this world, naked and old and bitter."

"From my food? You've got to be kidding." Paul waved now. "Who would have thought of such madness? In all my years I have never heard ..."

"It was Frank's idea. He's down there somewhere." Verbolana peered over the side and waved, too.

Paul stood in mute amazement. The car rocked and he stumbled across the cushioned seat until he plopped down into Verbolana's lap. "It doesn't get any better than this," and he gave her a long, passionate kiss. "Thank you for everything." He pulled away and looked long into her eyes. Then, in one motion, he pulled himself up into a crouch on the seat and as he launched over the side, Verbolana heard him scream, "God, let me die before I hit the ground!"

Without a thought, Verbolana lunged for him, trying to grab a leg or foot. When she missed, she launched over the side of the car. She fell headlong into the lighted night. "Paul!" she screamed. Outside herself she felt her body gaining Strength as she watched Paul fall flailing toward the trees. Suddenly his clothes vanished, and in that same instant, his body, a wrinkled emaciated corpse, hit the upper branches of a spiky tree. Verbolana watched his body almost snap in half, and then careen off a branch, only to hit another. She felt a sudden chill but couldn't be bothered, as her eyes followed the skin sack of broken bones that was a moment ago her lover.

The first branch that struck her jarred her from her vigil. Sliding down her falling body, it ripped and abraded with every touch. Her mind focused now, almost against her will, on the threat she faced. The next branch came and she was ready. With outstretched arms, she cushioned the branch into her, slowing her fall while guiding the branch past. She jackknifed her legs into her, and in spite of the terrible rending of the flesh of her hands and the wrenching her shoulders took as her falling body obeyed gravity, she held on. With Strength, she controlled her wild swinging, then dropped, from branch to branch through the tree, her focus back on reaching Paul before …

She reached the ground only to be surrounded by gawking, horrified friends. Knocking a few to the ground with her Strengthened intent, she pushed others aside, wading through the crowd, searching for one last glimpse of Paul.

"Verbolana, Verbolana!" Frank's voice floated to her. "There's nothing. The branches." As if that explained things. "Just bones. Honey, we have to get you back. You're hurt, you're bleeding."

Wild-eyed, Verbolana turned on her friend. She recognized the voice, but not the man who stood before her. Wrinkled, balding and stooped. Verbolana wanted to grab him by his skinny neck and shake an answer she could comprehend out of him. His appearance shocked her into some semblance of understanding. Anger and Strength evaporated, and without that she crumbled to her knees into a ball of convulsing grief.

She felt Frank's hands at her sides, trying to right her, bring her to her feet. Then more hands, some with the strength of youth, pulled her up and landed her on her feet. Wobbling and still bent near in half, she allowed them to guide her through the trees.

"Over here, quickly!" she heard voices urging.

"She'll be fine once we get her inside!" another voice shouted. "I'm back in. Over here."

Panic rushed across Verbolana's muddled brain. *Paul, I cannot leave Paul!* Strength surged, limbs flailed, determination steeled.

The enemy was all around her. They must not take her—not there. She could not go *there*. Not now, not ever!

"I must stay with Paul!" she screamed, as she shed the hands that held her captive. Spinning, knocking, punching, she escaped the surrounding bodies and bolted into the forest.

"Verbolana!" choruses of voices followed her.

"Somebody get her!" she heard Frank's frantic voice. "My feet. I've got to get back inside. Somebody, please."

Verbolana felt the flesh of her own feet tearing as she bolted deep into the trees, though it was hardly a distraction. Paul was still out here, she felt it. And something else. The cold night air dimpled her skin. The pain, breaking out from so many spots, brought focus to her brain. Something else washed through the scent of the green forest, through the filtered light of the giant moon that floated above. Her brain suddenly lifted from the fog. She stopped running. No one followed, just their voices. Their silly ignorant voices. She felt Paul's eyes on her. She closed her own eyes and sucked in his love. Grief fell away with each inhalation, the cold air scouring her lungs. She threw her arms wide, her face to the sky. For the first time, she realized her body had aged. Through the pain that screamed all across her skin and deep into her bones, she felt a peculiar calmness and sudden lack of urgency. She dropped to her knees, naked and bleeding to the world and felt God's presence.

Though she knew the answer, she screamed to the night sky, "God, what are you doing here?"

There was no answer.

Slowly, Verbolana stood, pain exploding through her rapture. "You never were," she mumbled under her breath as she turned her back on the city of marvels and trudged deeper into the forest.

# Chapter 46

Trake's greasy black hair fell into his face as he slumped. Swiping listlessly with the edge of his sword, he seemed almost unaware of his blocked vision. The arena, lit with smoking torches crammed between broken rocks, danced with shadows and gloom anyway. Not much to see. Just another blade attached to arms and legs that could not destroy him, as much as he tried to let them.

*What do you want?* He screamed to the inside of his head. *I have given you everything I ever had, yet still you want more. My shame is all I have left. Find a new pawn and let me die. I can be of no use to you any longer.* However, when the next strike came, his arms responded. He blocked and lunged, crossed and stepped with casual abandon. Strength coursed, lightning erupted and another man lay bleeding across the ground. Cheers and jeers filled the cavern as onlookers perked or slumped at the outcome of their wagers.

Trake stood stock still, blade point casually thrust to the packed earth. Peering through his tangled mop, he wondered idly about the stench around him. Vaguely he knew it was his or at least something that followed him. He couldn't imagine how he could give off such a stink when he barely even existed.

"Come on, Trake," a familiar voice echoed between his ears. "Let's get a drink. We're set for a week after that one. Your opponent was well known in these parts. Got three-to-one from some of these yokels." A hand grabbed his arm and led him out of the makeshift arena, down a few broken steps, then into a dank, torch-lit tunnel. "Sure you don't want a girl? Saw some in the stands eyeing you."

"Had a girl."

"Yeah, I had a girl too. Want another," Artent, his new best buddy, responded through rotting teeth. "Look, I know you had a bad shake; can't change that. You killed the guy, right? Can't do nothing beyond that."

Trake glanced sideways at the guy who had attached himself a week or month ago. "Exactly," was his only comment.

"Well, I'm gonna buy you a bath. And a girl to scrub you, so you might as well scrub her right back."

Trake walked on. "You said something about a drink."

"Yeah, just up here. Bathhouse with booze. Doesn't get any better." The man skipped ahead, apparently impatient with Trake's plodding. "Might want to put your sword away," he suggested.

Trake realized his right hand still clenched the dripping weapon. He thrust it into the sheath strapped to his waist, thinking that if the next man wanted to die from a clean blade, then he would have to wash it himself before the fight. The thought brought a rare smile to his lips.

"You fool them every time," Artent kept up his running babble. "Look like hell, you know. Maybe you shouldn't get a bath. Nobody thinks a man who looks like you can fight." They stopped in the bustling corridor as Artent regained his bearings. "Place is so confusing. Don't know why they don't run wires down to the arena. Guess nobody wants to pay." He made a decision and explained it to Trake, as if Trake cared. "Yeah, the bathhouse is down here." He pointed to a long avenue of well-lit shops, their colorful lights beckoning them onward. "Checked it out while you were sleeping. Got some lookers." He prodded Trake forward. As they walked, Artent continued his interrogation. "Just occurred to me. You're not into boys, are you? Is that the problem? Haven't given you the right temptation? You were Honored; should'a guessed."

Trake put one foot in front of the other. "Said there'd be drinks," he mumbled as if in answer. "How much further?"

"Just up the road, I tell ya," Artent shot back defensively. "If you don't want to talk, just tell me."

"I don't want to talk."

"Well, how am I supposed to know what you want if you don't tell me? I'm trying to look out for you. You're kinda pathetic, ya know. Great with the sword, don't get me wrong, but not much else goin' for ya."

Trake's mind wandered. It was something that still marveled him. Unless he had enough drink in him, he still wondered. Things such as, where exactly was he? How did these people work the lights? How did they grow food and make clothing under the constant watch of the Honored? Was all this leftover from before the Cleansing? Where are the Honored blimps, and why don't they put an end to such blasphemy? And why did he insist on calling it blasphemy?

"Are we closing in on that drink?"

* * *

"I don't know who he is or what he wants," Artent whispered, crouched next to Trake, who lay on the low mat of his rubble-walled room, nursing an uncooperative stomach. "The guys he sent are just flunkies. But he did send this." The bare bulb hanging from the low ceiling glittered across a coin that held no interest for Trake. "I'm sure there will be more."

"The price is always higher than the reward," Trake intoned with slack conviction.

"The price is what keeps us alive. It is always that way."

"Exactly," Trake agreed, though he stood anyway. Artent was a good friend, and if for nothing else, he would go along for a friend.

"Good thing I bought you that bath." Artent jumped to his feet and followed Trake to the door. "Wait," he lurched back into the room. "You almost forgot your sword. By the way," he added, "I cleaned it up for you. That guard was stuck to the scabbard with all that blood."

Reluctantly, Trake accepted the weapon and hooked it under his belt; their burly escorts watched every move from just outside the curtain. In spite of himself, Trake's Strength perked as he watched the men outside fall into proper military step: two to the rear and two in front, their distance appropriate and their attentions acute. Trake let his mind painfully expand through the pinlights that fluttered behind his eyes. To his surprise, he felt others, an advanced guard as well as a well-hidden rear. *Am I that important, or are things really that treacherous? This could be interesting.*

Trake had no idea and no interest in how big this city was, though he was getting an impression anyway. Most of it was underground, it seemed, but every hundred feet, the labyrinth of corridors opened up to a sunlit pile of rubble or a small covered courtyard with a tree and maybe a few scraggly bushes. And the wealth impressed him. Fully clothed, pudgy people scurried everywhere. They sat, with tables and chairs, in little groups with people who served them food. Apparently many of them bathed regularly in warmed water and most carried large satchels to hold even more luxuries. He wondered, as he walked, whether he could be happy with some of these things. Even as an Honored, such decadences had not been available. Hadn't he wanted these things at some point? He searched back through muddled memories. Vaguely, faceless forms coalesced behind his eyes. Shadowy bodies mingled, fingers and mouths touched his memories. He shook himself violently, almost knocking into Artent. The guards fore and aft bristled. Trake gave a rare laugh that burped out hoarse and graveled along with a little bile that burned as he swallowed it back down.

"You all right?" Artent nudged him with a bony elbow.

"Just remembering," Trake intoned.

"No time for exorcising demons," Artent warned.

"I don't pick the times," Trake explained.

"Well, hold it together for now, would ya? I don't want to get in your way when you decide to self-destruct."

Trake smiled again, two times in one day. "Aw, that's not much of a friend. You don't think I could take these guys before they got to you?" Purposefully, he said it loud enough for all to hear.

Artent followed suit. "Would you please shut your trap? We don't want any trouble."

"It would be no trouble, really." Trake was actually enjoying himself. Suddenly alert and full of Strength, he noticed they had entered a room easily as big as half a deck. Floor to ceiling windows ringed the perimeter with lush greenery beyond and large, freestanding sculptures scattered in the foreground. Such a display of wealth made Trake certain they had arrived. The small group approached an ornate central column Trake recognized as an elevator. His observations were confirmed when the lead guard pushed a lighted button beside two shining panels. Without further thought, Trake shouldered Artent violently to the ground and drew his weapon. Full comprehension only came to the remaining guards when the spurting head of one of their compatriots rolled across the floor. Trake stopped his arc short and plunged his blade in and out of the second guard before the man could even raise his weapon. Trake turned and smiled at Artent's horrified face. "See, no trouble at all," he announced as he advanced on the remaining two guards.

Simultaneously, the stunned guards fell back as each screamed for backup. Both drew their swords and sidestepped, giving the other room to move. Trake stepped between them, his sword casually dripping at his side, his eyes glazed, staring off into nothing.

"What have you done?" Artent moaned, choosing to stay on the ground where he had fallen. "You will get us killed for sure! Sirs, please, I have no quarrel with you. I barely know this man." Then he skittered across the floor as one of the guards circled near.

Long before backup arrived, Trake felt their stealthy approach. From both corridors leading to the large room they came, arrows notched in drawn bows. He heard Artent whimpering and directed a modicum of his attention in that direction. One of the guards slowly closed on his friend, obviously intent on lessening the odds. It was as good a time as any to move, though he waited another moment. When he felt the man's attention shift fully to his defenseless prey, Trake feinted to his right, and then plunged to his left. As expected, his swift movement brought instinctive action from the archers. With ethereal vision, Trake tracked the path of the archers' extended intention while still concentrating on the job in front of him. Seeing that the arrows would miss, Trake sighted on the raised sword of the guard as it was about to drive downward. Trake swung high and wide, lopping the sword and hand at the wrist. It was such a clean slice that apparently the man had not noticed, for with great force he brought his pumping arm down in a mighty swipe, covering Artent in a warm shower of crimson blood. Both men screamed as Trake scrambled to retrieve the fallen sword. Before either victim could recover, Trake had run the guard through and handed the dripping weapon to Artent. Another sword lay abandoned close by, so Trake picked it up as well, before turning to face his opponents. He realized he was having more fun than he'd had in a long time.

Both archers had reloaded and Trake observed that others had arrived as well. A little more fun, and then they would have to leave. He lamented for a moment. If Artent hadn't been with him, it might have been fun to see how far he could get through this force before they cut him down. Trake heard the elevator doors slide open behind him.

"Artent, you're fine. Slide over and get in the elevator!" The screaming continued, so without looking, Trake lashed out with his foot and brought the man to new attention. "Artent, we gotta go. Move your ass!" The screaming stopped. To Trake's relief, he heard Artent clambering behind him. He felt the doors starting to close and stepped back. Too late; they bounced back open. Trake faced the rushing figures as men moved into position. Artent sat stunned as he watched Trake swipe two arrows from the air with his blurred swords.

"Push a button," Trake urged, as the archers reloaded.

Two more arrows whizzed as Artent came to a low crouch in the far corner. As Trake's blades calmed he screamed, "Now!" Artent leaped for the buttons and crumpled immediately to the floor as Trake's swords sliced again. The doors whooshed closed and the car lurched upward.

Artent wasted no time with his recriminations. "What have you done? They will execute us for sure!"

"Ya think?" Trake responded.

# Chapter 47

"What button did you push?" Trake asked, as if he did not hold two dripping blades.

"The one that's lit," Artent answered as he tried to rub the blood from his face.

"I think we ought to go to the top," Trake postulated as he pushed the last button.

"Are you crazy? We gotta get out of here. We gotta find a place to hide, then wait for nightfall. I don't give us much of a chance. Maybe we should split up."

"And leave all that money behind? You said you wanted the money, that we needed it. I just thought I would raise our asking price a bit."

Trake placed both swords on the elevator floor. Then methodically, he unhooked the scabbard from his belt and placed that beside the swords. "Stand up, man. We gotta make an entrance!" He felt the car slowing, "Quick with you," he quipped as he squared his shoulders.

The doors slid open as Artent was just straightening up. To Trake's surprise, no one confronted them. Apparently, the alarm had not yet reached the top floor. What did confront them was a vision of decadence beyond belief. Verdant green, deep golds, brilliant sapphire blues and whites so bright they hurt the eye. Trake had no experience with such beauty. His immediate thought was of the illicit stories of his childhood, of the upper floors, and he realized that was exactly what he saw. It, of course, was not a tower of the Chosen, so his second thought was of shame and anger, and hideous waste. He stepped onto the green floor, and his foot cushed. Artent hung back, but that did not deter him. He took another step. He thought of the forest where, every so often, Father's gifts conspired to make a step or two as soft. He looked further. Where he had expected to find guards with steel, he saw low puffy cushions on raised platforms inviting him to shed his anger and fear, and sleep in comfort. The golden brocade beckoned his weary body in a way no sight had ever done. Atasha, her lush body naked, waiting, enticing. It was the only comfort that compared. And since his mind dared go there, he saw Atlana, barely denting the cushion, in more luxury than she had ever known.

"You like what you see?" A voice bounced off the expanse of glass in front of him. It was as if the snow-capped mountains that commanded the view had spoken.

"Your vision is no doubt different from mine," Trake answered truthfully. "What I see is waste and decadence. Coveting for the sake of coveting."

The mountains laughed, deep and echoing. "You are still Chosen, after all you have seen and done. You are not daunted by the lies?"

"I am daunted only by the hypocrisy," Trake returned, though he was confused and more than a little concerned. There was no energy signal for the voice. His ears and eyes instinctively triangulated on the voice and ferreted out the only possible source, but that was hardly the point. No one had successfully hidden his signal from him since that first time, that man who had destroyed his life.

A man stood from a high-backed chair and faced Trake. "Then you are daunted by human nature. Every man, no matter how humble or pious, craves comfort. I dare say you have found none yet. That is a sad thing."

The man was tall and thin, fit and handsome. He continued, "You see, I know a great deal about you. I have spies in every corner of every land. I have heard you are a man of broken faith, yet you speak to the contrary. At least the reports of your skills are accurate. How many of my men did you leave alive?"

"Do you care?" Trake stalled as he tried to get a read on this man's intentions.

"I suppose not terribly, though I do not like being made to look a fool."

"That would have only happened if you had been surprised by my arrival without them," Trake observed.

"And you sense I was not?" The man stepped around the chair to reveal a sword dangling from his left hand.

"That is what I sense," Trake lied.

Trake heard the doors behind him trying to shut and Artent's fumbling movements.

"Come out," he commanded. "We are as safe here as anywhere."

Emboldened by the seemingly benign scene, Artent ventured forth, his bloody hands thrust before him to show he carried no weapon.

"You are a sight, young man. Are you wounded?" For the first time, Trake noticed that the man was considerably older than he was, graying at the temples with a slight, wrinkling of his hands.

"I—I don't think so, Your Highness. Someone else's blood, though I had no hand in getting it there." Artent took another step forward. "And I don't wish to drip on your carpet."

"Very thoughtful," the man conceded, then looked at Trake. "Though little help in a fight," he observed. "Trenta, Velenta," the man called. Trake looked in the direction the man indicated and for the first time noticed the room was divided by a floor to ceiling curtain. Through a hidden break, two girls that even Trake's nonexistent libido acknowledged skittered into the room. "Take this man off for a bath and a new wardrobe," the man commanded. "And feed him if he so desires."

Artent looked sheepishly at the girls and back at the man. "Thank you," was all he said before the girls playfully guided him back through curtains. A startled squeal from one of the girls reached Trake's ear before the curtain closed.

The man laughed lightly. "Comfort first, even in the face of danger beyond his description."

Trake ignored the obvious affirmation. "Who are you and what do you want?"

The man laid his sword against the chair and sauntered across the room to a row of bottles and glasses. "Drink?"

"Not quite yet," Trake answered, surprising himself.

He watched the man's movements. Trained, he concluded. And obviously some understanding of the Strength. But does he have it? Trake could not tell.

"My name," the man continued after pouring an amber liquid into a bowled glass, "Will mean nothing to you, so I will not bother. What I want, however, could be of great interest to you." He turned from the bar and confronted Trake eye to eye for the first time. Casually, he took a sip of his drink and placed it back on the bar. "We have mutual enemies, you and I, and I was thinking we might join forces."

"Enemies? How can a man with no allies have enemies?" It seemed to make sense until he said it. Trake shrugged to himself and moved on. "Let's try this: 'When everyone is an enemy, how can one have allies?'" Then he added, "I desire nothing but death."

"Not even revenge?"

"I have gotten whatever revenge is available."

"You think so? What was taken from you could never be avenged by the death of one man. Why do you think you walk around as you do? Revenge for such a massive loss must be taken on a massive scale. It is the only way to recover." The man looked in astonishment at Trake's ignorance.

"What do you know of loss?" Trake surprised himself with the question. This man must be hitting a nerve.

"The world is an evil place. I have lost and regained and lost again more than you can imagine. Anger fuels my every action. As I alluded to earlier, only my desire for comfort outweighs my anger. That is where you and I appear to be different. Though I doubt you have ever seen the comforts that are possible. This," he spread his arms. "This is nothing."

Trake took it all in, let the words and options percolate. He reached back in his mind, pictured his loves; their soft bodies, yielding flesh, bundled devotion. But no faces. He searched for his swaddled daughter, felt her warmth, connected with the love eternal, but could not discern her face. He touched his wife, felt her passion and connected with her wonder, but not her eyes. Then he went where he always went, to Verbolana. Lost before her time, stolen without the words ever being spoken. He saw her hair, the almond shape of her head, her laugh carried across the deck, but not her lips. Anger or maybe guilt washed though his body. It didn't matter which; they felt the same.

Trake became aware of the man's eyes on him. Feeling naked to his gaze, he asked, "What do you have in mind?"

"I am building an army. One that this world has never seen. I want your Strength at the vanguard."

Somehow Trake was not surprised. "And for me?"

"Let's sit and we can talk. Naroma, Glartanya, bring us food."

# Chapter 48

W hat did you expect to find out here?" a grizzled man sat on a fallen log, the bark black with the first rain of autumn.

"Not this," Verbolana's answer came slowly to her sun-chapped lips. "When I first left I did not expect anything, just death. I had seen a display, years before, of glorious bloody death. That's what I wanted."

"And when it didn't come?" the man's voice smiled patiently. "You could have gone back."

"No, no, I couldn't. My betrayal had been completed." Verbolana, too, sat on the sopped log and tried to ignore the itching wetness that spread across her backside. Instead, she concentrated on the view, let the greens and browns of nature pull her thoughts outward. She felt the recently cleared crisp blue sky open and cleanse her mind. She laughed with the simple joy brought by a simple life.

"You find that funny? Being betrayed?" the voice next to her asked.

"I was just remembering," she answered, as her eyes wandered to the distant hills. "It was a drink Paul and I discovered, or concocted, I think. Can't really remember. But anyway, this drink had tiny bubbles and the base was Cranstal Root or some such. Anyway, when I drank it, it felt much like this view makes me feel. Does that make any sense? You know, clean and fresh. Cleansing."

"I don't know the drug you speak of. I was only in that wretched city for a short time."

"Why did you leave?" Verbolana asked.

"They said God was there, but I knew better."

"He says he created us," Verbolana stated.

"Tell me how that matters," Altef, the old man, demanded.

"Well, he is certainly powerful."

"That he is," Altef conceded. "But that does not make him God. Not to my way of thinking. I will not pray to a God who has no forgiveness."

"Forgiveness? He has nothing but forgiveness. That is his weakness," Verbolana lamented.

"You mistake acceptance for forgiveness," Altef persisted. "With total acceptance, there is nothing to forgive. My God has expectations for each of us. He even has expectations for that creature they call God. Though I do believe forgiveness has its limits. I would not wish to be 'God' when God comes calling."

"But how do you know these things?"

"You have felt them. You know as well as I do. You simply don't believe yet." Altef turned to search her eyes. She gave him nothing. She had been cheated too many times.

"Tell me about your forgiveness," she inquired instead.

"Forgiveness is the ultimate gift one can give oneself or another. As I have said, the universe is a cruel and bitter place, giving each of us more than enough to lament. No matter our gifts, there is not a creature in all of creation that does not want more. It is the way of survival, and the way of progress. What one man builds, another man covets."

"Ah, yes," Verbolana remembered. "Coveting. My people know about coveting. They have long listed it as one of the five evils."

"And you believe this?" Altef asked.

"Of course," Verbolana responded, eager to please.

"So you embrace the evil within yourself?" he persisted.

Verbolana sat silent, open to his teachings yet confused by their meaning. Fearlessly she burrowed down into her simple life. Her meager hut that hardly blocked the wind or the rain, her itchy bed of straw and stiffly cured animal skins, her rough clothing that she had helped to spin and sew. She had little, but wanted nothing more. She remembered the gnawing hunger that came every winter. She knew that others hoarded stores, though she did not investigate or enter into the gossip. She saw her hunger as her penance and almost welcomed it. She thought of her friends back in the city and found no jealousy there. Something dragged her thoughts back to her sorry bed. She felt the cold in her joints and, without warning, felt the emptiness of her arms, the screaming of her skin, the longing in her lips.

"I am certainly lonely," Verbolana admitted after a long pause. "I can touch my feelings of abandonment. But I do not covet what anyone else has. I do not desire to take anything away from anyone. I do not waste or horde or collect. I merely want what I can never have. For the most part I am satisfied with that."

"Really?" Altef seemed to wonder. "Let me tell you what I hear. You left the city with a desire to die. When you did not die, you came here. You have joined in with the work, you have learned our language, you have even shared in our defense, but you have never joined in the celebration. You wander to your bed alone and cry yourself to sleep."

"I do not!" Verbolana exploded.

"Of course you do. Your tears may be dry and your heart numb, but it is all the same. You covet not what man has, or what God can give you, but what the universe has stolen from you." He waited for a minute, watched the first rays of the morning sun play across the village below. He watched Ral, one of his neighbors who, after ten or so years in the village, had still not learned the communal language. Ral hiked up his nightshirt, squatted over a freshly dug slip trench, and relieved himself. Altef watched as Ral spit on two fingers and reached down to clean himself, careful not to let his nightshirt fall into the shallow trench.

"Coveting is a celebration of your existence," he finally stated. "A desire for something you do not have is the origin of passion. And as long as you are ashamed of your desires, you will be ashamed of your core being. Hence you will never find your true passion."

"You talk in circles. Evil is good; good is evil."

"What I suggest is that the universe is what it is. If you need to change something or someone, change yourself. Forgive yourself for being a part of the universe – a part of the evil and a part of the good."

"And how is that different from acceptance?"

"Forgiveness is active; acceptance is passive. Forgiveness acknowledges the concept of evil, the ideas of right and wrong. Acceptance requires no such judgment."

"So you say to forgive myself and find my true passion, and that will guide me." Verbolana thought through her next words. "What if my true passion is to kill others?"

"Then I would submit that you have not looked deeply enough. It is my belief that true passion cannot exist to the detriment of others. True passion must, by its nature, be in concert with those around you."

"So what is your true passion?" Verbolana demanded.

"To understand the nature of God. To live in concert with the nature of the way things are and with those around me."

"And yet you have killed. I have seen you."

"I did not say that I desired to change the ways of the universe, just my own ways. I can forgive myself and I can forgive those around me."

"Even as you are running them through with your pike."

"Yes," the old man answered.

"I will have to think on this," Verbolana admitted.

"Of course, but can I make a suggestion?"

"You have already made many," Verbolana observed with a smile.

"Indeed, but this is one of process. As you consider these concepts, breathe into your belly, deep and long and release slowly and completely. That is all I ask."

"Yes, I am familiar with this technique. I use it when I gather the Strength."

"Oh, yes, your Strength. That is what we came up here to discuss in the first place. Look at this old man, so intent to teach, he forgets to be the student." He laughed at his own arrogance.

A terrible racket jolted them from their discussion. Someone, across the valley and into the hills beyond, yelled and thrashed through the underbrush. "Get away! Help! Stay back! Someone help!"

Verbolana scoured the distant hill, looking for movement. She assumed whoever it was had just crested the hill, since no noise had come to them before and now the woman's voice was quite plain.

"There!" Verbolana pointed. "Directly above the commissary, twenty feet from the ridgeline." She was already on her feet, loping down the hillside.

"You'll have to go without me. I'll be preparing for her care." He was also already in action, though his careful picking ways would be of no immediate help. "Can you see what is chasing her?"

But Verbolana was too focused and intent to answer. Instead, she screamed, "Come straight down the hill. There is a path about halfway down. We are on our way!"

She forded the creek, then headed up the rise into the village. Sleepy men bolted from their huts, weapons drawn if not pants or shirts. Verbolana spotted one man brandishing a long pike and as she passed, she ripped it from his hand. "Bring more!" was all she gave as explanation.

Verbolana shot through the village and headed up the trail before she heard the first echoing basal snarl of a giant cat. A second surge of Strength bolted her up the hill and as she rounded the first corner, she nearly tripped over a bleeding scrambling girl as naked as nature allowed. Verbolana hurdled the whimpering form and took up a defensive posture. In her days fresh from the city, she had tangled with a similar creature, and had learned then that many of Father's creatures have a Strength of their own. She did not underestimate their peril.

"Move!" she screamed. "Down the hill—go, go!" When the girl did not move, Verbolana kicked at her to get her attention. "I don't wish to die here, girl! Get up and run!"

The frightened girl came to her hands and knees and scurried away from Verbolana's prodding feet. She tried to gain her footing, but stumbled and went down again.

From the brush, the cat launched. Verbolana spun her pike, planted the tail end in the ground and ducked to the ground. She felt the pike sink deep into the animal, and then heard the handle crack and then snap as the mammoth cat fell upon her. She pushed off hard as the beast's back claws raked down her sides. She ducked again and rolled in the direction the cat had come from. Somehow, she avoided the crushing weight of the falling cat. She jumped, empty-handed, to her feet. The animal writhed on the ground, with as many as eight arrows protruding from its side, each with its crimson splotch.

Men rushed to Verbolana's side, noisily checking her wounds and jabbering among themselves about the early morning excitement.

"Get away from me! What are you saying? What are you doing?"

For the first time, Verbolana realized the girl was speaking in Verbolana's own native tongue. "They are just concerned. They will not harm you."

"Finally someone who understands me. Tell them to back away. I am naked!"

"They can see that. It is not uncommon here," Verbolana tried to reassure her.

"You must be Wretched then," the shaking girl concluded. "Just my luck."

Verbolana erupted with spontaneous mirth, startling the men around her. "It is difficult to imagine those terms even still exist. There are neither Wretched nor Chosen here." She took a few steps toward the girl. "Blessed Militia, I assume," Verbolana concluded after observing the girl's hair and tattoo rank. "I somehow hoped women would not have to die in battle as I did. Wishful thinking that there would only be two."

"Only two?" Verbolana felt the girl's eyes searching across her face, drilling into her eyes. "Blonde hair, pouting lips ... *Verbolana*?" she muttered. "Could it be?" The girl dropped to her knees in the inch-thick dust of the worn trail.

Verbolana stood, blood oozing down both arms and legs, perplexed.

"*The Cannons of Courage.*" The ragged girl spoke with obvious deference, the men gathered around silenced by the scene. "You are Verbolana, yes?

*Obstinate teacher with the whip marks to prove it,*
*Swinging to battle with everything to lose.*
*Wexi, your love, only moments behind,*
*The devil incarnate is all she would find.*"

She recited. "It is you, isn't it?"

"I am Verbolana, and I was a teacher, but what is this?" she stammered in confusion.

"*The Cannons of Courage*? Every school child learns that song."

Another great commotion arose. The women of the village approached in excited turmoil with bandages and a covering for the mysterious girl.

# Chapter 49

Verbolana sat with the jumbled feelings of an old friend come to visit, only to bring bad news. Though Trake, Treena and Wexi were never far from her thoughts, they seemed more abstract now, frozen in time and space with their sparkling eyes and spirited gaits all she could really picture. But this girl, Fletta, who sat across from her, bundled in the only non animal-skin cloak Verbolana could find, had brought her old friends into new and painful focus. Trake and Treena would be in their late forties by now, if they were still alive. And from what this girl told her through the day and into the evening about her home world, she doubted there was anything left of their sparkling eyes or spirited gaits. The last time she had seen Trake, he was swaddling a newborn; one that now could be in the thick of battle next to his father. Or worse yet, swiping at Chosen in revenge for a fatherless childhood.

Verbolana realized, as they sat around her tiny stove, soothing tea warming their hands, that Fletta was still rambling, recounting histories of people and places Verbolana did not recognize.

She nodded in polite acceptance and then admitted, "I knew some of this, but I didn't know the battle had gone so wrong. I remember telling my friend Treena before I died, that it wouldn't be that hard for the Wretched to take a tower. I went back and watched some, but like you, found it was painful to see my friends struggle; to know of all the deceptions and not be able to open their eyes."

"Yes." Fletta sipped her tea in contemplation. Verbolana watched the girl's eyes flit from one memory to the next and was suddenly thankful for her growing forgetfulness, for even joyous moments remembered could hold such pathos. "The Wretched have no concept of the truth. To watch our leaders compromise and negotiate with those animals; it makes me sick. I couldn't watch the betrayal any longer. The Chosen will be swallowed up whole and spit onto Father's skin."

Verbolana sipped her own tea, fighting back a sudden chill. She looked across at Fletta, the exposed flame of the stove bounced in her youthful eyes. She noticed the girl's jaw working and the set of her lips. Fletta looked up and caught her watching.

"Are you ready for bed?" the girl asked, misreading Verbolana's interest. "We would have to be careful; we're both pretty banged up."

Verbolana smiled in surprise. The thought of sex came so seldom these days. "I was wondering, in your trips back, did you ever get to know any Wretched?"

The girl wrinkled her nose in disgust. "I got to know enough Wretched once I got up here. Father-raping heathens! Why would you ask? They are all ignorant, evil savages."

Though she had prepared herself for the answer, Verbolana dropped her eyes to the onslaught. "I knew one," she stated, without the least bit of shame or embarrassment. "I knew and loved him."

"Him?" Fletta jumped to her feet, preparing for flight. "How can ...? What are you ...?" she stammered.

Verbolana looked up to meet Fletta's daggered response. "When I spoke of deception, I was referring to God's deception, not the deception of the Wretched. God has never stepped one foot on our home world, yet all who live there think they know his desires."

"God or Gods," Fletta spat. "May the Gods be damned. Our people tell stories for the easily deluded; bedtime stories with silly twists that only a child could truly believe. All people do that! These deceptions come from the brains of selfish or inspired people, not the Gods. The only real question is which side you are on. Do you follow the selfish or the inspired? Truth and righteous rage are all that win the day."

Verbolana sighed deeply, her rage long since vanished, "And what is the truth, sweet Fletta?"

Apparently Fletta took Verbolana's resignation for condescension, for she nearly jumped across the small room at Verbolana. "You! You must know, great warrior that you are. Why else would you live out here? I thought for sure, sitting here, in this place, that you were one of the few. One of the only ones who truly understood."

She stood sputtering, struggling to declare the obvious. "Father—Father is all that matters. All the rhetoric, all the rules, all the sermons, all the fighting, yet very few truly understand. Even I, when I lived my life down there, I could not see. Mankind is stupid, greedy and ignorant. Every one of us struggles in a pathetic myopic haze, trying to carve out a little comfort and a little happiness. We all look at our own little piece and say, 'Oh, I can't make that much of a difference.' The Directors say they care, but they've already carved out their little piece. The Generals spout lines from the Great Dramas while only really having a heart for battle. Meanwhile, the rest of us follow along with their sermons bouncing around in our heads, trying desperately to stay alive in the face of swinging steel. Everything is Za shit compared to the needs of Father. The Author was right. His brilliance is unmistakable, but apparently his execution was slightly inadequate. Somehow we must finish the job, that is all."

"And how do you plan to do that from out here?" Verbolana appreciated the anger that flowed through this girl's veins. A memory from a long time ago, for sure, but she still identified with pieces of the rage.

"I don't know that," Fletta deflated a little, seemed to take her first breath of the last few minutes. "I have come out here to study Father, hoping to find some answers. So far, I have been a little too distracted." Fletta sat back down.

Verbolana watched the girl's zeal fade, through either resignation or calculation, she wasn't sure which. But in a moment the girl confirmed her observation.

"I'm sorry for the outburst. You saved my life and have been nothing but kind. Without you, my search would be over, permanently this time. Maybe we should get some sleep. You look tired, and I have imposed myself enough."

Though she agreed with almost nothing the girl said, Verbolana felt a growing kinship with this struggling soul. "I appreciate your passion and your fresh look on an ancient problem." Then she surprised even herself. "And I would welcome your warmth tonight."

A sly smile broke across Verbolana's face with the dawn. Her wounded legs could not compete with the comforts of snuggled warmth and adoration. She lay, collected the thoughts that had coalesced through the night, and wondered which route she would follow today. Altef said that morning was the time for reflection and projection, and that seemed particularly fitting today.

*Can I give Fletta any of the comfort I have found? She is so raw, the struggle still piled so high before her. And yet there must be a shortcut, a way to heal without the years of agony. Altef would insist the key is in forgiveness. I can see a piece of that; but it all seems so passive.* Verbolana circled the room with her eyes, forgave the fire for not lighting itself and forgave her ceramic pot for the thin sheet of ice that covered her water for tea. As she stirred to rise, fiery pain shot across her skin. She winced, sucked her breath and pulled her legs free of the covers and Fletta's enveloping warmth. Huddled naked on the edge of the bed, she pulled her cloak over her shoulders before slipping her feet into her waiting shoes. *If Altef had his way, would I forgive or accept these insults too?*

She hobbled over to her rickety stool, leaned over the stove and examined the ashes. With a stick of kindling, she gently brushed at the coal bed, searching for a flicker of life that would give her a head start toward one of the only comforts she had in this harsh life. She uncovered a glowing jewel and blew gently across its surface as she added tiny shreds of twig. When they caught, she layered a few full-sized twigs, then chips of dried branch until she had a good flame.

She allowed her thoughts to fall into the flame as she automatically retrieved the teapot that lived on the shelf next to her meager food stores. She set it over the fire while she watched the building flames.

*Elemental,* her mind repeated over and over. *Natural, unavoidable. Fire is the first creation. Do I forgive the creation or the creator? Or do I accept? What was Altef trying to say? Can fire be evil? Fire just is. That must be accepted.*

"Augh." Verbolana peered through the gloom and encountered fierce, frightened eyes. Apparently Fletta had awoken from a fearful sleep.

"Fletta, everything is fine. You are safe. The cat is dead," Vee breathed across the room.

"Are you really Verbolana?" The intensity of the question surprised, then puzzled Vee.

"I am," Vee stated, then remembering the song. "Does that really matter? I have never thought of myself as worthy of song."

"I dreamed you went back." The girl ignored her question. "That you saved the Chosen with your knowledge from above."

"Hah!" Verbolana laughed despite herself. "Whatever your songs say, I am not a hero, and neither was Wexi. Just two young girls frightened beyond words, caught in a terrible situation."

"Yes, the songs tell of your fears." Fletta, still sleepy, seemed to reach back, maybe into her dream, maybe back to Father. "They also sing of your determination and your sacrifice. How, with the last ounce of Strength, you outwitted the scoundrel and secured the evil machine. And how, after a lifetime of sacrifice, you lay under the sword of the scoundrel to give yourself to Father."

For the first time in many years, Verbolana looked back at the scenes surrounding her death. Shame and regret were tough emotions to accept or forgive. Even with the cushion of time and the conviction that someone else's lies, not her true feelings, had driven those moments, she couldn't help but cringe. Poor Trake and poor Verbolana, doing the best they could, with both coming up short. Then Fletta's little story sunk in. Verbolana realized the death in the songs was not her true death. And who was this scoundrel the story spoke of?

She played along, not wanting to crush Fletta's fragile hold on normalcy. "Yes. Did the machine turn out to be important?"

"Important?" Fletta was now fully awake and sitting up in the chill. "Capturing that machine saved many lives for many years. Without your bravery, most feel all the towers would be conquered by now."

When Verbolana frowned, Fletta continued, "I don't know exactly what happened, but the Directors say the Gods allowed them only that one machine. They were never able to build another."

"That sounds like something the Directors would make up. I wonder what really happened?" Verbolana asked. "Doesn't really matter, I guess. I am still getting used to the idea that my people thought I did something great. It was all Trake, really." The comment brought a blurred vision of Trake standing over her, directing her not to move, sword held high.

"Trake? Who was Trake? The songs do not mention a man other than the scoundrel."

Verbolana busied herself with their tea. She carefully crumbled three different leaves into the bottom of two mugs, poured the boiling water and covered them each with a small plate to steep. When she was sure the mugs were both secure on her ancient cupboard, she turned to Fletta. "Trake was the blimp captain who truly saved the day. He engineered the securing of the weapon and defended it until reinforcements arrived. He and I test-fired it for the Generals. Then he hooked it up to be hauled off. It was all Trake, really." Verbolana watched Fletta's eyes turn from confusion to alarm.

"That can't be right. You, of the Blessed Militia, fought the traitorous scoundrel, matching Strength to Strength in an epic battle and after placing the last hook, he finally overwhelmed you, threw you to the ground and ran you through."

"But that ..." Verbolana blurted.

"This man Trake. He must be the scoundrel. That is who you fought, who you outsmarted, and who, after a valiant struggle, killed you!" Fletta screamed with certainty.

Verbolana sat slack-jawed, trying desperately to understand a world she vowed she would never bother herself with again. *What were the Directors doing? Why did they change the story?* she breathed, unwilling to ask the questions aloud.

But Fletta was Chosen and picked up on every breathed word. "What are you asking? Was it not that way? The scoundrel was certainly evil. You must have fought him. He could not have done what you said. It would make no sense."

"What you say makes no sense. Trake was a kind and gentle man. I watched him for years afterward. You can't be talking about the same man. He learned on his own about the lies. He lived with the Wretched and learned to love and be loved. I saw him. I cheered for him." And without hesitation she declared, "I loved him."

"He killed you," Fletta persisted.

"No, that was a ruse," Verbolana admitted. "I was furious at the time. I thought he was selfish, keeping me from my Encore. But I learned later he did it because he loved me, too. He was not willing to die before he told me." Tears streamed down her wrinkled cheeks. "He was right. The Gods lied, the Directors lied, Father lied. Only he held true to what he believed. And he believed in love.

"Then why is he trying to kill us all?" Fletta demanded.

# Chapter 50

Everything here is yours," Verbolana declared as she packed what she thought she might need for the trek. "If I make it back, I can always start over."

"What did I say? I did not mean to upset you." Fletta stood naked in the tiny hut, her goose-bumped flesh forgotten in the moment.

"I have to see for myself," Verbolana explained, not wanting the young girl to feel guilty. "Trake is not the scoundrel you sing of, and if he is, something has gone terribly wrong."

"I'm sorry I have brought you such distressing news. I feel responsible. You were settled, happy."

"I was neither," Verbolana stated; only at that moment realizing her declaration was true. "I have longed for something for so long it lost its name. He lost his name. But you brought him back to me. And if I have to bring *him* back from wherever he has fallen, so be it." Fueled with bewilderment and anger, and a surprising sense of joy, she dressed in silence, layered all the clothes she owned against her damaged body. "You have given me a gift so precious I did not even know it existed. Be at peace, young Fletta. I will set things right."

Verbolana threw a few items into the shoulder pouch she used to harvest her garden and stepped toward the door. "Take care, learn the language and respect the laws of Father. All else will come to you — or not. Leave that up to the swirling universe."

451

She walked out the door into the crisp thawing village. Her first stop was the village commissary. Under the astonished eyes of her neighbors, she stuffed her satchel with whatever would travel. "I have left my hut and my share of everything to your new resident. I will not be returning." Without a glance back, she called upon the Strength and hiked up the same path from which she had fetched Fletta the day before.

The first few miles whirled by as Verbolana's thoughts jumped ahead of her feet, almost dragging her along the mountain trail. The sun seemed to lie forever on the horizon. It reminded her of those precious moments of luxury a lifetime long ago, snuggled with Treena and Wexi under layers of privacy.

*I could visit with them. Rekindle my love. Wallow in true comfort. But Trake! I cannot leave Trake for another moment. Something has happened. Poison has bewitched him. His woman has turned against him, corrupted his mind, made him stoop and fetch for her pleasure. Evil, evil. How could she do that? I saw the love, the dedication, the true adoration in his eyes. How could she turn that power so? It must have been a plan all along. A Wretched conspiracy to steal the Strength. What can I do? I must see what happened and devise a plan. Devise a plan. See what happened. Devise a plan.*

*Thwack!* Verbolana, at near a run now, slammed straight into a low-hanging branch. Her feet continued as her head snapped back, tearing the skin of her forehead and sending her sprawling on her back. Surprise quickly gave way to concern. She had landed on her satchel, squashing everything inside. Mingled fruit juices soaked through her layers of clothing. The pain in her forehead and back reminded her of the gashes in her legs and, now in concert, brought her mind back to reality. Moaning, she rolled off her precious stores and came to her hands and knees in the thin mud of the melted frost.

"It is a good two days to the city," she grumbled to no one. "You must take more care." Blood dripped into the dirt between her hands as other rivulets stung her eyes. It was then she heard the low extended growl.

As she panicked the Strength vaulted her into a low crouch as she wiped frantically at her blurred eyes. Unable immediately to clear them, she scanned the forest with her mind. Thirty feet into the bushes lay a large intention. Verbolana immediately thought of the mate of the great cat they had killed the day before. They traveled in pairs and were known to be quite loyal.

With all hope that the cat could sense her energies, Verbolana focused every malevolent thought she could muster toward the animal as she pulled her sleeves down and cleared her eyes. She pulled her bag closer and rummaged for her stone dagger. The cat moved closer and the sound of breaking brush filled Verbolana's ears. She stood now, crouched and armed, and remembered Trake and her mission. Somehow, she knew she must defeat the undefeatable, only so she could face a bigger challenge.

She heard the great rumbling before her mind registered the moving threat. Devoid of options, she found herself rushing to meet the demon. They sprang at each other just off the path. But the animal outweighed her by three. Flying backward suddenly, Verbolana stabbed at whatever she could reach. With Strength, she stabbed and stabbed, landing blows even as the cat pummeled her into the ground with explosive force. Blinded by fur and fighting for breath, she continued stabbing.

The cat seemed unaffected. It pulled back and took a mighty swipe at Verbolana's face. Vee's raised arm took most of the blow, but through the ringing and blinding pain she felt her arm open to the two-inch claws and pump blood fat upon the ground. Reared up as the cat was, they came eye to eye. In that instant, Verbolana searched deep into the soul of the magnificent creature. No fear, no hatred, no remorse. The way of the universe was all there was.

"Thank you, God, for my time here." Verbolana spoke into the face of the void. The cat took no notice and sank its fierce teeth into Verbolana's exposed neck.

* * *

"Take this to General Pournat on the right flank." Trake handed a hastily scribbled note to a scruffily dressed runner.

"Your will." The runner stood tall, turned smartly and departed.

Trake stood, then called after the boy, "Wait for his response."

Trake strolled out of his tent and across a small clearing, his men camped all around, grabbing whatever rest they could after the forced march. It seemed the way with war, moments of frantic activity surrounded by days upon days of waiting or maneuvering. And that annoyed Trake. Not that a year or two ago his life had been any different; it was just that now the waiting bothered him. His mind constantly whirled with the possibilities of the next battle. He was always anxious to engage. Anxious for death. He cared little who died or why, or how many. He had already avenged everyone who needed avenging, had killed whole clans for merely defending themselves. He had vanquished his home tower and summarily put each Deck Director to a horrible death. So now, it was just the blood and the screams he craved. Though only from the men. Strict, extremely unpopular orders had gone out with his first command. Upon death, he ordered all the women and children spared. Even those under arms were not to be harmed or molested. With great care, they were merely detained.

Trake smiled into the thin cold air as he remembered back. The Colonels had been the most rewarding for him. With concern for their men as their stated goal, they had revolted, but their honor would not allow them to attack en masse. One by one they had confronted him, and one by one they had died. The Generals had been less satisfying. They sat watchful and complained to his back, yet they would not confront him directly. Trake tested his food and drink and set his Strength to watch while he slept, but no challenge ever came from those in real power. They recognized and appreciated his successes, at least as long as they had common enemies and men who would still fight.

Surprisingly, the rank and file seemed to love him and seldom tried to kill him. Trake knew they appreciated that, unlike any of their other superiors, he was always in the thick of the battle, and he killed five or ten for any one they downed. He saw their eyes as the enemy wilted before his blurred swords. Even those with the Strength did not stand long. He was the undisputed master, and every foot soldier knew he was safe if he stayed close to Trake.

Trake topped the small rise with his entourage in tow and looked out across the expanse of farmland below. Crops and domesticated animals crowded the landscape. Only in the distance, on the far side of the river, did he see any evidence of the army they would fight. Tents and cooking fires dotted the treed buffer that ran the length of the river before the next farms spread to the horizon.

"They say ten thousand?" Trake shot over his shoulder.

"That was yesterday's estimate, my liege. Every day we delay, their numbers grow. The scouts counted another two thousand arriving in the night." His adjunct was another disaffected Honored warrior who stood a solid hand taller than Trake and was blessed with a healthy dose of the Strength.

"Perfect," Trake commented. "They appear to be taking the bait. Any preparations for attack?"

Swallert stepped up beside Trake, pointing as he spoke. "The bridges at Gronant's Corner and Trelant Pass are still up and heavily guarded. The ford at Swelton Shallows is wide enough to pass a large force and there is some evidence they are building boats in the barns to the east, but I doubt seriously they will attack while we hold the high ground." He waited for Trake to respond. Once Trake grunted he continued, "I think we will have to feint an attack across the bridges before they will commit any arms. If we do that, it will appear as though our forces have split and induce them to ford in the center with their primary force to attack our exposed flanks. If they are truly that stupid, we can call up our reserves and box them in. If they smell the trap, we can withdraw from the bridges with little lost."

"Exactly as I have communicated to our Generals," Trake nodded. "I will lead the center attack."

"As expected, my liege." Swallert bowed with respect. "Will you honor me by allowing me to accompany you?"

"I would wish no less." Trake felt a surge in his loins that he decided not to resist.

# Chapter 51

White void greeted her opening eyes. Instinctively she ran her mind over her body. No pain. Her hands brushed her thighs as a double check. No marks, just smooth, youthful skin.

*"Welcome back."* God's voice filled the empty space.

"I was coming to you," Verbolana responded, still in dream. "At least coming to the city," she clarified. She moved her head in the faint hope of gaining her bearings. She noticed she was lying on a soft white pad, in a soft white room, alone. The knowledge helped a little.

**"On a mission to save your world? What gave you the impression you could do any more than what you did before? Did you think your new anger, your new determination, was different from anything I have seen before?"**

"I knew I had to try." Verbolana wilted under his scrutiny. Then, in a moment of hope, she queried, "What were you doing watching me anyway? I thought you didn't watch what went on in the Wilds."

**"Of course I do,"** God answered. **"Did you think my people would have remained so primitive if not for my help? Did you think they would not have forged metals, developed glass, split atoms? There have been people living in the Wilds for forty thousand years. Without my help, they would have developed beyond almost any world by now."**

"More tricks, more lies," Verbolana moaned as she sat up. "Can you do nothing with honesty?"

**"Well, I honestly wish you were happy,"** came his gentle voice. **"Apparently that is not to be."**

"I died my second death."

**"I changed the rules."** God answered her unasked question.

"Then you want more of me?" She sat straighter, stretching her back as if she had been sleeping for a very long time. She looked down at her perfect skin, a moment before ravaged with open wounds.

**"I brought you here for a purpose; that is true. I do not squander my resources."**

"Purpose! What purpose? You have always stated your only wish is for our happiness," she spat. "Yet you throw us on cold planets to be ravaged by disease, eaten by wild animals, frozen or starved. Then you pit us against each other and laugh while we slaughter in the tens, or tens of millions, for your pleasure."

**"Happiness is my truest desire for you and all my people,"** God returned, then changed the subject. **"You were returning to the city to fulfill your journey?"**

"To happiness? Hardly!" Verbolana exclaimed to the ringing voice in her ears. "I left the only happiness I had ever come close to finding to try to help a friend."

**"And that would not bring you happiness?"** God queried.

"I doubt it. Knowing you and the world you built, I expected only more frustration and sorrow." She bowed her head in recognition of the truth.

**"I was watching your shift in thinking. You were receiving some good tutelage. What if I told you there were other possibilities?"**

"I would tell you that you are a poor excuse for a God," Verbolana answered honestly.

"I would agree. But once you got over yet another disappointment with the universe — what would you say then?"

"I'll tell you when I get there," she sniped. "Or not."

"The time is now, Verbolana. Do you think you are the first to come to me with such drivel? You want me to be universally kind or manically evil. And when all evidence points to the contrary, you expect me to answer for my shortcomings. Have I asked that of you? Haven't I always accepted you for who and what you are?"

"You did not create me?" she asked, looking up for the first time.

"I did."

"And then you wonder at my questions?"

"I wonder at your expectations. Does a father expect his children to be perfect when he, himself, is not?"

"I wouldn't know. You saw fit to raise me without a father — or a mother."

"I did this?" God pressed.

"Yes, you!"

"Because I have the power?"

"Yes," she mumbled.

"And you had none."

"I had none then," she responded. "I feel stronger now."

"And what gives you the impression that I have that power?" the voice insisted.

"You can do anything."

"Many of you say so. And yes, I can do many things. I can see so much, yet not nearly enough."

"Can you see into my heart?" Verbolana asked.

"Yes, I can."

"Can you understand my words?" she continued.

"I believe I can."

"Can you not see where my thoughts will take me?"

**"That is the key, Verbolana. No,"** God admitted. **"I cannot."**

"Even I can see that!" she shouted.

**"Can you really?"** God responded with raised voice. **"Ten years ago, when you walked out of my city, did your thoughts allow you to know that you would be here, now, talking to me? Yesterday, did you see that you were going to make this journey to confront me? I certainly did not see it. Your development as a person and as a species is still a complete mystery to me."**

"So you let miseries upon miseries fall upon your creations because of your endless curiosity?" Her accusation fell without echo into the white universe.

**"I can see how you would think that."**

"What other explanation could there be?" she demanded.

**"Is that as far as your imagination will take you, or are you merely afraid to look further? I created you better than that."**

"Did you, oh Father? You flatter yourself!" she mocked. "Apparently your creations are not worthy of your praise. We are flawed, shortsighted, clumsy creatures, and we look to you for the Plan."

**"That is a mistake. In many things your teacher was right. The universe does not allow for plans, not even mine. You are a speck of dust on my grand and regal robe. I am a smaller speck of nothing to the universe. You expect me to have a plan. What would be your plan?"**

"I don't have a plan."

**"You must. You traveled here for a reason, and so far you are afraid to ask. Have courage, for you have nothing to lose."**

Verbolana sat for long moments, weighing what few options she had. "You can read my thoughts. You see my struggle. I know I can help. The suffering of my people is so great. You have never helped us. You owe us."

"What? What do I owe you, Verbolana?"

"You owe us a savior. Send me back!"

"You? A savior?" God exclaimed. "Why would I want to muck around in your world like that? From your world's suffering could come greatness. Look at your friend Trake. Who can tell? His suffering has been immense. Yet, he may well unify a world. He may push an entire civilization to greatness."

"What? What have you done with Trake?" Verbolana asked accusingly.

Suddenly her mind filled with Trake's history. She felt his suffering, saw his losses. With frantic determination, she galvanized her thoughts, keeping in mind that she was on trial. "And equally likely, he will push the people of my world into many more years of suffering," Verbolana countered.

"That is true. So what is your plan? You expect me to have one. What is yours?"

"I would like to give my people forgiveness."

"Forgiveness!" God laughed. "You think you know of forgiveness?"

"Fuck you, God!" she screamed. "Yes, I know of forgiveness!"

"Forgiveness is a powerful thing," God agreed. "Can you forgive the universe?"

"The universe? What is to forgive? The universe is what it is," she concluded.

"Yet your teacher says the universe is a cruel and vicious place. How can you forgive that?

"It has no consciousness."

"At least none that you are aware of," God kept prodding.

"That's right."

"So do you forgive the universe?" God continued.

"I guess. Yes, I forgive the universe."

"What else—*who* else might you be able to forgive?"

461

"I forgave Trake a long time ago," Verbolana ventured. "And I can forgive the Deck Director and all the Chosen for what they have done."

**"And the Wretched?"** God asked.

"Yes, yes, the Wretched. I don't see much to forgive them for."

**"And yourself? Can you forgive yourself, Verbolana?"**

Tears suddenly pooled in her eyes before spilling down her cheeks. "I don't know. I see so many things I could have done better. My failings are so profound. I can see myself failing even now, at this moment; knowing the answer you need to hear and yet still not able to give it."

**"Because you have the power,"** God concluded. **"You and I, we have the power. You can forgive everyone else, because all you see are their actions with only a glimpse at their motives. But you and I are different.**

**"You can feel your own power; you can feel yourself making choices, blundering with your ignorance, railing at your stupidity. And me! You assume, since I created you, that I have powers beyond ... what? Anything? And therefore I am immune to your forgiveness?"**

She shrunk, knowing her answer would doom her mission. "Yes."

**"And yet you want me to send you as a savior?"**

"Have you had any other volunteers?" Verbolana asked in dejection.

**"But Verbolana, forgiveness is not an outward occurrence. Even your teacher spoke of this. It is a journey inward. Sit with the universe. Look inside. Breathe and relax. I will return.**

Verbolana did not bother to appeal; she felt a force leave the room. In turmoil she sat, then stood, then paced through the void, always finding her way back to the single mat that was her only companion. She asked for a windswept mountaintop and received nothing. She pleaded for Altef, her teacher, but no one came. She was alone. Never more alone.

*  *  *

*I am a mote, on a mote, on a mote.* Verbolana sat straight-backed on her thin mat, her breath deep, her arms limp at her sides. *The universe, either by design or by chance, is a cruel and violent place. I am a creature of limited skill with an even greater limitation of imagination. I was born, I have lived and I have died with little control or power. That is the way. That is the way, and I cannot change that.*

*What I can do is fill my heart with love. I cannot fill it with happiness, or contentment or fulfillment, for I must rely on others to help me with those emotions. I cannot change my world, mold it to my liking, but I can change how I look at it.*

*So, pull Verbolana, pull! Pull the love you saw in Treena's eyes. Pull it into your heart. Fill your heart with Wexi and her last moments. Collect the flashes of laughter that rang across the deck when a child completed some forbidden prank. And Paul, harvest, one by one, the sweet fruits of touch and taste, of hot breath and patient understanding. Feel his appreciation of who I am, his total acceptance and approval. Lastly Trake, watch him glance, with eyes flashing. Drink his gentle touch as he swaddles his newborn, flesh and blood expressions of his passion for life.*

*Then, Verbolana, set all those cherished holdings aside. For as valuable as they are, they are only examples, examples of the capabilities of my own heart. Breathe, Verbolana, breathe deep and filling. Feel the love that is all around you. The infectious germ that lives in every breath. Feel it creep through your nose, through the tissues of your brain, as it passes down, through your throat and into the cavity of your filling heart. Feel it well with your lungs, pushing fear and contempt deep into your bowels. Feel your core free and your Strength rise. Let your Strength rise and merge, this time with the glow filling heart. With each breath let this furnace grow, feel it spill from your hands and your chest and your face. Watch the fire hose vortex open through the top of your head, filling and opening to the heavens.*

*Release the voice, let all thought wash into the tornadic flow, and sit in wordless beauty.*

# Chapter 52

G od," Verbolana lay weak on her mat. "Am I undeserving of your gifts?"

*"You rejected my gifts."* His voice was soft to her ears.

"I am weak with hunger and thirst and my universe smells of urine and feces."

**"Does your hunger focus your thoughts?"**

"My hunger distracts and discourages me," she whined.

**"You are not happy or content with your new knowledge?"**

"Happy? Content? I am hungry and I stink. And I want a toilet!"

**"Do you know how many of my people live without toilets, without enough to eat or drink? You ask for the mundane."**

"I ask for only enough to survive so I can carry on my search."

**"What have you found?"** God asked.

"I have found a universe of love and strength inside myself. And it is withering from lack of nutrition."

**"Many find great power and insight in your condition. Visions and grand awakenings from a state of want."**

"Illusions and hallucinations are more likely," Verbolana muttered, too weak to fight. "I do not oppose the universe. It is what it is. I need food and drink."

*Good,* God intoned, as a table appeared laden with fruits and beverage.

Verbolana pulled herself to her feet and reviewed God's offerings. "I need the meat and milk of other animals," her instincts screamed.

God laughed as bloody browned flesh appeared with a pitcher of pale liquid.

**"Tell me of the Strength you feel,"** God prompted as Verbolana sat and dug into her meal.

"The Strength? I have always had that, at least since my home world. You must see that in many people," Verbolana managed between mouthfuls.

**"Illusions and hallucinations mostly. Many of my people on many of my worlds talk of great powers and some have developed amazingly, though none quite like yours. Your people are unique in that way."**

"Really?" Verbolana wondered. "Out of so many worlds, mine is special?" She thought for another few moments. "And mine is one of the only worlds you have not helped? I find that odd."

**"Very odd indeed, odd and troubling,"** God admitted. **"And now you are asking me to help your people. It is a great thing you ask. There is so much at stake."**

"At stake?" Verbolana screamed to her emptiness. "What games are you playing?"

**"A game you could never imagine."** God's voice dropped. **"As I have said, and as you know, the universe is an evil place."**

"And how—how can I—how can my people—how can the limited power of any human fit into these mammoth games?"

**"As I say, you could never imagine."**

"I demand to know what you are up to!" Verbolana screamed through a mouth crammed with meat; her chin dripped with its juices.

**"Good for you. I need your spirit. Who knows, if you keep looking, you might find the answers for yourself. But I have**

more immediate needs. Tell me, if I grant your wish, if I send you back, what could you bring your people?"

"Happiness."

"Happiness!" God exclaimed. "And what would they do with happiness?"

"Live in as much harmony as this universe allows."

"And you think this has not been tried before? I would simply repeat my past errors. I have built a whole world, filled with comforts and happiness. I have sent thousands of saviors to a hundred worlds and the results have been unsatisfactory in every case.

"Then, one of the only worlds I never touched develops a power beyond any. And it is not a power of love or happiness. It is a power built on death and pain. You developed your Strength from extreme challenge in order to kill. I think it no coincidence that your friend Trake is the one most blessed with the Strength, yet he is also the most conflicted. Why, on the brink of success, would I make such a gamble?"

"Because you care for your creations."

"You are but insects to me. I would wipe you all from the galaxy if it met my desires."

Verbolana was at a loss. She sat, filled with food, waiting for energy to return. Nauseated, she stumbled back to her mat and lay, thinking. Finally she asked, "God, where does the Strength come from? Why were we able to develop something no one else has?"

"I believe it comes from your unique living arrangements. You spend your entire lives up in your towers, separated from what you call your Father. We have long known of the power available to many life forces from the connection to a planet. I have never seen a people live close to, but not on, a planet. I have set up scenarios elsewhere to study this phenomenon, but it may take generations."

"And what—you don't have the time?" Vee wondered aloud.

**"I have time,"** God returned.

"And you don't yet have what you need, or you wouldn't still be looking." Verbolana concluded. "And you would not be wasting your breath with me, one who has rejected you."

**"You are not so important."**

"It is true that the Strength was born in blood," she continued as if she did not hear him. "However, I have learned a different Strength. I have the Strength of Love."

**"If I send you back to them, what will you say of me?"** God asked.

"I will say that there is no God worthy of worship," Verbolana concluded.

**"Then they will make you their God and build their dogma around you."**

"I require no dogma, no rituals, no restrictions," she argued.

**"But they do."**

# Chapter 53

Signal lights winked across the rolling hills as Trake applied his night paint.

"All report ready," came word from outside his tent.

"Launch the left and right flanks," Trake muttered as he dabbed the final colors on his chest.

"You look absolutely menacing tonight, my liege."

Trake closed his eyes, imagined a different woman in his bed, and strode from the tent without response. Numb to the sudden blowing cold, he slung the offered quiver of poison-tipped arrows around his shoulder and then did the same with his bow, having no real intention of using such a long-range weapon. He drew his sword and examined its edge, anticipating the soft, liquid plunging and raptured eyes of those who would stand before him tonight.

"Advance the archers with absolute stealth," Trake ordered to the throng around him. "On pain of death for a cracked twig."

Trake hiked to the crest of the hill to gaze through the intervening trees. Pre-battle silence enveloped the countryside as he pulled on the Strength. Father flooded him with his love, steeled his arms and legs and sharpened his every sense. As the first sounds of battle reached him, his awareness expanded even without his command. To his left he saw, as if with his eyes, his forces surge into heavy resistance, individual energy signals merging into long undulating snakes of slithering activity. To his right, the surge of his men advanced unopposed and reached the bridge before encountering any opposition. He watched sparkling rockets of intention launch from the ranks of archers and the huddled response they enticed. He watched the voiding and filling as one man fell to his death and another took his place, always pushing from the rear, eager to engage the monster of death.

Trake stood motionless, impatiently waiting, those around him completely uninformed except by the screams of warriors on both sides that echoed across the mile-wide battlefield.

Trake took pity on those without his skills. "General Pournat is halfway across the bridge, with his archers in position along the shore. He will have to stall where he is if we are to provoke the response we desire. General Farnal to the left appears disorganized, breaking under the pressure. Send in his reserve regiments."

Minutes ticked by, with only faint screams of activity to mark the seconds. Trake monitored the different fields as the others waited on shuffling feet for the order to charge. Finally, Trake broke his silence. "A force is forming in the middle of the enemy line as we had hoped." That was all he said for a good five minutes. "It is larger, much larger than our spies reported. They appear to be waiting. I am guessing they anticipated our trap. Their intentions are alert, but languid." He turned to a runner. "Signal General Pournat to advance with all haste and take up position a quarter-mile downriver from the bridge. Send eight more regiments to General Farnal and order them to cross at any cost!

"Swallert, bring our archers up to the tree line. Make sure they make just enough noise so the fiends across the river detect them. Tell the troops our charge is imminent. Feel their energies and rally them. Add your intentions to theirs and project pending attack. Though I cannot feel it yet, it appears our foe may have

Strength beyond my expectations. They lie in wait instead of attacking. A logical approach, more akin to the Chosen."

Bloodlust unexpectedly gushed through Trake's veins at the thought of a true challenge. He felt the new energy merge into the whirlwind of his Strength, fortifying its foundation, amplifying its range. The battle evolved as he watched, surging like a creature alive with torment. Chosen lay in wait; he knew it beyond any proof.

*I wonder, in the years I have been gone, have any of their powers grown as mine have? Do I dare hope for death today? And that song. Do I even care about Chosen propaganda? They sing of Verbolana and that other girl as if they know what really happened. Though it turns out they were right to fear me. Their punishment comes from their own lies and misquotations of the Gods. I will see my Encore and be rid of this sorry place as soon as the Gods allow.*

Trake felt the two bridges were now his. His ranks of archers stood ready, Swallert lending his heart to the deception. Yet nothing of import changed across the river, though Trake's forces were now split. They would have to make a decisive strike or withdraw from the field. And withdrawal was not an option.

"Ready the men. Leave nothing in reserve. We strike across the river in ten minutes. Signal both Generals. Tell them to stick to the shore and come in fast and hard. If these farmers are smart, they will seal us close to shore so we cannot ford our entire force."

Soundlessly, Trake bounded down the hill as if a child headed to play, leaving his astonished men to divvy up the tasks. He found Swallert dividing his archers into blocks, leaving clear lanes for the infantry to advance through the ranks.

"We attack in seven minutes," Trake announced, his excitement obvious. "They are not going to move, and the sky will soon brighten. I want to be across the river before they can see well. Start your fires for the signal corps and stand ready for my order."

Reverting to a professional demeanor, Trake strolled to the head of the ranks. Without warning, he bellowed; his lungs filled with Strength. "Be ready, you mother fuckers! We come for you!" Then he strolled out onto the rocks. Moonless and striped with bands of milky stars, the sky sucked at his eyes. He frowned. *Glorious!* was his first thought. *Where did all those stars come from? Have I slept my life away not to have noticed? The moon was not like this last night or the night before. Or is it me? Has the Strength given me new eyes?* He heard Swallert falter across the loose rocks.

"Is it my eyes?" Trake asked before immediately regretting a possible sign of ignorance.

"It is not," Swallert answered. "I have come to tell you. Many have noticed the change. Even the wind and rain have never scrubbed the skies so. The men are grumbling. Some say it is a bad omen."

"Indeed." Trake removed every ounce of wonder from his voice and improvised. "Humble Magician," he bellowed into a sky cleansed of death. "You honor me beyond words. You have told me on many occasions that, upon the final battle, you lifted the curtain and watched from the front row. Welcome, to all. The performance is about to begin."

He turned to his men. "Take heart," he bellowed. "For after tonight, you will return to your families as wealthy men. Those who have followed me with bravery and tenacity will be favored beyond all others in this new performance the Gods will write for us. Talsartts to the fore!"

Battle cries of every pitch and volume erupted across the lines. Wild shuffling echoed through the night as lancers took up position. Many splashed into the edges of the river to make room for those behind. Trake bathed in the spirits he felt all around him, more alive than he had felt since — then.

He waved to Swallert, and the arrows flew. Without a moment's delay, Trake felt the far bank launch its response. Trake watched sharpened stone rain upon them with sparkled starlight, a sight not seen on this world for a few eons. He threw his intention wide and the twinkles bounced and slid harmlessly down the invisible umbrella.

"Advance!" Trake ordered across the lines as he took to the water himself. "Push through; the Gods are watching." Knee deep, waist deep, then shoulder deep, they advanced. Many lost their footing. Amidst cries and confusion, Trake's Strength shrunk in his concentrated effort. Then chest deep, waist deep, and they were running, with Talsartts searching for leathered chests.

Trake felt the enemy surge, then heard them splashing into the shallows. The first cries and clinking of hand-to-hand combat rejuvenated his Strength and he sent his intentions surging ahead. With sword bared, he shouldered his way into the fight and slashed his first victim deep. Warm blood splattered across his face, painted his chest. He smiled, sucked the allure of death to him, felt her cold lips and marveled in the heat of her breast. He sliced the next man to appear, and shook with passion. A farm implement probed toward him. He blocked, spun and sunk his weapon deep then pulled free for the next thrust.

"Aha!" Trake yelled aloud. "I am here!" A Strength signature appeared before him.

The force came in silence. Trake parried an incidental blow and slithered through the frantic conflict around him, dodging slashes from both sides in the battle. There was no room to fight with any grace, so he approached this new foe with direct and relentless purpose. His disappointment wilted his passion when he realized the life force before him was so puny. He wondered idly if it wasn't a Wretched trainee just learning the Strength, though he, himself, had had little success with such training. Regardless, he met the man sword-to-sword in respect for Father. Ten seconds and the man stood holding his arm at the elbow, his sword and forearm somewhere in the ankle-deep water. Trake ran him through without comment or salute, then hacked unnecessarily in frustration at the corpse as it fell.

Pikes and Talsartts came at him from every angle. An arrow buzzed his ear. Trake took scant notice that he had outrun his troops and pushed ahead alone. Another Strength signal was close. Before he located it, he was awash with signals that glided in fast from overhead.

"Battle blimps!" he screamed in warning, as if his aft commanders could do anything of real value. Thrilled, Trake fortified the Strength around him and turned back to the river. He sloshed through blood and floating bodies for a clear view of the blimps' arrival. They came in low, three of them, at swing height. Trake let out an involuntary cheer and waved his sword. "Here—I am here! Send me your best!"

But the blimps flew over the melee in the river to advance immediately on the rows of archers. Trake waded toward the new fascination. He recognized from the bustling Strength within the vessels that these were not captured blimps. Honored battle awaited if he could catch them in time.

He was shoulder deep, in full retreat, when the aft cannons of the middle blimp blew shrapnel, exploding the water around him. Trake felt chunks of chain and jagged shards of scrap metal penetrate and brush past him. "No! I will not die with glory so close!"

For the first time since he was a child, Trake wondered about the limitations of his Strength. Of late, it seemed that every time he asked for more, the Gods accommodated. He pulled now at their Strength and counted down to the next blast. He glanced at the other two blimps. Their angles were wrong; they were aiming at different targets. Now only ankle deep in the river, Trake sprinted to shore to stand directly under the big guns, immune for the moment. As the battle raged, Trake stood calmly, breathed the balletic beauty of the three crews in full swing. Something tugged at his heart, a remembrance, days of laughter, his friends gathered, simple, focused and dedicated. In that moment, between his ranks of archers and those who forged through the river, calm reigned. He dropped his sword arm to his side while waves of grief pummeled him.

"It's a beautiful thing, is it not?"

Trake turned to the voice, recognizing immediately his old friend, his old lover. "Erox!" Trake was suddenly ecstatic. The Gods sent his perfect executioner. "Take me away, my old friend."

Erox scowled. "Do you have any idea what you have done to me?" Trake recognized the signal, Strength mixed with anger and betrayal. "Take up your sword and die like a man! Your cowardice and treason will have their day!"

"Take me! Take your revenge! I have no apology for you; I have never given your situation the slightest thought. I have missed you, but I only realize that now." Trake did not raise his sword. "I feel, though, that your Strength has grown healthy with your anger."

"They are all watching. You will not cheat me of my revenge! Take up your sword and fight!" Erox breathed his contempt.

"It will not help, believe me." Trake lowered his voice, conscious of their audience. Then, as he realized Erox's dilemma, he raised his sword and proclaimed to all, "Let the Gods and all men witness the death of yet another Honored devotee!"

Trake rushed Erox with a vicious, explosive attack, cutting Strength to Strength, blade to blade. Erox answered with parries that slid seamlessly into lunges and lunges that danced into parries.

"You have studied, old man," Trake chided with quiet laughter. "Roasted Milnox agrees with you. Can you smell the roasted flesh on my breath? Every bite of Father's gifts grows my Strength." They danced and swiped and danced. "There was a time when I claimed the Gods guided my sword. I searched and I found great truths that I'm sure, to you, would be betrayal." He swung, grunting with the effort, stepped back and reengaged. "I lost all truth along the way, but you need not. Open your mind and question the skies. The Encore is there for us all; of that I am certain."

"Shut up and die!" Erox answered as they grappled close.

"I guarantee that," Trake promised.

"As do I," Erox grunted. He pulled back just enough to draw his dagger. Trake sensed the shift and smiled. His friend's penetration completed the circle, and with a feeling of newfound justice, Trake crumpled to the blade.

The skies clapped with thunder as all minds filled with the sight of Trake falling to the ground. Blinded by the vision that suddenly connected every living soul on the planet, all fighting halted, men swung to a stop, cannons quieted.

Trake lay on the pebbles as Erox wobbled above him, similarly stricken with the vision. To a million gasps, Trake rose, his aft skull freshly shaven, his foretuft blowing free. He stood beside his downed form, his hairless chest sculpted and unscarred, his arms tight with muscled youth. He looked down at his broken, sagging body and smiled. "I was right. We all have Encore."

A few steps past Erox, Trake noticed the sled, the Beasts of Ansett stamping in the loose rock by the river flowing with blood.

# Chapter 54

Unaware that an entire world watched his every move, Trake stripped his pants to leave them on the beach. He would take nothing from this world with him. He would meet the Magician, pass his Trials and forget.

Before Trake could step a foot on his sled, the skies burst from a cloud that had not been there when he last looked. Thunder shook his chest as lightning blinded his eyes. With spots floating through his sight, he doubted his vision. He looked harder and the dancing image cleared. Another sled sat waiting in the sky, its animals rearing in protest from their sudden and violent halt. With unknown Strength, Trake zoomed his sight in on the rider, expecting the Magician.

*Verbolana? How could this be?* Her angelic face was unmistakable, though, even after so many years. She looked as peaceful as in his dreams; vibrant in her youth, steeled in her posture.

"I will have no more of this!" Her voice rang to every ear, her face full before every eye. "The Gods have returned me, so you are all now my charges." With a flip of her powerful intention, she switched the direct access she had manifested over to Trake, who still had his one foot on the sled. "Trake, come to me. We have work to do. But first, we must love, for all the world to see. We must rejoice in a union to reshape our world!"

The world watched Trake's face as clearly as a mirror would show its own reflection. Confusion and suspicion flitted through his eyes before he was overtaken by bold determination. He stepped resolutely on the sled, took up the reins and whipped the beasts to a gallop. His eyes never left what he fervently hoped was not an apparition. As he gained altitude quickly, he took a moment for his first prayer in many years. "Gods," he proclaimed aloud. "I do not know what you have in store for me. What I see before me is more joy than the Blessed Amnesia could have ever brought. If you have chosen this as my Trials and it is but a trick, I will gather my Strength, defy every dictum of man, the Gods and the universe. I will hunt you down and kill every last one of you! This I promise."

As Trake approached, Verbolana carefully directed the feed to the world through her mind's eye. Her message must be clear. Five years, ten years, one hundred years from now, the drama of the day could fade. Myth or political convenience, she knew, could change miracle to mundane and vice versa, even in the eyes of the devout. Yet even with her months of preparation and covert manipulation, she was not ready for Trake. His fiery eyes, his sleek bulging arms and hairless smooth chest. His persona stoked her belly with passion, heated her heart and loins to a point where she almost feared his touch.

The two sleds drew closer, and Trake's flooding eyes never left her. Years of pent-up passion streamed down his cheeks. He felt cheated and desperate, ashamed and vindicated, weak and powerfully hungry, deserving and suspicious. Thoughts ricocheted through his filling mind with only one constant: the vision before him. He whipped the animals mercilessly and then stopped as he remembered Chosen dogma; then he found himself whipping them again.

Verbolana grew the tension for her audience, while finding herself suddenly separate. What did God have planned for this day? He had spoken of a higher purpose, importance beyond her understanding. Had the Author been right? Were there bigger battles on fields beyond the stars? Verbolana realized she had been so pleased and so excited by his agreement that she had spent no time thinking of the consequences. As she directed Trake's final approach, switched angles and froze expressions for her audience, she wondered whether her muddlings were all merely selfish desire. If she could manipulate an entire world of souls for her exclusive pleasure, were her motives pure?

She smiled with abandon and threw her lavish robe wide. Ripe with youth, Verbolana bared her body to the world and her arriving Trake.

"I forgive myself!" she sang through to the population and dismissed all misgivings. "I fill my heart with love and forgive myself. I love myself so I can love you!"

She watched Trake's eyes, and for the first time they diverted.

Trake pulled his steady sled beside his love's and dropped to his knees before her overpowering beauty. He shook with trepidation. "I am not deserving. I am too damaged, my love. I have squandered your gifts, stomped them into the mud of my own urine."

Verbolana cut him short. "I am not a God, my love. You need not fear me. The Gods see your weakness and revel in it. They forgive you and ask you to forgive yourself." She waited for a moment, letting her drama build, allowing her words to sink into a million ears. "The Gods have chosen you, as they have chosen me. They have gifted you with Strength beyond any others, you and I both. They direct us to build a new Strength, one that rejoices in love, that embraces passion and builds tolerance."

Still unaware of his audience, Trake stood. "It is not a trick?"

Verbolana smiled, touched his shoulders as she had in her dreams and sunk into his streaming eyes. "It is not a trick," she assured him as she stepped to his sled to comfort him.

Trake crumpled into her arms and slowly they dropped to the padded floorboards, both now sobbing.

Verbolana abandoned her directing and let the feed run. She held nothing but Trake, felt nothing but Trake, loved nothing but Trake. She ran her fingers down his arms, up his back to his tufted hair. On a whim, she grew his hair to his shoulders and ran her fingers through the black velvet. She drew his face to her chest, willing him to suckle. When his lips finally touched her mounded flesh, her heart jumped and her breath caught. She hugged his head tighter as she fell to her back. She needed his touch to envelop her, needed his weight to smother her, needed his fingers to probe her, needed his cock to fill her. She felt his face wet against her chest and she breathed patience and compassion — and the sweet melancholy of his fragility.

In all her preparations, she had not foreseen this. She had imagined him stoked with frantic urgency, yet now he sobbed and burrowed, cuddled and curled into her. Her heated passion evolved and she stroked him like the baby she had never, until this moment, even considered.

Verbolana paused the world feed, unsure of what to do next. With a force of will, she hunted through her thoughts and released her fantasy of what could have been. A nagging disappointment still lingered. She could feel it bubbling through her body like one of Paul's special drinks. She sat with the emotion for a moment before plucking a single tear from Trake's cheek. There was no room in her love-bloated heart for anything but compassion and forgiveness. With a deep sigh, she felt the emotion float up and release into the blue sky above her.

Suddenly she knew what Trake needed. She remembered her first days in that place some called Heaven. She stroked Trake's head. "Feel the pain, know the wrongs, picture the tragedy. Revel in the certainty that the universe is a cruel and bitter place and just live with the knowledge that the injustice will continue.

"Then feel my hand," Verbolana continued. "Hear my heart and burrow to my heat. I love you. I have always loved you; I will always love you. I have studied your life, walked by your side, lived with your sword. And I love you. The Gods love you.

She waited a moment. "Feel my love as you feel my hand. Go to my breast and suckle my desire. Embrace my passion as your own."

"But how can I ...?" Trake's muffled voice wondered.

"Pretend," it occurred to Verbolana. "Pretend to feel my love. Pretend to open your heart. Pretend to embrace the power. Pretend to accept this universe of evil. Linger in a make-believe world of peace and forgiveness. That is all for now. Sleep or cry or rant. These are all wonderful things."

She shut her mouth and sat with him.

* * *

Trake did not shy, but sat cocooned in her arms, knowing beyond any doubt that he was undeserving of her love. The Gods smelled his disease. This woman, whoever she was, did not know him. How could she have walked with him and still love him? How many had he killed without a care? How many nights had he blinded himself with drink? How many friends had he betrayed for his self-righteous pain? Without the Blessed Amnesia, there was no love possible, no forgiveness, not from the likes of her.

*But I could pretend*, he realized. *It would be nice to pretend. Take her as in my ancient fantasies. This is my right, for a life so miserably dumped upon me. I could pretend she loves me, pretend her body aches for me, imagine her eyes sparkle with lust instead of fear and loathing.*

She was so close and so tender; his hands ached to run up her sides, cup her perking mounds and hunt down for her well of pleasure. He turned and looked into her eyes, pretending, imagining, but not believing. He watched her eyes wash across his face and back to drill into each eye. Her smile came soft to her lips as her hand cradled his chin. She bent to meet his mouth while he pretended there was no alternate meaning, no hidden agenda. He accepted her tongue across his lips and let his hand wander casually, without commitment, up her arm.

"Suckle me, my love." She dropped his cradled head to her breast. "Take me gently into your mouth. Feel my response." He felt her shudder when he latched on and pretended her reaction was something other than disgust. His hand reached her shoulder, then up to her cheek.

"Grow your hair as you did mine," he found himself requesting.

Without thought, Verbolana plunged her waving blonde hair down to her shoulders, then down to tickle his face. He combed it back from her cheek, marveling at its Za softness.

"Are you ready for more?" she asked, her breath catching. "I yearn for you. I have yearned for you for—my entire life. Let me stroke you, my man. Let me feel your lust."

He was suddenly frightened. "It has been a long time. I don't know that it still operates."

Verbolana glanced down and smiled. "Oh, it still operates," and latched as gently as she could onto his stiff cock.

Verbolana started the world feed again. It was essential for the Chosen to see that a man had a place inside a woman and a woman could be filled with a man.

# Epilogue

Verbolana sighed in resignation as she surveyed the hundreds of unopened gifts that had arrived over the last few days strewn across the top-floor deck of their new home. Enclosing Za curtains fluttered in the gentle breeze of the warm summer day and Verbolana could hear the disciples who insisted on serving her scuffling behind them in preparation for the noon meal. "Who would have thought there could be such luxury in this world? Can we send these things back? We are drowning in gifts"

"People are just trying to show their appreciation for what you have brought them. You are the Savior of an entire world. You have brought God, for the first time, to unite with Father," Trake pointed out again, his head comfortably propped on her belly. "Share in their joy. After all, accepting the generosity of others is part of your message."

Ensconced as she was in a pile of lavish pillows, Verbolana did her best to shoot him a disapproving glance. "I didn't consider the sacrifices we would have to make." Then she raised her eyes from his to assess, again, her surroundings. "I feel truly ashamed sometimes. Look at this place, Trake. How many live like this here on Father?" She threw her arms accusingly at the patterned Za curtains, the deeply stuffed pillows, the separate, curtained futon on which they slept. "And what are we going to do with that fountain?" She pointed at the newest arrival taking up one whole corner of their cordoned off space.

"It makes a wonderful sound," Trake defended. "Helps keep me out of my body."

"And apparently in mine," Verbolana returned, and shot him a lighter glance.

"They are all very thoughtful gifts, designed to make our lives easier," Trake insisted.

"That's exactly my point." Verbolana could not let go of her frustrations. "I long for my frozen chamber pot and my too-thin blankets. I miss my dawn hikes to the top of the hill with only the stickers in my butt as my reward."

"Oh, do you, now?"

"Of course I don't, and of course I do. It is hard to feel my gratefulness amidst this bombardment of comfort. I forget all the misery that is possible, all the misery that still plagues our planet. Sometimes I forget that our work has just begun, that many still fight and die for the ways of the past, that so many have heard the words of God but still do not believe!"

"I don't forget," Trake assured her and breathed deep this still new loving Strength she brought him. "I can see how this isolation could frustrate you. We live where we need to live; we do what we need to do. Humans are born with free will. It is a blessing and a curse. It has been less than a year. We can only reach those who will listen … those who *can* listen."

"You do not need to remind me of that. I am just complaining."

"Ah," Trake laughed. "Feel the misery; be the misery. What happened to 'accept this universe of evil'?"

"You shit!" Verbolana cracked a little smile. "You mock me. Do you think I don't have to relearn the lessons every day, just like everyone else?"

Trake placed his head back on her stomach. "It does surprise me sometimes. The woman who teaches a world is still a student."

"Just like you, the man who leads a world to peace is still a warrior." The lament was obvious in her tone.

Trake's thoughts roved about in his head. "Maybe, just maybe, this one will struggle to his feet in a world full of loving Strength." He turned his head and kissed Verbolana's swollen belly.

"Just imagine," Verbolana muttered as she snuggled back into the cushions and closed her eyes.

## To Be Continued . . .